Praise for

TRUST
ME

"An unstoppable ride to the very last page."   —Wendy Walker

"Tense, suspenseful . . . A killer plot twist."   *—Real Simple*

"A sinister story that readers won't be able to put down."
                                                                    —Mary Kubica

"First-rate psychological suspense."   *—Booklist* (starred review)

"A revealing light on the nature of truth."   *—Publishers Weekly*

"Stellar . . . 'Trust Me' when I say that her latest is her best novel to
    date."   —Associated Press

"Her latest is a winner, it'll be a major crime not to read *Trust Me*,
which by far is one of the best thrillers I've read in years."
          —Andrew Gulli, managing editor of *The Strand Magazine*

TRUST ME

HANK PHILLIPPI RYAN

A TOM DOHERTY ASSOCIATES BOOK

NEW YORK

This is a work of fiction. All of the characters, organizations,
and events portrayed in this novel are either products of
the author's imagination or are used fictitiously.

TRUST ME

Copyright © 2018 by Hank Phillippi Ryan

All rights reserved.

A Forge Book
Published by Tom Doherty Associates
175 Fifth Avenue
New York, NY 10010

www.tor-forge.com

Forge® is a registered trademark
of Macmillan Publishing Group, LLC.

The Library of Congress has cataloged the hardcover edition as follows:

Names: Ryan, Hank Phillippi, author.
Title: Trust me / Hank Phillippi Ryan.
Description: First edition. | New York : Forge, August 2018. | "A Tom Doherty
  Associates book."
Identifiers: LCCN 2018023298 | ISBN 9780765393074 (hardcover) | ISBN
  9780765393081 (ebook)
Subjects: LCSH: Psychological fiction. | GSAFD: Suspense fiction.
Classification: LCC PS3618.Y333 T77 2018 | DDC 813/.6—dc23LC record available
at https://lccn.loc.gov/2018023298

ISBN 978-1-250-23272-4 (trade paperback)

Our books may be purchased in bulk for promotional,
educational, or business use. Please contact your local bookseller
or the Macmillan Corporate and Premium Sales Department
at 1-800-221-7945, extension 5442, or by email at
MacmillanSpecialMarkets@macmillan.com.

For Jonathan, and Justice

It's no use going back to yesterday, because I was a different person then.

Lewis Carroll, *Alice's Adventures in Wonderland*

It is easy to say you believe a rope to be strong and sound as long as you are merely using it to cord a box. But suppose you had to hang by that rope over a precipice. Wouldn't you then first discover how much you really trusted it?

C. S. Lewis, *A Grief Observed*

It is only prudent never to place complete confidence in that by which we have even once been deceived.

René Descartes, *Meditations on First Philosophy*

PART 1

USING ONE forefinger I write on the bathroom mirror, drawing through the steamy condensation left by the shower. This morning's number is 442.

Four hundred forty-two days since the car accident that destroyed my family. The crash that took Dex and Sophie from me. The numbers disintegrate as I write them. They melt into watery tears, then disappear.

I would give anything, *anything*. I would *do* anything. Longing—unbidden, unwanted—hits me hard as I look at my reflection. We make those offers every day, filling in our own personal blanks. If you make this happen, we promise, I'll give up drinking. Or speeding. Or whatever. If only you'll give me what I want, I'll be a better daughter. A more reliable husband. A more devoted wife.

Make my wish come true, and I'll do . . . anything.

We bargain. Negotiate. Make deals with the universe. Eventually, certainly, inevitably, we'll get what we want.

Then the universe laughs. And we are left to bargain with ourselves.

CHAPTER ONE

DO YOU KNOW ME? Of course I'd seen those billboards, the posters, the full-color composite drawing plastered on every TV screen and newspaper—so has everyone else in Boston, if not everyone on the planet. *"The poor little girl,"* everyone said. "Who *is* she? *Someone* must miss her." And those who still had daughters of their own drew them closer, or whispered warnings, or kept one protective hand on the cart as they shopped for groceries.

"Mercer? Can you handle it?" Katherine's voice on the phone softens with concern. "You need to get back to work."

I guess I've been silent, thinking about "Baby Boston" longer than I realized.

"You okay?" she persists.

"Yeah. I'm fine." So Kath wants me to write the inside true story of this gruesome crime. I sink into my chair in the study. Can I handle it? To be honest, I'm not sure.

"The book will be an instant bestseller, kiddo. It'll put you back on the map." Katherine charges ahead, persuading me. "Toddler killed and dumped in Boston harbor? And now the mother's on trial for the murder? Sorry, I'm horrible. And I know it's short notice. But you're the only writer who can do this justice. Can I tell them yes?"

Good thing she can't see the look on my face. Having the sensationally tragic murder of a child be the best thing that's happened to me in a while is probably not socially acceptable. Since people finally left me alone, I've gotten out of practice being socially anything. I hadn't heard from my former editor for months. Not since I stopped returning calls. And now this. A job offer.

All I'd have to do, Katherine Craft explains, is–starting tomorrow– watch the courtroom testimony through the same video feed the TV stations use, then write an "instant book" about the Baby Boston murder trial. "Of course you could watch it on regular TV," she says. "But what if some moron producer decides it's boring? Or they cut away for the dog in the well or some phony news? Can't rely on *them* deciding what to broadcast. So getting you the full feed is perfect. I tried to get you a seat in court, sweetheart, but it was too late."

Just as well, I don't say. Face all those people? Kath then offers me fifteen thousand dollars up front, with another fifteen thousand after the verdict when the book hits the market. Hefty royalties after that. I do need the money.

"Unless she's not guilty." Katherine goes on, her voice infinitely dismissive. "Like that's gonna happen. But when Ashlyn Bryant is convicted? You'll be Mercer Hennessey, bestselling author. I promise."

That'd be good. More important, though I'll never admit it to Kath, the book might give me a reason to get up in the morning.

"It's *never* the mother, right?" She keeps up the pressure, and assumes she knows best. "The boyfriend, maybe. Or the father. But the mother? This is pure crazy."

Right. It's never the mother. Except when it is.

In this case, it is. And yes, pure crazy. Kath's in her Back Bay office; I'm in my little suburban study. But I can picture my former editor's expression. It's the same baffled one I see on the TV talk shows and when I fidget in line at the coffee shop. People asking each other: what kind of monster mother could kill her own two-year-old?

"She's . . ." I search for a gruesome enough word. The mother *is* definitely guilty this time. I'd already devoured every newspaper and magazine article and watched every newscast and feature story revealing every heartbreakingly disgusting detail about the missing-then-found little girl, even the online TV stories from the Ohio stations. At first I couldn't stop weeping for that poor dead child. Then more tears as I shared her mother's certain anguish. Easier to fill my brain with someone else's grief, hoping to replace my own. Not completely successful, but better than emptiness.

When Tasha Nicole was finally identified, I actually considered calling Ashlyn, thinking (ridiculously) I could comfort her by sharing some maternal bond, each of us lost in grief and mourning our treasured baby daughters. Now it turns my stomach to think of it. How she duped me. Duped everyone. After the breaking news of her arrest? I could have murdered Ashlyn myself.

And no jury would have convicted me.

"Merce? You there?" Kath's in full pitch mode, as if we still work together, still talk every day. "Go for it, honey. Say yes. It's been long enough. You have to get back to work. You have to *do* something."

Do something? *Do?* I almost yell at her. But she means well, and she'd stuck by me through the days the sun went out and the shadows closed in. Kath understands, as much as anyone can. It's unfair for me to take my grief out on her. Is she right? Is there something I can do?

Maybe—for Sophie? And for Dex. Maybe to make up for what happened to them. To accept that I'm the one who's left alive. I'm not fooling myself; I can never actually accomplish that. But at this moment, I feel Dex. Urging me to do it. To use my words to right a wrong. To strive for justice, like he always did. *What's more, he whispers, you could at least honor Sophie's memory.*

Yes. Dex is right. Yes. I'll do it. To avenge Baby Boston. And I'll secretly dedicate this book to Sophie. To every little girl unfairly wrenched away from the world. The more I think about it, the more I know I can do it. I *yearn* to do it. Physically, mentally, emotionally *do* it.

Plus, writing a book beat the options I'd already contemplated. *Maybe I'll burn down the house.* I'd actually said that out loud only a few days before Katherine called. Though there was no one to hear me.

I'd visualized the flames, too. Visualized the nursery furniture, its pink rosebuds and indulgent ruffles, blackened by flames. The sleek suits Dex wore to court, and Sophie's daisy jammies and her plushy animals, the wedding photos and the toothbrushes and the . . . there's so much of our stuff. What would I feel as the Linsdale firefighters battled hellish flames and choking smoke, attempting—yet ultimately failing—to save any evidence the Hennessey family existed? I wouldn't live to find out.

That was the point.

"Merce?" Katherine prompts.

Putting Kath on speaker, I get up from my desk chair and retie the strings of my sweatpants, yanking them tighter. The sweats, black and soft and now grotesquely too big for me, are XL. Not mine. His. Dex won't be needing them. No matter how many days go by, I'll never get used to that.

"Yeah, well, maybe." I pace to the bookshelves and back to the desk. Trying to gauge whether *I'm* the crazy one.

"Come on, Merce. The jury's chosen, all the boring motions out of the way. It's all on camera now. You just dig up the deets on the nutcase mother." Katherine's voice follows me, reprising the fast-talking cajoling-editor tone she'd used on me and her other underlings, when we were all at *City* magazine. This year she began acquiring for Arbor Inc., the mega-co that owns *City* and a bunch of other publications, including Arbor's true-crime imprint.

"I know, you're like, *another* body in Boston Harbor?" She goes on. "But you gotta see this one's different. It's not a Mob hit on a snitch, not some heroin addict's poor abused child, not a gang turf war. The killer is the gorgeous young mother next door. *Ashlyn,* I mean, even her name is perfect. You can't turn on the TV without seeing that clip of her, all petulant and pouting off to jail. So we'll need you to convey, you know, the secret torment of the seemingly typical suburban family. Give it the feel of real."

The feel of real. Got it. I'm a writer. I'm a storyteller. I take the facts and make them fascinating. This story doesn't need much help in that department.

"Like *In Cold Blood*," Katherine continues, as if I've said yes. "Narrative nonfiction. Reportage. Truman Capote simply imagined half that stuff. Made up dialogue. How else could he write it? But you can do it, Merce, I know you can."

"Well . . . okay," I say. "Deal." She thinks she's convinced me. I'll let her believe that.

"Terrific. I'll email the paperwork. There's no one better for this job. You'll kill it." Katherine says. "Oh. Sorry, honey. But you know what I mean. You okay?"

"Sure." She doesn't know the half of it. "Talk soon."

I hang up the phone, looking out my study window, down our—*my*—flagstone front walk and our—*my*—quiet neighborhood, still serenely green on a September morning, as if nothing has changed. As if my Sophie were still alive, and Dex, too. Funny what strength there is in purpose.

"Rot in hell, Ashlyn Bryant," I say. And then, "This is for you, darling ones."

But of course they're not here to thank me.

CHAPTER TWO

You Mercer Hennessey?" A guy in a blue windbreaker consulted a clipboard as I opened my front door. "We got your courtroom feed stuff, ma'am. Where do you want it?"

Katherine must have been pretty confident I'd say yes. By 7:15 Monday morning, I'd signed for eight cardboard boxes of video equipment, and clutching my coffee, tried to stay out of the way as a phalanx of flannel-shirted guys hauled everything to the study. They unpacked a silver monitor, a silver mouse, two aluminum speakers, and two black routers; then uncoiled orange cables and white cords and plugged it all in, connecting the raw broadcast from the courtroom the same way the TV and radio stations receive it. Now my study is a snake pit of multicolored wires and power strips. I'm hooked up for a front-row seat at the Baby Boston trial.

"Is there a way to record the trial on all this? Not just watch it?" I'd asked one of the techs.

"Yeah, there is a way," he said, texting someone at the same time. "But you don't have it."

Fine, I'll record it on my iPad. Crude, but the tablet's adequate for quote-checking or review. The trial starts in ninety minutes.

After the guys leave, I swoop up all the bubble wrap and Styrofoam packing they'd strewn around, and drag it through the dining room and down to the basement. They'd told me to keep the packaging for when the trial's over.

"Why can't they take it themselves?" I mutter into cardboard, as I lug the stuff down the dusty back stairs. Snap on the light. "Can't believe I have to go down here."

The basement is the burial ground for my other life. Whenever I can't bear to look at something, but can't bear to throw it away, that's where I stash it. Sophie's first crib, the same white wicker one Dex used. His mother presented it to us, tears in her eyes. Sophie in arms, we'd accepted it, all enthusiastic. When she left, Dex lugged the deathtrap fire hazard into the basement, trumpeting how it was a father's job to protect his family. Gramma's gold-rimmed wedding china was my mom's contribution. Mom's will's, at least. Most of Dex's mom's tea set is here, too. There's the album of our wedding, which Aunt Someone told me—incorrectly—would be the best day of my life, a windswept October in Nantucket, where we'd all shivered in blankets, rushed out to 'Sconset beach, then, gasping in the cold, thrown them off to get one gorgeous moonlit photo of me barefoot in white tulle, laughing in Dex's arms. It wasn't the best day, because every day was better and better, until Sophie, another best.

Then it all stopped. There were no more good days.

I dump the boxes at the bottom of the steps. Click the string that turns off the basement light. Turn off that part of my life, too. I tramp up the darkened stairs, through the dining room and into the kitchen.

Baby Boston.

I don't need a Psych 101 textbook to explain *transference*. But now Ashlyn Bryant is no longer an emotionally problematic and potentially unhealthy distraction. She's my job.

I slam some bread in the toaster, make coffee, then wait, because the toaster is cranky, then tote it all to my desk. I am *on* it. I am going to be me again.

Back in the study, sitting in my desk chair. I jiggle the silver mouse and crank up the volume. The monitor screen stays opaque. Silent. Blank.

Like my life? No. I have a purpose again. The little girl whose body washed up on the beach at Castle Island.

Baby Boston.

And the murder trial of her mother. That woman's been held in a cell for the past year, and deservedly so. With many more years to come, if all goes as it should. She'd killed her daughter, and then for at least a month, lied to everyone about it. Actually pretended Tasha was somewhere else. According to the police, there's no one but Ashlyn with motive, means, and opportunity. Lucky for writer-me, Ashlyn Bryant's defense attorney is an old colleague of Dex. *Lucky*. Right. Dex gets killed. I get a source.

But, luck without irony, the unfolding case is now even more blanketed, wall-to-wall-to wall, by newspapers and radio and TV and internet. Strangers in elevators, I bet, find instant kinship in hatred of Ashlyn Bryant. When that monster goes to prison for life, it'll give this suburban tragedy its inevitable ending.

"Guilty!" I say, punctuating the word with one finger. Though, yeah. There's no one to hear me.

BABY BOSTON TRIAL—DAY ONE, I type the header on my laptop.

The real headlines don't call the victim "Baby Boston" anymore, not since the same cops who named her that proved her real name was Tasha Nicole Bryant.

Two months later they arrested Tasha's mother. Kath's right, I watched that almost-medieval thirty-second clip on the news over and over. The once supposedly gorgeous Ashlyn Bryant in handcuffs, crying, her tight black T-shirt rumpled and twisted. Humiliated. Scrutinized. Shunned. Led away to penance for murdering her own child. How many times did I wonder, sitting alone, how she felt?

Ashlyn Bryant. The most reviled woman in Massachusetts. In the entire country, possibly.

Anticipating the swarm of single-minded reporters and photographers descending on Boston, Judge Franklin Weems Green demanded that the four courtroom cameras–including one dubbed "Ashlyn-cam" focused only on the defendant's face–be locked down. Each allowed to show only a severely restricted shot of Suffolk Superior Courtroom 306. No jurors' faces. And no shots of the spectators.

They'll all be asking the same question I am.

Why would she do it?

Sophie used to say that one word. *Why?* Endlessly. Well, not endlessly, as it turned out. It only seemed so at the time. *Why?*

We thought she was so dear, so funny, and so brilliant, even as a shy almost-three-year-old. Her tawny curls and deep brown eyes. Those eyelashes. Dex and I would whisper "why?" to each other before we fell asleep–a ritual, a married thing. Laughing at our joy and our luck and our future. Four years ago, hoping for a Sophie, we'd found this quirky gray one-level ranch in Linsdale, and I'd happily gone suburban. Happily turned my back on my magazine career. Quit my plum job as a writer for *City* magazine to become a full-time wife, a full-time mom. To have a full-time family.

I had no idea that "full time" would be so brief.

I stare at the still-dark screen. *Everything ends.* It's the when and the how that surprises us.

"One minute. And counting." The disembodied voice coming from the tinny speaker near my computer yanks my brain back to reality.

"Ready," I answer, as if the voice can hear me. I've cleared my desk of Sophie's framed scribbles and all the photos of Dex, even the one his mother took at law school graduation. Gone, too, is the tiny nubbin of peat Dex carried home from Scotland, and the grapefruit-scented candle he brought me from Harrods. I kept only one remembrance, a dappled fist-size rock he'd found, its bulky heft smoothed by the Aegean.

I blink away tears. There'll never be another gift from him.

"Thirty seconds," the voice announces. I envision an assistant director in a plaid shirt, maybe tortoiseshell glasses and unruly hair, seated at a flickering console inside the mobile broadcast studio, an unmarked white van parked in the lot behind the courthouse.

Is there truly a white van? Is there truly a flickering bank of controls? Here at my desk, I conjure the aging stone and granite courthouse, the constant battle for parking in a crumbling asphalt lot, pungent and sticky in Boston's ridiculously unbearable September. The reporters, lugging tote bags and cell phones and spiral notebooks. I've seen these things so many times, why should it be any different now?

But maybe the van is blue. Maybe everything is different. It is for me.

"Attention stations," the voice says. "You may roll tape. We're about to hear the opening statement from District Attorney Royal Spofford."

CHAPTER THREE

"They found the decomposing remains of that beautiful child in a garbage bag," the district attorney told the jury. The full-color crime scene photographs—grotesque and unforgiving—glowed on the courtroom projector screen.

I'd closed my eyes against them and listened to the DA. Until I couldn't bear it. Now, balancing one hand on the cool porcelain of the toilet, eyes closed again, I wipe a slimy strand of hair away from my face. I can't breathe. Or think. Or see straight.

My imagination is holding me hostage.

The pictures DA Royal Spofford showed were as real as if I'd been standing on that beach at Castle Island. As if I'd seen the choking strands of seaweed twining around that pink-clad leg. As if I'd been there when the black Labrador found her. Bloated. Murdered. Dead. In a trash bag.

My stomach wrenches again, gags with the memory. That woman, dumping her own daughter. Her own daughter! A little girl is not disposable.

My knees ache, even though my bathroom rug is thick and soft. I'm fine now. *I'm fine.* With one last wrenching breath, I push myself to my feet.

I stand, almost dizzy, my vision dim and my back aching. I feel my heart struggle, my brain unable to focus. My mouth tastes disgusting.

Royal Spofford had assured the jury, and all of us watching in bars and offices and livingrooms, that he would prove only one person responsible for that poor little body.

"*Only* Ashlyn," the DA told them, "had the access, the motive, the opportunity, and the power to snatch life from angelic little Tasha Nicole. You will hear how Ashlyn Bryant decided the daughter she brought into the world hindered her nightclubbing lifestyle. You will hear how Ashlyn Bryant, with malice aforethought, extinguished that child's innocent life with chloroform and duct tape. Then, thinking only of herself, tried to cover up her unspeakable crime.

"Only Ashlyn." He made it a mantra, shaking his head. "Only Ashlyn."

I wipe the tears from my eyes, flap down the toilet seat, and flush, my body dank and clammy, my T-shirt clinging to my back. I picture my darling Sophie, all of us, on that very beach. The wind in her curls, and the sun spackling the harbor. Dex and me, hand in hand, knowing we'd all live forever.

"I love you every day," I whisper. "I am so sorry."

The only thing that'll make this better—and I apologize mentally to the otherwise-admired Quinn McMorran—is the bullshit I am about to hear from Dex's pal, the defense attorney. My tablet had taped her opening statement for me as I sprinted to the bathroom.

I can't wait to hear *that* load of alternative facts. My darling Dex would disapprove of my scorn, but I still wonder how Quinn McMorran can defend such scum. I'm supposed to talk to her on the phone "possibly Wednesday." She'd made it clear she agreed only as a "favor" because of her respect for Dex. I get ten minutes. Fine.

I peel off my T-shirt, yank on a clean one, make some tea, go sit at my desk again. It's late, after four, and trial's in recess until tomorrow. I'm okay. I really am.

"Let's hear what you can do, Quinn," I tell the screen. "May the jury sneer at your every word."

I touch Dex's heavy Aegean rock for luck, take a breath, and push Play.

On the video, a navy-suited Quinn McMorran stands up. Her short auburn hair, now unabashedly showing its gray, illustrates her experience on the legal battlefield, case for case as much a veteran as her DA adversary. She places her hand on Ashlyn Bryant's shoulder. Ashlyn's about half her age, twenty-four. The papers report they're "like mother and daughter." Ashlyn looks up at her as if it's more like savior and victim.

"Gimme a break," I mutter. But I'm riveted.

"I'll be brief," the defense attorney promises the jury. "You don't need me to tell you that under our Constitution, a person is innocent until proven guilty. Our legal system makes it the prosecution's burden to prove—beyond a reasonable doubt—that the defendant is guilty. That means they have to prove every element of the crime beyond a reasonable doubt. That the defendant killed the victim without justification, and that it was premeditated. That she *intended* to do it. With premeditation. With atrocity and cruelty. Bottom line, they must prove how and when Tasha Nicole was killed. And how 'only Ashlyn' could have done that."

Quinn lets out a breath. The courtroom is so still, I can hear her whoosh of air. She lifts her chin, then points to Ashlyn.

"Sitting here, facing you, my client Ashlyn Bryant is innocent. Neither she nor I have to prove that. *It is already a fact.*"

Quinn McMorran lays out her defense case for seventeen more minutes. No witnesses, no fingerprints, no DNA, no hair samples, no surveillance. No evidence whatsoever linking Ashlyn Bryant to the death of her beloved daughter. Apparently the director is having trouble following her movements and cueing the camera changes, so I see her back, then her face, briefly out of focus.

She finally faces the jury full on. "Over the next week or so, my learned colleague will try to dazzle you with computer searches and scary words and some family disagreements. But every time, ask yourself, so what? What does that prove?"

"Puh-leeze," I say out loud. I punch off the video and talk back to the blank screen. "It proves the monster is guilty as hell."

CHAPTER FOUR

It's not like I *can't* leave the house. I do it when I need to. Even drive. But when I do I can't avoid seeing the driveway, and our street, and that tree. Four hundred and forty-three days ago they took away the crumpled car. Took away my family, too. When I'm out in public, I can't avoid people asking if I'm okay. I'm not. Of course I'm not.

But now, alone at my desk and ready to write, I can focus on another little girl. Thanks to the relentless coverage, I've compiled a gold mine of material. Interviews. Photographs. Video from local and national news. Katherine had dropped off a stack of revealing documents, including the Dayton police reports and inside investigative stuff her sources gave her, so now I'll devour that, too. I'll double-check the facts when I can. It'll feel real, all right.

Instead of using today's opening statements, I'll open the book with an inside look at Ashlyn Bryant's parents. A personal take on their then-missing granddaughter. After a chapter or two of buildup, I'll do Day One of the trial.

It's tricky.

The order of the book, chronological from beginning to end, won't follow the actual order of the trial, which will go witness to witness. Two stories underway at once. Mine, and Ashlyn's.

Two weeks after the verdict, Ashlyn Bryant will be sentenced. As soon as the judge sends her away for life, the publisher wants my book ready to go. That means the two weeks between verdict and sentencing will be a writing marathon. And of course, I'll have to add the ending.

Ending? She killed her own daughter! My brain almost screams at me. *While you were burying yours.*

It had almost confused me, if I could have been any more confused fourteen months ago, when news broke that they'd found the body of a little girl on the beach. A spectacular June day—sunny, and sadistically gorgeous. I had just managed to walk out of Dex and Sophie's funeral. With everything else going on, Dex's mom had tried to keep the story from me, best she could. Someone at the cemetery, I forget who, actually told me about Baby Boston. Of course back then, no one knew who she really was.

Well, Ashlyn did.

I look at my almost-blank laptop screen. I delete, letter by letter, "DAY ONE." I replace it by typing something else in the manuscript. The title I just thought of.

LITTLE GIRL LOST

Where was their Tasha Nicole?

Sun-battered and dry as only western Ohio can be, Dayton was breathtakingly hot that summer day. Inside their modest Laughtry Drive split-level in a beige and concrete suburb, the little girl's grandparents, Tom and Georgia Bryant, were telling a story that made no sense.

Georgia—pale lipstick, a hint of brown eye shadow, and wearing a sleeveless top studded with tiny pink pearls—was a devoted homemaker. Solicitous and insistently helpful. She looked too young to be a grandmother. Tom, a retired insurance adjuster gone gray, sat silently beside her on the gold damask couch, stiff-backed in shorts and a knit polo shirt, a glass of iced tea sweating in his hand.

Georgia's words tumbled out, as if she couldn't reveal the mystifying information about their daughter, Ashlyn, quickly enough. Ashlyn Louise, their only child. "I'll start at the beginning," she said to a reporter.

Since the moment Ashlyn gave birth to Tasha Nicole, two years ago August at Edgewater Hospital, the sunny good-natured child filled her grandparents' lives. Ashlyn and Tashie didn't move out of the Bryant's house to an apartment until a year or so ago, after Ashlyn insisted she was "too old to live with her parents."

"At age twenty-two? I had to admit she had a point," Georgia said. "But Tashie needed us. I insisted we see her. Every day."

And to the Bryant grandparents' joy, every morning at 8:45 Ashlyn dropped off the little girl. Tom scooped the child up in his arms the moment she arrived, and she'd coo with delight. The doting couple would read Tasha Nicole picture books. Laugh as she learned to count. An adorable girl, a darling girl. They couldn't get enough of her.

But one morning, Tasha and Ashlyn didn't show up. Ashlyn called and made an excuse. Again, the next day. Then every day for a week.

"I kept asking Ashlyn, where is our Tashie?" Georgia's worried eyes filled with tears of anxiety as she remembered. "Didn't I, hon?"

Tom nodded, silent.

"Ashlyn *always* had an answer," Georgia went on. "She was in day care. On a playdate. Once Ash said she wanted Tashie to bond with her new boyfriend. Remember that, hon? In that mocking voice she always used. 'Don't *worry* about it,' she said."

But Georgia had worried. Days went by. A week. Two. Ashlyn eventually ignored Georgia's calls. "Tasha sends love," Ashlyn once texted. "See you soon." Three weeks passed.

Georgia drove to Ashlyn's apartment at all times of the day and night. Called, too. But no one was there. That is, no one never answered the door. Or the phone.

Where *were* they?

Tom sipped his tea. Shooed away one of their pesky spaniels. After ten years in the insurance biz back in Minnesota, he knew about family troubles. This had the makings of disaster. But he let his wife talk.

Yes, she admitted, she and Ashlyn had their moments. Ash was headstrong. Manipulative. Demanding. Ambitious. Yes, Georgia was sure she'd been too easy on her only child. But Ashlyn always wanted to be "free" of her "loser" family. She had quit college, and was always on the hunt for a new job, a new life, a richer man.

Georgia picked up a small silver-framed photo. Ashlyn Louise Bryant. Slim, hazel-eyed, pouting glossed lips, and a clinging V-neck sweater. Now she did some part-time work in some—someplace. It was never clear where. Ashlyn would never talk about Tasha's father. She still had a room of her own, though, here in the house where she grew up. Tashie had a room, too.

"Ashlyn loves Tasha Nicole, I know she does." Georgia's voice caught. "And Tasha loves her."

Georgia opened a pink leather-bound album, "Tasha Nicole" embossed in script on the cover. She turned to a recent photo where her granddaughter, wide-eyed, honey hair, tiny teeth, and wearing Hello Kitty overalls, stood on the seat of a backyard swing set, a chain gripped in each pudgy hand. In another photo, she clutched a purple crayon, a coloring book of baby animals open on a table in front of her. Tasha was too young to stay in the lines.

But now—where was she?

"Where was she?" I ask the question out loud as I type, then lean back in my chair, stare at my words, and read my first scene again. I'll have to check on the timeline, but I mentally pat myself on the back. Pretty good for a first draft. And I don't feel like throwing up anymore.

"Good job, Mercer," I say. Since there's no one else to say it.

It's ten after two in the morning. Court recessed yesterday at five. I've been writing almost nonstop since then. I should sleep, but I'm too revved.

I'll make a list of questions so I won't forget anything.

Tasha Nicole's father? is first on my yellow legal pad. *Who is he? Where?* From all accounts, the unmarried Ashlyn never told her parents who the child's father was. Some stories implied she didn't know. More than implied. WHO'S HER DADDY? one headline sneered.

MURDERED TOT HAS MYSTERY FATHER! But certainly that will come out at trial. Will the "mystery father" be called as a witness?

I sip from my second, okay, third, glass of pinot.

This is a challenge. I've got to re-create reality, so, unavoidably, I'll have to imagine much of it. In other words, make it up. Some scenes that I'll describe, like the one I just wrote, will be near-fiction. I've never been in the Bryant's suburban living room, but I'm relying on magazine pictures and TV reports. Is that fair? Too late now to second-guess.

Besides the duel of opening statements, two moments of Day One caught my ear. Made me lean closer to my monitor.

First—when Ashlyn Bryant walked in. Not wearing her orange prison jumpsuit, Quinn McMorran would never have allowed that. The defense attorney is obviously trying to bamboozle jurors with her client's loose dark sweater, baggy skirt, and black tights—it's still like summer!—hoping sartorial modesty shorthands her client's innocence. It didn't fool me.

The other moment—and maybe this was also at Quinn's direction, but I bet it was Ashlyn's own personal power move—Ashlyn had angled her chair so her face was off camera.

At one point, though, Ashlyn deliberately turned *to* the camera. She tucked her now-darker hair behind one bare ear, then looked up from under her lashes. The photographer seemed to get her come-hither signal. As he zoomed closer, Ashlyn's face, a makeup-free mask of phony cinematic sorrow and, I had to admit, almost beauty, seemed to entreat the lens. Caress it, as if to promise— *I did nothing wrong, I'm simply a grieving mother.*

Yeah, well, I thought. Join the crowd.

CHAPTER FIVE

"appy Tuesday, trial-watchers. Got your coffee? You may roll tape in black," Voice breaks into the morning silence of my study. "Fifteen seconds."

I'd tried to name the voice. Give it a personality. But every name I came up with haunted me. Mickey—too much like Dex's beloved Yankees. Mr. Darcy—never. Tigger? Never.

So he's just Voice. That way he doesn't have to be like anything else. "Thank you, Voice," I reply. Might as well be polite, even to an empty room.

I'm prepared for Baby Boston Day Two, back at my desk, laptop open. Two cups of French roast. Toast, burnt around the edges, easier to put up with it than to fix the toaster. I have no idea how to fix a toaster. Dex would have taken care of it. And I'm not much interested in food, anyway, since everything. The video monitor pings its welcoming trill, but the courtroom is still in black.

One big question: will Ashlyn eventually testify?

If I'd been accused of killing my daughter, I'd leap right on to that stand. I'd demand my day in court. How could any parent not do that?

Unless they're guilty.

I'd love to hear her, though. Hear her attempt to testify her way out of this. It could provide an entire chapter on self-delusion and self-centered melodrama. *Ashlyn testify?* I write on my list.

Talk about drama. If District Attorney Royal Spofford stays on schedule, we're about to hear from the woman whose curious black Lab wouldn't stop barking at something on the beach at Castle Island.

I stare at the dark monitor, envisioning it. The woman, khaki pants and fleece vest, maybe, walks the expanse of rocky shore, smelling the salt air, maybe picking up shells, the newly risen June sun sparkling on Boston Harbor, her dog frolicking, then stopping, barking, insistent. Poignant, and intensely disturbing. Because every reader will know what her dog found.

How did body get to beach? I write. *Tides?*

Today's other testimony will be from Bryce Overbey, the Boston detective who opened that green trash bag to find a murdered child. He's the one who dubbed the then-anonymous victim "Baby Boston." I hope I can stand it. I have to, though. It's the truth.

Why hasn't court started? In the pixelated blackness of the video screen, I imagine Ashlyn's face. Not good-girl Ashlyn from yesterday, all demure for the camera. The other Ashlyn. The schemer, the bad seed, who'd finally exploded after a big fight with her mother.

I open my *Little Girl Lost* file, switching my brain into storytelling mode. I'll use this time to write about how even before Tasha's body was found, Ashlyn's mother began to get suspicious. I type in a new chapter heading. This time, I get to be Ashlyn.

MOTHER KNOWS BEST

"Holy crap." Her mother? Her freaking *mother*? How had Georgia found her here at Ron's apartment? Ashlyn held the grungy blinds away from her face to peer out the second-floor window. Saw her mother's white Honda at the curb. Watched the woman in those too-tight capris slam the car door behind her. Ashlyn recognized that walk. Mother was on a freaking mission. Good thing her new boyfriend wasn't home.

Ashlyn took the stairs down two at a time. Her mother ruined everything she touched. She yanked open the front door, hoped no one was watching.

"What the hell, Mother—" Ashlyn began.

In a flash, Georgia had grabbed Ashlyn's arm. Pulled her across the sidewalk and into the front seat of her Honda.

"Are you *mental?*" Ashlyn didn't fight her, didn't want some nosy neighbor to call the cops. "You're embarrassing me. Making a fool of yourself."

"You need to start answering my questions. Right now." Georgia clicked the car doors locked. Started the engine. Pulled away from the curb. "Take me to my granddaughter. Now."

Ashlyn weighed her choices—fight, or play along. When her mother was in a snit like this, play along was the only way.

"Okay, don't have a cow. I'll take you to Tasha." Ashlyn tried to sound like she meant it. Her mother's veiny hands clenched the wheel. Her jaw was set, she'd seen that expression a billion times. "She's at Valerie's. The babysitter. Turn left."

"Why didn't you leave her with us?" Georgia's voice had the whiny tone Ashlyn hated. "Why do you always lie?"

Shut *up,* Ashlyn thought. If her mother didn't stop nagging her, like constantly, she'd go nuts. "Take me back to Ron's. Then I'll tell you where Tashie is."

"No. Ab-so-*lutely* not. We're going home. I want some answers. No Ron. *No.*"

"No." Ashlyn mocked her. She was such a witch. "Ron's first. Or I won't tell you. What're you going to do about *that?*"

"*Love*ly creature," I say out loud. I hit Save, then read over what I've written, making sure I've captured Ashlyn's persistent deception, her reliance on delusion, her narcissistic self-confidence. I wasn't making up the episode itself–the specifics came from a surprisingly revealing interview Georgia Bryant did with a Dayton cable station. After this encounter, Georgia tries to take Ashlyn to the police station. If she'd succeeded, maybe Tasha would still be alive. Maybe not.

Someone's at my front door.

"Katherine?"

She shoulders by me as I open it. Comes inside. Already talking.

"Is your phone off? Aren't you watching TV?" Katherine asks, as if I know what she means. She's predictably unpredictable, we used to say.

I roll my eyes behind her back, following her. "No, sister, I'm writing. Like you're paying me to do. The feed's still in black. But, no, my phone isn't off."

She's heading for the living room. I trot to keep up. "Kath? What's with the suspense?"

"Turn on your TV." Katherine points to it. "I was in the neighborhood, lucky for you. Or you'd be totally clueless."

I click the remote. The TV powers up. "Geez, Kath. Why didn't you just call me?"

"See for yourself." Kath gestures to the screen.

Breaking news. Courthouse evacuated.

Bomb Threat at Baby Boston Trial.

CHAPTER SIX

"Pure crazy." Kath, in black leggings and a pink blazer, plops onto my couch.

I'm standing in front of the TV, remote in hand. "I *know*."

A Channel 5 reporter in a khaki blazer and red tie, stands in front of the gray stone courthouse. I know him, Howard Frisch. "As you can see," Howard says, squinting into the morning sun, "officials ordered an immediate evacuation of the building." He steps out of the camera shot so viewers like us can see live pictures of people in suits and high heels, some with briefcases and all with frowns, swarming down the broad front steps.

"Smart man," Kath says. "No one wants to miss the shot of the courthouse blowing up."

"And here comes the bomb truck," Howard continues. "You'll soon see the bomb techs in those white moon suits."

"This sucks." Kath pulls out her own phone. Punches numbers.

"Are you calling someone there?" I ask. I realize Kath's the first visitor I've had since . . . I don't know. My house looks the same, I guess, imagining it thorough her eyes. Just emptier. Without the toys.

"The other black van carries the bomb-sniffing K9s," Howard's voice goes on. "They're blocking off access, so we won't be allowed to stay at this vantage point much longer."

"You think it's a real bomb?" I ask. "Who're you calling?"

"Huh?" Kath click her phone off. "Turn the channel, see what the others have."

It's the same video on Channel 4. "Fourteen jurors," their reporter says, "twelve plus two who will eventually be alternates, were exited via the back door, loaded onto a bus, and driven away."

Kath's now texting. I switch the remote again, then again, but nothing new. Cameras stay trained on the courthouse.

"It's probably nothing," Kath says.

"Yeah." I have to agree. Still, a bomb threat is a big deal in Boston.

"Ashlyn Bryant," the Channel 2 reporter is saying, "is in protective custody, whereabouts unknown."

"She's probably loving this," I say. "Ha. I bet she called it in herself. Or duped someone else to. You know? To put off testimony about finding the trash bag."

About finding her decomposing daughter in the trash bag I don't need to say. *That poor innocent girl.*

A cloud of sadness smothers me as the room seems to go darker. I sink onto the big chair. *Sophie.* And Dex. In one random miserable moment they were taken forever.

I'm not close to fine. No matter what I try to tell myself and everyone else. I pull myself back to the present.

"Ashlyn did it? Love that idea." Then Kath waves it off. "More likely it's dumb kids."

"Yeah." Not someone targeting Ashlyn, or sabotaging the trial. "Probably a stupid prank. There's been a bunch of those, right? Kids not wanting school to start or whatever? TV's just repeating stuff now."

"Yeah. It's gotta be nothing. You okay?"

"I'm fine," I lie. "Seriously. You want coffee?"

"Nope." Kath tucks her cell into her carryall, pulls out sunglasses. "You need to write. Hey, awesome job on the first chapter. You nailed Dayton. I don't miss my hometown, gotta say."

She gives me a hug as she leaves. Which is strangely weird. When was the last time someone hugged me? Or touched me, in fact, at all? Sometimes I sleep on the couch, hoping the lack of space beside me will help me forget. How Dex breathed. His heat, his skin, his laugh, his footsteps coming down the hall to find me. But I won't forget. Can't. We never said goodbye. The memories, and the sound of Katherine's car driving away, almost bring on the darkness again.

No. I close the front door, and shut off my sorrow. For now, at least, I need to care about someone else's history. I march myself back to my study, back to my assignment, back to reality. I'll leave the TV on in the unlikely event they find a bomb, but while cops investigate, I need to write. About Tasha Nicole Bryant, victim of her mother's toxic life. It's empowering to know that my words will become history. Become the truth.

I open my manuscript. With a shiver of almost-anticipation, I slip back into Ashlyn's head.

THE FAMILY CONFRONTATION

It totally sucked that she had to come back to Laughtry Drive again, especially after she'd finally convinced her mother to lay off. Mom had changed her mind about going to the cops, pretty darn fast, after Ashlyn reminded her it'd be in all the papers, and her country club friends would gossip about her. You could always get her with stuff like that.

"Two minutes," Ashlyn promised herself as she strode up the front walk. She patted her pocket for her secret key. Get in, get the stuff, get out.

But the front door opened. And her mother started in on her. "Where is Tasha?"

Before so much as a hello. Showed you who was important in this family.

"She's with the sitter, Valerie, what d'you *think*? She's taking a nap. You honestly want to wake her up? How selfish is that?" Ashlyn tried to squeeze by her. But her mom was blocking the way.

"I want to see my granddaughter." Georgia stood, hands on hips, in a terrible flowery blouse thing and pitiful jeans.

"It is not. A good time." Ashlyn spit out each phrase. "Can't you understand?"

"Here's what I understand, missy. You're a liar. I want my granddaughter. And I'm calling the police." Georgia pulled out her phone.

Was she punching in numbers? *Shit.* Ashlyn turned her back, ran down the hall to her old bedroom. She yanked open her dresser drawers, pawed through.

"Ashlyn? What the hell is going on?" Her father's voice.

Tom Bryant stood in the bedroom doorway. Wearing one of those gross country club shirts he thought made him look rich.

"Why do you always fight with your mother?" He took a step closer to her.

Ashlyn slammed the drawer. Whirled. Faced him down. "Why do *I* fight with *her*? Because I'm a spiteful bitch. Like she always says."

"Where's Tasha?" he persisted. "Who's this Valerie?"

Shut *up,* she felt like saying. But maybe she was handling it wrong. She let her shoulders drop, and put a defeated expression on her face. "Daddy? You've got to help me. Val's a babysitter. Listen, I needed to get away from the whole motherhood thing. Just for a while. Mom'd never understand."

A noise in the hallway. Georgia.

"I *heard* that! I'd never under*stand*?" Her mother stomped in, slammed a hand on the bed so hard the throw pillows jumped. "*Try* me, young lady. Where *is* she?"

"Mom, listen, Tashie's fine." Ashlyn kept her voice soft. Maybe this could work. She held out both hands, like, begging. "I'm so sorry. She's with Valerie. If I promise—*promise*—that you can see her tomorrow, will you trust me?"

As for Georgia. She looked at her daughter, the one she'd cradled in her arms, the one who'd fussed over the Gerber pears, the one who would only sleep with her grubby teddy and the blue blanket.

"Why'd you lie all this time, then?" Georgia believed and didn't believe, both at the same time. "Why make us so upset?"

"You made *yourself* upset. You made more out of it than it was. Daddy? Tell her." Ashlyn turned to her father for backup. But Tom was gone.

Good. Now Ashlyn only had to deal with Georgia. She plucked at the flowered coverlet. "*You* were such a good mother. But I—got scared. They're in Chicago, okay? Listen, I'll call Val. You'll see Tashie tomorrow."

Georgia held up her phone, brandishing it like a weapon. "Why did she take Tasha to Chicago? If you are lying to me—"

"Mommy. I'm not lying." Ashlyn had almost convinced her, she could tell. "I'm so, so sorry I made you upset. Valerie's mom lives there. She's like, Spanish. They might go to the zoo. Tasha's safe. She's happy. Trust me."

"*Trust* you?" Georgia, still frowning, jammed her phone back into her pocket. "Okay. Tomorrow. But if you're lying, I'll call the police. I swear. If something's wrong with my Tashie, I swear I will not protect you. Never, ever, protect you. I'll see you rot in hell."

You'll get there first, Ashlyn wanted to say. But out loud she said, "I promise, Mommy."

Not bad. Do I make a convincing Ashlyn, or what? I forgot to mention that she'd driven there to Laughtry Drive, but I'll put that in later.

With Ashlyn's audacious lies and omissions, and knowing what I know now, that scene is especially chilling. But back then, only Ashlyn knew anything was wrong. So I'll present it like that, with Tasha safe and happy. It might even have been true. Georgia— and Tom, apparently—believed it was.

What up w/ Tom? I add to my list.

"She's gotta be a monster, you know?" Katherine had said on the phone the other morning. "What mother could stay sane, being *told* her child is dead?" Then she'd paused, mid-pep-talk, silent for a beat. "Oh, I'm so sorry, honey."

There was no way to paper over reality. I let her off the hook.

"I'm fine," I'd lied, for the billionth time.

It's my job now to create the monster's story. I'll make it impeccably researched. Authoritative. Compelling.

And then I'll see Ashlyn Bryant sentenced to rot in hell.

CHAPTER SEVEN

A hoax," one news anchor pronounces, all chunky eyeglasses and inappropriate cleavage on tonight's seven o'clock news. "The bomb squad found nothing."

TV commentators are going nuts. Talking heads brand Ashlyn "the symbol of selfish post-millennials" and "the poster child for failed motherhood." Some advocates try to get a word in about the difficulties of a mother's role and the postpartum pressures on an inexperienced mom. No one is buying that.

Was Ashlyn depressed? I mean, at one point I'd seriously considered burning my own house down. Who knows what may have driven her? She's eleven years younger than I am, and her family life apparently pretty loveless.

A pang of potential sympathy tries to weasel a foothold in my brain. I push it away with a click of the remote.

On another channel, a fusty red-faced pundit complains about the money wasted evacuating the courthouse and delaying the trial. "Taxpayer dollars down the drain," she sneers. "Let's get on to the guilty verdict."

Charming. But I agree.

I mute the sound, thinking about the role each of us is playing. The murderer, the lawyers, the jurors, the journalists. No one really knows anything about anyone else. How can we understand motivation unless we *are* that person?

But I'll do my best. Soon to come in the trial is the part of Ashlyn's story—and Tasha Nicole's—that prosecutors promise will focus on motivation. On malice aforethought. That's got to mean the Skype chat, the one Georgia Bryant tearfully described on Dayton TV news. The local paper, conveniently, printed a transcript.

I twist the cap off the bottle of pinot noir that I put—when?—on the end table with one stemmed glass. I can drink and write at the same time. After all, I think as I watch the red liquid flow into the curved glass, I do know how to tell a story.

GOTTA LOVE SKYPE

"Is that real?" Georgia Bryant couldn't hold back her suspicions. Most computer things confused her. But there on the screen, in living color, clapping her sweet little hands and giggling, was her adorable darling granddaughter.

She'd secretly feared Tasha Nicole was dead. A grandmother thing. An instinct. But here she was. Alive as alive could be. "Is it truly real?"

Ashlyn, sitting in Tom's desk chair, didn't answer. Instead, after throwing Georgia a *give-me-a-break* look, she leaned closer to the monitor in her father's home office, clicking the mouse. She fluttered her fingers at the screen. "Hi Tashie, sweetheart, it's Mommy," she cooed.

Georgia crowded in closer, Tom behind her. They'd closed the scarlet and gray curtains—the colors of Tom's beloved Ohio State—to keep out the morning glare. Put the spaniels in their crates.

"Gotta love Skype," Ashlyn muttered.

"Mommy! I see you!" That voice, a sparrow's chirp, almost broke Georgia's heart. But there she was. Not dead. Not—not anything but fine. Far away, but fine.

"Hi, darling!" Georgia said. Even with the distorted computer lighting, the child's face shone bright and clean, and her soft sandy hair looked shiny and curled and bouncing. Her pink overalls, the ones she and Tom had given her for no occasion but just because, looked properly ironed.

"I see you! Do you see me?"

"Gampy's here, too." Georgia kept talking, gesturing behind her, gathering her husband closer. "How are you, honey?"

"We saw animals!" Tasha's eyes focused on the screen, then she seemed to be distracted. "Oh and we—what?"

The child's image left the screen. Now there was only a stretch of flowered wallpaper.

"Where'd she go?" Georgia demanded. "Who's she talking to?"

"Valerie, of course," Ashlyn said.

"We want to talk to the babysitter." She turned to her husband. "Right, Tom?"

"She's shy," Ashlyn said. "And's not comfortable with English."

"*What?* She has got to come home, Ashlyn." Georgia was laying down the law.

"I see you!" Tasha was back on the screen.

"I see you too, honey," Georgia said, lilting her voice to a more Tasha-appropriate tone. "We want you to come home, and you can play with Gampy." She felt Tom close behind her. "We want you to—"

"I'll come get you, and bring you to Grammy," Ashlyn interrupted, almost blocking Georgia's view. "Okay, honey?"

That was the last thing Georgia expected.

"Really?" She whispered the question.

"I'll come get you tomorrow, I promise," Ashlyn went on. "Bye-bye, honey." Ashlyn clicked the mouse, and the screen went black.

"Why did you end it?" Georgia said. "I didn't get to say goodbye."

"Can it never be enough? No matter what I do?" Ashlyn crossed her arms in front of her. "I promised you'd see her. You totally see she's fine. Exactly like I tried to tell you. But you never *never* believe me."

Tom stepped closer to her. "I believe you, Ashlyn," he said.

"See?" Ashlyn touched his arm. "Thank you, Daddy. At least someone stands up for me."

"That's not fair, Ashlyn." Georgia looked at the now-dark computer screen, remembering the little face she'd just seen. "I *do* stand up for you. I've stood up for you for twenty-three years! And to prove it, you don't have to drive to Chicago to pick up Tasha Nicole. I'll make your plane reservations, and we'll pay your airfare. Both ways."

Ashlyn blinked. Lifted her chin. "And Valerie's."

Georgia glanced at Tom. Didn't wait for a response. "And Valerie's."

A slash of soft light filtered through a crack in the curtains. Like a ray of hope, Georgia thought. A sign.

"Okay," Ashlyn said, drawing out the word.

"Tomorrow. Or—" Georgia's heart lifted with her good idea "—or right now! After you change clothes, of course. I'll take you to the airport!"

"Tomorrow." Ashlyn ended that part of the negotiation. "And there's one more thing."

"Gotta hand it to ya, Ashlyn," I say, saving my pages to the chapter file. If I'd been Grammy Georgia, would I have believed everything was fine? In the movies, it would have been a Tasha Nicole lookalike on Skype. Or the session faked somehow. But in this case, that *was* Tasha. Or so I'd read in the papers. Had Ashlyn already planned what she was about to do?

What no one but Ashlyn knew: that Skype call was the last time her grandparents would see the little girl alive.

If I had known that Saturday was the last time I'd see Sophie alive, what would I have done? I certainly wouldn't have yelled at her when she spilled her milky Cheerios. Wouldn't have griped about being late. Wouldn't have criticized Dex for dressing her in mismatched ruffly socks. I would have made sure to say—well, *I love you* is so obvious. And I'm certain they knew that. Would I have done anything different? Oh, yeah. I sure would. But I can't allow myself to think about that. I *don't* allow it.

I yank myself back to the book. Hating Ashlyn is so much more rewarding than hating myself. Having her call him "Daddy" might be over the fictional top, but people like Ashlyn are always Daddy's girls. Father-daughter relationships are the Freudian seeds of manipulative behavior. How girls learn to deal with men. Especially aging once-handsome gents like the gray-templed, golf-playing, country-clubbing Tom Bryant.

If I'm wrong, I'll change it later.

The lives of the Bryants are becoming so real. As if their stories are all playing out in my head and I'm simply transcribing. I can smell the lilac air freshener Georgia sprays; see the lines on the carpet she's vacuumed. Count the array of stuffed toys cuddling in Tasha Nicole's silent room. See the sneer on Ashlyn's face, the peachy-pink of her lip gloss. Her tight jeans.

The one thing I still can't channel is why. Even cautiously accessing my darkest thoughts, my most bitterly depressed moments or—I try to come up with a description—my blackest night of the soul, I can't understand *why* Ashlyn would do it. How could she?

I wipe one tear, determined. This is my job. As long as this book takes, I'll think of Tasha and Sophie. Think of them, but not think of them. I'll think of justice. Dex would want me to.

CHAPTER EIGHT

Last night, for the first time in I can't remember how long, I slept through the night. No nightmares of shattering glass and sirens. No thrashing off the covers and crying out loud, no waking myself up in chills and terror. Just sleep.

What's more perplexing, even disquieting: this morning my first thoughts are of the trial, not of Dex and Sophie. I write my numbers on the mirror, more deliberately than usual, 445, drawing my grief back into place.

A whisper of conscience trails me to the kitchen, prods me as I make my coffee, haunts me as I carry the steaming mug to my desk. *Sophie.* What would she look like now, more than a year older? I'd slogged through her birthday, pretending the day didn't exist, wrapped myself in blankets and shut the blinds and ignored the phone. Sophie will be three years old forever.

Dex's birthday was a wine-sotted nightmare.

On the anniversary of the accident, 365 on the mirror, Dex's parents called from Scottsdale. Katherine called, too, and a few brave friends. I hadn't picked up for any of them.

I sit in my chair and click on the computer, suffocated by what will never be. Dex will never be thirty-six. Sophie will never be four. Tasha Nicole Bryant will never be three. I'll keep changing, though. And keep wondering why.

"Attention, stations."

I flinch at Voice's interruption.

"For you early birds this Wednesday morning," Voice continues, "the clerk informs us trial will begin as scheduled at 9 A.M. Recess for the day at 5 P.M. Here at Ashlyn Central, we're in standby until approximately 8:55."

That means I have just over half an hour. In my old life, this time of morning, I'd chat with Sophie, have her put the breakfast napkins on the table. Together "his girls," as Dex called us, would get him off to work. First blueberry muffins and coffee, then a kiss from each of us.

"How're you going to drive?" I'd call out.

"Drive!" Sophie'd say. Another ritual.

"Carefully!" he'd reply. And off he'd go.

My magazine colleagues were incredulous. *You're giving it all up?* Far as I was concerned, I wasn't giving up anything. I was making a choice. Family.

So much for that plan.

I scroll through the Internet updates on the trial. My new life.

BOMB SCARE BOZOS headlines one local tabloid. Less yellow journalism described law enforcement reassuring the public there was no danger, and that the "small-potato troublemakers will be brought to justice." In Ashlyn news, the defendant is safe, the jury untainted, and the trial scheduled to continue.

Thirty minutes, now, until the day's testimony. I open my *Little Girl Lost* file and reset my brain to my narrative of another family's past.

According my research, Ashlyn's monstrous cover-up shifted into high gear when Georgia dropped her at the Dayton airport. I type as fast as I can to get to that part.

ONE MORE THING

"Remember I told you there was one more thing?" Ashlyn checked her hair in the passenger-side mirror, then flapped the sun visor back up.

Her mother steered the Honda to the curb at Departures Drop-Off. Five minutes more, if all went as planned, and Ashlyn would be out of here.

"Of course, honey," her mother said.

In that phony-gushy voice Ashlyn hated. But she wouldn't have to hear it for long.

"I'm worrying that Tasha and I . . ." Ashlyn pooched out her lips, frowning as if she was in deep thought.

"You're worried?" Georgia stopped, shifted into park, then turned to her, reached out a hand, touched her bare arm.

"Yeah." Ashlyn tried not to flinch. "I'm worried Tasha and I don't get enough time together. That's why I packed for two. And that's why I'm having—difficulty."

She checked for her mother's reaction. Was Mom buying this? Georgia loved Tasha. Fine. But Ashlyn could not handle her mothering. Her smothering. Her constant snooping. Meddling disguised as concern.

"That seems wise, honey," her mother said. Like she knew what was wise, for crap sake. "It's always better to have quality time with your children, especially when they're young. Like Tashie is. And you're still young, too."

Ashlyn almost gagged. But she could get through this. She had to. "So, Mommy, I need your advice. You really think it's good if Tasha Nicole and I have quality time?"

"Oh honey, yes, sure it is." Her mom had turned to face her, the skin on her neck quivering. Her teeth were so yellow. "Nothing would be better for Tashie than to be close to you. Bond with you."

Ashlyn put her hand on the door handle, clicked it open. She heard the hum of the air conditioner and the rumbling idle of the car and the distant roar of a jet engine.

"Wait a sec while I get my suitcase," she said. "Pop the trunk, Mom, okay?"

When Ashlyn rolled her suitcase back to the open passenger

door, she leaned in over the front seat, keeping one hand on the car's roof.

"Okay, thank you, Mother." Her mom was a silhouette, backlit by the sun's glare. Which meant she didn't have to see her face. "For your advice. And your permission."

"Per—?"

"I'm not coming back," Ashlyn said. "And Tashie isn't either. Like you suggested, I'm taking her. We're going on vacation. We've already bought our tickets."

"Like *I* suggested?" Her mother reached out her hand, but Ashlyn backed a step away.

"It was your idea, right? To 'bond'? And don't try to find us," Ashlyn went on. "If you do, we'll stay away longer. I told you I was packing for two, didn't I? But you didn't notice. Because you never listen to me."

"But I *never*—"

"Bye, Mom. We'll come back when the time is right." And she slammed the door.

"What a complete and total manipulative bitch." I say it out loud, realizing I've been typing faster and faster, my manuscript filled with typos and misspellings as the scene pours out. Ashlyn twisting her mother's words. Lying about taking a flight to Chicago. Laying the groundwork for her bogus story.

I tilt my head back and forth, contemplating the final sentence. Maybe it needs one more line? About looking back, or something. Except Ashlyn would not look back. Unless, maybe, in triumph?

"Attention stations." The voice interrupts my decision-making. "We'll have video in sixty seconds. The judge polled the jury on whether they've read anything about what happened yesterday. They've all said no. There are no motions pending before the court. Stations, forty-five seconds."

I click on my tablet, ready to record the video.

"Assistant District Attorney Royal Spofford—again, that's o-r-d,"

Voice goes on, what would I do without him, "has indicated his first witness will be Estrella Amador, the woman whose dog Frisco found the garbage bag in the—stand by please, stations. Thirty seconds."

I hit Record.

"And we're on in five, four, three—" Voice counts down.

Poor Estrella Amador. Talk about having a bad day at the beach. I feel the hint of an unworthy smile. Ashlyn Bryant is about to have a pretty bad day herself.

CHAPTER NINE

Estrella Amador, silver gray chignon and sensible shoes, steps to the witness box. Raises her right hand to take the oath. The blue-uniformed clerk opens her mouth, but in that instant, Quinn McMorran stands up.

"Your Honor," she says. "May we have a sidebar, please?"

"Oh, come *on*," I complain to the screen. "I want to hear this!"

The courtroom camera pulls out to a wide shot. Ashlyn, alone at the defense table, is holding her head in her hands. *Tough luck, sweetheart.* Reap what you sow.

Judge Green has ruled they can't broadcast sidebar audio, so the feed goes into almost-silence.

I fiddle with a pen, resist the urge to get more coffee. Do I have time to hit the bathroom?

"Attention, all." Voice is back. "We're in recess, gang. We've got to stop meeting like this. Stand by for updates."

Recess? Why? It can't be another bomb threat. Or can it? If it is, there's something seriously scary happening. Or something incredibly annoying. To stay productive, I start reading a bunch of the stuff Katherine brought, grand jury testimony and police reports. I know it'll be juicy, but I'm so distracted I'm not comprehending the words. I feel my foot jiggling. Why was there another recess?

The phone rings. I'm so startled I stand up from my desk chair. "Hello?"

"This is Miyoko Naka?" the woman says. "Lawyer McMorran's secretary?"

Like everything is a question. Quinn's secretary? "Yes?"

"She's asking me to tell you she won't be able to talk with you today, Miz Hennessey? And she asks could you please postpone?"

"Until when?" Quinn putting me off? A recess? Not good.

"She will call you?" the secretary says. "Thank you."

I stand there, listening to the dial tone. Stare at nothing. Worrying. I'm a storyteller. I can think of a million reasons court screeched to a halt. Each of them disastrous. At that moment, 9:27 Wednesday morning, all of them parade through my mind. What if . . . ? Panicked, I stab in Katherine's phone number. Be there. *Be there.* Keep me sane.

"This is Kath—"

"Listen," I interrupt. "I'm freaking. What happens to the book if Ashlyn admits she's guilty? What if she went crazy at the idea of hearing Amador, and decided she can't stand any more horrible body-found testimony, and offers to plead to, say, manslaughter and the DA agrees and the trial is over? Does that mean the book is over, too?"

My chest aches, thinking about it. It's been only four days since I signed up for this job, but I've conscripted myself, enlisted myself, pledged myself. For Sophie. The muscles in my back tense so tight I have to sit down. Four days, and I'm hooked. Physically and emotionally addicted to Ashlyn Bryant's comeuppance. Hell, *punishment.*

Katherine makes it clear that Arbor Publishing wouldn't want a book about a woman who hadn't fought for her innocence.

"A plea deal? That'd suck," she says. "It makes Ashlyn, I don't know, too sympathetic."

"Sympathetic? *That* woman?"

"Or pitiful." Kath puffs a breath. "Yeah, I'm disgusting. I'm the media. But listen, kiddo, we can't sell a book about a contrite and remorseful victim of postpartum depression. Or whatever excuse she pulls." She pauses. "Unless, I don't know, you want to make it into a book about redemption? Redemption sells."

Could I write a book about redemption? Ashlyn's attempt at redemption? *Gah.*

"Gimme a break." I say. "Redemption is a lot more than simply admitting you did it."

"Not in our legal system," Katherine answers. "Let's wait and see. Talk soon, kiddo."

A squawk from the speaker. The courtroom video goes to black. Then color bars.

"Attention, all." It's Voice. "Trial's in recess until Monday, at 9 A.M. If you're wondering why, join the club. Gotta stop meeting like this. See you next week, gang."

Next week? Kidding me? Monday? Four days from now? I stare at my manuscript, my words blurring. What's the point of working? If this all falls apart, there'll be no book. All of this will be for nothing. Three glasses of better-than-resorting-to-Ambien wine later, I give up. I skip dinner, who cares, and stare at the blank TV.

The next thing I know is the light.

I blink, trying to figure out where I am. And when it is. Couch. Morning. Thursday. But my dream still wraps around me.

I'd dreamed . . . Sophie. I try to retrieve it. Retrieve *her.* Sophie . . . yanking green garbage bags out of the bottom drawer in our kitchen. Unspooling a whole roll of them, one after the other, and twirling herself into them, laughing and laughing, until finally, her spinning made her dizzy and tipped her onto the floor. Except, wait. In the dream, it was not floor. It was sand. Or broken glass? "Look Mommy, I'm Little Mermaid," she'd said. And then it was wet, so wet, everything was wet. That's when I woke up, I guess, morning sun in my face, and I knew it was my own tears.

A thunk on my front porch saves me from the rest of the dream. Wiping my eyes, still bleary and uncertain, and a little bit grateful to have seen my daughter, I pad out to retrieve the Thursday morning newspaper. The headline jolts me into reality.

Ashlyn Bryant Ill, Trial Delayed. Underneath, in a smaller font: Court to resume Monday. I scan the first paragraph, standing in my entryway, before I close the front door.

"She's sick?" I say it out loud as I read, only the universe hearing my skepticism. I close the front door with a hip check. "Oh, *right*."

Joe Rissinelli got the scoop, of course. He always does. Joe Riss works freelance now, doing undercover investigations, so talented he can write his own ticket. These days he's on the team covering the trial for the *Boston Globe*. Joe and I know each other in passing because we'd crossed paths at *City*. After I left, I still followed his bylines. He's a relentless journalist who drives me crazy with his sources. But at least now I can stop worrying about a plea deal.

I'd stampeded myself into believing something I made up.

Truth is, Joe's exclusive explains, right before Estrella Amador came to the stand, Ashlyn started writing notes to Quinn McMorran. They weren't about pleading guilty. They were complaining about her stomach ache.

"What a *liar*," I say out loud. That's *my* verdict. But Joe's a reporter. He has to report what his subject says.

I skim more of it, heading to the kitchen, needing coffee. Joe Riss's article reports Ashlyn has "mild food poisoning." Apparently it'd been "all the defendant could do not to get sick in the courtroom"—I assume that was Joe's polite way of saying *throw up*, another thing she and I apparently have in common.

I flip to the jump page. Stop in the kitchen entryway. *Joe.* How does he know this? He could be pals with the judge. With Quinn McMorran. Or with Ashlyn, for all I know. I pop in a coffee pod, assessing.

Maybe Joe Riss has been cultivating Ashlyn from the start. Sending her letters in jail. Maybe visiting her. Seems like she's always, from my research anyway, attracted to handsome and powerful men. Not sure how powerful Joe is, but he's handsome enough. He's married, and more than twenty years older than Ashlyn, but hey, if she could use him, that wouldn't have deterred her. So I've read.

Maybe I'll call him? Ask him? Wonder if Katherine knows Joe. We'd all worked at *City*, though at different times.

But bottom line. All good. Rescued by Joe Rissinelli. I postpone coffee, take my shower, and write my numbers extra-large on the foggy mirror. 446.

As always, I take a quiet moment to honor what they signify. Not forgiveness, certainly. I'll never have that. There's only loss. And remembrance. And love. As they fade, I believe the ghost of each number remains. Will always exist, like the ghosts of Dex and Sophie will always exist with me.

Back in the kitchen, clean and back to semi-normal. Out the window, the morning is blue-skied and sunny, the neighborhood traffic clattering by. That's the real world. No one knows what's going on in *my* world. In my house. Or in my head.

The fragrant caffeine splashes into my mug. And the phone rings.

"Told you so," Katherine says, before I get my cell all the way to my ear. "The great Joe Riss strikes again, and all is well. Except for our defendant, of course."

"Yeah. And good morning, Kath."

"Food poisoning?" Katherine goes on, her voice a sneer. "No way. She wanted to avoid hearing the details. Seeing those photos."

"Makes sense, but even so. I had my whole book on redemption plotted out," I lie. "And I'd get the kill fee, right, if the book doesn't go? A thousand bucks?"

"Kill fee my ass," Katherine says. "Listen, you win, kiddo. The trial's delayed until Monday. That means you get more time to write. Count your blessings, Merce."

"Counting," I lie again. I have no blessings. I douse my coffee with milk, head for the study. "But Kath? She's 'sick'? And those baggy clothes? Speaking of counting—what if she's pregnant?"

"The true facts are awful enough," Katherine says, "without you making stuff up. Plus, she's been in jail for a year. Listen, no need to send us any more chapters as you go, okay? It's great. Just write. Now back to work. You owe me a book."

I'd already opened the *Little Girl Lost* file as she hung up, planning my next scene. One of the important unanswered questions—one that should help explain why the murderer could be "only Ashlyn"—is where did Ashlyn go after she lied to her mother and left the Dayton airport?

From all accounts, that police investigation started when Georgia Bryant demanded the Dayton cops "find" her granddaughter.

The detective who caught the case, a mid-level journeyman named Wadleigh Rogowicz, started his investigation at Hot Stuff, the skanky Dayton nightclub where Ashlyn hung out.

Rogowicz predicted a textbook mother-daughter squabble. "Families are complicated," he says in the *Dayton Sun*. "I have a daughter myself."

For a heartbeat or two, that stops me. I don't.

CHAPTER TEN

What was it like at Hot Stuff? I pay the club a visit by way of a grainy cell phone video on YouTube. I'd hoped Ashlyn would be in it, but it's impossible to recognize anyone in the flashing lights and shaky pictures. Watching it, I can almost smell the sex. And the weed. It's a throbbing mass of sweating twenty-somethings, cruising and dancing and slugging down, I don't know, Moscow Mules and Tito-sodas. Rock star wannabes in sunglasses leading alcohol-fueled partiers in ear-splittingly loud and indecipherable song lyrics. Everyone wearing as little as possible.

I jam in my earbuds and play it again, cranking the volume, loud, *louder*, so loud the music blocks out everything else. Blocks out reality. I transport myself. Change myself. I'm not me.

I'm Ashlyn Bryant at Hot Stuff. Glossed lips, tank top clinging, hair damp at the nape of my neck. I'm the thump of the music, the harsh sexy fragrance of sweaty bodies, the mind-numbing swirl of lights. The alcohol, seductive, sugar and lime. And drugs, the sweet whisper of marijuana, or the unmistakable dice of a razor blade through chunks of white powder laid out on a mirror. A twenty-dollar bill rolled up as a tube.

The video runs out. Silence. Back to being just me.

And, okay, no one's ever specifically mentioned drugs.

"It's a club, right?" I defend myself to no one. I yank out the earbuds, dismissing my own hesitation. "There's gotta be drugs."

The real Ashlyn apparently frequented Hot Stuff at all hours, made up and dressed to kill (oooh). A few stories reveal Ashlyn Bryant was not only a regular, but she and others sometimes pitched in to crank up the fun as unofficial "hostesses." Hostesses were told to buy a bottle of top-shelf mezcal, then sell it, shot by upcharged shot, to patrons who wanted a hot drinking partner. Ash was "awesome" at it, club owner Ron Chevalier was quoted as saying. "Customers loved her."

So where was Tasha Nicole during all this awesome clubbing? With the friend-babysitter-whoever she is?

Where is Valerie? I write on my list.

I look at the clock. Still early. Too early for wine, especially on a Thursday. Okay, then. Still working.

MAKING THIS STUFF UP

"This had better pan out." Detective Wadleigh Rogowicz, muttering to himself, slammed his cruiser door and headed toward the front door of the south Dayton apartment building.

He'd been optimistic about the Skype lead. Until the Skype people informed him calls weren't recorded. As for "Valerie," Georgia Bryant had told him the babysitter's last name was "something like Lucio or Luciano." Spanish, maybe. Italian. She "wasn't sure." He pictured a girl on a student visa, maybe, or illegal. Valerie Luciano in Chicago? Needle in a freaking haystack.

But Facebook might save him. One of Ashlyn Bryant's friends had posted that on the night of June 16, her pal Ashlyn and Hot Stuff owner Ron Chevalier were at the movies. In Dayton. Rogowicz checked his "Ashlyn calendar," a grubby paper printout he kept folded in his wallet. The sixteenth was two days *after* Georgia Bryant dropped Ashlyn at the Dayton Airport.

But the friend's cell phone video recorded Ashlyn and Ron arriving arm in arm that night for the midnight showing of an R-rated thriller called *Joy Ride.*

The video'd been posted by a Sandie DiOrio, a Hot Stuff hostess who also worked at the Upton Cinema. DiOrio had apparently let the pair in free, and was boasting about it. *Social media,* Wadleigh thought. People post anything. Even things that will get them fired.

Now he'd see. If Ashlyn was in Dayton, that was big. It meant she was lying.

He knocked on apartment 4B. A young woman opened the door. A white cat in her arms writhed away the moment it saw him. The woman admitted being DiOrio, even offered him a seat on her cat-hair-covered couch.

"I'll pay the company back, I promise." DiOrio, instantly capitulating to his inquiry, obediently transferred her cell phone video to him. She fussed with the strap of her revealing tank top. "And I'll never let anyone in free again. Am I in trouble?"

Gotta love it. The old tank-top move. Everyone was hiding something. It made them so helpful. And dumb. DiOrio was so skeeved she didn't ask why he wanted the video. Simply assumed her employer had discovered her petty larceny.

"In trouble? Well, that's kind of complicated." He scratched his head, pretending Sandie's future depended on what came next. Then he lied. "Ashlyn told us you *hadn't* let them in free. Why would that be?"

"She was just trying to protect me, I guess. She used to bring Tasha over here, you know? And the three of us would play on our laptops and phones and whatever. But, um, once? Like, two months ago?" she said. "I was driving. Ashlyn was on her cell."

"Go on," Rogowicz said. "By the way, was Tasha in the car, too? Do you know who Ashlyn was talking to?"

Sandie apparently thought the answers were on the ceiling of her pre-fab condo.

"No," she said. "Tasha wasn't there. And Ashlyn was talking pretty soft. The only thing I remember about it, was after."

"After?" Rogowicz looked up from his pad. Pencil poised.

"Yeah." Sandie was still not quite looking at him, obviously picturing it. "After Ashlyn hung up, she threw her phone on the dashboard. Then she laughed. Like, laughed. And I'm like, 'What?' And she's like, 'Holy crap. I am so good at making stuff up.'"

I did not make up that quote. Sandie DiOrio had said that, word for word, to Rogowicz, and he had told the *Dayton Sun*. "Holy crap. I am so good at making stuff up." I cut and pasted the quote into my manuscript from the newspaper's website, changing only the font to make it match.

So far, this story feels like it's on track. But is what I wrote in the right order? Ashlyn, making stuff up, pretends to leave Dayton. She's actually still in Dayton. For a while, that is. Tasha is apparently in Chicago. Georgia goes to the police. Rogowicz begins the hunt. But Ashlyn—now with Tasha?—has disappeared. Two weeks later, Baby Boston is found. That's when the misleading composite gets issued. I'm getting ahead of myself, of course. I haven't put that in yet. Eventually, a thousand miles apart, Dayton's Detective Rogowicz and the Boston cops will put two and two together. Search, arrest, custody, no bail, trial.

Okay, it works. Now I've got the whole weekend to work on the book.

Though what I'm writing is all basically true, I am really good at making stuff up.

CHAPTER ELEVEN

Welcome back, stations." Voice greets me at my desk Monday morning. "As you no doubt are aware, both sides have stipulated to Estrella Amador's testimony, and she will not take the stand. Court resumes on schedule at zero-nine hundred hours. That means? You have five minutes to get your morning coffee. Hope you had a great weekend."

"Thank you, Voice," I say to the empty room. "And yes, I got a lot done on the book this weekend, thank you very much." I'm disappointed Amador isn't testifying, but I suppose her discovery of the garbage bag on Castle Island beach doesn't provide anything probative to either side. I'll still put her and Frisco in the book. It's such a disturbing story.

There was never a trial about Dex and Sophie's deaths—it wasn't murder, unless an oak tree can be a murderer, and rain its accomplice. The police told me Norwalk Street was slick, and their accident-reconstruction team suspected an animal darted out into the road. Though no animal was found. Dex would always slam on the brakes for an indecisive cat or a dopey bird. Once a wild turkey strutted out onto our street. We'd all burst out laughing. What does a turkey say? Gobble Gobble! Why did the turkey cross the road?

Dex put it on Facebook. I don't go on Facebook anymore. People there are too happy.

"All rise," the court officer announces.

I start my tablet recording. Ashlyn, in her usual phony-innocent outfit, sits at the defense table beside a gray-suited Quinn McMorran. She hasn't returned my calls. I hate using Dex as leverage, but Quinn promised to talk to me. And I'm going to hold her to it.

"The Commonwealth calls Detective Bryce Overbey," Royal Spofford says.

Overbey is the first cop who saw the green trash bag. Craggy, middle-aged, and wearing a tweed sport coat, he strides to the witness box.

And my phone rings. The landline. Caller ID says GWP. Gorin, Willberg, and Pritchett. Attorneys at Law.

I can't breathe. I haven't seen this caller ID in—I try to do the subtraction, using the instant of silence on the other end of the line—but I can't. Hundreds of days.

It takes two more rings before I can convince my muscles to move. Before I can make my brain remember what to say.

"Hello?"

"Mercer?"

I recognize the voice, too.

"Hi, Will." The nickname strikes me for the very first time as the most awful name ever. Why a trusts and estates lawyer named William Pritchett wouldn't call himself Bill or even William, is beyond my imagining. Will is, was, Dex's law partner, and the lawyer for our . . . estate. Such as it is. Will did our wills.

Now what? I hear him preparing to speak, so I wait.

"Anyway, Mercer," he says. "This is as hard for me as it is for you."

My brain explodes as he talks, blotting out his words. No it *isn't* "as hard" for him, not at all.

". . . and so we just wondered when," he's saying, "or if, you'd like any of the items—his case notes and calendars, correspondence, memorabilia—from, ah, Dex's office."

"Office?" I picture Dex's office, a room in a dream. Bookshelves and windows and diplomas. Framed news clippings from his big criminal acquittals. Photos on his desk. Both of us in Nantucket wearing silly hats. Our wedding. All three of us at the hospital with brand new baby Sophie, that stretchy pink bow Mom sent us perched around her fuzz of pale hair. Arm in arm, in mourning black in front of my childhood home in Ithaca, right before Mom's funeral. With no one left to live there, we sold the house soon after. I close my eyes, try to erase the image.

It does not exist.

And it doesn't, I realize, my heart hitting the floor as Will's voice buzzes in my ear. There's no "Dex's office" anymore. It's a room, a vacant room filled with items that don't belong to anyone who's alive.

The monitor on my desk shows the trial is underway, Overbey still on the stand. I know his testimony today is only to describe seeing the garbage bag and calling in the medical examiner. The investigation part will come later in the trial. Still, I am missing important stuff. But the past is on the line, the past is calling me. And won't let me go.

". . . we waited, as you know, Mercer, in an effort to spare you from . . ."

I let him talk. It doesn't matter what he says. On the monitor, I see Royal Spofford gesturing at blown-up photographs of the green bag on the shore.

"Thank you, Will, that is thoughtful of you," I reply when it must be my turn. "I'm working on a project, though, so I could pick it all up in say . . ." I calculate. "A month."

Silence on the other end.

"What if we delivered it?" He finally says. "We need–"

I don't care what they need, but I don't say that. "Fine." I remember my manners. "And again, you were so kind about the . . ."

I can't say the f word. Funeral. So I stop.

Apparently Will doesn't want to say it either. "How are you, Mercer?" he asks.

"Fine." I am just making stuff up. On the monitor, Quinn

McMorran approaches Overbey for her cross-examination. *Get in, get out,* Dex would have suggested to her. McMorran will probably remind the jury that Overbey, at this point in the case, had no evidence connecting Ashlyn to the murder. He didn't even know whose body it was.

"Yes," I agree, quickly as I can. The trial is taping, but I've *got* to get off the phone. "If someone brings it over, it would be—"

Then I hit a vocabulary wall. What word can I choose? It would be good, fine, perfect? Nothing seems good or fine or perfect, especially in describing how my dead husband's possessions are about to be put in a box, and—in a box. Just like Dex.

"It would be *okay,*" I say. My eyes are drawn to the monitor, where, as I predicted, McMorran has already finished, and now Medical Examiner Barbara Zimbel, a slim dark-haired woman, quietly professional in long-sleeved black and glasses on a silver chain, takes the three steps up to the witness chair. She raises her right hand to be sworn in. Coming next is the part that'll make headlines. And break jurors' hearts.

"Will? I *have* to go." It's easier to handle TV death. It's my job to handle it.

"I understand," he says.

He doesn't. I hang up, I fear, in the midst of his gratuitous attempts at conciliatory goodbyes. I stand there for a moment, lost in time. The trial is taping, someone else's life, and someone else's death, and I am tangled in memories and confusion and uncertainty. Only one thing is certain. The verdict. Which brings me back to real life.

Dr. Zimbel is talking, and her voice comes up mid-sentence as I unmute the volume and lower myself into the chair.

". . . opinion, a body is more likely to exhibit advanced stages of decomposition if it has been in water than if it has been, for example, on the ground."

"So to be clear. A body decomposes more quickly in water," Spofford translates into plain English.

"Yes."

"Meaning a body could be in water for a very short time to exhibit the level of decomposition that little Tasha Nicole's body presented?"

"Yes."

"As a result of your experience," Spofford goes on, "can you give us an opinion of *how long* the victim had been dead?"

"Your Honor!"

I understand where Spofford is going. And why Quinn McMorran wants to stop it. It's about Ashlyn's alibi. If they pinpoint a time of death, they can pinpoint where Ashlyn was at that time. The more imprecise the time of death, the more difficult to prove Ashlyn is responsible.

What could anyone say that'd convince me she didn't do it? I suppose if Ashlyn points to the "real killer." Or if someone else confessed. Honestly? I still might not believe it. I know guilt when I see it.

"You may answer," the judge says.

The medical examiner looks at the floor. Maybe she understands she's on the verge of revealing something so irrefutable, it'll clinch Spofford's case. I'd kill to know what Ashlyn Bryant is thinking.

"It depends on the temperature and the tides," the medical examiner says. "It's not an exact science."

"It's not an exact science," I repeat out loud. No, sadly, it's not. Like justice.

The trial goes on, clinical evidence and inescapable sorrow, for more than an hour. I watch, transfixed. And then my doorbell rings.

CHAPTER TWELVE

The doorbell? I stop, fingers poised over my keypad. Katherine again? She's been here more in the past couple of days than in the past six months. I wait. No more doorbell. Maybe I'm wrong?

"You're losin' it, sister," I say aloud. Still, I'm out of practice with visitors. My friends from the magazine stopped visiting months ago. I knew they felt uneasy. Sensing my unpredictability, their common ground with me became unsettled, rearranged by what had happened. No one seeks out regret. Katherine's visits trailed off–until recently. Dex's parents almost smothered me with a few months of hovering, but they've now decided to give me my space.

We live in such fragile equilibrium. When one thing changes, everything else has to readjust, same as when a new person steps onto an elevator. People move, shift positions, make sure the remaining room is properly allocated. Most people in my life have decided to leave me alone. It's my fault, I understand that.

The doorbell rings again. I'm aware of my sweatpants, my random hair. Did I brush it today? I lift a hand to check.

One look through the peephole reveals it's Theo Ballero, the law firm's messenger-assistant-gopher. Everyone loves Theo, always in a button-down and loosened pastel tie, polished loafers. No aspirations but to please the man, his reach not exceeding his grasp. But why is he here?

"Hi, Ms., um," he attempts as I open the door. "I have your boxes." He gestures toward a silver minivan idling in the driveway.

The willow in our front yard, in full tender leaf, rustles in a puff of breeze. The sprinklers had come on mid-morning, the last of the droplets now glistening on the grass and on that bush with the feathery leaves in sweetly fragrant bloom. What a pretty yard, passersby used to tell us. And it was. Pretty, like our home and our family, exactly what everyone wants. Too bad we don't fully appreciate our joy until it's too late.

"Ms. Hennessey?" Theo is saying. "Hope I'm not bothering. There are three boxes, and . . ."

He stops. Maybe reading my expression.

"That was fast," I say. Will must have had the boxes ready to go. "I must admit I wasn't expecting anyone. So soon."

"I'll bring them in for you?"

Theo's no threat, just doing his job.

"I'll help," I say. Faster the better. Get this over with. *Will.* What a liar.

Theo hefts a brown carton from the back of the van, hands it to me. It's flapped closed with one strip of tape, not too heavy. I take a deep breath, cardboard pressed against my chest, maybe searching for a scent of Dex. But it only smells like box. Theo stacks the other two, slams the van's door with a shiny loafer. Lugging both boxes, he lets me go first through the front door.

I'm relieved Theo won't think–if guys think about this stuff–that I've turned into a slob. Dining room, as we walk by it to the hall, abandoned, a bare oval table set only with pristine white candles in Dex's heirloom silver candlesticks. They've stood there, off duty, for four hundred and fifty days. It's easy to keep a house in order if it's only you.

At least my desk looks as if someone works there.

"Watching the trial?" Theo asks, cocking his head toward the muted feed monitor.

"Isn't everyone?" Theo doesn't need to know what I'm doing. No one in my world, other than Katherine and the publisher, is aware of this project. Oh, except for Spofford and McMorran.

And the judge. And probably Voice and the video guys. So it's really not that secret.

"Poor thing." Theo lifts a knee, hoisting the box he's carrying. "Poor little Tasha Nicole."

We stash the containers in the guest bedroom. As if I'll ever have guests. Three boxes, law firm logo on each side, corrugated cardboard, lightly taped so they can be opened easily. They're numbered one of three, two of three, three of three.

"Need help opening them?" Theo dusts his hands on the back of his khakis.

I blanch at the thought. But he's only trying to be nice.

"No, thanks." I close the guest room door and lead him away. As he backs out of the driveway, I'm thinking: I'm never going in that room again. Never opening those flaps, never ripping off the tape, never looking into those boxes. Never ever.

And now I've missed my morning's writing.

In real life, the trial's in recess, set to reconvene after lunch. I'll rewind my video; see what I missed. Because of those boxes. A shadow crosses my heart, the darkness calling to me, pulling at me. Dex's stuff. Sealed up. *Like he is.*

"Dexter Liam Hennessey." I say his name out loud. He wouldn't want me to "schmull," as he used to say. He'd want me to get the hell on with it.

Getting the hell on with it, I defrost a container of condolence soup someone left for me. The label has peeled off, so it's also surprise soup. Chicken, I smell, as the microwave does its thing. I remember that fragrance.

"Soup!" Sophie would crow from her Piglet booster chair, holding up her special bunny spoon in delight. "Super duper!"

The bunny spoon is in the basement now. In a box.

I shake it off, the darkness, best I can. The darkness will not conquer me. I bring my soup into the study for a working lunch, prop my tablet against the still-black monitor, and fast-forward to video of this morning's proceedings. Medical examiner first. The tablet has a smaller screen than the monitor, but this is about the words, so it doesn't matter. I hit Play, guessing on the timing.

". . . explain the process?" A miniature Spofford is asking an equally small medical examiner. "After you received the body, what did you do first?"

Still holding my spoon, I fast-forward again. I need to hear the pivotal "cause of death" testimony before the trial starts live. Guessing on the timing again, I hit Play.

". . . drowning?" Spofford is asking.

"The lungs were not sufficiently intact to allow such a judgment," Dr. Zimbel answers.

"Were there any specific indicia of trauma? Broken bones?"

"No."

"Internal injuries?"

"Because of the victim's condition, I–no. Not that I could tell."

"Bruises?"

"Again. Because of the victim's condition, no."

"Were there signs of choking or suffocation? Petachiae in the eyes?"

"There were no eyes," the ME says.

My soup spoon clatters on the hardwood floor. I leave it. I'll never eat again. My tablet's speaker is feeble, but I hear the audience react, and then the gavel banging to silence the horrified murmurs.

"I see." Spofford shuffles his pieces of paper. Clears his throat. "After you completed the autopsy, ah, in your opinion, then, what was the cause of death?"

The courtroom goes silent. I move my disgusting soup out of the way, and lean in toward the tiny screen, as if getting closer could allow me to hear what Dr. Zimbel is thinking. She knew, when she conducted that autopsy in the dank, steely basement of 94 Albany Street, masked and gloved, smelling the morgue's disinfectant and decomposition, with the tiny body of whoever it was–a little girl, a little dead girl–on a sleek slab of aluminum, that she'd be called on to do her job. To understand the death. Describe it. Possibly convict the person who erased an innocent human being from existence.

"Homicide," Zimbel says.

"Not an accident?" Spofford asks. "Why?"

"Attention stations," Voice interrupts. Real life is starting again. "Court will resume in one minute."

And now I've missed Zimbel's answer. I push Rewind. *Accident.* I hate that word. But I have to focus on this, not on my Sophie, not on Dex, not on my own life, not on the terrifying uncertainty of random disaster that steals our loved ones from us. I could *kill* Ashlyn Bryant. It's heart-twisting enough when it's an accident, when everyone says it couldn't have been prevented, but how does the mind grasp the reality when a monster, a real actual *monster* like her–

I fumble with the tablet, my fingers not obeying. I need to hear this.

"Thirty seconds, stations," Voice says.

"Dr. Zimbel," I hear again. "Not an accident? Why?"

The ME puts on her glasses, takes them off.

"Mr. Spofford?" she says. "She had been put in a trash bag."

I hear a choked-back sob from someone–and realize it's me.

"No further questions," Spofford says.

"You may roll tape in ten seconds," Voice says.

Next will be Quinn McMorran's cross-examination. After that, the sketch artist.

But I am crying too hard to listen.

CHAPTER THIRTEEN

If I let my emotions derail my assignment, it'll prove I can never be me again. That's—well, I was going to tell myself *that's pathetic.* On the other hand, it's true. I never will be that me again. That's what I have to get used to.

I'd lost it again after the medical examiner's testimony. Buried myself in bed, a blanket over my head. Now I have to come back to life. Because I, at least, can.

So now, even though my eyes are puffy and all I want to do is keep sleeping—maybe forever—I convince myself to get out of bed. I make coffee. Pour wine. Open a pack of saltines with my teeth, and force myself, at ten thirty at night, to listen to today's trial recording. And work on my book.

Are the jurors asleep now? I think about those fourteen souls as I flip on the study light, and click open my manuscript, brushing salty crumbs from my lap. The jurors are at home, not sequestered. They're forbidden to talk about the trial, read about it, or watch it on TV. *Right.* The whole jury system is based on impossibles.

To avoid the incessant press coverage, Quinn McMorran had argued to move the trial out of town. But change of venue motion got denied—without explanation—in about two seconds. I'd agreed with Judge Green's unspoken reasoning. What good would moving the trial have done? Everyone everywhere knows about Tasha Nicole Bryant. And Ashlyn.

The judge finally asked each juror: "Can you put aside any

preconceived ideas about the defendant, listen to the evidence, and render a verdict based on that evidence alone?"

All of the seated jurors said yes. How many lied?

I open my tablet to watch the recording. I push Play. I'm ready. Nothing happens.

"What?" I ask it. I try again. "Come *on*."

One frame of video is clearly there–I can see Barbara Zimbel, the medical examiner, ready for her all-important cross by McMorran. If they had time, sketch artist Al Cook would come next. But although I push Play, nothing happens. After that one frame, my recording ends.

"What?" Did I do something wrong? I fiddle with the tablet, do a sound test.

"James James Morrison Morrison, Wetherby George Dupree," I recite the snippet of poetry toward the embedded mic. What I used to read with Sophie at bedtime. *Though she was only three.* I rewind. Push Play. "James, James . . ." I hear my own voice.

It works perfectly. I apparently don't.

"Shoot." This is bad. I take one sip of cabernet, then another. Then coffee.

Wait. I reassure myself. It's fine.

I can find Zimbel's testimony online. And I don't really need to hear Al Cook. A slew of blustering interviews and blistering articles revealed how his drawing of Baby Boston went so disastrously wrong. When I saw it, I assumed, like everyone did, the poor child was Hispanic.

The mess it caused should be the next chapter. I mentally sketch it out.

First, the Do You Know Me posters went up, illustrated with Cook's full-color drawing. The city buzzed, nonstop, about the girl's poignant wide-eyed expression, her dark curls, her purple butterfly barrettes. I obsessed about the ominously disturbing family drama implicit behind it.

No one knew her name, but Boston adopted her. Mourners

made pilgrimages to Castle Island Beach, bringing candles and teddy bears. When TV cameras arrived, the crowds increased. The hashtag #WhoIsShe? trended nationally. Was the poor girl Amanda Sue Rogers, who vanished from the Gloucester cliffs while her family picnicked twenty feet away? But Amanda was not Hispanic. Was she Liliana Paradol, who'd been abducted from that playground in Everett? But Liliana was seven. Was she the accidentally drowned child of undocumented immigrants, her parents terrified to identify her for fear they'd be deported?

It wasn't only Boston PD on the hunt. The Foundation for Missing Children. The Portuguese Friends of the Harbor. The Sons of Barcelona. One newspaper story reported that suspicious residents were paying attention to their Hispanic neighbors for the first time, trying to remember—had they ever seen a child like that? Maybe they should have been more vigilant. Maybe everyone should have been more vigilant.

What I didn't know then—Boston Police Detective Koletta Hilliard had sent hair and tissue samples, and a snippet of the victims clothing, to a state-of-the-art forensics lab in Utah. At Hilliard's insistence, they expedited the tests.

It took two weeks. According to a police report Katherine gave me, after scientists measured the hair for "carbon and oxygen isotope ratios," they theorized she wasn't a New England native, and had been in that area fewer than three months. Their forensic pollen expert—who knew?—tested her leggings, and discovered traces of pollen that occurred only in the Midwest. Specifically, the Ohio Buckeye tree. "Pollen, under the right preservation conditions," his report read, "is virtually indestructible."

Koletta Hilliard then decided to call every PD in Ohio. Asking about missing little girls.

On call number 17 of 131 she got Wadleigh Rogowicz.

"Amazing," I say out loud. I can't help but punch a fist in the air as I reread that report. Then, even though I'm alone and no one witnessed my moment of personal satisfaction over a tragedy, I lower my fist, embarrassed. Katherine is right, writers are scum.

Still, a good story is a good story. I type my chapter heading.

WERE THOSE HER REAL BARRETTES?

Sometimes my brain goes so fast my fingers can't keep up. It takes about fifteen minutes to write the whole thing. The sketch artist had screwed up, big time. He'd drawn the hair and the chubby cheeks correctly, but his possibly Hispanic, approximately five-year-old Baby Boston looked nothing like the pale, blue-eyed, almost-three-year-old Tasha Nicole Bryant.

But that's who she was. The inaccurate Baby Boston sketch, drawn from misconception and assumption, was such a career-ending error that Al Cook instantly retired.

The barrettes, though, Cook had copied from reality. And Wadleigh Rogowicz recognized them.

This book is going to work.

CHAPTER FOURTEEN

This book is not going to work!" I plaster a pillow over my face to silence my own whiny outburst to the bedroom ceiling, and flat on my back, breathe into the pillow's dark softness. The evidence is coming in too fast, information overload. Why I thought I could write an intelligent and compelling true-crime book about the life and the murder trial of a now-internationally notorious mother and the beloved daughter she killed and do it successfully in a single month—even six weeks—is beyond my comprehension.

I cross my arms over the pillow, keeping the world out. I know it's only 6 A.M. I cannot sleep. I can't even try.

My decision-making capabilities were skewed when I said yes to this book, of course. My whole damn world is skewed. I'd decided I could reclaim my life. Find forgiveness. Well, that particular moment is most assuredly gone. But my responsibility isn't. Now I've agreed to a job that might be impossible. Now I have no choice.

Fine. I'm up.

T-shirt on. Sweatpants tied. Flip-flops. Advil. Water. Onward.

Today is 451. I acknowledge this as I draw the numbers, as always, onto my medicine cabinet mirror, which obediently steams up when I shower. For a moment, flip-flopping down the hallway toward the kitchen and coffee, I wonder about my counting-the-days thing. Is it healthy? Am I simply reminding myself to be unhappy?

But we need rituals. Rely on them for sanity. And I see it as tribute, an acknowledgment that Dex and Sophie existed. *Exist*. And are not forgotten.

Anyway. In the trial, it's Day Five. I twist the gas on under the teakettle, self-diagnosing. Maybe all the coffee is making me jittery. Or maybe it's that my mental focus is on a missing little girl, a dead little girl, at exactly the time I am trying *not* to think about that, not every single minute of every single day. Now it's my *job* to think about it.

I feel a flare of anger, a darkness, my brain twisting words into italics. Anger at *Katherine,* for offering what she knew would be a painful assignment. Anger at *myself,* for taking it. Anger at *Ashlyn,* for destroying the one beautiful thing in her life that could never be replaced.

Setting the tea on my study desk, I'm careful not to clatter the fragile china cup and saucer. A gift, heirloom Havilland, from Dex's mother. The rest of the set is in the basement. It calms me, now, to see the painted lavender flowers and pale-green tendrils. Reminds me how life itself is fragile. How we must embrace love. And beauty. Try to find meaning. Leave legacies. I sit, gingerly, hands propping up my chin. Okay. I forgive Katherine. She's only doing her job. But I will never forgive Ashlyn. And I don't need to.

I toast heavenward with my teacup. "For you, darling ones."

Granting myself a change of venue to look online for Quinn's cross of the medical examiner, I take my tablet and laptop into the kitchen. As Dex insisted, we'd painted the room all white. Which, after Sophie, I'd soon regretted. Now I regret every time I'd been annoyed by her grubby fingerprints on the bottom cabinet doors. Wish I'd never cleaned them off. I kept the childproof door latches, though, after. Couldn't bring myself to remove them, despite knowing I was embracing the pain every time I had to deal with them. Black stove top, chic black oven, Swedish dishwasher. Oh, we were textbook. Until we weren't.

My cell phone rings. The caller ID says Quinn McMorran.

"Hello?"

"Is it too early?" It's odd to hear Quinn's voice directly, not through the speakers of my monitor or on tape. Maybe she couldn't sleep last night, either.

"Of course not," I say. "Thanks for calling."

I look at the clock. 6:42 A.M. She'd told me she'd give me ten minutes.

"How are you, Mercer?" Her voice is softer than the one she uses in court. "I was . . . surprised you'd taken this assignment. Are you all right?"

"I'm fine." I shake my head. No matter who it is, they ask the same thing.

"I'm sorry I missed the funeral." She says another of the usual post-Dex phrases.

"I understand," I recite back my line. I wonder if this is coming out of my ten minutes. "Anyway, Quinn, thank you for calling. I know you're so busy, but I wanted to ask you about—"

"About Ashlyn. About your book exposing the 'unthinkable crime.'" There's a darkening in her voice, but I wait. "I assume you're portraying her as guilty."

I wish I could see Quinn, maybe already dressed for court. Maybe in her office in the super-gentrified South End, bars on the brownstone windows, gorgeous high ceilings, original fireplaces. She's appointed to this case, I know, but she's had some big-bucks winners. Or maybe she's in her kitchen at home in suburbia, like I am, in sweats and a T-shirt.

"Not at all," I lie.

"It's a good case, Mercer." Then silence.

"Yeah, I'm—well, the book is my way of trying to come back." I feel guilty as I play my sympathy card. It's true, though. "Into the real world. Understanding that other people face sadness, too."

"I see," she says. "And truly, I am so sorry. It must be so difficult for you. Dex was such a fine—"

"Thanks. He admired you, too."

"There's a lot more to this case than I can talk about," she says. "I'm sure you understand."

"Do you think she did it?" I wince at myself. I'm feeling pressured by the clock, but that's pushing it. "I mean—"

I hear her sigh. "Look. I know I agreed to talk to you. And I'm so sorry about Dex. And your daughter. And you. I am. But I don't think there's anything I can tell you."

"Maybe about when you *met* Ashlyn?" I can tell she's about to hang up. I can't let that happen. "Remember, this won't be published until after the trial. And it'll show you in action as a skilled and zealous—"

"Ashlyn Bryant is innocent until proven guilty," Quinn interrupts. "This is thin ice for me."

"Trust me, Quinn. Maybe tell me how you met. What you noticed. Nothing specific about the case." It's silly to try to manipulate her. She's got more tricks than I do. And twenty years more experience.

Silence. I hear her breathing. She must have *some* agenda. She called me, after all.

"You have seven more minutes."

"Deal." I'm not tired any more. I need to get what I can get while I can get it.

We talk for much longer than seven minutes.

NO ONE WILL EVER KNOW

The morning Quinn McMorran met her newest client, Ashlyn Bryant arrived at South Bay House of Correction's attorney room with the collar of her orange jumpsuit popped and the short sleeves rolled up.

"I'm Quinn McMorran," the lawyer said. "Appointed to represent you."

The gray metal door clanged shut. Ashlyn took a seat in a dingy metal folding chair.

"My parents will pay you." Ashlyn didn't say hello. Didn't stand or offer to shake hands. "Like, pay you extra."

"I don't work harder based on what I'm paid." Quinn tried to stay cordial, even sympathetic. She sat down, set her briefcase on the conference table between them and clicked it open. Time to set boundaries. "I'm hired by the state. It's your right. But if your parents *can* pay, you'll have to hire an attorney. Is that what you're saying?"

"Listen." Ashlyn leaned forward. As the top snap of her jumpsuit gapped open, Quinn saw the rise of her full breasts, her creamy un-freckled skin, the tiny tattoo of an almost-invisible pink star. "No one would have to know about the extra money."

"I'm here to save your life, Ms. Bryant. Not ruin mine." This girl—half her age—seemed oblivious to the prospect of spending the next forty years behind bars. "Let's talk about your situation. Shall we?"

Ashlyn shrugged. Quinn could almost hear her thoughts. *Stupid lawyer,* maybe. Or *Sucker.*

"First, why didn't you report your daughter missing?" Quinn asked.

"Because she wasn't."

"Where was she?" Quinn asked.

"With my boyfriend. Sometimes the babysitter. Valerie. She was fine. I talked to her."

Quinn nodded, took notes on her yellow pad. "Who's this boy-friend? Where is he?" To have a Mr. Reasonable Doubt, that's exactly what they needed. "And the babysitter?"

"Where? I . . . don't know," Ashlyn said.

Bullshit. She hated bullshit.

"Listen," Quinn said. "If a 'boyfriend' had your daughter, or 'took' her, it, *he's* who we should go after. You want to get out of here? Tell me who that is. And where he is. You called him? What's the number?"

"Yes, of course," Ashlyn said. Palms open, explaining. "But Luke's phone stopped working."

"Luke? Is it Lucas, or Luther? Or just Luke? Last name? Do you have a DOB? Address? How about Valerie's last name? And contact info? How do those two know each other?"

Ashlyn seemed to search the scarred tabletop for an answer.

"I see." Quinn put down her pen, laced her fingers in front of her. This woman was digging her own grave. Luckily Massachusetts did not have the death penalty. "You understand why this matters, Ms. Bryant. If this Luke had your daughter, he's your reasonable doubt."

"But what if Luke Walsh is a made-up name?" Ashlyn's voice caught, then she began again. "I don't know. I can't take it. Everyone hates me. And I did *not* kill my daughter."

"I understand, Ashlyn." Quinn remembered that moment with infinite clarity. "In the eyes of the law, you are innocent. It's the Commonwealth's job to prove you're guilty."

"They *can't* prove it," Ashlyn said.

Interesting answer. "Ashlyn," she urged, "If you know anything, let's talk about that. If you had anything to do with this—"

"I get it." Ashlyn stood. Her eyes narrowed. "Even you hate me."

CHAPTER FIFTEEN

know I'm in trouble as I save the chapter to its file. You don't want to interrupt a scoop, so I'd let Quinn talk. But I'd been surprised she divulged what she did. Maybe she felt sorry for me. Maybe she thought she could convince me to help her client. Maybe she wanted publicity for herself. At one point, when I guess she realized how much she was revealing, she'd backpedaled.

"I should never have told you that," she said. "It's off the record. The money, the tattoo. Her attitude. All of it."

"But it's true, isn't it?" I'd said. "Seems like Ashlyn tried to manipulate you from moment one."

"I'm done." Quinn's voice went tough, and I could hear imminent dismissal. "I'm truly sorry about Dex and your daughter. I know you're having a difficult time. But about Ashlyn Bryant? Or anything about this case? Let me make it clear. Do. Not. Ever. Call me again."

She'd pretty much hung up on me.

So. Using that scene might create a problem, although I think retroactive off-the-record doesn't count. You say it, it's said.

I'm also bummed because I hadn't gotten a chance to ask her about Valerie and Luke. I write on my list: *Where is Valerie? Luke Walsh?*

And I'd never asked Quinn if she knew about Tasha's father. *Who is Tasha's father?* I underline that, then roll my eyes. As if I have to be reminded that it's important.

I'll work on that later. Right now I have twenty-five minutes to watch (and write) as Quinn McMorran (on video from a local TV's website) cross-examines the medical examiner. Because of our conversation, I can more authentically imagine Quinn's thinking.

For the book, I'll pick up the action in the middle of the testimony. When it gets really good.

CALLS FOR SPECULATION

"Objection!"

Quinn McMorran felt a laser-shot of animosity from Royal Spofford as the DA got to his feet.

Quinn smiled at the jury. As if—can you believe the DA is objecting? Don't we *all* want this to be fair?

The medical examiner, straight-backed in the witness box, fussed with a gold earring.

"I'll allow you some leeway in cross-examination, Ms. McMorran," the judge said. "Proceed."

"Thank you, your honor. So. Dr. Zimbel. Could *little* Tasha Nicole ... ." McMorran pretended to consult her yellow pad, but was actually allowing Spofford to understand that she'd not only won, but appropriated his diminutive. "Could little Tasha Nicole have been abducted? Even by someone she trusted?"

"Objection!" Spofford was up again. "Really, your honor, that is beyond the scope of—"

"Ms. McMorran, please rephrase," the judge interrupted.

"Thank you." This was shaky legal ground, but Quinn needed to plant every possible alternative scenario in the jurors' heads. "Was there anything that *precluded* the possibility that she'd been abducted and killed by someone *other* than my client?"

"No, but I—"

"How about a head injury, doctor? Could she have hit her head, fatally, while, say, falling? Maybe off a boat? Possibly whoever's boat it was who then tried to hide her body?"

"I suppose, but again. As I said, I cannot state the cause of death. Other than homicide. So . . ."

Quinn saw the witness silently implore the DA to rescue her. "Dr. Zimbel? You don't need to check with Mr. Spofford before you respond. I'm sure you can answer on your own. Since you testified that you cannot state the cause of death, could Tasha Nicole have choked? Maybe, on a hot dog?"

"Yes."

"Could she have had incurable cancer and died in her bed at home? Or drowned? And her loving family decided to bury her at sea instead of in a cemetery?"

The DA's face was seriously crimson, redder than Quinn had ever seen it. "Objection." Spofford spat out the word. "Your Honor, I ask you! Cancer? A *hot* dog?"

"This is not at *all* speculative," McMorran persisted. "And is, in fact, *narrowing* the scope. If the medical examiner can *exclude* a cause of death, shouldn't the jurors hear that?"

Judge Green closed his eyes, an infinitesimal second. "You may proceed, Ms. McMorran. But the door is closing."

Quinn nodded. She'd get that door slammed in her face for the next question, if Spofford even sat still long enough to let her complete it.

"Dr. Zimbel. Might the victim have been the daughter of an immigrant, coming to the United States to secure a family's future, and tragically, become gravely ill? Or fallen from the boat her parents engaged to bring them all to safety?"

Spofford was on his feet. Quinn ignored him, talking faster.

"And then, after that, they'd been so terrified of being deported they'd—with prayers and anguish—wrapped her in plastic and buried her at sea?"

"Your Honor, I object. In the strongest way." The DA's voice cracked with derision. "The DNA from the hairbrush proves she is *not* the daughter of—"

"Isn't it true *that* is the conclusion your own police artist came to, Dr. Zimbel? A conclusion you were once sure was correct?" Quinn knew her time was running out. "And now you're equally sure is *not* correct? How can that be?"

The prosecution had done this to itself, and it was Quinn's responsibility to illustrate how uncertain the DA's office was about the evidence surrounding the child's death. Of course the DNA test proved Tasha was not an Hispanic immigrant. The point was that the prosecution's *own* artist had speculated she was. Add that ambiguity to the ME's inability to pinpoint the time of death and the cause of death, and the result was inevitably reasonable doubt.

The judge's gavel silenced the rising buzz from the audience.

"Move away from this, Ms. McMorran. The door is closed. And locked."

"Thank you, Your Honor." At least the jury heard it. "One last question, Dr. Zimbel. In your examination, was there *any* physical evidence—hair, cells, blood, tissue, or fingerprints—on Tasha Nicole that connected her death to my client? Let me list that again: Hair, cells, blood, tissue, fingerprints. Linking the deceased with my client. Yes or no."

The ME looked at the DA, a momentary flicker. "No," she said.

"Thank you. No further questions." *Gotcha, Royal,* Quinn thought. That's reasonable freaking doubt.

"You need coffee?" Voice asks. As if he's talking to me. "Praise this morning's delay, team, you've still got fifteen minutes."

"Thanks, Voice," I say. "Good idea."

I'm proud of myself for that chapter—it proves I'm being fair, highlighting what Quinn must think are her strong points. I don't want her to hate the book when it's published, so I'd written her a moment of victory in what she certainly knows is a lost cause.

As the coffeemaker heats up, I look out the window, touching base with reality. We're in full late summer, the spiky early-September dahlias beginning to reveal their colors. Maybe I should take a walk? My legs—used to running 5Ks, then running with health-nut Dex, then running after Sophie—have spent most of the last year pacing, or sitting, or lying down.

"I've got to get out more."

I've got to get out more? Did I just say that?

Yeah. I admit it. And it's not only about exercise and fresh air. I'm obsessed with seeing Ashlyn Bryant in real life. It would make the book better. Make my writing more vivid. More authentic.

The cool part: She'd see *me,* but wouldn't know I'm the one writing about her.

"Ten minutes, stations." I can hear Voice all the way down the hall. I've cranked the volume to make sure I don't miss anything. Maybe Katherine can get me into the courtroom. Even only one day.

Today—I'm back in the study. Notebook open. Laptop open. Mug of coffee. Tablet ready to record. I look over what I wrote this morning, imagining it through a reader's eyes. What would they think is true?

Dex, who handled his share of controversial criminal cases, would have laughed. The verdict isn't always the truth, he'd remind me. And sure, it depends on the particular combustion in the particular jury room—the unique crucible where evidence meets emotion. And the law. But even Dex would have to agree this one was inevitable. No matter what bottom-scraping theories Quinn McMorran floats.

If Tasha had been abducted in Boston by some stranger—even the elusive Valerie, or Luke Walsh—why didn't Ashlyn Bryant report her daughter missing?

And if she'd choked accidentally on a hot dog or accidentally drowned or accidentally any number of things, why didn't someone call 911?

Tasha died.

No one called anyone to save her. Instead, someone put her in a trash bag.

Her. Own. Mother.

End of story.

"Five minutes," Voice warns. "Stand by, please, stations."

I lean back in my chair, stare past my lacily curtained windows. The willow is rustling, its graceful branches lifted by the breeze. I'm genuinely trying to come up with any reasons why Ashlyn would have kept silent about her own daughter's kidnapping. Or death.

There are none.

CHAPTER SIXTEEN

Surprise, surprise, right? She'll be testifying in ten minutes, gang," Voice says. "Never a dull moment."

It was supposed to be disgraced sketch artist Al Cook on the stand—but the Associated Press bulletin says "a family emergency" is keeping Cook from his court appearance in the order DA Royal Spofford scheduled, and he's now slotted to come later. Family emergency. *Right.* If I were Al Cook, I'd have headed for the hills long ago.

Now Georgia Bryant will take the stand. I cannot wait.

I bet the DA's goal is to distract the jurors from some imaginary hot dog and boat and grieving family. To focus them on the girl in the trash bag. To make them remember Tasha didn't choke on junk food, or drown by accident. Spofford needs them to remember it was murder.

And who best to sock them in the gut with that reality?

The murder victim's grieving grandmother. The defendant's own mother.

A witness for the prosecution.

My monitor screen is black. The white noise of the open feed is silent. For one hushed moment I'm in limbo, staring at my study wall. Trying to picture it. Trying not to.

Would my own mother have testified against me? Who would do that?

Only someone who loved a child so passionately she'd do anything to avenge her. Only someone who believed she was guilty.

I know the feeling.

"Attention stations," Voice says. "Me again. There's some sort of delay with the Bryant testimony. So we're in a thirty-minute recess. Back to you at 10 A.M."

As the audio fades, I wonder about Georgia Bryant. Hearing the incomprehensible and impossible news that her granddaughter was dead. Murdered. And her daughter the main suspect.

Boston Detective Koletta Hilliard clinched that case. And Wadleigh Rogowicz became her Dayton bloodhound. His police report—thank you, Katherine—tells the whole story. I don't need to hear any testimony to write that part.

I type *Notes to self.*

Rogo screens surveillance video from Hudson News kiosk at Logan Airport Terminal B. Writes: *Possibly Ashlyn in Cubs hat. With child, possibly Tasha.*

TSA tracks Ashlyn back to Dayton. Three days later. Alone.

What happened? How did Tasha end up in Boston Harbor—and Ashlyn back in Dayton?

Maybe Rogowicz walked the streets, thinking if he could only put himself at the right place at the right time, he'd see her. But he didn't.

Rogowicz tells Georgia: "Ashlyn is here in town somewhere." Then has idea.

He tells Georgia to text Ashlyn, say relative died, say Ash getting bequest from will. Need to discuss in person. Big money. Ashlyn replies, cell phone pings in Dayton suburb.

"Oldest trick in the book," Rogowicz tells the chief. "Can't go wrong with greed."

Rogo makes phone call to Boston. Five hours later, Koletta Hilliard arrives in Dayton.

I read over my outline. It could work. And I'll expand it later. It's always tricky deciding how many details to use.

Should I describe Rogowicz showing Al Cook's composite drawing to Georgia? Georgia shrieking, and trying to rip it in half?

Should I include the moment she gasped with devastating heart-break, identifying the barrettes? How, without Rogowicz asking, she'd brought out the slick cardboard that still held the third and fourth of the four-barrette set? The indentations of the missing butterflies almost proved that someone in the family had clipped them into Tasha's curls.

CHAPTER SEVENTEEN

I head back to the kitchen, thinking about monsters. How often has a mother deliberately murdered her own child? I know about the woman who drove off the pier with her kids in the car, left them to drown. The one who murdered her daughters in the bathtub. Each mother was found guilty, if I remember correctly. Not "not guilty by reason of insanity."

Ashlyn INSANE?? I add that to my list.

Casey Anthony, the archetypal example of a young woman charged with murdering her toddler daughter, was found not guilty several years ago in Florida, of course. To everyone's horror and derision. But I do not put *Ashlyn innocent?* on my list. I am only including realistic possibilities.

Is Ashlyn truly a psychopath? Or a sociopath? So what if she is? I open the fridge for milk. Quinn McMorran is not arguing insanity. Ashlyn is pleading straight not guilty. I understand that doesn't mean she didn't do it. It means only that she's willing to risk that the Commonwealth can't prove her guilt beyond a reasonable doubt.

I stir my fresh coffee, settling myself in my book's reality. My questions are intriguing, but I keep forgetting I don't have to answer them. I only have to listen to the trial and write. During which, I must say, I'm feeling increasingly claustrophobic. I need to ask Katherine about getting into court.

Too bad it won't be this afternoon. I'd love to see Ashlyn's mother throw her under the bus.

The maternal betrayal—the second one—is the key to the whole arrest. Ashlyn *knows* Georgia Bryant was in on it. More than "in on it." Georgia actively tricked her daughter into incriminating herself.

THE DETECTIVE IN THE CLOSET

Standing in the open front door of Laughtry Drive, Georgia lifted a hand, waving hello. Trying to behave normally. It was harder for her to playact than for Ashlyn, she bet. Which nauseated her.

Tom, as usual, was not home. Georgia hadn't told him about this. He'd have tried to talk her out of it. Tell her she was unfair. Disloyal. Emotional. That Ashlyn was *their own daughter.*

Piff. Had she not thought *exactly* that? Had she not slept a damn wink the night before trying to figure out what the hell to do? She'd deal with her husband when they knew more. All depended on what happened now.

Ashlyn half-waved back. Her hair was that crazy blond again. They wouldn't let her bleach her hair in jail, that was for sure. If she went to jail.

It was all Georgia could do not to glance at the front hall closet. She'd stashed the first row of coats in the guest room, so the extra space in the closet could be occupied by Detective Rogowicz, the sad-eyed cop who'd returned to their home the day before with that horrible drawing. He'd insisted on the closet. Said he needed to hear what Ashlyn said if she thought she was talking only to her mother.

The other detective, that nice young black woman from Boston, sat out of sight at the kitchen table. Georgia had made her iced tea. If need be, they'd decided, Georgia could say she was a friend.

Her daughter approached, in clothing Georgia didn't recognize, high-heeled sandals with white jeans. She supposed she should feel sadder about this. But how could a broken heart become more broken? Georgia was already living in hell. Her only salvation was that Ashlyn would soon be there, too.

Whatever happened, it was Ashlyn's fault. This ruse was the only way Georgia would get to the truth. Find out what happened to the dearest, sweetest, cutest granddaughter who ever lived, who would still be alive if Ashlyn had left the poor child where she was supposed to be, in the care of her loving grandmother. It made Georgia's blood boil.

"Hi, honey." Georgia felt like an actor playing a role. Which she was.

"Hey, Mom." Ashlyn arrived at the front door. Hugged her mother, briefly.

So briefly Georgia had no chance to hug back, which, she guessed, was a blessing.

"Where's Tashie?" Georgia, acting, peered down the walk as if she expected her dear darling dead granddaughter to skip up the begonia-lined path as she always did. After Ashlyn stepped inside, Georgia closed the door. She was about to throw up. But now she had to be brave.

"Sweetheart? It's been weeks, honey. How's my baby girl?"

"She's fine." Ashlyn scanned the living room, then sprawled onto the brown wing chair. Her toenails were painted bright blue. "So what's the deal with Aunt Marie? I thought she was, like, fine."

"Where's Tasha Nicole?" Georgia asked.

"Mom." Only Ashlyn could drag that tiny word into so many syllables. "Do we need to go over this again?"

Georgia waited. Tried to compose her face, look like the old Georgia. The grandmother. The dupe. The person who would never again exist. Ashlyn's next words might be the answer to everything.

"Geez. You worry too much," Ashlyn said. "Tasha's in Chicago, she's always been in Chicago, she loves Chicago. With Valerie. If you want to do another Skype with her? Fine. I'll arrange it."

"Will you tell her I said hello?" Georgia hoped her face didn't betray how she felt. Drained. Worried. Horrified. She tried to look normal. "And that I love her?"

"Sure," Ashlyn said. "She said to tell you she loves you, too."

"Oh. That's wonderful." Georgia's throat was closing. Maybe she'd misunderstood. "She said that today?"

"Yes. Before I left Chicago this morning. Okay?"

"You saw her today?" Georgia talked louder than usual. She hoped the detective could hear this. She hoped she wouldn't faint.

"Yes, for crap sake, what do you think?" Ashlyn's face darkened, then the sun came out. "I'm so sorry about poor Aunt Marie," she said. As if she'd changed into another person altogether, the grieving niece. "So what did they tell you about the will? I can't believe she left money to me."

"You've been in Chicago, too, all this time? Since you left me at the airport that day?"

Ashlyn stood, wobbled a fraction of a second on those strappy heels. Georgia saw her pinkish underwear through the jeans.

"What're you getting at?" Ashlyn's eyes darted around the room—bookcase, front window, hall table, closet door. Landed on Georgia.

"Nothing, honey, just making conversation." Georgia retreated. Let it go, the detective had instructed her. *If you get close to the truth and she balks, don't push. Let her talk. Talk about the 'inheritance.'*

Georgia started again. *"All* that money. So lucky you answered my text, hon. I tried to call you before, but it was disconnected."

"Yeah, I'd lost my phone. In Chicago." Ashlyn slid a phone out of her back pocket. "I told them to shut it off. Then I found it again. Like, yesterday. And had them turn it back on. Then I needed a new battery. What a pain. But yeah, like you said. Luckily."

Georgia's own cell phone rang. She answered it. "Hello?" She knew full well who it was. And what it was. The signal from the detective in the closet.

Is that right out of a movie, or what? Quinn McMorran had tried her best to keep it from the jury, but her motion to suppress the "unconstitutional" use of Georgia as a "de facto police officer" was denied. The jury will hear about how Wadleigh Rogowicz, warrant in his pocket, breathed cedar chips as he eavesdropped through the closet door, his bare forearms scratched by nubby wool winter wear, his body cushioned by slick puffer jackets. How he heard every word Ashlyn said.

They'll hear how Detective Koletta Hilliard waited in the kitchen, afraid to stir her tea for fear the ice cubes might rattle and alert her prey.

They'll hear how Georgia Bryant must have tried, repeatedly, to reassure herself—as I must realistically portray her doing—that her once-beloved Ashlyn might plausibly have no idea what happened to Tasha. But then, gradually and inexorably, the truth settled its gruesome self into place. Her daughter might be a murderer.

Ashlyn had told her mother she'd talked to Tasha Nicole "that very morning." As if she'd just left her in Chicago. Georgia knew that could not be true. So did the detective in the closet.

I remember when they came to tell me about Dex and Sophie. Actually, that's not true. I don't really remember. I can still hear that knock on the door, 451 days ago. I remember seeing two police officers. After that, everything is pretty much fog.

Like my life, this story turns on moments. On choices we make, whether we know it or not. What happened to my family. Of course, now I would have made completely different decisions that day. Would Ashlyn?

And if Georgia hadn't chosen to nag Wadleigh Rogowicz, he would have told Koletta Hilliard there were no missing little girls reported in Dayton. No little girls with barrettes. But Georgia Bryant had decided to take action. In this part of the story, she acts again.

Soon, in real life, she'll swear to tell the truth. Tell her story to the jury that will decide the fate of her own daughter.

There I go with the drama again. Not fate. It's *fault*. Ashlyn's own evil fault.

CHAPTER EIGHTEEN

'll have to leave some parts out. "No one wants to read about process," Kath once imperiously informed me as she spiked my feature on the abuses of the public-records law. She was probably right, if entertainment is the goal.

Now, not only to please Kath but because interstate law enforcement is a morass of red tape, I'm skipping the details about how Koletta Hilliard had to get a warrant, then notify Dayton police, then how Wadleigh Rogowicz had to get a special fugitive warrant before that closet episode could happen.

After it all went down, Ashlyn was held in lockup until a judge could hear the rendition request. Hilliard then applied for a special governor's warrant in Massachusetts, which also had to be approved by the governor of Ohio. Process.

All that legal wrangling left Ashlyn in the Dayton House of Correction for a few days. I tried to imagine what it must have been like, stewing in that smothering (I guess) eight-by-ten cell (according to the Department of Correction website), eating cheese sandwiches and milk, fuming about how her own mother had set her up with the cops.

Georgia told scrumming reporters she herself had sobbed throughout the entire arrest. "But what could I do?" she'd wailed. "She said Tasha was with Valerie Luciano, some name like that, but I knew that wasn't true. Was I supposed to let Ashlyn disappear again? What if she could have helped bring the real murderer to justice?"

Exactly. Why hadn't Ashlyn confessed to being a—well, not a bad mom, but simply an overly trusting one? Why hadn't she owned up to having left her daughter with fill-in-the-blank turned-out-to-be-bad-person and pinned the murder on him. Or her?

But in lockup, Ashlyn continued to insist she knew nothing about anything, and that as far as she knew, Tasha was fine, and that she *had* talked to her—okay, by phone, that very morning.

That could only be classified as delusional. More than delusional. Disgusting. Ashlyn had to know her daughter was dead. And exactly how she died. Since she didn't know the extent of the cops' investigation, she tried playing her hand the best she could.

But it was game over. Rogowicz read her the Miranda rights and arrested her. She's replied with one word. "Lawyer."

She did, however, talk to her mother once on the phone. And those phone calls were recorded. A Dayton weekly newspaper somehow got hold of a certified word-for-word transcript. Unbelievable.

A HUGE WASTE

She had no idea what this was all about. Ashlyn would stick to that story.

She stared at the stupid bars of her stupid ugly pitiful cell. They actually wanted to send her to Massachusetts, to another jail! No freaking way. She had to get out. Fuming, Ashlyn called her mother from the greasy wall phone in the cinderblock common room. Her family had screwed her. Big time.

"You had a cop, a freaking cop, hiding in the freaking front hall closet," Ashlyn yelled.

Georgia Bryant clutched her cell phone. Looked out her kitchen window at their empty backyard. Walked an impossibly fine line. Yes, the closet part was true. And yes, except for her secret collusion with the Dayton Police Department, her daughter would not be in jail.

"You have to get me *out* of here!" Ashlyn's voice grated in her ear.

What was also true: if Georgia hadn't told Wadleigh Rogowicz her granddaughter was missing in the first place, no one would have connected Baby Boston to Tasha Nicole.

"Don't yell at *me*, Ashlyn. It's not up to me," Georgia replied. That part, honestly, was a relief. "If you want help, why don't you just tell me what—"

"Because I don't know what 'happened' to her," Ashlyn interrupted, her voice rising, taut with scorn.

"Ashlyn, don't shriek at me," Georgia said. "Are you blaming *me* that you're sitting in jail?"

"Effing right," Ashlyn retorted.

"Blame yourself," Georgia snapped. "For telling lies."

The phone went silent.

"Ashlyn?" This was her daughter, after all, but it was hard to juggle her emotions. After—whatever happened. "You told me you'd seen Tasha that morning. I knew that wasn't true."

"You are such a moron," Ashlyn said. "Just because I tried to make you feel better? That doesn't mean *any*thing. How do we know that's Tasha in whatever picture they have? They're trying to screw with us. And now look where I am. Because of you, Mother. Because of freaking *you*."

Silence again.

Georgia could not think of one more thing to say. Her eyes filled with tears, and she could almost see Tasha Nicole's dear face in front of her, hear her peals of laughter on the swing set, smell her strawberry bubble bath. She'd lugged that silly flop-eared stuffed rabbit everywhere. Rabbie. Now she'd never see Rabbie again.

"Do you have Rabbie?" Georgia said it, out loud, without thinking.

"Are you kidding me?" Ashlyn's voice peaked again. "Hey. Hang on. Was that whole thing about Aunt Marie not true? You said she was dead, but she isn't? Oh, that's just freaking beautiful. So *Mother*, tell me this. You lied to me too, right? Right? You told me Marie was dead, and she wasn't. What if they're lying about Tasha, too? And answer me this. How is it not okay for me to tell you a fib, to get you to calm the hell down, but it is okay for *you* to lie to *me*?"

Was Ashlyn right? That composite didn't look like Tasha, not that much. Could it be? Tasha was alive? And the dead girl was another toddler with barrettes?

No. Ashlyn manipulating her. Again. Lying. *Again.* Although in a case like this, anyone, even Ashlyn, might be forgiven for being in denial. It was a stage of grief, wasn't it?

"Honey, I know you're upset, but . . ." Georgia began.

Then Georgia stopped, soon as she heard her own words. In truth, Ashlyn wasn't upset. Not about Tasha Nicole. Ashlyn was concerned about one thing only. Herself.

And she wanted her cell phone. "Get them to give it to you," Ashlyn whined. "All my numbers are there."

Georgia didn't trust herself to answer.

"Can you not hear me?" Ashlyn's voice was derisive, dismissive. "I have *no* idea in hell what happened."

"Whatever's going on, we're going to find out, Ashlyn."

"There's nothing to find *out,*" Ashlyn insisted. "Not from me, anyway."

The perplexing thing about this phone conversation, I think as I read over the transcript, is that it is so subject to interpretation. Reading it one way, it's exactly what an innocent person—upset and confused and terrified—would say. *I don't know what happened. There's nothing to find out from me.*

But what would a guilty person—frightened and nervous and conniving—say? Exactly the same thing.

On the other hand. And it's a big hand. Even O. J. Simpson had vowed to find the real killer. Not Ashlyn. She wasn't concerned about what happened to Tasha Nicole at all. Didn't ask where she was. Or seem worried.

Did she honestly not believe Tasha was dead back then? Or

know she wasn't? But if her daughter wasn't dead, that'd be the instant proof this whole thing was a ghastly mistake. If she knew where the little girl was, holy crap, as Ashlyn might say, no better time than this to bring her out.

It was a big rabbit hole—*Rabbie,* I thought, like Sophie's Bunno—to think that way.

Writing scenes like this make my brain fry, because I have to juggle what I know now with what was known at the time the "scene" took place. At the time of the jailhouse phone call, Ashlyn's appointed lawyer, a hotshot Dayton guy named Teige Duffy, was preparing to fight the police department's request for a court order to take DNA from Ashlyn to confirm the victim was her daughter.

The judge ordered the sample anyway. The DA's office told reporters they were "expediting the hell out of it," but the DNA results still haven't been returned. Those could also prove who the father is, but only if his DNA is on file somewhere.

Ashlyn/father DNA? I write on the list.

But to prove it was Tasha, all they needed was a hair from her pink Pooh hairbrush. They compared that to the DNA of Baby Boston. And it matched. I figure only the lawyers, and possibly the jury, care about the DNA results. Tasha was missing. The dead body on the beach wore her clothing. The rabbit. The pollen. The blanket, which I haven't put in the book yet. It's Tasha. *Was.*

I cross DNA off the list.

Did Ashlyn know jail phone taped? I write that instead. What if she was trying to *use* the calls? To create a framework to argue for her own innocence? Or maybe she wasn't using them at all. Maybe she was telling the truth.

That'd be a first.

CHAPTER NINETEEN

No peace shall I find," my song trails off as I open my front door, feel the noontime sun on my face, wave at my across-the-street neighbor Liz Rayburn who's power-walking her snuffly beige cockapoo. Liz waves back and for a tiny moment, there's a feeling of nice neighbors, nice neighborhood, normal day. But I smile as I realize what song has been going through my head, and why. Georgia *is* on my mind. Voice told me she's scheduled to take the stand in twenty minutes, at 1 P.M. I open a can of tuna, very glam, and pour a glass of iced coffee, and set my lunch provisions on my desk. Soon I'll hear the most anticipated testimony since the trial began.

I check the mailbox on the front porch, a habit I wish I could break. The only mail we—I—get is depressing. Stabbingly upsetting catalogs for baby clothes and toys. Dex's law school alumni fundraisers. The bills always remind me I'm alone. Today there's one from the water company. I'm ashamed to admit that 451 days ago, I would not have known how much our water bill was, or our light bill. Dex took care of that, took care of all the money. I did food and shopping, and my brand of house cleaning. Dex handled car and finances. Every time I wheel the blue plastic trash bins to the curb now, Thursday mornings, I think about how this silly chore was so much a part of his life. He never complained, never missed a Thursday, and I never gave it a second thought. Now I do.

Today is no different. No mail at all. How bleak is that? Like I have nothing, and no one. Even my mail has given up on me.

I almost don't hear the car pull up, but then it turns into our driveway, tires crunching on gravel. Katherine. She pops out of her white Lexus, slams the door, and trots up the walk.

"Nice look," she says, eyeing me. "Sweat pants, very hip."

"Gimme a break, Kath," I say, patting my fleeced thighs. "I'm working, not out having glamorous fun in the real world. Because of you, remember. And this completely impossible assignment."

Katherine, white jacket, dark-wash skinny jeans, bright blue heels, holds out a manila envelope. "You've got mail," she says.

I take it, puzzled. I just checked the mail. "What is it?" I gesture to the still-open front door. "Want to come in, watch Georgia testify? She's on in fifteen."

"Nope, no can do," she says. "But take a look at the goodie I just brought you."

I bend up the metal prongs to open the envelope. "What is it?" I rip up the sealed flap.

"I got it from a friend of a friend," Katherine says. "I had to come over. I wanted to see your face when you opened it."

I draw the piece of paper from the envelope.

"We're not releasing this," Katherine goes on. "And we're not sure if anyone else has it. We're crossing fingers it can be exclusive for your book. Maybe the cover."

It's eight-by-ten, heavy paper. I turn it over. It's a photograph. In color.

"What on earth? It's Ashlyn, right?" A sign on the wall behind her says something that's partly obscured. *STU* is all I can make out. But I can make out quite a bit about Ashlyn.

"Yupperoo," Katherine says. "Wet white T-shirt. Apparently our girl entered a contest. Like, last year."

"S-T-U is Hot Stuff, don't you think?"

Kath nods. "Unbelievable, huh?"

I look at it, picturing how it must have happened.

"Good thing we didn't have cell phone cameras when we were that age, right?" I say. "Not that there'd be anything like this. And I always wore underwear in public. But—is it fair to make her a murderer because she was partying?"

"You wanna fight the optics battle for Ashlyn?" Kath interrupts, raises an eyebrow. "It is what it is."

And with that she's gone, her car a flash of white and chrome disappearing down Norwalk Street.

I stand in the doorway. Staring at the photo. If Katherine has this, does Royal Spofford? What would the jury think?

Ashlyn's wet, laughing, lip-glossed, and wearing a truly translucently glistening T-shirt in front of a room full of Hot Stuff partiers—I guess, because you can't see anyone else in this shot. But does that mean she killed her daughter? It doesn't. It's one of those things Dex would call phony-relevant. It seems like it matters. But it doesn't.

What definitely *is* going to matter—Georgia Bryant's testimony. I click on my computer. She's about to tell all.

Five minutes in, I'm riveted. Ignoring my lunch. I can't even write. This is too cinematic, like some 1940's Joan Crawford melodrama. Georgia Bryant, the suburban mother who's made an unimaginable choice. Grandchild over daughter. Justice over loyalty. Her blue skirt does not quite match her too-tight jacket, and there's a dusting of what might be face powder on one wide lapel.

So far what she's telling the jury, sometimes wiping tears with a shredding white tissue, exactly corroborates the way I'm telling the story in the book. That's reassuring. But I'm obsessed with Georgia's state of mind. How can she do this?

For the millionth time, I look for emotional clues in the family photos published in *UpClose Magazine*. Preteen Ashlyn in curls and silver ankle bracelet, soaking wet, posing at some swimming pool. Ashlyn as a teenager, high-kicking in a cheerleader mini, pale-pink V-neck sweater just a bit too tight. Ashlyn as a chubby new mother, radiant, I have to admit, with a tiny Tasha Nicole in her arms and a beaming Georgia hovering behind them.

But Ashlyn had become a self-styled seductress, who had decided—if you buy the Commonwealth's theory—that her own daughter's very existence was an impediment to her party-girl fun.

How does a mother—a grandmother—live with that?

"Why did you agree to let that detective hide in your closet?" Spofford is asking.

"Because the police said they needed to hear what she told me," Georgia answers. "They said—"

"Objection!" McMorran sounds angry. Even I know that calls for hearsay.

"And after that," Spofford carries on after the judge sustains, "what did you learn?"

Quinn plants her palms on the defense table. Ready to leap up at the first inadmissible word.

"Well, that police detective showed me the drawing, and that little girl had the same barrettes as Tasha. I knew it was Tasha. But Ashlyn said she saw her alive that morning."

"And what did that mean to you?"

"It meant Ashlyn had to be lying. Because I knew Tasha was dead."

CHAPTER TWENTY

Quinn McMorran. Georgia Bryant. Ashlyn Bryant. The three women create a chilling legal triangle. In one corner, a defense attorney preparing to destroy the direct testimony of the woman in the opposite corner, the person who should be Ashlyn's prime advocate–her own mother. At the apex of the triangle, Ashlyn herself, in a central-casting neutral sweater and virtuous gray skirt, listening to every word. Glued to my desk chair, I'm listening, too. Quinn's talented, but her client is a monster.

Quinn starts her cross-examination with some predictable questions, clearly designed to lay the defense groundwork–ridiculously shaky as it is–for "good mother Ashlyn." Quinn gets in a couple of successful moments, I have to admit. She's certainly making Georgia look less sympathetic. But she can't make Ashlyn look less guilty.

No matter what happens in the courtroom, I figure mother and daughter will never speak to each other again. Talk about betrayal.

HOW DID SHE KNOW THAT

"Let me ask you this." Quinn McMorran's tone revealed a hint of scorn, her antagonism showing through her practiced politeness. "You never witnessed your daughter Ashlyn abuse Tasha in any way, did you?"

Georgia Bryant shifted in the hard wooden chair. She hated that look on the lawyer's face. Like somehow something was Georgia's fault. Which it most certainly was not.

"No, I did not." This was the truth, certainly, if she meant hitting Tashie. Ashlyn never did that. That she'd seen.

"And Tasha never went without food or shelter or anything she needed in life?"

"No, she had everything." *Tom and I made sure of that,* she wanted to say.

"Did Tasha love Ashlyn?" McMorran asked.

"Oh, yes. Yes, she did. She's her *mother.*" So now it had to be over. Ashlyn herself could not criticize her mother's answers. Georgia felt better. No one could say she hadn't defended her daughter. Nauseating as it was.

"Just a few more questions, Mrs. Bryant. First, were you and your husband attempting to trademark Tasha Nicole's name?"

She heard the rustle from the courtroom audience. Her husband was staring daggers at her. They hadn't told anyone about this, not even Spofford. Certainly not Ashlyn. How could this woman know?

"Yes." Georgia said. Spofford had told her only to answer what was asked. But she couldn't stand it. "But it never actually—"

"I see." McMorran didn't let her finish. The attorney picked up a manila folder. Opened it. "And finally, this copy of *UpClose Magazine.*" She held it up, showed it to the judge and jury. And the TV camera. "This is marked exhibit M, your honor. May I approach?"

She came so close to Georgia she could smell the woman's perfume. "Now Mrs. Bryant, this is an article about this case, correct? With, among other things, family photos of Tasha Nicole as a baby, and my client as a high school cheerleader. Are these from your family album?"

"Yes." The woman could not know about this, could *not!*

"Isn't it true," McMorran went on, "that you sold these family photos to the magazine?"

She knew. How did she know that? "Yes," Georgia said.

"For how much money?"

There was no way out of it. "Twenty thousand dollars."

"Let me clarify," Quinn said. "You sold your family photos for twenty thousand dollars?"

"Objection," Spofford barely looked up. "Asked and answered."

McMorran gave Georgia a look. *Gotcha.* Georgia shot one right back. *Bitch.*

"Nothing further," McMorran said.

Thank God. Georgia tried to calm her breathing, still her heart, quiet her frazzling nerves as District Attorney Spofford approached her again. She knew this was called "redirect." At least he was on her side.

"One question," the DA said. "Isn't it true. . . ."

His voice sounded funny, she thought. It had a little undertone.

"Isn't it true that you believe your daughter killed Tasha Nicole?"

"Objection! I move for a mistrial!" Quinn McMorran leaped out of her chair, almost knocking it over as she protested "What Georgia Bryant *thinks* is inadmissible. As counsel is well aware."

"And what's more"—McMorran settled a palm on Ashlyn's shoulder—"I demand the district attorney be sanctioned for prosecutorial misconduct. This is cynical. It's manipulative. There's a human life at stake."

Ashlyn's life, she meant, but I figure everyone in the courtroom was thinking about Tasha Nicole. I had never seen a defense attorney leap up like that, shouting. *A Perry Mason moment,* I bet TV will call it. If anyone remembers Perry Mason.

I feel my foot jiggling under my desk. I didn't start it on purpose. This isn't about me, I know that, but for me, a mistrial is the worst thing that could happen. If there's a mistrial, my book dies. Or gets hooked up to life support.

The monitor shows Judge Green on the bench, paging through papers. The courtroom is silent, everyone in place.

Would he do it? Send the jury home and force the Commonwealth to start over? A second trial is a defense attorney's dream.

It's a second chance. Why would Spofford take such a risk with that question? Everything is stopped, now, while the judge decides.

All this gruesome testimony, the evidence and objections, the backstage wrangling, the journalists' predictions. It's toxic. I'm immersed. And more toxic, I'm isolated. No one knows I'm watching, a voyeur with a secret agenda. To punish Ashlyn Bryant. To avenge Tasha Nicole.

My little girl is gone forever, too. But I, at least, admit why. Although not in court.

I feel my eyes narrow. There has never been a guiltier person on the planet. A mistrial would put Ashlyn one step closer to getting away with murder. I can see that murder so clearly, it's almost as if I witnessed it myself.

The judge's gavel jolts me from the mental picture of the decomposing Tasha Nicole. "We'll be in recess until tomorrow at nine," he says.

CHAPTER TWENTY-ONE

In fifteen minutes I'd washed my face, yanked on jeans and a T-shirt, combed my hair, put on real shoes, and I was outside. The air is heavy with the waning summer, the lacy pillows of lavender hydrangea on our—my—next-door neighbor's hedge sweet and buzzing with satiated bees. Once in the car, I drive up Norwalk Street past the square of stores in the town center, striped awnings and forest green benches, pots of fuchsia begonias trailing ivy along each side of Lincoln Avenue. I blink in the late afternoon sunshine as I arrive in the grocery parking lot, getting my new bearings.

"Shopping," I say out loud. "In the real world."

Dex's parents, who I know were trying to help me, showed up with the little Subaru a month or so after the accident. Someone—maybe them, I don't know—had done something with that wrecked Volvo. Patrick and Lita Hennessey, they meant well, had insisted I needed a car, and the pale gray sedan showed up soon after. I had sworn never to drive again, which was self-defeating and ridiculous, but for a few months I felt like it gave me some control. The Subaru keys sit on my dresser. I do use them, times like now. Or when I go to the cemetery. Or the wine store. It's not *that* car I think of when I drive.

Patrick and Lita are on a cruise. Somewhere. Aruba, I think. Probably, like I am, still trying to forget. It's reassuring that they're together. I count my blessings that my own parents, long departed from this world, were not alive for Dex and Sophie's deaths, or to witness their daughter's despair. Mom would have insisted I move back home to Ithaca. Dad would have tried to distract me with hiking or tennis. I would have said no, but I miss my parents. I sure would like someone to talk to. To hold on to. To be a family.

The air goes cold as I swish through the revolving doors of DeMilla's, the locally owned mini-grocery favored by harried professionals and overscheduled parents picking up forgotten milk or cheese or necessities like wine and diapers. And coffee. I grab a black plastic basket, hang it over my arm. I've shopped plenty of times in the past 451 days. But the world is still not quite—reliable, is the word, I guess. I still look over my shoulder at everything. Hearing noises. Half-seeing movements, that when I turn to confront them, vanish. Waiting for someone to ask me something. Pull the rug out.

"Get over yourself," I mutter as I select two cans of chicken gumbo soup, then a minestrone, plunk them into my basket. Maybe my frustration is a sign. Maybe I'm weary of sorrow. But I can't allow it to vanish. That's disloyal. Grief is what keeps Dex and Sophie real.

Ice cream next, mocha chip. A bag of almonds. People learn to live with grief. Their lives go on after a loss, even after a devastating loss. They have to keep living. I suppose.

"Thanks," I say to the mom in the messy bun and khaki shorts as she moves her double-seated stroller—twin girls—out of the way. "Cute," I say.

See? I can handle the world.

I'm in line at the register, the guy in front of me unloading Doritos, an avocado, and wheat germ, when I spot the rack of eye-candy tabloids set up to tempt impatient impulse buyers. MURDERING MOM's SECRET CONFESSION, one headline reads. It shows a blurry silhouette of someone who may or may not be Ashlyn Bryant possibly kissing someone whose face is also blurry. Another one, with a picture of Anna Nicole Smith, says TASHA: NEW VICTIM OF

Curse of Nicole. In the holder beneath it, a glossy magazine, *Insider,* promises Tasha Nicole's Secret Brother with the subhead Is he also in danger?

This I cannot resist. I know it's complete bull. There is no brother. I put my basket on the conveyor, walking beside it as it creeps forward. I flip through the slick magazine pages, looking for the "Tasha's brother" story.

"Horrible, right?" says the cashier. She's maybe seventeen, attempting suburban Goth, wearing a black T-shirt under her bright red DeMilla's apron. Her name tag says Carmendy. "To murder your own child?"

Horrible? *You have no idea* goes through my mind. "Yeah," I say out loud. "Can't believe I'm reading this."

"Everyone does. Reads it, I mean." She scans my soups with a beep, picks up the almonds, beeps those too. "She's so guilty, right? Ashlyn?"

First-name basis, I think. Charming.

"It'll be interesting to hear what the jury decides," I say. If the judge decides to let them decide.

Carmendy's almost finished with my checkout, and I put the magazine back in its metal rack, careful not to dent the pages.

"Well, yeah. My friend's mom is on the jury." She waves the ice cream over the red light. It beeps. "She says she says the whole thing is awful."

She says she says? I untangle her sentence.

"You mean your friend's mom, the one on the jury, said to your friend that—" I stop.

"Yeah." She rings up my celery, and my Syrah. The conveyor rolls forward. "My friend told me."

This is uncharted territory. A juror is not supposed to be talking to anyone about anything related to the trial. Now what do I do?

Grabbing some random gum from the colorful candy rack, I put it on the belt. I retrieve that tabloid with the brother story, slap that on the conveyor, too. A flavored lip balm, peppermint. One gilt-wrapped square of Northern Delight dark chocolate.

Someone is in line behind me, huffing dramatically as I add to my purchases. I stolidly ignore her, hoping Carmendy will continue to talk.

"*So* guilty," Carmendy says with a roll of her eyes. "And it's hard for her to get to work."

"Your friend's mom?" Using a time-honored journalism technique, I pretend to misunderstand. I'm not going to do anything with it, but if I can find the friend, I can find the mom. And then I'll know one of the jurors.

"No," Carmendy says. Like, *idiot customer*. She's packing the last of my groceries into a second brown paper bag, putting the three cans of soup and the ice cream on top of the eggs. "My friend. She works at Home D, you know? And now Kelsie has to Uber to classes, because her mom needs the car for court. Which they both hate."

My brain is on fire. "Thanks." I say, picking up the two bags. *Kelsie. Home Depot.*

"Hi," Carmendy says to the huffy customer.

How about *that*. The revolving door whirls me back into the waning summer afternoon. I stash my stuff in the car, and make a plan, waiting for a desultory landscape truck to mutter by. There are seven women on the jury. Now I know one of them told her daughter the whole thing is "awful," whatever that means, and "hates" it, whatever that means. She's also told her daughter about what she thinks about Ashlyn. Which is, apparently, guilty.

CHAPTER TWENTY-TWO

The hardware store, with few customers this time of day, is scented with newly sawed wood and peaty fertilizer. It's like the trial come to life. A display of plastic trash bags. Shrink-wrapped rolls of silver duct tape. Rubber gloves.

I shiver, haunted that I still have to write the chapter about the crime scene testimony. Pushing a rattling orange shopping cart, hoping the ice cream I left in the Subaru won't melt the backseat into a sticky disaster, I now pretend I'm scouting for hardware items instead of for a certain college student. I see no name tag with Kelsie. No Chelsea, or Chelsie, or anything like that.

A clerk whose tag says Loris, her logoed baseball cap barely fitting over her gray curls, is zeroing in on me.

"May I help you?"

"Oh, thank you," I flutter. Here I go. "Um, my husband was working with a 'Kelsie'? He said to ask for her."

People always believe it if you say your husband told you to do something.

"Which Kelsie?" Loris, tilting her head, wants to be helpful. "There are two."

That narrows it down. Good. "Oh, gosh. She's in school."

"Kelsie G," Loris says. "Sorry, though, she's not here."

"Kelsie G, yes." I smile. "How *do* you spell her name? I'll tell the hubs for next time."

"No idea," she admits. "It's one of those names."

One of those names. Starts with G.

I look at my watch. "Oh, the time," I say. "Got to start dinner. He can just come back himself, then. Men, right?"

"Men," Loris agrees.

By the time I get home, the afternoon is fading into a shimmer of twilight. The days are getting shorter, a few seconds each evening, but it's still stubbornly summer. As if to prove it, the crickets are "cwicking," in Sophie-speak. Dex and I once Googled to remember how to calculate the temperature by counting cricket chirps. Someone's mowing a lawn, someone's cooking out with charcoal. The fragrance makes me almost woozy. Dex insisted on grilling, although everything came out charred. I hope I never complained.

I shut off my brain before I get to Sophie and the toasted marshmallows she craved. My ice cream, mushy and sweating, fits into the freezer after I shove over Liz and Ezra Rayburn's condolence lasagna to make room. A puff of condensed cold hits my face as I close the door.

One of those names. Starts with G. Do I have any responsibilities about Juror G? To get her removed?

If I call Quinn . . . should I call Quinn? She ordered me never to contact her again.

I open the swivel cabinet next to the fridge, stack in the soup cans. Jurors are not supposed to discuss their case. With anyone. Does "hate it" count as discussing? It might simply be a throwaway.

But I know that a female juror whose last name begins with G is talking to her daughter about the trial. And that daughter is casually chatting about those opinions—"guilty"—with at least one of her teenaged BFFs who, in turn, is casually discussing that with strangers.

I stash the celery, which, as always, does not fit into the vegetable drawer. Is Juror G's behavior outrageous? Or insignificant? Meaningless? Or illegal?

Dex would remind me that it's a violation of the juror's oath to voice an opinion—even *have* an opinion—before all the evidence is presented. If Juror G already believes Ashlyn is guilty, Dex would insist Quinn McMorran should know. It would mean that juror was not impartial. It would "infect" the deliberations.

Royal Spofford would certainly like to know, too. Wonder what he'd do? Knowing a juror had already been convinced? Or didn't need convincing?

I take my last purchase, the Syrah, out of the bag. I hide it behind the toaster, out of reach.

Hey. If Juror G thinks Ashlyn Bryant is guilty, she's nothing but right. Who am I to interfere? Not my responsibility.

Pulling out Dex's kitchen chair, I sit at the table, click on my tablet, and with a last longing look at the wine, choose a trial segment. The crime scene evidence. This'll be a test of so many things. My stomach, and my determination, and my sanity. And maybe Ashlyn's.

I'll turn off my emotions. Pretend it's not real. That's how I'll deal with this. It's a story. I push Play.

In the video courtroom, I see a glowing laptop that's cabled next to a gizmo in the center of a wheeled metal cart. Full-color photographs, in excruciating detail, are projected onto a big screen, one after the other. The green plastic trash bag, shredded and torn. What was left of Tasha's face, pale bone showing through matted sandy hair. One purple barrette, hanging on for dear life. *It's not real.*

The photos are in sharp focus. Tasha's skull, whiter than white. Dense brown debris cocoons it, embeds the vacant eye sockets. Filmy tendrils of seaweed twist around the longer bones. The TV camera shot shifts, thank heaven, to show viewers the witness and the district attorney.

"What are these?" DA Spofford touches the screen in three places with a wooden pointer.

"Bites." Crime scene tech Patricia Ruocco sits on the stand. Shoulders square. Severe black-rimmed glasses, white shirt. All business.

"Human?" Spofford asks.

"No. The markings indicate aquatic creatures."

Ruocco confirms the plastic bag also contained three strips of duct tape, a disintegrating white blanket, and what looked like a once-pink water-soaked stuffed animal.

"What kind of a stuffed animal?" Spofford almost whispers his question.

"Possibly a rabbit."

I cannot watch this. A rabbit? *A rabbit?* I try to still my heart, try to stop my tears. Lots of little girls have stuffed rabbits. This is not Sophie. This is—was—Tasha. I sit up straighter, as stiff-backed and steel-willed as the crime scene tech. She and I have exactly the same job. To let people know this murder will not be tolerated.

The rabbit picture clicks away.

But now we see a close-up of those pink leggings, a jagged rip in one side seam. The striped T-shirt, disturbingly tiny, soaked out of shape. I count to five, take a sip of water, look out the study window into the twilight. The pictures are not real.

"What is that?" Spofford points again. "That, and that?"

"Duct-tape glue," Ruocco says. "On the victim's lower mandible."

"Chin, mouth, and nose?" Spofford translates.

"Yes."

Duct tape. I feel my stomach turn, almost hearing the sound of the tape tearing, tasting how it would feel to have it plastered over my mouth. Sophie's mouth. I can't breathe.

Ashlyn has pulled her cardigan up to her chin. She's head down, huddled, and wiping away tears. The judge had warned people to leave if they worried they could not handle the photos.

"Too bad *you* can't leave, you witch," I tell the screen.

And it gives me some horrible pleasure to know that there's

one person in the jury box who I know agrees with me. Juror G thinks Ashlyn Bryant killed her daughter. I will happily chronicle the day the jury verdict confirms that.

I push Stop. The final gruesome images, skull and seawater, fade to black. I take a deep breath, trying not to think about crime scene photos. I never saw the ones of Dex and Sophie, after the tree, although they must exist. My entire life faded to black after that. I never read the newspaper stories about it, never watched the TV coverage. If there even was any. I don't talk about it. Not ever. What happened was an accident. No one's fault. The final police report confirmed that. But now, it seems, my conscience is coming to life.

In the stillness of our kitchen, I can almost hear Dex's voice. He'd remind me that if someone hears about the biased juror *after* the verdict, and as a result McMorran appeals, Ashlyn could get a new trial.

That would completely suck. Plus, my book would be toast.

Should I tell Quinn McMorran? She insisted that I never contact her again, so hey, if I don't, it's her own fault. Right. I'm not gonna call.

A car alarm goes off outside. It shatters the silence, clanging for attention. A car. Alarm. A warning. It's a message from Dex. I know it is.

Fine. Okay. I hear you.

"Hi, Quinn. It's Mercer Hennessey." I keep my voice casual as I leave the message on her cell. "Sorry it's so late, but I thought ten might be okay. I know you told me not to call, but it's . . ." I hesitate, wanting to entice her to call me back without giving anything away, ". . . truly something you might be interested in. Call me, okay? Any time."

That was two hours ago. I waited in my study, working, but now it's too late for her to call me back. At least I tried. And I finished writing the scene revealing the moment police found the smoking gun. Ashlyn's computer searches for chloroform.

Chloroform? I write on my list. That is . . . perplexing. Everyone in the world—don't they?—knows prosecutors still believe the notorious Casey Anthony killed her daughter with chloroform. Like Ashlyn, Casey was charged with her young daughter's murder, but Casey Anthony was acquitted. Ashlyn must have been aware of that—she was, maybe fourteen when it happened? As in Ashlyn's case, the press coverage was relentless, the grisly details irresistible water-cooler scandal.

Casey and Ashlyn's lives are similar in other ways too, now that I think of it, but so are the lives of any number of pretty-ish nightclubbing man-hungry party girls. Still. Did Ashlyn do research on Casey? Study the endless TV documentaries and step-by-step dramatizations? Did she take how-to-get-away-with-murder lessons from the case of the not-guilty Casey Anthony?

Murder lessons. That makes my skin crawl.

According to my research, it takes five minutes to incapacitate a person with chloroform. Five horribly unimaginably writhing minutes. A shorter time, my online medical text explains, if the patient's body is very small.

I pause for a second, imagining small bodies. Take a sip of wine, but my glass is empty. I can almost hear the buzz of the halogen light pin-spotting my desk. Sophie was so small, both of her feet would fit into one of Dex's shoes. *I still have those shoes.*

Times like now, right now, my therapist had told me, I have to pull myself out of the darkness. Back to reality. Ashlyn Bryant is on trial for first-degree murder. With premeditation, malice aforethought, and extreme cruelty. Duct tape. And chloroform.

I look at my silent phone. Apparently Quinn doesn't care what I have to say about the talkative Juror G. Does anyone?

And then I have an idea. But too late to do it now. Tomorrow.

CHAPTER TWENTY-THREE

No answer on the first ring. I hear the second begin as I jam my cell phone to my ear, watch the newspaper delivery guy toss the Wednesday morning *Globe* at my porch, and reassess my decision. A reporter calling another reporter? I'd gotten up earlier than usual, surprisingly awake, surprisingly—to me, since there's no one else to be surprised—eager to begin my day. Third ring now.

The numbers had remained on my mirror this morning a tiny bit longer than usual. Maybe the weather is changing? I watched, as always, as the lingering numbers began to fail, using the time to say hello to Sophie and Dex.

"I miss you every moment," I said aloud. "And everything I do, I do for you." The numbers disintegrated as I talked, making me hurry to finish. "Dex, honey, thank you, I'm using what you taught me, too. It's all for you, all for you both." I paused, the numbers almost gone to memory. "You know I love you," I whispered.

By then it was 7:30. I made the call. The fourth ring doesn't finish.

"Rissinelli," a voice answers.

What if he doesn't remember me? "Hi, Joe. It's Mercer Hennessey. I'm—"

"Hey. Mercer. Long time." A pause. "Ah. How are you?"

Of course. "Fine," I say. "Listen. Uh, just between us?"

"Well, probably." Joe takes the middle ground. "What's up?"

I'd considered how much I could tell him, how much it would take to lure him into talking to me, how much it might matter in the long run. I'd practiced the conversation last night in bed, mentally playing both roles as I always do before an important interview.

"About the Bryant trial. I'm–and please keep this under your hat–writing about it." I'll let him assume it's for the magazine.

"Okay."

"I'm not at the courthouse," I go on.

"I was just thinking that."

"And I know you have your real work to do there. But I'm hoping you might let me interview you. Give some of the vaunted Rissinelli perspective."

Silence. It's tough for a journalist to convince another journalist to talk. All the usual gambits fail, because the other guy sees them coming a mile away.

"Unless there's a mistrial of course," I go on, like we're big news buddies. "Then we're all doomed."

"Look, Mercer," Joe says. "I'm interested. I'm a fan, used to love your stuff. Why don't we grab of coffee at Courthouse Square deli? At like, 9:15. Before today's session starts at 10. On background. Go from there."

Gotcha.

"Sure," I say. "Meet you then."

HOTTEST TICKET IN TOWN

Every court has its regulars. There are the retired sixty-somethings who don't want to be cooped up in some apartment. The detective wannabes. The *Perry Mason* fans and the *CSI* aficionados who think they know about crime scenes and forensics. The sickos, and the ghouls. Those looking for cheap thrills, and those hoping for justice.

"What kind of mother would murder her own child?" one woman in a green *Criminal Minds* T-shirt told a reporter. "This is the hottest ticket in town!"

Some days people camped out, stayed overnight on the bumpy

concrete tundra of Courthouse Square, sleeping on inflated air mat-
tresses under the buzzy security lights and the September stars
interrupted by the Boston city skyline, then making a mad dash to
the ticket line when it assembled at 5:30 A.M.

After the first day, trial-watchers figured out their own system for
keeping the first-come first-served situation fair. A flame-haired woman
they called "The Sharpie Lady" wrote indelible magic marker numbers
on the back of attendees' hands, indicating their place in the line.

By 9:05, I've typed that scene on my laptop, sitting in a ridiculously uncomfortable metal chair at a tippy wrought-iron table
on what Courthouse Square Deli calls its "deck," more accurately
the restaurant's pigeon-magnet outdoor-seating area.

The deck gives me an unobstructed view of the courthouse
plaza. A single line of courtroom hopefuls starts up at the big double doors, continues down the ten or so shallow marble steps, and
spreads out onto the concrete courtyard. The sun is already blasting, and a few attendees carry shade-providing umbrellas. I squint
to see if they have Sharpie numbers on their hands, as the *Herald*
described, but I can't see that far. I'll confirm it with Joe. That'll
be a good way to start the conversation, let him be the smart and
knowledgeable one.

All seems peaceful on Trial Day Six. I attempt to sip my bitter
deli coffee, in a paper cup just in case.

The morning shadows shift, and I scoot my chair a half-turn to
keep my eyes on the front door and the pack of wannabe attendees gathering. If the judge decides that Spofford asking Georgia if
she thought her daughter killed her granddaughter is objection-
able enough to call a halt to the entire trial, everyone will have to
go home. The idea is more bitter than my coffee.

Driving here, my radio's morning news was full of speculation.
Speculation is all anyone has.

"I mean, if Ashlyn Bryant didn't do it, who did?" one commentator sneered. "The poor defense attorney is grasping at straws."

I see both sides. If there's a mistrial, clearly the Commonwealth will bring charges again, and it'll all start over. On the other hand, if the jury can't make a fair decision, the legal system *requires* a do-over. What if I were the accused? What would I believe was fair? What would I want?

That's why I have to tell Joe about the juror. Dex would want me to.

My cell phone pings a text. It's Joe. SORRY, it says. Call u later.

I frown. *Sorry?* And, call you later? Why'd he change his mind? What's more, something's happening on the courthouse plaza. A hum from the line of spectators, like a buzz of instant conversation, is growing in intensity.

My reporter instincts are killing me. Maybe the Sharpies have gotten wind of something. I stash my still-wrapped bagel-with-light-cream-cheese in my tote bag, then peel a two-buck tip from my wallet and tuck it under the faceted glass and chrome saltshaker. And go.

I smile at the Sharpies as I reporter-walk past them up the courthouse steps. "Press," I explain, so they don't call the line police. I have on my confident look. *Done this a million times.* "What's up?"

"No comment," one man says. He turns away from me, adjusting a black baseball cap.

I try not to laugh. Like I care what this guy's comment would be. People watch too much TV. Scanning the next few people in line, I try to detect someone who's civil and rational. "Why all the buzz?" I ask a young woman in red jeans. "Is anything special going on?"

"Not that we know of, ma'am," she says. Her hand shows a black inked 7. "Around now's when we get to see the lawyers come in. We're all saying there's gonna be a mistrial, and—"

"Not *all* of us," the man turns back, interrupting. His hand is numbered 2. I don't see a number 1.

"Thanks." I power through the heavy front door, revolving out of the morning sunshine and into the dusty gloom of the dark-paneled courthouse. Formerly an expanse of black-diamond marble floor and lofty architecture, the grand entryway is now blockaded by an ugly gray metal detector, a rubber conveyor belt, and two grim-faced rent-a-guards. Just a week ago there was bomb threat here. False alarm or not, I feel the lingering edge of suspicion.

"Hi guys," I'm smiling and congenial to the guards, *nothing to worry about here,* as I dig for my press pass. The scene is so familiar, my muscle memory slips back into journalist mode. Joe Riss didn't show, but since I'm here anyway, maybe I can get a seat at the actual trial. I'd love to see Ashlyn in real life. Georgia and Tom, too. If there's a mistrial, it'd be Georgia's testimony that caused it. Wonder how she'd feel about that? The trial she essentially started—*ending* because of her?

I hold out my laminated press credential to the guards, showing them my happy-looking photo and affiliation with *City* magazine. If they notice the expiration date, I'll act baffled and figure something out. I put my handbag on the conveyor belt. The belt doesn't move.

The shorter one, name tag Silvio Ortiz, takes my credential, almost looks at it, hands it back. "Where're you headed?" he asks.

I know that. "Three-oh-six."

"Where's your Bryant pass?" the tall one asks.

"Oh," I say.

"Yeah. Sorry." Ortiz glances away as we hear the whisk of the revolving doors. "Miss? Can you step aside, please?"

I turn to see who's getting priority.

Well, well.

"Hi, Quinn," I say. Quinn McMorran. Accompanied only by two bulging black leather briefcases. Quinn was my first phone call about Juror G. And now, here she is. *Sorry Joe.* You just lost a biggie.

"Hello, Mercer." The sleeves of her black blazer are pushed

up over her elbows, pearl earrings match her necklace. The life-changing mistrial decision is looming. This is probably not her most approachable moment. But it's the moment I have.

"Did you get my message?" I ask. "Do you have two minutes?"

"Not now." She puts down one briefcase and swipes her bangs out of her eyes. I'm sure she has associates, but I've never seen them. Maybe they're out of camera range in the courtroom. Maybe she wants Ashlyn to appear vulnerable.

"Big day, as you know," she says. "Mistrial decision. Whatever you have can wait."

Okay, fine. First Joe bails. Now Quinn McMorran's entire body language is announcing *I am outta here.*

And you know, I mentally shrug, if she doesn't care, who am I to force her to hear this? Juror G would probably be replaced by someone else voting guilty.

My conscience–Dex–pokes me. Hard. If I give up on this, it betrays everything he stood for. "There's no true justice without the rule of law," he'd say. "Playing fair is how we demonstrate faith in our system. How we honor it." I let Dex down once. I swear I will never do it again. Quinn ordered me not to call her. But I am not having this on my conscience.

"Quinn?"

She frowns, as if I've overstepped. "Goodbye, Mercer."

"Quinn." I take a step toward her, then another. "Wait." A few more people, I don't recognize them, are yanking off belts, then plunking wallets and cell phones in gray metal-detector bins. The guards focus on them, and they focus on the guards and the conveyor belts and their destination inside, so Quinn and I are–for the moment–ignored.

"Listen." I lower my voice, aware of the others, aware of the un-predictable acoustics of the cavernous lobby. "It's about a juror."

"You're sure?" she asks when I've finished. "A woman. G."

"Well, no," I whisper back. "Not sure at all. But that's what she said she said. What she told me."

She stares at me, then looks up and to the right. "Could she have said Grunewald? Or Galanopoulos?"

"The person didn't say the name," I remind her. Wonder if she just handed me two jurors' names. "Just indicated a G name, hard to spell."

"G as in guilty, apparently." Quinn rolls her eyes.

"I have no idea." I don't really know anything. I'm truly speculating. "I only thought . . ."

"You did right, Mercer. Dex would have—well. Approved. Thank you."

I've never seen that expression on anyone's face before. Gratitude. Fear. Light-speed assessment.

"See you in court," I say to her back. I won't, of course, because the guards aren't letting me in. If I don't get home soon, I'll miss the fireworks.

CHAPTER TWENTY-FOUR

needn't have hurried home. It's one in the afternoon, I'm back in my sweats, and the trial hasn't started yet. Nothing from Joe. Nothing from Quinn. Nothing from the judge.

I'm stolidly pretending my life is not on the line here. Proceeding as if the trial will proceed as well. If the world worked the way it should, what would I write next? I sit at my desk, open my tablet to the video of my unwatched testimony, then open a manila folder full of snipped-out clippings and forensics files from Katherine. *Perfect.* The duct tape.

ALL DUCT TAPE IS NOT THE SAME

"Perry Chaudhary." The man in the white coat stated his name as Royal Spofford requested. "Evidence analyst for the State Police Crime Lab."

He'd brought a regular sports jacket to court, but the district attorney rejected it. *Wear your whites,* Spofford instructed. *Makes you look more credible.* Chaudhary'd gotten a haircut, too. Unfortunately.

He sat in the witness box, trying not to look at Ashlyn Bryant. Kept imagining what she must have done. And how. He knew he had to be clinical. But it was difficult.

"So Mr. Chaudhary." Spofford pointed to a poster-board exhibit showing a cross-section of duct tape. "To the untrained eye, all duct tape looks the same. Is that true?"

"No. All duct tape is not the same," Chaudhary replied.

"Why is that important in this case?" Spofford asked.

"Only one manufacturer uses the kind of powdered aluminum that gives that silver-gray color. A company called Adheeso."

"Was the tape found with little Tasha Nicole manufactured by Adheeso?"

"Yes."

"How available is Adheeso tape? If you know?"

"Yes, I looked into that. And it's, well . . ." Chaudhary paused. "Rare."

"Adheeso is—*rare*?" Spofford raised his eyebrows at the jury, confirmed they were paying attention.

"It is," Chaudhary said. "It's available, but very local. You have to be where they sell it."

"I see." Spofford appeared to be thinking. Then, "Could you buy it in Ohio?"

"Yes," Chaudhary said. "Ohio is the only place."

Spofford turned away from the witness, as if he had finished. Then he turned back, raised one finger at Chaudhary. "One more question. Was there anywhere else, besides with the victim, that you found this 'rare' duct tape?"

"Yes." The lab tech tugged at the hem of his suddenly too-small white jacket. "On the refrigerator of the Bryant home. Detective Koletta Hilliard had seen duct tape there when she waited in the Bryant's kitchen, and asked Ohio law enforcement for a sample. And" He swallowed. "It matched."

"Nothing further," Spofford said.

Quinn McMorran was on her feet before Spofford settled in his chair.

"Mr. Chaudhary," she said. *This damn duct tape.* "The tape on the refrigerator—what was it doing?"

"It appeared to be securing a ventilation grate."

"I see," she said. "The Bryants used their *own* tape to fix their *own* refrigerator. Now. That tape in the green plastic bag. Were there traces of clothing fabric on that? Or skin?"

"No," he said.

"I see," she said. "Now, it's difficult to use tape, especially the kind you tear, without leaving fingerprints on it, isn't that true?"

"Yes."

McMorran cleared her throat, looked at Ashlyn. Ashlyn, as instructed, was using her best posture, keeping her face composed, her eyes focused.

"Two final questions, Mr. Chaudhary. Yes or no. My client was fingerprinted after her arrest? Correct? Her fingerprints had not been on file prior to that, correct?"

"Yes."

"Exactly. So, again, yes or no. Did you find any of her fingerprints on that duct tape? Just yes or no."

"No."

"Nothing further." McMorran almost made it to her chair before Spofford stood.

"Redirect?" Spofford said. "Mr. Chaudhary, did you find *any* fingerprints on the duct tape?"

"No."

"So since *someone* used it, she might have been wearing rubber gloves?"

"Yes." Chaudhary said. "She might."

"Recross?" McMorran barely waited for the judge's approval.

"Mr. Chaudhary, you said *she.* How do you imagine Ashlyn Bryant got the duct tape from her parents' home all the way to Boston? You think she packed her suitcase with a roll of local duct tape?"

"Objection." Spofford sneered out the word, didn't bother to stand. He rolled his eyes at the jury. "Your Honor. Please. Absurdly argumentative."

"Withdrawn," McMorran said. Let the jury mull *that* one over, she thought. But she was worried. This duct tape could sink her client.

Duct tape. I write that on my list. Spofford had hit this one out of the ballpark. *Ohio* duct tape? Brilliant. No way Quinn McMorran could undo that inescapable connection.

As a writer, I can think clinically about that duct tape. How and why it was placed on Tasha's face. The evil it allowed. In my writer role, it's a compelling story.

But in my mom role, it's unthinkable. When I imagine—and I can't help but do so—that happening to Sophie? My very consciousness would crumble, or explode, or both. How is Ashlyn standing this, hearing—and seeing—graphic representations and unflinching testimony about her own baby girl?

Ashlyn is so adept at keeping her face off camera, it's all the more riveting when I do catch a glimpse of her. The day McMorran called for the mistrial, Ashlyn looked, only once, right at Ashlyn-cam. As if she were telegraphing—well, triumph? But that interpretation may be my own skepticism.

One thing for sure. It was not a look of grief. I'd recognize that particular look. I see it in the mirror every morning.

CHAPTER TWENTY-FIVE

The suspense about the mistrial is driving me crazy. I should be thinking: the longer the delay, the better for the book. Instead I'm thinking: hurry the hell up. It's now almost three in the afternoon. Nothing from the court.

Fine. I'll work.

TOM BRYANT, I print on my legal pad, then list bullet points. *Father. Retired. Accountant. Pilot. Babysat.*

From all accounts, he and Ashlyn did not get along. Why? *Tom relationship w/Ashlyn?* I write on my list.

If I believe what I read in *Insider*—I know it's the most unreliable source ever, but at the grocery I can't resist—the reason Ashlyn *might* have hated her father was that he was cheating on Georgia. I write *Affair?*

Maybe in Boston? Was Tom Bryant ever in Boston? Someone must have checked. While I wait for the judge to rule, I could pre-write a Tom Bryant on-the-stand scene. It's not clear that he's going to testify, and if he doesn't, that scene won't matter. If there's a mistrial, none of this will matter.

I am weary of making things up.

I need food. I need exercise.

And I'm lonely. I stop in the center of the kitchen, realizing I could scream and shriek and go totally bananas, and no one, *no* one, would know. Maybe that's what I'm really doing these days. Screaming. And shrieking. But now there's no one to hear it.

"O-kay, Mercer," I say out loud. "Get over yourself." I put one hand on the refrigerator door handle, thinking. Maybe I should get a dog. Or a cat? The random cat begins to coalesce into a specific cat. A rescue. A sweet fluffy tortoiseshell rescue. I begin to pull the door open, then stop, shaking my head with a smile. Silly, Sophie is allergic to cats.

I stand there for a beat. My hand clenched on the fridge door is all that keeps me from collapsing onto the floor.

It doesn't matter anymore that Sophie's allergic to cats. The weight of that is almost—but I'm not going there.

I'm not.

I'm trying to write a book. I'm trying to find a life. For now.

Bottle of water. Apple. It'll have to do. I trudge back to the study, still feeling blue about the cat.

"If you're still with us?" Voice interrupts my gloom. "It appears the judge has a ruling on the mistrial motion. We're back live in ten."

Of course that's when the doorbell rings. And the phone rings. It's not Quinn McMorran because she's in court, so I let my cell go to voice mail. But I've gotta answer the door. Since the trial is starting in ten minutes, I have eight minutes and thirty seconds to find out who the heck is here and tell them to go away.

As I arrive at the front door, the phone rings one more time before giving up.

I look through the peephole.

Joe Rissinelli?

"This is *your* doing, isn't it? Is *this* what you wanted to tell me?" He's talking before I get the door all the way open. A silver Mini Cooper is in my driveway. "About the juror? That was me calling you, by the way."

"Hi, Joe." We're face to face, him on the outside, me on the in. Him in Levis and a sport coat, me in sweats. Both of us wearing wedding rings. *His* spouse is probably alive. "Tell you? About . . . the juror?"

I know I floated the idea of doing an interview with Joe, but did I use the word "juror"?

"Yeah," he says. "The juror. Sandra Galanopoulos."

He smiles. A nice smile, but I bet it's the one he uses on interviewees. To get them to talk. I smile back, exactly the same way. I absolutely never said a juror's *name* to him, because at that point I didn't know a juror's name. Quinn McMorran mentioned two last names at the courthouse. *That* I remember perfectly. Galanopoulos was one of them.

"Sandra Galanopoulos?" I repeat the name he said. "The trial is about to begin, so—"

"Is it?" Joe says. "Want to invite me in?"

I'm baffled. I'm not sure what's happening in court, but whatever it is, it's four minutes away.

"Sure." I wave Joe toward the living room. "I just have to, uh, save something." I gesture, vaguely, down the hall. I'll start my tablet taping, at least. "Have a seat. I'll be right back."

"I know you have video feed," he says to my back as I head down the hall. "And I know about your book."

"Hang on, okay?" I trot to the study, not acknowledging what he's said. I'm not going to play this game. Someone told him everything, or enough, and the list of the possibles is short. Maybe it doesn't matter. All that matters is the book.

"All set," I say, as I come back into the room. Joe's on the couch, tapping on his cell, but clicks it off and stashes it into his jacket pocket.

"I'll tell you something if you tell me something," he says. Smiling again. Lots of smiling going on. He points me to the wing chair across from him, as if he's in charge.

I burst out laughing, can't help it. I don't sit. "That's certainly putting it all out there."

Joe stops smiling. "Here's how it'll work. First, I promise I won't say I got it from you if you promise you won't say you got it from me. You tell me about the juror. And I'll tell you about Ashlyn's pregnancy. And who she says is the baby's father."

I blink at him, remembering my own speculation that he

had an *in* with Ashlyn. Maybe they've had a jailhouse rendez-vous? Or several? He's a reporter, a very good reporter, so there's got to be more to this than is evident. Because right now nothing is evident.

"It's about two minutes until the trial starts." I'd adore to know what he's offering to tell me, but his arrival doesn't make sense. Especially right now. "I'm surprised you're not there to hear the judge's ruling in person."

"The judge is gonna rule there's no mistrial. But he's not doing that until four," Joe says. "He's replacing Sandra Galanopoulos, but *he's* not explaining why. I'm thinking *you* can. And he'll put the trial into recess until tomorrow."

"What?" I'm surprised Joe knows all this, but he's Joe Riss, so it's possible. I lower myself into the chair, conscious of my sweats and stupid furry slippers. Good thing I have on underwear.

"Recess. Which means we have time to talk. Trust me." Joe makes himself at home, leans back against the white couch cushions, crosses an ankle over his knee. Fingers a smudge from his loafer, like he's noticing my feet. Smiles at me. Again. "And oh, that 'in-depth perspective interview' you wanted to do with me? Bull. Good try, Mercer, but that's the oldest trick in the book. What did you really want to talk about?"

Busted. But I was going to tell him anyway, I bargain with myself. If I tell the "Carmendy at the checkout" story—leaving out her name—and as a result he tells me something good, what could that hurt?

"Want some coffee?" I ask. Which reminds me. "And hey, what were you 'sorry' about? When you texted?"

A shadow passes over Joe's face. "Personal thing I had to take care of," he says.

Personal is the line I won't cross. "Cream and sugar?" I fill the empty space.

He follows me down the hallway to the kitchen, and he's prob-ably inspecting all the family photos lining the wall. He's a reporter, and I'd do exactly the same thing at his house, but I walk faster to give him less time to visually invade my privacy. As we pass the study, I see they've posted a graphic on the court monitor. It says: COURT WILL RETURN AT 3:45. Has Voice lost his job? But Joe seems to be right. Again.

"How'd you know?" I ask.

"Lucky guess," he obviously lies. He takes a chair at the kitchen table. "But our deal. To show my goodwill, I'll go first."

No one else has sat there for the past year or so—that fact does not escape me. It's Sophie's chair, and the padded seat still has four indelible dents from her pink Piglet booster. But he doesn't know that, and I cannot ask him to move. I stab the coffee pod into the machine, recognizing the emotional land mine, defusing it. "Deal," I say.

"Okay. So—and again, you didn't get this from me," Joe checks to confirm I'm consenting, then drums his fingers on the white tabletop. Stops. "About Tasha. At first, Ashlyn tried to hide being pregnant with her. She gave all the predictable excuses for her weight gain."

"Uh huh," I say, lifting the container of skim milk, inquiring.

"Sure," he says to the milk. "When it got too obvious to ignore, Georgia asked Ashlyn, flat out, who the father was."

As the coffee gooshes into a cup, I imagine that dysfunctional family dynamic. I put in a pod for me. "She's never had any other kids, has she? Ashlyn?" I ask.

"You've been reading *Insider,* I see." Joe laughs. "Anyway, she first told her mother it was Jeff Prechack, a guy she knew in high school. But bummer for Ashlyn, Georgia knew this Jeff's mother, and knew Jeff had been in the army, stationed in Kabul for the past six months. Since Ashlyn was four months, that was impossible."

"Whoa." I put down the mugs, pull out my chair. Ashlyn's duplicity is never-ending. And naming a guy as the father? Who *isn't* the father? Typical Ashlyn self-centeredness. "That's harsh. And stupid."

"She's a piece-of-work," Joe says. "Quoting Georgia herself. Says she 'makes her own reality.' Anyway, then, with much emotion, Georgia told me, Ashlyn confessed to her that the father is a guy she met at Hot Stuff–you know it?–a guy called Barker Holt. From Dayton. She apparently told Georgia that 'Bark,' who she called 'incredible,' had been killed. In Dayton. In a car accident. Before Tasha was born."

"Killed." This is so beyond. "In a car accident."

Joe flinches. "Sorry."

I put up a palm, absolving. "So, before Tasha was born, then?"

"Yup. But I got a copy of the birth certificate–it's impounded now, in evidence–but there's no father listed."

"Was there really a person named that?"

"Who knows?" Joe shrugs. "I can't find any death notices for a Barker Holt, but that doesn't mean anything."

"What did she tell *you* about it?"

"Right." He toasts me with his mug. "Good try. Now it's your turn."

We each take sips. I tell him a sanitized version of the juror story, and he seems satisfied. Anyone seeing us would say we look like two pals, chatting over coffee in a world that doesn't revolve around baby killers or murder trials. Or lying twenty-somethings who get pregnant and then decide their lives are too complicated with a child.

"Have we lost sight of the little girl on the beach?" I ask him, surprised I said it out loud.

"Probably." He shakes his head. "Remember all those teddy bears? They were supposed to leave the WE LOVE YOU BABY BOSTON signs and tributes on Castle Island until after the funeral, but at some point, like, overnight, everything got put in plastic bags and disappeared. 'Bad for tourists,' one administrator actually told me."

"Bad? For tourists?" I envision it, the gut-wrenching makeshift altar on the beach. Stuffed bears. Homemade signs. Flowers, wilting and desiccated. Some suit deciding it was bad PR and getting a lackey to broom it away. "Pretty cynical."

"I know. Anyway, that's when people started clamoring for 'closure.'" He rolls his eyes. "Thing is, they couldn't actually have a full funeral until the trial ended. In case there was some evidence that needed to be retrieved, or a test re-done. So they compromised on that memorial service."

"So sad. Did you go to it? In Dayton, right? I know Ashlyn didn't, although I read they'd have let her."

He nods, stares into his coffee mug, like it's a mirror. Then looks up. "Yeah," he says, in a different voice than before. "I did go. Very tough."

He's a respected reporter. He was there. No better research method than that. I could have found out about this a million ways. He'll never know. I'll write it up after he leaves.

My turn to smile, so sympathetic and understanding. "Tell me about it?"

Three hours later, alone again, my eyes are blurring the letters on the screen. I almost wish Joe hadn't told me about the memorial service. And in such tragic detail. It's unfair to make me write this part of the story. How can I not relive Dex and Sophie?

Somehow I planned their funeral. I don't remember the process. People came, Dex's parents and his entire law firm, if I remember correctly, which I probably don't. My colleagues from *City,* some neighbors. I spent a solid week writing thank-you notes for flowers and cards and casseroles, every note a triumph of euphemism and a sledgehammer of emotion. Thank you so much, I'd write, and wonder, *what am I thanking you for?* For reminding me my how my family died? That they were wonderful? And now they're gone forever?

It's long turned dark outside. I missed dinner, writing this scene. Haven't budged from this desk.

The funeral. I spent days, weeks, recalling it, replaying it in my head, over and over, trying to remember and trying to forget at the same time. I have to say—and I'll never repeat this—I understand why Ashlyn might have avoided Tasha's memorial. Why sit there, surrounded by sad people, all of whom are crying and mourning your loss? They'll all go home, and be happy they're not you. You'll go home and have no other choice but to *be* you.

I know this from experience.

I close my eyes, think of the beach at 'Sconset. Nantucket was our respite, for as long as we had it, our tiny but gorgeous wood-shingled rental in the island's most popular village. In the dark of my private self, I hear the gulls, and smell the oceany brine, feel the sun on my shoulders and think of the Perseid meteor shower that regaled us every August. Sophie saw a shooting star, just that once. We'd let her stay up ridiculously late, a special occasion. She jumped up and down, clapping her hands at the bright lights that fell from the sky.

CHAPTER TWENTY-SIX

Whoo hoo for no mistrial, right?" Katherine's too-cheery voice trills over the phone. "That judge had me going for a while last week. Sorry I've been out of touch. We almost got screwed, all I can say. Anyway. You keeping up? It's going fast, right? How are you, kiddo?"

"Tired," I say, trying to use as few words as possible. It's ten at night, Thursday, after Trial Day Twelve. Which I know only because I'm keeping track. Otherwise, the days would all run together as a blur of testimony and note-taking and taping and research and writing. It's now day 460 on my mirror. Finally sick of soup, I lunch-subsist on coffee and peanut-butter toast. I've given up wine. Mostly. Every night I order pizza, and I'm probably getting fat. At least they deliver.

But Joe had been right. The judge ruled no mistrial. Juror Sandra Galanopoulos was excused, and replaced. The trial continued with just one alternate. But I had told the truth as I knew it. That was a good thing, right?

Katherine is still talking. She hadn't interrupted me for a few days, and that was also a good thing. Now I wish she would chill. "Keeping up" isn't the half of it. I worked like crazy through five more days of the prosecution's case. We're now three days into the defense.

Quinn McMorran got the cops to admit they didn't know where Ashlyn was every moment in the weeks before Tasha was found. Where Tasha was, either. The TSA admitted Ashlyn might not have been on the plane to Chicago, and they couldn't be sure about the identity of a lap child, or if one was even on the plane. Al Cook, doddering and probably drunk, admitted he'd created the missing-child poster mostly from his imagination. Ron Chevalier said Ashlyn "seemed to love her daughter" but had told him she was "in Chicago or someplace." And Ashlyn's dimwitted pal Sandie DiOrio reiterated how "Ash and Tashie" were inseparable. Until Tasha went "away."

"Where did she go?" McMorran asked.

"Ashlyn didn't say."

"Did Ms. Bryant seem nervous or worried?"

"Not at all." Sandie went wide-eyed. "She *loved* her."

Everyone on TV is gagging over this "good mother" testimony. I am, too. But Quinn has to do her job. For what it's worth. My favorite part was when Spofford got DiOrio to relate Ashlyn's "Holy crap, I'm so good at making stuff up" statement.

I'm still waiting to see if the boyfriend, Luke Walsh, shows up. And Valerie, the babysitter.

"I have book scoop," Katherine is saying. I try to concentrate as she prattles in my ear about proofreaders and page galleys. About cover art and liner copy.

I pepper our "conversation" with *greats* and *terrifics* while I multitask, yellow-highlighting the trial notes I've printed out. I think about the trial every waking moment. And every sleeping moment.

Last night I dreamed Barker Holt came to the witness stand, draped with dripping seaweed like something out of Dickens. No one seemed to notice. He told the court he had died with Tasha, but no one had found his body. *This is a dream,* I told myself in the dream. When I woke up, it took me a second to remember that hadn't actually happened.

"Can I put you on hold for a sec?" Kath asks. "Can you hang on?"

"Sure." I don't try to keep the sarcasm out of my voice, but Kath is already elsewhere.

To remind myself of trial reality, I now keep a chart of the major witnesses. None of them wore seaweed.

The accountant. Spofford called her to testify that Ashlyn changed the Chicago plane ticket her mother bought for her to a Boston ticket, but hadn't used the return. That was supposed to convince the jury Ashlyn was in Boston at the time of Tasha's death, and so could have been responsible for it. That strategy hit a snag during cross-examination.

"Did she use her credit cards in Boston?" Quinn McMorran asked. "Was there any trace of her?"

"No," the accountant admitted.

"Did you find any financial footprint of her in Boston? Or anywhere near there?"

"No," the accountant said again.

I know that was designed to convince the jury there was no proof Ashlyn was ever *in* Boston, so couldn't be responsible. Spofford had not introduced that Hudson News kiosk surveillance video, which I thought was strange. He'd tried to neutralize the credit card testimony, asking if there was any way to trace cash. "Absolutely not," the accountant said.

The forensics guy. Spofford called the technician who tested for chloroform in Ashlyn's car. Was chloroform present? Inconclusive.

Quinn McMorran asked him only one question. "Did you find any trace of chloroform, anywhere, connected to Ashlyn Bryant?" He said no.

A Coast Guard oceanographer testified to tides and drift analysis. Where could a body have been dumped if it washed up on Castle Island in June? "Would it necessarily have come from Boston?" McMorran asked. "No."

Boston Police Detective Koletta Hilliard. The prosecution's final witness. I'd transcribed her most devastating testimony word for word.

"What was the bottom line of your investigation?" Spofford had asked her.

"I followed every lead to answer one question: If Ashlyn Bryant didn't kill Tasha Nicole, then who did?" Hilliard said. "There was no alternative. Ms. Bryant took her daughter to Boston. She later lied to her mother about seeing Tasha alive the morning we knew she was already in a garbage bag on Castle Island beach, and had been dead for some amount of time. Why would she lie? Only Ashlyn could have done it."

Only Ashlyn. I underline that. The very words Spofford used in his opening.

Kath still has me on hold. What the heck is she doing?

Quinn McMorran—known for her blistering cross-examination skills—barraged Detective Hilliard, nonstop. Asked about Ashlyn's boyfriends. And babysitters. Not hiding her derision.

"Did you find *them?* Interview *them?*"

"No."

Did you suspect Ron Chevalier, the owner of Hot Stuff? Did you ever suspect Tom Bryant? Georgia Bryant? McMorran asked all of those questions, rapid-fire, with growing incredulity, but Detective Hilliard stolidly testified all investigatory roads led to Ashlyn.

It felt—in my opinion, which doesn't matter—like grasping at evidentiary straws. What motive would those people have to kill a little girl?

All the news commentators agreed with me. They went nuts over the prosecution's case. *She's so guilty,* they all said. The lies, the deception, the duct tape. And if she's *not* guilty, they agreed, she's *got* to take the stand. They all echoed Royal Spofford's opening mantra, which also became a 46-point headline in the *Herald.* ONLY ASHLYN.

"Gotta call you back," Katherine's voice squawks through the speaker.

"Great," I say. "Lovely talking to—"

But Kath is gone. At least can look at my defense case notes before the morning session. And—radical idea—hope for some dreamless sleep.

The legal net under Quinn McMorran's tightrope is that she doesn't have to prove Ashlyn didn't do it. She doesn't have to prove where she was or what she was doing, or even who did kill Tasha. She only—only!—has to make the jury see reasonable doubt. That someone else, *anyone else,* might be the murderer. She doesn't have to prove who that someone might be.

But I know there *is* no one else. Only Ashlyn.

CHAPTER TWENTY-SEVEN

My desk phone rings again. It's 11:45 P.M.

"You still up?" Kath doesn't break stride. "So like I was saying, they're now working on the title, and–"

"What do you think happened with the boyfriend and the babysitter?" I interrupt. "Remember the people I told you Quinn told me Ashlyn told her about?" I stop, playing that question back to myself. "Know what I mean? Why doesn't Ashlyn tell Quinn where those people are? They might totally corroborate her story."

"Maybe Ashlyn doesn't know where they are," Katherine says. "Or maybe Quinn's avoiding them. A 'boyfriend' might be a defense lawyer's hero, for sure. Especially if he could give our girl an alibi. But–he also might be a villain. And that babysitter–the news articles all have her name, right?–might go either way, too. She might be, I don't know, the evil nanny. But she could be a big time witness for the prosecution, too. Maybe she knew Ashlyn was unfit? Or neglectful."

"Right. The Dayton cops were looking for her," I say. "But Spofford didn't call a babysitter either."

"Whatever. Ashlyn's a big fat liar, and soon to be a permanent resident of the slammer. I was just thinking, Merce. Could Tasha talk yet? Maybe Ashlyn worried about that."

"Whoa. That's creepy–you think Ashlyn worried Tasha would spill some secret?" I spin my pencil on my desk. It hits a pad of yellow stickies, knocks it on the floor. How well *could* Tasha talk?

I can hear Sophie's voice. Trying out her words. "Why? Why, Mama?" She had intent. Imagination. What might Tasha have said?

"You can't just make people up, though," I say, retrieving my notes. I write *Tasha talk?* On my list. "Luke and Valerie are *some-where*."

"Hey. Like Quinn said, the woman has issues. Maybe . . ." Katherine sounds distracted. "Can you hang on? Sorry. Call waiting."

Sure, heck, I'll hang on. What else do I have to do?

McMorran's opening statement *did* promise we'd hear Ashlyn has issues. What issues? And when? Drug abuse? Child abuse? Is there some repressed-memory thing? Something about that Hot Stuff nightclub? *Family* issues?

Hmm. Family issues.

I tap my pencil point against the yellow pad, then flip it to tap the eraser. Point, eraser, point. Maybe with her father?

Speaking of fathers. How about Tasha Nicole's? Talk about "issues." How can his identity not matter?

"Merce? Are you there?" Katherine's back.

Where else would I be at this time of night? My rear is permanently attached to this chair. My fingers glued to the keyboard.

"Yup. I'm here."

"Will Ashlyn testify tomorrow? You think?" Katherine goes on, picks up a new topic as if she hadn't parked me on hold.

Another great question. Again, what I think doesn't matter.

"She's such a self-absorbed bitch," I say, then remember what Joe Riss told me. "Her mother says she 'makes her own reality.' Maybe she thinks she can outmaneuver Royal Spofford. Wouldn't you love to see that?"

"He'd rip her to shreds," Kath says. "Wouldn't it be awesome if he shows the jury the wet T-shirt photo? There's gotta be more copies."

"Yeah," I say. "I think her only play is to shut up. We'll know tomorrow. Now can I get back to writing? I'm terrific after midnight."

We hang up, and I go back to the manuscript.

"Five minutes," Voice says. But that's got to be a dream. "This is a dream," I mutter, then realize I said it out loud, into my arm. Which is resting on my desk. I've slept here—all night? I blink, sitting up in my chair. It's morning. All the lights are on.

"I was just resting my eyes," I explain to no one. I'm still not sure I'm awake or asleep.

"Four minutes," Voice says.

Awake. And late. Heart pounding and head still bleary, I race to the bathroom, touch the mirror for luck. I know it's 461, but no time to make steam to write in. "Love you!" I say out loud, make it to the kitchen, slam in a coffee pod and race back to the study. I yawn, stretch, struggle to clear my head.

When the feed comes on, Ashlyn-cam shows the defendant sitting, posture perfect, in an ice blue sweater and pearls. The shot changes as Quinn McMorran rises from her chair.

"The defense rests," she says.

I'd guessed right. Ashlyn is not going to take the stand. I mean—smart girl. What could she possibly say? What reality can she create? Dex would remind me that constitutionally, the jury can't hold her silence against her, but they've got to wonder why she's not defending herself. This decision was a lose-lose for Miss Ashlyn. Exactly what I hope for her.

I mean, pearls? Puh-leeze.

"And we're in recess until Tuesday," Judge Green is saying. "Counsel, we'll take administrative matters first. Closing arguments will begin at ten on Tuesday. Jurors, as always, you are not to watch any news stories about the case, or discuss it with anyone. That includes fellow jurors."

The gavel bangs. The audio stops. The video screen goes dark. All that's left is the verdict.

My world comes to a halt.

I stare at the black screen for a moment, mesmerized by the silence, the gravity, the infinite nothing, thinking of the dark dark water, black as that screen, and a little girl. Of *two* little girls. When I slide under my white comforter, exhausted and so alone, it doesn't matter that the morning sun is beaming through my bedroom window. I'm engulfed in the darkness, too.

CHAPTER TWENTY-EIGHT

Closing arguments are the whole ball game. This morning Royal Spofford has to prove that a crime was committed, how the victim was killed, and that beyond a reasonable doubt Ashlyn Bryant was responsible. The defense—which goes first in Massachusetts—has only to convince jurors there's reasonable doubt. Sometimes that is tough.

It's the lawyers' last chance. The defendant's, too. This is a chapter I cannot write in advance, because those words no one can predict.

I worked the whole weekend and all through Monday, trapped by torrential rain and a relentless deadline. Joe's on the way—he called to say the paper assigned someone else to court this morning. Then he asked if he could bring coffee and watch the closings with me. On regular broadcast TV, not the feed. Every station is carrying it, of course. So, sure. Whatever. Maybe Joe likes having someone to talk with about the trial, too. Or maybe he's angling to get more page-time in my book.

I'd changed into jeans and one of Dex's oxford shirts. Combed my hair.

Theo from Dex's law firm called five minutes later, saying they had two more boxes of possessions and asked to bring them over. Why not. Party at Mercer's house.

But at 9:45, Joe notwithstanding, I'll focus on the closing arguments. Today is when the case of *Little Girl Lost* will be won—and lost.

I can almost hear my deadline clock ticking. I head for the living room to turn on the TV. It all depends on the jury.

The jury. Thirteen men and women now—twelve eventual jurors and one alternate. People whose faces I have never seen. I think about ex-Juror G, Sandra Galanopoulos, probably watching the trial at home. Because of me. And not having to decide whether Ashlyn Bryant would spend her life in prison. Wonder if she's happy about that?

What if her one vote would have made a difference?

I stop in the middle of the hall. What if Ashlyn walks? Because of me? What if Ashlyn's acquitted, the only thing in the world I could not bear to happen, and it turns out I *made* it happen? Because Dex would have wanted the trial to be fair, I ratted out Juror G. I did the right thing for Dex. But what if it was the wrong thing for Sophie? Did I ruin everything? Again?

Unsteady on my feet, suddenly, I touch the wall for equilibrium. I see my reflection in the front hall mirror, then think—*mirror.* Today I wrote 465.

The doorbell rings. Joe already? I flip on the TV. Go to the door. It's not Joe.

"Katherine, honey," I say. "What's wrong?"

"Let me in," she says. I've never seen Katherine's hair so chaotic, or her face so drawn. Her chic cropped jacket is yanked off one shoulder by the strap of a heavy tote bag, her sunglasses dangle from the collar of her silky shirt. "Someone's following me."

I step out onto my front porch and Katherine slips inside. "Following you?" I ask. "Who?"

"Come back inside," she hisses. "Don't let them see you."

I look up our street, then down. No one unusual. I come in, close the door. Katherine is unsettled, her eyes darting in a way I've never seen.

"Who?" I say again. "Why would anyone—why were you coming here, anyway? Anything up?"

"In a silver car," she says, not answering me. "Some kind of silver car. Was behind me the whole way. Crazy-driving."

We both flinch, startled, as a horn honks on the street outside. A snazzy Mini Cooper pulls into my driveway.

"That car?" So much for the scary stalker. "That's Joe Rissinelli. He was on his way here."

Katherine gives me a look, blinking. I can't tell whether she's assessing his arrival, or deciding whether it's his car she saw. A Mini Cooper is pretty easy to recognize.

"Not sure," she says. "The publisher got a bomb threat, *he* thinks it's about the book. *Cops* say it's a hoax, but I guess it's making me jumpy. Shouldn't even have told you. Morons. But I did see that car."

"What?" I say. "A bomb threat? Because of the book? *My* book? Listen, that's—incredibly disturbing."

Joe trots toward the front door, khakis and loafers, carrying a cardboard container with three coffees. Reporters always worry there won't be enough coffee.

Katherine, still regrouping I guess, adjusts her jacket, smoothes her hair.

"Hi, Joe," I call out from the doorway, lifting a hand in greeting. I explain to Katherine, keeping my voice low. "We're watching the closings on regular TV together, his idea. Because I'm interviewing him for the *book*."

A horn toots out on the street, a hand waved from the driver's side window. A silver Audi pulls into my driveway.

"Who's *that?*" Katherine recoils, steps out of street view as Joe comes inside. "Listen, I need to talk to you," she says.

"And I need to talk to you, sister," I say. "*Bomb* threat? And that's just Theo from Dex's law firm," I say. "Bringing me boxes of his stuff. Stupid, because I'll never open them. Hey—is that who you saw? Silver car?"

"Maybe," Katherine says.

She peers around the doorjamb as Joe arrives with the coffee. Theo pulls into the driveway behind the Mini. Awful lot going on for 9:25 in the morning.

A flurry of introductions—though Joe and Katherine know each other, of course—and I send Joe (and his coffees) to the living room and the big-screen TV. Theo is pulling a wheeled cart up the front walk, two oversized cardboard boxes bungeed to it. I have about ten seconds until he gets to the door.

"Kath?" I grab her arm. "Bomb threat?"

"Forget about that, cops insist it's nothing."

"Kidding me? A bomb is not nothing."

"It's *not* a bomb. It's nothing. Like the other day at court. I shouldn't have mentioned it. And listen. We may have found the babysitter."

"Valerie?" I ask, dumb question, because there are no other babysitters. "And who's 'we'?" I look out the open front doorway, briefly scanning for silver cars. And bombs. Theo is five steps away, but turns to adjust the boxes.

But whoa. Babysitter Valerie could confirm where she'd taken Tasha, the little girl's relationship with Ashlyn, and how Ashlyn explained Tasha's whereabouts. Maybe she could explain Ashlyn's "issues." And Luke.

My brain is going at light speed, weighing the possible outcomes at this point in the trial. This is going to be a holy mess.

"Does Quinn McMorran know?" I ask. "Does Spofford? Where is she?"

"She's dead," Katherine whispers.

"Dead?"

"Hi, Miz Hennessey." Theo's at the front stoop. He points to his cart. "These are kind of heavy. Want me to bring them inside?"

"I have to go," Katherine says. "You have too much company."

I grab a box from Theo's cart and plop it down inside, blocking his entry and Katherine's exit. No way she's gonna leave me without explaining *that* breaking news. Dead? Valerie is dead?

"Thanks, Theo." I take the other box, too, pretending it doesn't weigh a ton, and stack it on top. "I'm sure you have to get back to the office. And I'm in a meeting."

I close the door with as believably polite a smile as I can muster, shutting him out and Katherine in. She cannot leave. Not after that breaking news.

"Valerie's *dead?*" I whisper. Put two and two together. "Was it a *bomb?*"

"They're starting!" Joe calls out.

"Tell you later," she whispers back. "But Merce. Trust me. There are no bombs."

Katherine, who still seems freaked out from her "silver car stalker," makes the morning even nuttier by settling herself on the couch too, and the three of us have a closing-watching coffee klatch. I'd put my tablet on Record in the study so I could watch the closings with Joe, Kath, and everyone else on the planet. Kath took one of the coffees. All good.

Ashlyn-cam is trained on her face, and the defendant closes her eyes as Quinn McMorran begins her closing.

"What showboats, right?" I wave off the drama. No one answers me.

At least Ashlyn had the self-restraint not to fold her hands in pretend-prayer. I have to believe that only some sort of *deus ex machina* can save her. The courthouse on fire, or someone having a heart attack. Even another bomb threat would merely delay the inevitable.

"The key question in this case can never be answered or proven," Quinn is saying. "That question is: when and how did Tasha Nicole Bryant die? And if you cannot answer that, you must acquit."

Wonder if Ashlyn would agree to a post-conviction interview with me? From prison? She'd probably love extending her fifteen minutes.

Joe and Kath are watching McMorran's closing in silence,

letting me take notes on my laptop. In about thirty minutes, I can hear Quinn building to the big finish.

"It's disturbing to think of a mother hurting her own child," she says. "But how disturbing is it to convict a grieving mother for that unspeakable crime—when she did not commit it? Ask yourselves, each of you fellow human beings, each of you citizens of the United States of America, ask yourself: do I have enough indisputable evidence, genuine facts, authentic truths? Has anything—*anything*—convinced you? You may not like her, ladies and gentlemen. But you are not asked to be her friend. You are sworn to judge her beyond a reasonable doubt.

"And you know, from sworn forensic testimony, that there are no fingerprints. No DNA. No witnesses. No hairs, no fibers, no evidence whatsoever, not even proof that Ashlyn Bryant was ever in Boston. There is no cause of death.

"'Only Ashlyn.' That's what the district attorney kept saying. But you know that's not true. And certainly not beyond a reasonable doubt."

I clap a couple of times, sarcastic applause, as she sits down. "When you got nothin', bring out the United States of America, Dex always said."

"Well, she's persuasive about the cause of death," Joe says. "And no forensics connecting Ashlyn, really, not in any way."

"Gah," I say.

"Anyone hungry?" Kath asks. "Merce? Okay if Joe and I go scrounge?" They head to the kitchen, discussing the proper preparation of peanut butter and jelly sandwiches as they go. They're all chatty, like they were both still working at *City*, like they watch sensational trials and make lunch together all the time. Funny to have people in the house again. Funny that we're brought together by murder. Very cozy.

CHAPTER TWENTY-NINE

Does it take this long to make sandwiches? Katherine better not be telling him about dead Valerie.

"You guys!" I call toward the kitchen. "It's on!"

I open my note-taking file. There's no way jurors can remember every word of evidence. Like all prosecutors, Spofford is hoping the jury's collective memory will forget the elements that hurt his case. And only remember those that help it.

I almost feel the warmth of Dex's body next to me. I certainly hear his thoughts. *It's all about which side tells a better story,* he'd say. I smooth the couch cushion beside me, imagining his favorite jeans, and his soft pale-blue shirts, and move my hand just in time for Katherine to sit down. She smells of peanut butter, and holds out an array of sandwiches, crustless triangles arranged on one of my mom's silver platters.

"Nice," I say, choosing one. Back to reality. "Where's—"

"Bathroom," she says.

I picture him there, can't help it, Joe looking at himself in my mirror. *Don't touch that,* comes to mind. When Joe comes back, I search his face for—I don't know.

He takes a sandwich, like we do this every day. Settles into the wing chair. Jeans and a tattersall oxford shirt. It's perplexing. Why is he here and not in court? The newspaper assigned someone else to cover the closings? Doesn't pass the sniff test. He knows I'm writing the Ashlyn book. What's his goal?

The TV screen shows the courtroom. The players, silent, all

in place. The microphones pick up that unmistakable court-room prologue—the rustle of papers, the adjusting of spectators' feet, a few muffled conversations. On the bench, Judge Green, his bright yellow tie peeking from the collar of his robe, turns pages in a file. Off camera, the jury must be seated in those thread-bare navy chairs.

The judge looks up.

"Here we go," Joe pops the last of his sandwich. Rubs his palms together, in anticipation, or to get rid of crumbs. "What do you think?"

"It's all about which side tells a better story," I say, thinking of Dex. "But she's irretrievably guilty. No one can story-tell me out of that."

"Guess so," Joe says.

"Yeah," Katherine says. "Seems like."

"*Seems* like?" My eyebrows go up at Kath's response. And I can write this scene as it happens. "Spofford is going to nail her. Don't you think?"

"Doesn't matter what we think," Joe says.

BE HER VOICE

"Good afternoon, ladies and gentlemen," Royal Spofford began. "Thank you for your infinite patience and goodwill." The veteran prosecutor came in smart, experienced, knowledgeable. He had to tell a story that would catch jurors' hearts and minds and persuade each one, beyond a reasonable doubt, that Ashlyn Bryant had thought about, planned, and then carried out a scheme to kill her own daughter.

The key to his argument was powerful. Heartbreaking. Compelling. That Ashlyn broke the sacred trust of being a parent. And deserved to rot behind bars for life.

"As we begin, let me show you something."

Spofford clicked a computer switch. A video montage of Tasha photos appeared on a screen set up to the right of the judge's bench.

"This is Tasha Nicole Bryant." He almost whispered, wanting the jurors to lean in to hear. Wanting them to be haunted by Tasha. See her as a real person. "*She* is why you are here. Here's her favorite stuffed rabbit. Her backyard swing set. Her doting grandparents. And—" He paused, not wanting to overdo. "And she was taken too soon."

He clicked again. The screen went black. "Who snuffed out the light in little Tasha's eyes?" He turned to Ashlyn Bryant, who, he assumed as instructed, looked at him square on.

"Ashlyn Bryant," he said, eyes locked on her, consonants hard. "Decided she didn't want to be Tasha's mother. Decided the child was *inconvenient*. A *mistake*. So she plotted and planned. She researched and she schemed. She erased the little girl from the face of the earth."

He turned back to the jury, added a tinge of sorrow to his voice.

"There's nothing wrong with drinking and dancing and having 'fun.'" Spofford smoothed the silky pattern on his crimson tie. "But as parents, we must change priorities. Ashlyn, however, was not ready for that. So Ashlyn decided—to make a change."

He paused, letting them imagine it. Nothing is more powerful than imagination. Terrible facts plus imagination always means guilty.

"Ashlyn Bryant is smart," he said. "When Ashlyn wants to do what Ashlyn wants to do, she finds a way. She creates a new reality."

He gestured, a fraction of motion, to Tom and Georgia Bryant, still in the front row, watching him, rapt. Georgia nodded, agreeing. *Even her own mother,* he wanted to tell the jurors, agrees with me. But of course he couldn't say that.

"Ashlyn led a life of lies and deception," Spofford went on, eyes back on the jury. "She lugged Tasha around, left her with sitters, who knows. Poor child, she didn't know what life was supposed to be. At her grandparents' house, lucky enough to be in their safekeeping, everything was fine."

Georgia reached for her husband's hand, clutched it.

"But Ashlyn knew," Spofford made his voice portentous, as if narrating a TV crime drama, "she knew her duplicitous life was inevitably coming to an end. Soon *everything* would have to change."

Every juror was listening, he could tell. Nothing beats a grisly murder story.

"Remember," he went on, "because Tasha was a two-year-old, only Ashlyn was capable of telling what happened in their lives. As long as Tasha simply said 'Gampy' and 'Rabbie,' no problem."

He took a deep breath, telegraphing that what came next clinched it.

"But Tasha began to say words. Make sentences. Become verbal. When Tasha starts talking the truth, Ashlyn's in trouble. Because Tasha's too young to understand 'secrets.' "

Reporters turned to each other, nodding. *He's right,* they mouthed. Tasha would eventually have blown it for her.

"The defense arguments?" Spofford's voice hardened. "An accident? A hot dog? Terminal cancer?" He shook his head at the absurdity. "That is a trip down a rabbit hole.

"If Tasha had died in a backyard accident, wouldn't *someone* have called 911?" Spofford ended this section of his argument not with a bang, but with a sneer. "But no one did.

" 'Only Ashlyn.' I spoke those words to you on day one of this trial—only Ashlyn could have caused the death of Tasha Nicole. Has anything—*anything,*" he deliberately echoed McMorran's construction, "convinced you beyond a reasonable doubt that it could have happened *any* other way?"

"Bottom line: Ashlyn changes the plane ticket her mother generously bought for her. Flies herself and Tasha to Boston, where they're unknown faces in an uncaring crowd. Somehow—could be any number of ways—she snuffs the last breath out of her own daughter with a chloroformed cloth and three strips of the duct tape she brought from home so she could not be caught on surveillance video purchasing it in Boston. Puts Tasha's little body in a plastic bag, maybe puts the bag in an inconspicuous tote, and carries her, like trash, to Castle Island. Perhaps she says goodbye, in a way we can only imagine, and returns to Dayton, free and unfettered, to the life she wants.

She makes a new reality by telling everyone that Tasha is 'someplace else.' Which, ladies and gentlemen, indeed she is. In Boston Harbor."

With those words, in a move orchestrated with his associate, the video came up again. A green plastic bag, rippling in the gentle waves, scarring the beach at Castle Island.

"There sits Ashlyn Bryant now." He pointed at her. "Silent. But you *have* heard her, from others who testified. There's one particular sentence I hope you will remember. Ashlyn said: 'Holy crap, I am so good at making stuff up.'"

That quote was a slam dunk. And now to nail it.

"Use your common sense, ladies and gentlemen. Only Ashlyn could have caused this tragedy, with planning and malice afore-thought. *Only* Ashlyn. Stand up for Tasha Nicole." Spofford paused in the hushed silence. One juror was crying. He had them.

"Be her voice."

We are quiet, quiet as the courtroom, when Spofford sits down.

"Well, that was a home run." I sip the last of my coffee, now stone cold. Spofford talked for ninety minutes, the full amount of time the judge allotted. We three remained silent throughout Spofford's presentation, riveted. I wrote as he talked, as much as I could, knowing I'll have to leave a lot of it out of the final book. Of course, I couldn't see Ashlyn's parents. Or the jurors. So I'll have to confirm that crying thing later. I'll make it work. "He got her, don't you think?"

"Up to the jury now," Joe says.

"Yeah," Katherine says.

"I can't believe you guys," I say. "How could you possibly think anything but—"

Katherine stands, dusts off her rear, looks at her watch. "You, my dear, have work to do. I should go."

"Me, too," Joe says, standing. "But now that the jury's out, hey. You want to have some dinner later?"

I don't get Joe, I have to say. Dinner? He's married, I know that. I looked up his wife online, out of curiosity, but there wasn't much. Joe's never talked about anything except the trial. Who knows, though. I'm out of practice at having friends.

"Tempting," Katherine says. "Merce?"

"Gotta work," I say. If he's just being friendly—I mean, dinner is dinner—then I may be overreacting. Dex would want me to "be happy," people try to tell me that. But it's too soon. Way, way, way, too soon. I'm thinking later will never come.

They walk to the front, skirting the stupid cardboard boxes from the law firm that still block the door. I kick them aside. *Stupid* boxes. Then, opening the door, I turn to Katherine. I need to ask whether she thinks an interview with Ashlyn might be possible. But first I need the scoop about Valerie's death.

Joe's back is to us. "Kath? Don't we have to chat? About—book things?"

"I'll call you," she says to me. And she's gone.

CHAPTER THIRTY

D on't you people have a brain?" I yell at the blank court monitor screen. Day Five of deliberations now, almost over. No
questions. Nothing. Not a peep. For five full days, I've sat at my
desk, writing like crazy and fueled by coffee and saltines and wine.
Going nuts.

What the hell is that jury doing?

"It means there's a holdout," one local cable commentator
pontificated this morning.

"You know *nothing*," I answered the television.

"There was no proven cause of death," the other suit agreed.

"So the hell *what?*" I debated him, too, jabbing at him with a
finger. "Dead is dead, and it was no accident. That child was in
a *trash* bag."

Moreover, I console myself, eating my salty cracker, it's definitely possible a guilty verdict is in the making. Jurors don't
want to convict someone—especially for a crime that carries a
life sentence—without appearing to meticulously consider all
the evidence. But the verdict could come any second.

Jurors took two days to convict Jodi Arias of killing an ex-
boyfriend. Four days to convict the Menendez brothers of killing
their parents. Eleven days to convict Scott Peterson of killing his
wife Lacey and their unborn child.

On the other hand. That idiot Florida jury only took about ten
hours to acquit Casey Anthony. To acquit O. J. Simpson, less than

four hours. *Four hours.* So a long deliberation has to mean guilty. I deeply relish that Ashlyn must also know that.

What if she gets off?

I would die.

"Hello?" I answer my cell before the ring is over. It's Kath.

"Listen, kiddo, I know I told you that Valerie was dead, but thing is. Turned out it was a different Valerie."

"Huh? A different?"

"Yeah. We'd been looking for her, trying to get the scoop for you. Our guy thought he had her. But turns out, nothing to do with Ashlyn. She's dead, yeah, but no connection. Sorry if I scared you."

"Yeah, you did, I've gotta say." If people connected with the trial were getting killed, not good. So, another false alarm. Not for poor dead different-Valerie, though, of course. Whoever she is. Was. "It's weird, though. Where's *our* Valerie?"

"Who knows. Yeah, weird. So. You're writing, correct? What do you think about the jury?"

"I think they better get the damn show on the road," I say.

After we hang up, I can almost hear a verdict clock ticking. I bet Ashlyn can, too. I picture her behind bars. Pacing. Fuming. Terrified, every second. Listening for the jailer's footsteps coming to get her. I can't wait to write that part. She deserves every bit of the misery.

At least the indecisive jurors are giving me more writing time. On my computer screen now is the chapter describing Tom Bryant's part of the story. Why didn't Ashlyn's father take the stand? One logical explanation—he must be equally harmful to defense and prosecution. Mutually assured destruction, so neither side calls him. Why?

Funny that I'm happiest, if that's a relevant word, when I'm trying to understand Ashlyn's life instead of my own. *How* could she do it? Maybe the jury can't accept that it's possible a mother would kill her own daughter.

That would be wrong.

Because Ashlyn lied. She said she'd seen Tasha the same morning that Detective Rogowicz hid in her family's front hall closet. But police are sure she knew Tasha was dead. Why would she lie if she didn't have to? Dex would call it "consciousness of guilt." Since she acted like she was guilty—it proves she is.

Should I give myself a treat and skip ahead to the verdict scene? I can certainly write what I predict will happen. But·what if it doesn't?

"Maybe I'll burn down the house," I say out loud.

THE DEFENDANT WILL RISE

When the word came, it was almost difficult to believe. Forty-one hours. Five days and one hour. They must have had a knockdown battle in that stuffy conference room. No windows, unreliable air conditioning. A whiteboard mounted on one wall, super-erasable markers so no snoopy eyes could decipher what they'd posted.

Did jurors make a pro-and-con chart, listing the elements of guilt or innocence?

Did they make a list of the reasonable doubts?

Reporters who crammed into the media overflow room speculated, endlessly, as they made their own lists. Journalists can't write their stories until something happens.

"No cause of death," one said, not looking up from her texting. "That's a big deal."

"No real forensics, either." The crime guy for the *Herald* punctuated his judgment by tossing a crumpled paper cup into the wastebasket. "Gotta be not guilty."

"Gotta be kidding me." The radio pool reporter untangled his electrical cords, made sure his phone battery was charging. "If Ashlyn didn't do it, who did? Only Ashlyn could have killed Tasha Nicole."

The court clerk's voice on the video feed interrupted their squabble.

"We have a verdict," she said. "The defendant will rise."

"Stations, we have a verdict," Voice says.

When Voice interrupts, I have an unsettling notion that I inhabit a parallel universe.

"Forty-one hours," Voice says. I put my hand to my chest, like some fluttery ingénue in a forties movie, startled and surprised. My manuscript mirrors reality—as well it should—but the concurrence of my imagined scene and the real-life courtroom action is unsettling. This is all I've been thinking about, besides Dex and Sophie, for the past thirty-two days—I counted, last night, as I tried to sleep.

This will be Day One of Ashlyn Bryant's new life. Every day of it behind bars.

PART 2

SOMETIMES I dream of forgotten rooms. Places that seem familiar, so familiar I could describe them down to the pattern of the creamy rug, the four-squared window, the sumptuous wallpaper, the sheen of the oaky wood armoires, and chests of narrow drawers. Thin, like map drawers, but these are lined with velvet, and always filled with pearls and scarves, paisley and silk. Laid out, displayed, organized, beautiful.

I could describe the broad curving stairway, chocolate brown risers painted with tiny flowers. A living room open and sleek, all leather and welcoming pillows. No curtains on the vast windows, and no houses beyond. The scenery is a still, shining lake, vast, and rising mountains. This is home. Sharply defined as a photograph. But it was never *my* home. I have no idea where it is.

What does it mean that I'm comfortable in places I've never been? That I yearn for them, call them home? What does it mean that there are beautiful things I recognize, that I know belong to me, even though I know they don't exist?

What about the rooms I haven't seen yet? Some hallway doors are closed, and I always pass them by. Maybe it means there are rooms still to be explored. Doors we have not opened. Secrets we have not faced.

I keep my eyes closed and pull the thin white summer blanket up to my chin, trying not to forget again, willing myself to hang on to the edges of the dream. Sometimes, in daylight and in real life, I remember the rooms. At those moments, I feel I can almost reach them. If I make just the right turn, choose just the right corner, or open the right door, there it'll all be, the velvet and the view and the mountains. And my family.

But then here is just here, and everything is as it is, and there are no mountains.

Dex is not here. Or Sophie.

I open my eyes, my real life floods back.

The verdict.

CHAPTER THIRTY-ONE

When the kitchen TV plays the breaking-news music, I barely comprehend it.

Not that it'll matter, but I lift the remote and click the volume. Not that it'll matter. You can't change a verdict. Not ever. Just like you can't change the past. Not ever.

"...here on her Newburyport home," a harried-looking twenty-something reporter is saying.

I recognize the reporter, Rachel Knapp. She's wearing a red sleeveless dress, her dark hair shifting in the slight breeze. Behind her, the corner of a white two-story Cape. I don't recognize the house, or the marigold-lined asphalt driveway, or the middle-class-looking neighborhood. Just another phony-sensational story about nothing. Typical. I grab a coffee pod, just out of habit. Not that it matters.

"No one was hurt, but our sources this morning say the vandals must have spray-painted attorney McMorran's home late last night," Rachel is saying. "They also smashed a window at the rear of the home, but were apparently scared off by her alarm system."

What? Some idiot tried to break into Quinn McMorran's house? Tagged it? I stand, coffee pod in hand, staring at the TV. *What?*

"We can't show you what they wrote." Rachel's tone and expression signal it's repulsive. "But as you look at the video we've blurred, we *can* say it's graphic and obscene, apparently scrawled by someone who did not approve of Ms. McMorran's defense of Ashlyn Bryant. Or of the trial's controversial verdict."

I take a step closer to the screen, leaning in to see better. I think about that courthouse bomb threat. They decided it was a false alarm. But now this?

The medium shot of McMorran's house shows gray splotches across white vinyl. I let it play for twenty seconds, pause the DVR, rewind, and replay it, frame by frame. Under pressure, the blurring guys sometimes miss a tiny bit. If I can get one frame to show–*ah*. There it is.

"Baby killer," it says. Then a scrawl of profanity. "Rot in hell."

"Sources tell us Quinn McMorran is now concerned about Ashlyn's safety," Rachel is reporting. "Police are investigating . . ."

"Yeah, well, life is hard," I remind the TV. I lower the volume. The book is dead. Whatever happens in those people's lives doesn't matter to me anymore. I'm sorry for Quinn, sure, but I don't care what happens to the disgusting Ashlyn. Or, in fact, almost anyone. *Baby killer. Rot in hell.* Could have written that myself.

I shower, because I need the steam. At least it's still morning, ten thirty-ish is still morning. Three days after the verdict.

I still hear those words. Still see Ashlyn burst into tears and fall into Quinn's arms.

I still see her walk out the courthouse door.

"I'm so sorry, darling ones," I whisper, as I write the numbers. Four. Seven. Five. And somehow my hand is heavy, almost too heavy to write. But this is my job now, remembering. My only job.

Coffee? Water rushes from the kitchen faucet. I flinch. I've turned it up too hot again. Too hot. Toast? I almost throw up at the thought of food. Who cares.

"Toast," I say. Queen of subtext.

The monitor in the study stays in black. Its job is over, too. They'll have to come pick up all that fancy equipment. No need for it here anymore.

When the phone eventually rings, again, it'll be Katherine, again. I imagine it as I pop a coffee pod into place. I'm avoiding her. Deleting her messages, unread. I cannot discuss it.

I'll finally answer, I suppose, because whatever. She'll commiserate, and congratulate me on a job well done, blah blah, a job that's now meaningless. All that research and painstaking writing, all that crafting a story from the facts and from experience, a story that's true enough to be a nonfiction bestseller. Now it's nothing.

"Adios to all that, sister," I say out loud as I get the milk from the fridge. I smell it, then recoil. The milk is bad.

"Seriously?" I ask the milk. "Is the entire universe fucking with me now, seriously?"

I dump it in the sink, the whole smelly curdling mess. Maybe I'll just go back to bed. Forever. But first I'll go to the study and superdelete the whole damn book. Into the oblivion of cyberspace.

Maybe I'll delete myself into cyberspace.

But I stand there, at the counter, disgusting sludge sliding down the drain.

Not guilty.

The bing-bong of the doorbell probably means I should answer the door. Odd, really, how my brain can conjure no circumstance under which this could be good news.

Hitching up my sweatpants—yesterday's, even the day before's, but "whatever," as the contemptible—and now-not-guilty! free!—Ashlyn Bryant so eloquently said. Or at least as I wrote she said. I trudge down the hall as the bing-bong sounds again.

"Whatever," I say out loud. It's like every damn thing is haunting me. Sophie loved the sound of the doorbell, and we'd let her press it until it drove us all crazy with laughter. Now I can't hear it without thinking of her.

It's Katherine, I see through the peephole. And—

It's possible my jaw drops.

"Hi, Mercer," Katherine says, all friendly, navy blazer and combed hair. She gestures to the woman standing beside her. Beautiful, truly, with a wan face and tired eyes, her hair pulled back in a soft ponytail. Some sort of wren-colored T-shirt dress, flats. "This is Ashlyn Bryant. Let us in, okay? Before anyone sees us?"

CHAPTER THIRTY-TWO

'm trying to be polite. I'm trying to act normal. But I'm in *The Twilight Zone*, certainly. Maybe also *Through the Looking Glass* with Alice. And a dash of Kafka.

Katherine is talking, sipping from a silver aluminum travel mug she brought. Next to her, holding the glass of fizzy water I served her, is Ashlyn Bryant. We're about the same size, I'd been surprised to see. The jailhouse weight gain I'd written about turned out to be wrong.

They're both sitting at my kitchen table, at 10:43 on this September morning. As if nothing happened, as if this time last week that woman wasn't in a dingy cell, awaiting a verdict on whether she'd smothered or strangled or drugged her own baby daughter to death, then tossed her into the ocean in a garbage bag.

No one's mentioned Quinn's house.

Did you see the graffiti? I want to say. *Calling you a baby killer?* But I don't.

Sitting here, on this otherwise ordinary Friday, she's now not guilty. And forever so. *There's no way she can be retried,* one track of my brain calculates as Katherine talks. I wish Dex were here to tell me the law, but I think it's legally unlikely that there would be a civil trial for wrongful death, like the one Nicole Brown Simpson's family brought in the O.J. case. (THE CURSE OF NICOLE, I remember that tabloid headline.) There'd be nobody to bring such a lawsuit, because Tasha Nicole's "estate" would include only Ashlyn, the accused-but-innocent killer. The only other person with possible legal standing to sue is Tasha's father, I suppose, whoever and wherever he is. Joe Riss told me Ashlyn said he's dead.

Could Ashlyn be completely and totally off the hook, no matter what happens? I'm no lawyer, but I'm pretty confident that's the reality. She's home free.

Ashlyn, I realize, could parade up Beacon Street yelling, "I did it, I did it, ha ha I fooled you all!" and nothing would happen to her. Except possibly a citation for disturbing the peace.

This morning, Ashlyn hasn't said anything but "hello" and "nice to meet you" and "thank you." I notice her teeth are nice, very white. She has split ends though, needs a haircut. And her fingernails are chewed. Her black flats look new. Snakeskin.

". . . redemption," Katherine is saying. I yank myself back, recognizing a negotiating tone in her voice. She gestures at me with her mug. "Isn't that right, Mercer?"

There's no way I can pretend I was paying attention. "Sorry," I say. "You mean . . ."

"Re*demp*tion, Merce," she says.

I can tell by her widened eyes she's trying to telegraph that there's something she knows I'm unaware of, at the same time trying to convey to Ashlyn that it's a done deal. When Ashlyn sips her water, I attempt a surreptitious *what the hell are you talking about?* look.

"As I explained to Ashlyn, you were writing about the trial," Katherine goes on. "A straightforward, objective view of the unfolding events. Right? And of course we're eager for you to continue your project. Of course."

That's the most ridiculous "of course" I've ever heard. Why didn't she call or email and warn me about this? Whatever "this" is. Although maybe she did. I'd deleted her messages.

"But now it becomes even more compelling." Katherine goes on, in full pitch mode. "Now we can use what you've already written to create a book that's . . ."

I know I'm frowning as she searches for a word. I am beyond

bewildered. The book is over, just like the trial. Katherine told me from the beginning the book was a go only if Ashlyn was convicted.

Katherine gives me a look full of subtext, then continues. "A book that's *big*. An important hardcover memoir that proves how a truly innocent person in partnership with a zealous attorney and a fair and just legal system can battle through a trial by fire and prevail. And Ashlyn, so tragically tested, has agreed to give us— you—us—her exclusive story. Her legal and emotional redemption. Her brave new start on her brave new life."

The light is beginning to dawn. I briefly check for candid cameras. Then realize the media winds have shifted. To flat-out sensationalism.

Katherine actually puts one hand on my arm and the other on Ashlyn's, like a bridge between two islands.

"As I explained to Ashlyn, we'll do the book with her or without her," she says. "But 'with' is better. I know you two will be a good match."

She pauses. I look at Ashlyn. Ashlyn looks at me. Weird, because I've contantly seen her, on TV and in newspapers, for the past thirty-some days. She's never seen me in her life. Katherine sighs, and I feel the pressure of her fingers on my bare arm. I wonder if she's squeezing Ashlyn's arm, too.

"You've both lost your poor daughters," Katherine whispers. "You've both had a miserable year."

It's all I can do not to burst out laughing. Oh, right, yeah, miserable. Precisely the word for what happened. Then I had to deal with the miserable reality of two cops at my door. Guess Ashlyn did, too. I swallow my reaction, trying not to yank my arm out from Katherine's clutches. Her grasp is verging on metaphor. This is a Journalism 101 technique, *create empathy*.

I imagine Ashlyn saying, "Oh, did you kill your daughter, too?" But she doesn't.

"I'm sorry for your loss," she says. "What was her name? How old was she?"

Okay. This is too much. I am not, I am absolutely *not,* going to discuss Sophie with this woman. Not a chance on the planet. It's disloyal. That's the only word I can think of. Followed by crass and hypocritical and phony. I won't say her name, not out loud, not to her. Not to this wretched woman who someday, I hope, will be justly punished for killing her own daughter, even if she doesn't spend another day behind bars. And now she has the nerve, that's hardly a strong enough word, to sit here at my kitchen table and ask me about Sophie.

As for Kath, she wins the prize for exploitive. As well as inappropriate, sleazy, manipulative, and duplicitous. Some friend. She and Ashlyn are quite the duo. Not even a warning phone call. Maybe.

Katherine clears her throat, lets go of our arms. "Sorry to cut to the business chase," she says. "But we're thinking this will be more successful—forgive me, Ashlyn, if this is difficult for you—as a sort of true-life legal thriller combined with an 'as-told-to' biography. We'll put both your names on the cover . . ." She looks at Ashlyn, who's nodding agreement, and then at me. Who, she must surely recognize, is still wondering if this is a particularly cruel joke.

"No problem," Ashlyn says. "If that's all right with you, Mercer."

I always envision myself on a tightrope, walking along, cautiously, step-by-step to an end I cannot see. Balancing, sometimes, but often, like now, struggling for equilibrium. I wait, as the high wire settles. Wait, as I accept the preposterous idea that this woman is calling me by name and asking me for permission, like we're at some tea party. I wait, recovering my emotional and spiritual footing.

"How does Quinn McMorran feel about this?" That's all I can think of to say that appears to be responsive, but actually is not. "I saw on the news—"

"Could you *believe* that? They—" Ashlyn begins.

"So wise of you to bring that up, Mercer," Kath interrupts. "I was going to mention that next."

Another journalism technique. Compliment the potential antagonist, try to get them on your side.

"Wise?" I'm not sure whose side I'm on right now. I'm barely staying upright.

"Yes," Katherine says. "Because of the—"

"I was *there,* Mercer!" Ashlyn whispers, elbows on the table, cheeks in her hands. "Actually there! How did those people *know* that? They, like, almost got *in!* It was—*so* terrifying. Plus they showed where Quinn lives. On TV. It's *so* awful."

"No one knows you were there." Katherine puts a hand on Ashlyn's thin shoulder. "And Quinn's left town for a bit. Until the smoke clears."

"Smoke?" I say. Was there a fire, too?

"Fallout. Reaction. Aftermath. Whatever." Kath dismisses me with a flip of a hand. "Anyway, now we need to make some new decisions."

"*So* terrifying." Ashlyn's continues her memory, shaking her head. "When Quinn's alarm system went off? I totally freaked. I'll never feel safe again. I can't believe how horrible people are. Can you?"

Am I supposed to answer that? On the muted television, I see the beginning of some syndicated courtroom show, Judge Some-woman-or-other, play-acting at justice. Outside the kitchen window, a cicada, some bug like that, flutters against the glass, then flies away.

"Which brings up my final point." Katherine takes a long drink from her mug, sets it back down on the kitchen table. I'm sitting in Sophie's chair, Katherine in Dex's, Ashlyn in mine.

"I had talked to Quinn about the book," Katherine goes on. "And she's aware. The plan was for Ashlyn to stay with her while you two finalized the manuscript. The book's almost done, of course, so we'd figured, if you both put your mind to it, it could take two weeks to repurpose. Sooner the publication, the better. But now that Quinn's unavailable, and her house, too, of course, the publisher and I think it might work if . . ."

She looks at me, takes a deep breath.

You have got to be kidding me. My brain is screaming "no," so loudly, I cannot believe these two women can't hear my thoughts. *Kath* wants me to do this?

"Well, we think it would be efficient." Katherine's face has an expression I've never seen before. "If Ashlyn could stay here, with you. To work on the project day and night. I mean, you have a guest room. If you can do it in two weeks, the publisher will pay double. Plus all the expenses, food, and whatever." She smiles. "Even wine."

I open my mouth to answer, but nothing comes out. Even for sixty thousand dollars, what Katherine's proposing is so outrageous . . . I stop. Rebalance. I think of Sophie's closed door. Dex's boxes in the guest room. My one bathroom. My mirror, marked this morning with 475. No. I'll say no. I have to say no.

"Ashlyn will be safe here," Katherine goes on. "It protects her from whoever has a grudge against Quinn. And from the drooling pack of reporters who'll be hunting her down. You remember how it felt after your . . . the accident. Right, Merce? How awful it was?"

I don't, actually. At least I try not to.

"Why doesn't she just leave town?" I ask.

"Exactly. And that's what we'll say." Kath nods, like I'm so smart. "We'll *tell* everyone Ashlyn's left town. No one else will even know she's here. And your book can be her lifeline. With her parents estranged and her family destroyed and her reputation in shambles, there's really no place else for her to be. Only with you, Mercer."

CHAPTER THIRTY-THREE

I let the shower sluice over my hair, my face, feeling the warmth and the steam. Washing away the sludge from yesterday's encounter. I feel confused. Defensive. What was I supposed to do? Tell Ashlyn, "No, go to the Holiday Inn, and I'll meet you every morning in the coffee shop?"

Maybe. But even with what happened to Quinn's house, I need the work. And the money, since Dex's insurance has to last my whole lifetime. I'd wanted to put the nail in Ashlyn's coffin, and somehow honor Sophie, but the ridiculous verdict put a stop to that quixotic idea. Plus, writers write.

Reporters get hooked on a good story. But "good" is sometimes negotiable.

So what do I do *this* time? Plenty of people are accused, unfairly, of crimes. Who am I to know what really happened? And shouldn't I be interested to find out?

I stick my tongue out at no one. Gah. I *know* what happened. But fine.

Ashlyn Bryant will now be living in my guest room. I cannot comprehend it. She'll show up later this morning. And we'll go to work. Plus, Katherine insists no one else will know she's here.

"She'll come tomorrow," Katherine had said. "Saturday. Deadline is—two weeks from Tuesday. First thing Tuesday. I promise I won't call and bug you. Just work."

As Ashlyn walked back to the car, I'd clutched Kath's arm, stopping her.

"What happened at Quinn's is scary," I said. "And now—Ashlyn in *my* house? I'm not sure that's, you know, prudent. To put it mildly."

"Sweetheart, forget about it. You're a writer, you can come up with every bad reality." She'd actually patted my hand. "Trust me. I got a text a second ago. It's nothing about Ashlyn. You'll probably see it on the news. The cops *caught* the guys. Stupid kids."

"Same as the ones who bomb-scared the court?" I'd asked. But she didn't know. And I suppose if the cops say it's fine, it's fine. Hard to think clearly about what's "real."

So it's a done deal.

I wrap the monogrammed white towel around me, then one-finger write, as always, on the steam-clouded mirror: 476. The start of another new real.

"Two weeks, darlings," I say out loud.

Last night, illuminated only by the glowing streetlight, I looked at the photo of Sophie I've tucked under my pillow because it brings me close to her in dreams. It's of her in Dex's arms, just a silly casual snapshot in our front yard, almost out of focus—maybe Katherine took it? She adored them both. It's one I might have deleted in another life. But now I'll never again delete another photo. There won't be any more.

I fluff my hair dry. Thing is, and it almost sickens me to consider this, but what if Ashlyn didn't do it? She appears pleasant enough. Not whiny or selfish or manipulative, not at all the "bitch" her mother described in interviews and on the witness stand. Hard to imagine this is the same woman who was photographed in the Hot Stuff wet T-shirt contest. Of course, maybe that's part of Ashlyn's con game, putting the other person off guard, then moving in for the kill. A chameleon.

"Try it, sister," I say out loud, half-smiling at my blurry reflection in the now-dripping mirror. I've handled worse. And it'll be interesting to hear what she says. I wanted her to testify in court, after all. Now she'll be testifying. But only to me.

To me.

I take a deep breath, reorienting my moral compass.

Testifying only to me. It could be a good story. A terrific story. It could give this manipulative bitch the punishment she deserves. International notoriety. Unending shame. I can bestow *justice.* I can't help Sophie, or Dex. Or change the verdict. But this—writing, story-telling, exposing the truth. This I can do.

By the time the doorbell rings, I'm ready. Ashlyn stayed with Katherine last night, so I guess she wasn't apprehensive about that, and Kath had texted me they were on the way. Kath waves as she drives off.

"I brought you coffee." Ashlyn's wearing tortoiseshell sunglasses, her ponytail under a Red Sox cap. "With skim milk. I saw the container on your counter yesterday. Nobody followed us, so that's a relief. Guess 'they' haven't found me. Reporters, I mean. No offense."

She smiles, handing me a cardboard coffee carrier with two covered paper cups, Starbucks ventis. A small black wheelie bag is beside her. It looks new. She's wearing jeans, which also look new. And a black T-shirt, respectable but snug. Wonder what she did with her dumpy trial outfits? I would have burned them.

"Thanks," I say, gesturing her inside. "Yes, reporters can be persistent." Which I know, from both sides of the notebook, is the truth. Sure, she was thoughtful—thoughtful?—enough to notice the skim milk. But I've decided to treat her as a subject, not a friend. Nor a potential friend. Not only because I still believe she's a monster. There are never friends in journalism, although considering the preparation and attention devoted to a big interview, sometimes interviewees get the wrong idea.

Fine with me. Old journalism technique, to allow the subject to believe the story is for *their* benefit, instead of for your own. The notorious Ashlyn—and little Tasha Nicole—will be my complete focus for two weeks. Then they'll be out of my life forever. Ashlyn's life will crash and burn.

Ashlyn eyes my front hall closet, and I wonder if she fears there's a cop hiding inside. I almost laugh.

"Let me show you the guest room," I say. "Then we'll start."

She's checking out the family portraits on the hallway walls as we walk by. Like Joe Riss did, I remember. Framed photos of Dex and Sophie, and me. Dex and me before Sophie. Paris in the rain, snorkeling in Bermuda, and two goofy yellow-slickered selfies at Niagara Falls. I regret that I didn't take them all down. Her scrutiny feels like an invasion of privacy.

She makes no comment, though, and neither do I.

I try to see the guest room through her eyes, the eyes of a woman who's most recently inhabited a windowless cinderblock cell. This room is pale yellow and white, ruffled pillow shams, white curtains. Bookshelves, filled. I thought about putting fresh flowers on one of the nightstands, but felt queasy about that phony hospitality.

"Bathroom's down that hall, white door." I show her the pile of yellow towels, not our monogrammed ones, on the corner of the bed. I hate that we're sharing my bathroom. For the first time it's annoying that this house has only one. I gesture to Dex's numbered cardboard boxes, still stacked one on top of the other, halfway up the corner wall. "Sorry about those. I have nowhere else to put them."

"It's all so pretty," she says. "So light. Thank you. You're so kind to—"

"I'll meet you in the kitchen in twenty minutes, okay?" Business, all business. "We can start talking. You'll find hangers in the closet."

Which I'd cleaned out months ago, in a tear-blinded flurry of angry despair, trashing everything except boxes of photos and newspaper clippings and some of my out-of-season coats and extra shoes. The study closet's equally un-Dexed. I don't want her in here or in the study or the kitchen or anywhere. I feel like putting plastic over everything. As I head down the hall, I'm fuming.

No one else has been in this house overnight for the past, well, year or so. Only me and my memories. And now this woman.

I slip inside my study and shut the door behind me, making a physical and mental partition. It's a job. Living two weeks in bizarro-world is only a job.

Someone might say—you're letting a murderer stay in your house? Possibly. The jury didn't think she was. And even if you believe Royal Spofford, she killed Tasha because her inconvenient daughter got in her way. I'm exactly the opposite situation. She thinks she needs me. She thinks she's using me. She thinks I'm her ticket to redemption. She's not gonna kill *me*.

Plus, she thinks I buy the jury's not-guilty verdict, and must realize I understand there's no legal process that can change that. All I need to do is keep her happy. Keep her thinking I'm her best friend. As long as I do, no one is safer than I am.

I flap my laptop closed, and next to it is the list I made as I kept track of the trial. All the unanswered questions.

Who is Tasha Nicole's father? That was the first one.
Ashlyn/father DNA?
Where is Valerie? Luke Walsh?
Tasha talk?

I scan the list, realizing I've created my own perfect road map for what I need to ask Ashlyn.

What does McMorran mean by "issues"?
Duct tape?
Did Ash computer search for chloroform? Why?
Why didn't father/Tom testify? What up with Tom?
Why did A go to Boston?
Why didn't A testify?
Why A not sad abt Tasha?
Ashlyn INSANE??

And the big one: *Who killed Tasha Nicole?*

I mean, I know who. That's no mystery. Now I need to know why and how.

I hear Ashlyn's footsteps on the hardwood floor, walking toward the bathroom, then hear that door shut. I close and stack my notebooks. Straighten my desk. I check that list again, memorizing, and, I realize, forming a plan. Then I fold the list in half and slide it under the closed laptop. Head for the kitchen.

And now I wonder, I just wonder, if this could turn out to be the best thing that ever happened. I've got her full attention, and soon her trust. There's nowhere else she can go, exactly as Katherine said. Maybe it was brilliant to have her stay here.

What Ashlyn Bryant doesn't know—I'm not about the law. I'm about the truth.

And I'll use every trick in the journalist's handbook to make her reveal it.

CHAPTER THIRTY-FOUR

t's nice here." Wearing her sunglasses and Red Sox cap again, her shoulders wrapped in a gauzy striped scarf, Ashlyn's received not one curious glance as we walk side by side up Lincoln Ave. She gestures at the Rayburns' gold chrysanthemums, the leafed out maples, a robin bouncing on a newly mown lawn. "So pretty. How long have you lived in Linsdale?"

"A while." I say. Small talk about me and my family is so not gonna happen.

It's our first day on the job. Two weeks or so until Katherine's deadline. We should be working. But when Ashlyn finally left the bathroom, then arrived in the kitchen, she asked if we could take a walk. I don't blame her. Being outside, being *allowed* to be outside, free, must be such a relief. And all good. I want her to be comfortable. Off guard. I need her to trust me. There's a dead baby sparrow on the sidewalk, one feathery wing extended. We each notice, but say nothing as we walk toward the town square. Things happen. As we both know.

"And we're going into town?" she says.

Duh. "Yup. Linsdale center."

"There's like restaurants, and stores? Everything in Dayton is malls."

"Oh," I say. I need to be polite. "We have those, too."

A few cars trundle by, families searching out bagels or the hardware store or the Saturday soccer game. We walk in silence, and I point the way.

Ashlyn will probably want real food more than I do, but I'm wary of taking her to DeMilla's. If Carmendy spots her, it might ruin Ashlyn's I'm-only-a-regular-suburban-nobody disguise. Especially if all the photo-laden morning papers are displayed at the checkout aisle.

Although. Watching Ashlyn read the articles about herself might be pretty fascinating. MURDER MOM WALKS was one snarky headline. The *Globe* stayed formal, with simply BRYANT ACQUITTED. Beneath, in smaller font, WHO REALLY KILLED TASHA NICOLE? Has she seen these? Did they watch TV at Katherine's? All the papers have a reaction from the victorious Quinn McMorran, who simply thanked the jury and asked for privacy. Nothing from Royal Spofford. He's reportedly "on extended vacation." "Possibly never to return." Poor guy. Defeated by a manipulative defendant and a jury of dupes. I wish I could call him and commiserate. He'd love my plan.

ASHLYN 1, SPOFFORD 0, so sneered the *Register*'s headline. I'll even the score.

Joe Rissinelli wrote an article about the deliberations. Not one juror said a word for the record, but Joe still made a story out of it. According to his two "sources"—had to be jurors or court officers—they argued for forty solid hours, with three holdouts for conviction. Then two. Then one. How they arrived at that "not guilty" in the final hour, even Joe could not confirm.

I keep thinking about Juror G. She haunts me, this woman I've never seen. Might she have held out, and caused a hung jury? Or even persuaded the others to convict? What if the only reason Ashlyn Bryant is right here, right now, strolling with me down a peaceful suburban avenue, is that *I* made a decision? I did something to win back Dex's approval. And that decision set Ashlyn free. What if—but *no*. Doing the right thing is never wrong. The miserably boneheaded verdict is not my fault. It feels like everything is my fault. *I am so sorry, Sophie.*

"Turn on Kenhowe Street," I say. "We're almost there."

Ashlyn nods, lost in her own thoughts. And free.

Stupid jury. I'll get Joe to give me the scoop, eventually, but I'll have to avoid him for the next two weeks. Right now it's only about me and Ashlyn.

"You okay?" I ask, as we head down the final block.

"Just being . . . outside," she says.

I long to ask—*don't you miss your daughter? How can you stand this? What really happened?* Soon, one way or another, I will. It'll be fascinating to hear her try to twist "they didn't *prove* I killed her" into "I *didn't* kill her." Especially since she did.

I'm also curious about how she looks at the world now. Is she afraid? Angry? If she meets a stranger, how will she introduce herself? Exonerated or not, the minute she says her name, there's only one thing people will think. *Baby killer.* How do you erase infamy and suspicion? Easier if you're actually innocent.

As we get to the town center, Ashlyn window shops, studying displays of new fall clothes, all plaid and tweed. A few yoga-pantsed moms sit with their fidgety preteens in Ristretto's outdoor café. No one gives us a second look. A young woman walks down the sidewalk toward us, pushing an elaborate big-wheeled stroller. As she passes, the child inside—a girl, I gather from the pink sleeve—tosses a green stuffed animal, a dragon or something, out onto the sidewalk. The little girl starts to wail.

Ashlyn stops. Stares at the toy, bright green on the gray concrete.

The mom grabs it, flustered, throws us an apology, then wheels away, comforting her child. The toddler's cry trails behind them. "Mommy! Want it!"

"What do you think when you see that?" I keep my tone objective with a touch of sympathetic, but I'm a writer, and everything is fair game. "Must be . . ." I let my voice trail off, let her fill in the silence. Old journalism technique.

"Hard to be a mom," she says. I can't see her eyes through those amber sunglasses.

I wait. Nothing. My turn.

"That little girl was putting words together." I'm thinking about my list. *Tasha talk?*

"Hmm." She seems fascinated by the paisley scarves festooned in the window of Verena's Boutique.

"Was your daughter talking?" I don't use Tasha's name.

She turns to me, sun glinting on her dark lenses. "Enough to make me miss it, and her, every day." There's a catch in her voice. It's certainly phony, but still elicits a tiny pang from my conscience.

"I know the feeling." I echo her tone. Ignore my conscience. "But—may I ask, do you remember the last time you talked with her? Where was that? When?"

"Of course I do," she whispers. "That age is such a critical time, you know? For talking? And she was learning lots of words. They mimic, you know?"

An ambulance screams by, siren wailing, and we both stop, turn to watch. The coffee shop people look up too. Disaster is always a draw. I wonder what they'd think if they knew who was standing here on the sidewalk with me. Just another Saturday, strolling with a murderer. Acquitted, but a murderer. Whose daughter was becoming proficient at mimicking "lots of words." Maybe like: *chloroform?* And *cocaine?* Just possibilities.

"I know we have to work, but is there a place to get, maybe, some take-out?" Ashlyn says. "I'm so sick of bad food. I can't wait to have, you know, bacon. Or a croissant. With butter."

"Sure," I say. She's changed the subject, major pivot, but she has to talk at some point. I can work with it. She's refused to let me tape her interviews, which is ridiculous and annoying and inefficient. But I'm a good note-taker.

By the time we get home, we've bonded over mothers. I mentally apologize to my own mother—I've been pretending she was a conniving bitch, completely not true, but I wanted to draw Ashlyn out, see how she'd hit the ball back. We'd taken turns in the bathroom. I'll never get used to that, and am planning constant

Cloroxing. Now we sit across from each other at my kitchen table, drinking iced coffee and eating ham-and-cheese croissants from Ristretto.

"My mother's dead, though," I say, gesturing with my sandwich half. That's true, certainly. "Which makes my life easier than yours." I take a bite, oh-so-pensive. "Anyway, maybe we should talk for the book? Where would you like to start?"

"My mother. On the witness stand, could you believe it?" Ashlyn dabs up a flake of buttery puff pastry from her plate with one finger, pops it into her mouth. She hasn't eaten much of her croissant, even though she's the one who asked for it. Her eyes are still tired. "Poor thing. She was . . . so incredibly weak."

That's surprising. "Weak? It seemed like she, forgive me, threw you under the bus."

"It did?" She looks into the distance. "Yes, I guess if you didn't know her life, it might seem like that."

"Her life?" I'm the writer, I'm allowed to ask. "With your father?"

Her face darkens. "Well, they weren't happy. *He* wasn't, for sure. He thought he was such a movie star, you know, all those good looks. But at his age? And that meant my mother, she, well, you know what, never mind." She offers half a smile. "Let's just forget about that. Not go there."

"Sure. It's your book." For a while. *Her mother on the witness stand.* "You know, I taped pretty much the whole trial."

"Yeah. Katherine told me she arranged some video thing." Ashlyn sighs, tucks a lock of hair behind one ear. "There was one camera right on me. Pointing at me every second of every day. It was just as much jail as that crappy cell. I couldn't get one second of privacy. Everyone was seeing me all the time. I'm on trial for my, like, freedom. And the frigging camera never leaves my face. It's like–thought police."

"TV." I dismiss it. "Relentless. But if you want, it'd be good to explore that emotion in the book."

Generous me. For now. But I'm certain she *used* that camera. Milked it. The jury never saw it, but Ashlyn's savvy enough to understand the court of public opinion. Was she sending messages to someone? A friend? Co-conspirator? But that's my writer brain going crazy.

"Did you think maybe your friends were watching?" Can't hurt to ask.

"What friends?"

Okay, another avenue. "Let's go back to your mother, then. She was so pivotal in all this. Did you feel she chose Tasha over you?" Let's see where this goes. "She didn't even try to defend you."

Ashlyn raises both eyebrows, which I notice have been carefully shaped since the trial. Maybe she and Kath went to some salon.

"Is that how you remember it?" she asks. "Is that how you *wrote* it?"

"Well—"

Her eyes narrow at me. "Mercer? I want to read how you wrote it."

CHAPTER THIRTY-FIVE

Hang on. Wait. Do you have *that* on *video?* My mother on the stand?" Ashlyn takes a bite of her sandwich. "Crap. That Spofford person twisted everything she said. May he rot in hell. *That* you can use."

"*We* can use. We're doing this together."

"Yeah." She rattles the ice in her coffee. "But when Quinn questions my mother. I want to see that."

"Sure," I say. Absolutely. Anything to distract her from the "I want to read how you wrote it" demand.

I open my tablet, find the file labeled McM cross GB. I've time-coded the most interesting segments. Is it cruel to make Ashlyn relive the testimony? Although she saw the whole thing in real life. I push Play, and Fast-Forward. And Pause.

Scooting my chair closer to Ashlyn's so we can both see the screen, I easel the tablet triangularly on its folded cover. Our shoulders touch. I try not to flinch as I move away. There's some kind of–heat? ice?–from her. Which is certainly my imagination.

The hollow muffle of the courtroom audio is almost nostalgic. The trial feels like the past. Another life. I haven't looked at these recordings for several days.

"Play it," she says.

The tinny audio begins, echoing off the kitchen walls. I feel Ashlyn breathing. Strange to be taken back to the courtroom, with her now beside me and on the screen at the same time. There's Georgia Bryant, on the stand, in that awkwardly mismatched blue outfit. I remember the fluff of powder on her lapel. Quinn McMorran, in pearls and impassioned resolve, approaches the stand, in the midst of her cross-examination. Her voice carefully polite.

"You never witnessed Ashlyn abuse Tasha in any way, did you?"

"No, I did not."

"And Tasha never went without food or shelter or anything she needed in life?"

"No, she had everything."

"Did you ever see Ashlyn do anything but care for her?"

"Well, no. But she told me that sometimes she felt–"

"Did Tasha love Ashlyn?"

"Oh, yes. Yes, she did."

Ashlyn touches Pause with one forefinger. Turns to me.

"So, Mercer? Did you hear one word that sounds like I was anything but a loving mother? You just said she didn't defend me–but you heard that, right? Is that how you wrote it? I think I should see the book."

Like all authors, I remember exactly what I wrote. I'd left out some of the testimony. And I'd created Georgia Bryant's inner dialogue for each answer, which was designed to cast them as evasive. Full of double meaning and rationalization and protest-too-much undertone. But taken on their face, I suppose, without my added interpretations, what she said could be heard as supportive. I suppose. If you look at it that way.

"Yes, of course you can read it." I have to say so, or she'll think I'm hiding something. Katherine had described the book as "objective." Which is true, if you mean I object to everything in Ashlyn's duplicitous life. But possibly–well, definitely–it's embellished toward Ashlyn's guilt. Since she's guilty. Given the turn of events, I need to keep that from her. Either she'll confess within our deadline, in which case all bets are off and I can write that block-buster; or she won't, and I'll have to bang out her warped version of the truth.

"As told to," Katherine also said. So it wouldn't be like I was writing something I knew to be false. It's just "as told to" me. I'd simply be the paid messenger.

But she'll confess. She has to. I can do it. I have to.

"Mercer?" She's dangling one flat off her toes, jiggling her foot. "I want to read it now."

"The chapters are all funky," I say, trying to change the subject like Ashlyn always does. "In separate files. Let me play more video first. Do you remember this part?"

I fast-forward to later in Quinn's cross-examination before Ashlyn can reply.

"Just a few more questions, Mrs. Bryant. First, were you and your husband attempting to trademark Tasha Nicole's name?"

"Yes. But it never actually–"

"Did you know about that?" I ask. "That they were trying to trademark your daughter's name?"

Ashlyn doesn't look at me as the video plays. "No."

"Really? What did you think about that?"

Ashlyn waves the question away. "How do I know what's in those people's minds? Tom always has some scheme. Mother always goes along with it. If they want something–money, especially– they go after it."

The late morning light shifts through my kitchen window blinds, and Ashlyn and I angle our chairs and the tablet screen to avoid the glare. Our croissant remnants are still on our plates, and the ice in my coffee is almost melted. Is this murder about money somehow?

"Next is the part where Quinn asks your mother about the *Insider Magazine* photos from your family album," I say. "Listen."

"Isn't it true that you sold these family photos to the magazine?"

"Yes."

"For how much money?"

"Twenty thousand dollars."

"Let me clarify. You sold your family photos for twenty thousand dollars?"

"Did you know that?" I push Pause. "I mean—before the trial? Did they give *you* any of the money?"

"No." Ashlyn is looking everywhere but at me.

"Your mother seems none too happy with Quinn."

"Yeah," Ashlyn says, with half a laugh. "I know that look. Mom's thinking: *bitch*."

"But what did *you* think? Listening to this?"

Ashlyn leans back in her chair, away from the little screen. Laces her hands on top of her head. "I thought—fan*tas*tic. My mother and stepfather are profiting off my murder trial. Cashing in on the death of their dear granddaughter. They always needed money, but crap. Even *you* couldn't make that stuff up."

I ignore her diss. "Let's watch the rest," I push Play again. "The redirect. When Spofford asks that one final question."

"Isn't it true that you believe your daughter killed Tasha Nicole?"

"That's when the whole mistrial thing happened," I click the video to black. "The judge didn't let your mother answer. What do you think she would have said?"

"Please," she says. "Don't you see? That woman was in an impossible situation. Impossible. Worse than mine, if that's imaginable."

"How worse?" I take my plate to the sink, but she still has croissant left.

"Mercer? If you wrote that she didn't try to defend me—that'd be wrong. She did. She totally did. She didn't know the real story, of course. But what she said was the truth as she understood it. I understand it kind of seems like two truths. But two truths can exist at the same time, you know? It's true to *her*, if she truly believes it."

She points a finger at me. "But you heard the part where Quinn asked whether I was a good mother. And Mom said yes, every time."

"Sure," I say. "And that's in the book."

"Yeah." She picks up her croissant. "I bet."

"No, honestly—" I stop myself. I hate when people say that, it always makes me wonder whether they weren't honest before, and I can't believe I've done it now. And the "good mother" part is indeed there. Just phrased differently. I need to keep her happy. "It's all there."

"What did you write about Tom?" she asks.

"Your father?" I'm relieved she keeps changing the subject, and think again of my list. *What up with Tom?* "Tell me about him. What role did he play?"

At that, I see her eyes dart, and somehow her head is shaking, like saying no a million times, very quickly, almost imperceptibly. She puts down her must-be-soggy half-eaten croissant, only two bites taken out of the remaining triangle. "Why?" she asks. "Have you talked to him?"

I haven't, but I don't need to say so unless I decide it'll be helpful. "Listen, Ashlyn." I make my voice businesslike. "We're doing a job. We're getting paid—sorry to be crass about it—to write a compelling saleable book. For you, it's to repair your reputation and reset your life. For me, it's how I make a living." I figure she'll understand mercenary. She apparently has no other means of support. "To make it work we have to trust each other."

"There are some things I can never talk about, never," Ashlyn says. "Not for the book, not for anyone."

I wait.

She waits.

She picks up her croissant again. Looks at the edges of it, pushes back some escaping cheese. "Yeah, well. Remember, in that opening statement Quinn gave? How she said I had 'issues'?"

"I do, sure." Ashlyn has "issues" with her family, Quinn told the jury. Issues we never really heard about in the trial. *Issues* is on my list, too.

"And did you ever wonder why I didn't testify?" she asks.

"Well, you didn't have to," I don't exactly answer.

"I *wanted* to," she says. "So bad. But if anyone had asked me about those 'issues,' I'd have had to lie. Or, you know, ruin my parents' lives."

CHAPTER THIRTY-SIX

I sit at my desk, computer monitor the only light in the study. I'm looking at the screen through the spaces between my fingers—because my hands are over my face. This whole thing would have been much easier if the jury had simply found Ashlyn guilty. Now I'm the prosecutor. And I have to prove she did it, even if Royal Spofford couldn't. But that's a slam dunk, because I'm the jury, too.

I've been gently trying to draw Ashlyn out about what happened. But this afternoon, when we hit the "issues" thing and she said she didn't want to "ruin my parents' lives," I'd asked what she meant. You don't just toss off a remark like that.

Her answer? She slugs down the last of her iced coffee, then says she needs a nap. Obviously pivoting again. That puts me back on the tightrope. To make this work, she has to tell me her story. She has to rely on me to be her biographer. To be her voice.

If she clams up, the book—justice—doesn't happen. If she gets angry and walks out, the book doesn't happen. So, sure, I'd told her, take a nap. She's out of jail. Avoided lifelong incarceration and permanent vilification. I suppose she should be allowed some personal space. If she doesn't trust me, this will never succeed. While she napped, I worked. I took my laptop to the living room couch and researched every online article about the trial I could find.

Eventually, about five, I hear the splatter and rush of the shower.

I imagine her in my shower, curtain fluttering, door closed. I imagine the bathroom mirror.

What if she comes out and tells me there were numbers on my mirror? What if she asks me why? I try to think of an answer. Maybe *Unlike you, I miss my daughter. And her father. My husband.* Maybe I should try the whole truth, and gauge how she reacts. That I'm doing this for Sophie. For all little girls lost. Because Ashlyn has to pay.

I go back to my reading. Eventually the shower goes off. All is silent for a bit.

"Sorry." She's standing in the living room entryway, wearing a plain pink T-shirt and reasonable jeans. "I guess I'm exhausted."

I click off the computer, flip over my notes, and stand, trying to look casual.

"Everything okay?"

"Eventually it'll be." She sits on the couch, all the way to one side. She politely turns down my potentially kind of tactless offer to watch the news. She does accept a glass of cabernet.

While I'm in the kitchen getting the two glasses and the bottle, I guess Ashlyn changed her mind about the TV. When I return, she's clicking through the channels. She mutes the sound, clicking the remote to something benign, a movie. Maybe she thought the room would be too empty with the two of us sitting solitary, *mano a mano,* in the last of the summery afternoons.

Or. Maybe she feels comfortable. Safe. And that's exactly what I want. When was the last time she'd felt that way? Maybe I can mine that vibe, her soul-crushing journey from carefree party girl to murderer to prisoner to wherever she is now, some private personal limbo. I hand her a red lacquer coaster, and she places her wineglass on it. I can be her protector, her supporter. Her– I hope–confessor.

"Do I ever get to start over?" she asks.

Her hair is still damp around the edges, making the dark roots seem darker. No lipstick, I notice, not a stitch of it. She's a lost forest creature, wary-eyed and vulnerable. Take off all that Hot Stuff makeup and there's a different person underneath. Or maybe this ingénue is the disguise, and the vixen the real thing.

"Start over my life, I mean," she goes on, not waiting for me to answer. "I heard what that Spofford said about me. Murderer. Selfish. Party girl. Whatever other gross and unfair words. How can I even use my own name? Will I be on the run forever, you think? Dodging questions about who I am? And how I'm 'doing'? I mean, how do they *think* I'm doing?"

I'd been wondering the same thing. About Ashlyn. And about myself. I sit opposite her on the couch, tucking myself into the diagonal of the corner. "I guess it takes time."

She takes a sip of wine. I wait. Wine can never hurt in an interview. Unless you're the interviewer. My glass stays on the coffee table.

I stick a toe into the waters of confession. "Time, and the truth, you know?"

She sighs, blows out a breath. "So here's a question. If I tell you something, does it have to go into the book?"

"Of course not," I instantly lie. No one but a journalist can understand the tension of this moment. But how do you catch a clever fish? Let out the line, make them feel free. Then reel it in, little by little. Then let go again. Then reel it in. At the moment the prey is close enough, grab it. I'll let out some line now. "Nothing has to be anything. It's *your* book, right?"

I pretend-sip my wine. It's a useful prop. She's on her second glass, probably catching up since there's no wine in jail. But I can't squander my brain on alcohol.

"It's just that we only have two weeks. Or we don't get paid." I smile, as if I just remembered that critical thing. The television is flickering an old movie, black and white, something with gowns and dancing. I turn to face her, tucking my bare feet underneath me, settling myself in. "So. You were saying. *Issues.*"

Ashlyn's propped the soles of her black flats on the edge of the coffee table, knees bent, and she's tucked a fringed throw pillow behind her. She's silent, staring straight ahead. Then she turns her face to me, inquisitive.

"How'd you write a book about me without ever talking to me? I mean, did you talk to my . . ." Another sip of wine. "Family?"

I explain the process of research, intense research, as quickly as I can. The framework, the trial, the timing. What *reportage* means.

She nods, as if she understands. "So you didn't talk to my family. You just took stuff that might be true and stuff that might not be, decided what *you* thought was true, or what you wanted to be true, and put that together into a story? So it came out sounding like it really *is* true?"

Sure, if you want to put it like that, I don't say. Like a jury.

"In a way." I try not to feel defensive, or sound it. "But it was only a first draft. Until the verdict, of course, I couldn't write the ending. Or give it context." Which, blessedly, *is* true. "So now we have the perfect opportunity for you to set the record straight."

"I suppose." She pours herself more wine.

Does she need convincing? Time for me to take control of this fish.

"Ashlyn? If there's an explanation about what happened . . ." I begin to reel her in, my tone gentle and tentative, as if I'm searching for the right words. "If there's something that can prove you didn't . . . I mean, if you can prove what really happened, that's what's missing. Proof. Yes, you're legally exonerated. But how can we get you—"

"Okay. Like we said before. *Issues.*" Her voice has hardened as she interrupts, as if she's made a decision. "My 'father,' so-called, is really my stepfather. Was that in any of the 'research' you did?"

I think. Feel myself frown. "No, I guess not."

"Not surprising," Ashlyn says. "They never discuss it. My mother volunteered at the hospital, I'm sure you remember that from the trial, and she met Tom there. He's a private pilot. You read that?"

"Yeah."

"He was an insurance guy, but now he's part of that program that flies sick kids to hospitals. Mercy Air."

"Yeah." I'm trying to sound confident, but I'm unsettled that I don't know that fact, either. Maybe it was never relevant? It seems like the kind of dramatic irony a reporter would highlight.

"So, they met when she worked in the children's ward. You knew that?"

"No." I'm actively wondering now, with more than a twinge of apprehension, what else I don't know. But maybe it doesn't matter. I should get a notebook, but I don't want to interrupt her.

"My real father died when I was pretty young, Mom always used her maiden name. It was just me and Mom. But then, Tom came into our lives." She shoots a forefinger, *bang*. "And, bang, she was all about Tom. We all became Bryant. Mom did whatever he said. I mean—what*ever*. I had to call him 'Daddy.' And what do you think it was like for me, a cute fifteen-year-old, suddenly having that man around? Calling him that?"

I blink. "Well . . ."

"As you remind me, we only have two weeks." The tone of her voice is new, and she's picked up the remote, flipping channels, the glow from the screen highlighting her eyes, then putting her face in shadow. She stops on some crime show, a police chase, the sound barely audible. "So let's just say, to make this all totally clear, he was an asshole and a jerk, and I couldn't get out of that house fast enough. It's no wonder what happened."

This time I take a sip of wine for real, trying to process. I put my glass down so I don't do it again. "Happened?"

A good interviewer sometimes lets the conversation go where the subject wants. Give the fish more line. Happy to do so.

"Whatever you're thinking? That's probably exactly right," Ashlyn says. "I don't want to say the words. I really—can't. My poor mother. I was fifteen when it started. Fif-teen. She's hated *me* ever since. Hated *me!*"

On TV a police car spins out, crashes into a light pole. Sirens, almost muted, fill the silence.

CHAPTER THIRTY-SEVEN

You go first," I tell Ashlyn. I'm not being polite. If she showers second, I don't get the mirror. When she's done, it's my turn. Monday, day 478. My family assured me they were at peace.

We pass in the hall, her in a towel, me in a T-shirt, like sisters in some horror-movie sorority. The entire energy of my house is off. My first two nights under the same roof with her felt like I was living someplace foreign or unfamiliar or besieged. Whenever I tried to sleep, an iffy proposition anyway, I kept hearing her moving around. Maybe in the bathroom, or getting water from the kitchen. Maybe I imagined it. The study door is closed, but I know there's no way to keep her out of there. The book manuscript is on my laptop, and when we're home, I keep it with me. Right now it's under Dex's pillow.

Ashlyn and I are walking, mostly in silence, toward Ristretto, because Ashlyn wants another croissant. She's again in her soccer-mom disguise, ball cap and scarf with her jeans and T-shirt. Our route into Linsdale center takes us past the oak where the accident happened. I won't point it out—my grief is shared on a need-to-know basis. A leaf, prematurely turned that luminous red, twists and spins as it flutters to the sidewalk. Slashed gouges, disappearing by the week, disfigure the trunk. That tree is taunting me, showing off the blood red leaves that prove even though its growing season is ending, it is still alive.

That tree is a murderer. Like my new companion.

"You want to talk?" I'm trying to craft a question about incest and child abuse. That's a tough one.

"Can we not?" she says.

"Sure," I say.

If Ashlyn was molested by her stepfather, which is all I can infer from Saturday's "conversation," that's horrific. But she still killed her daughter. If it's true, why didn't Quinn McMorran raise that abuse "issue" as a mitigating factor?

Okay, I'm not that cold. Okay, I feel bad for her. But she still killed her daughter.

Yesterday, Sunday, she'd slept in, not a sound from the guest room when I got up at seven. I'd made coffee for myself, and waiting for her, read my whole manuscript again, from the beginning.

Problem is, I realized, now that the primary source is right here, it's complicated. Reading it through her eyes, it's unsettling how my "pre-writing" seems less "feel of real" and more flat-out fiction. Now that the main character is writing the story with me, my journalistic freedom is over.

"Give yourself a break," I muttered out loud. And some of it inevitably *is* fiction. Informed fiction. No one can "know" the internal thoughts or motivations of others. And I probably have more information about the police investigation and the crime lab than she does. She wasn't there, so she can't criticize.

By Sunday noon I got so frustrated I cleaned the kitchen. Did laundry. Then I gave up. And waited.

She padded down the hall, finally, around four. Bleary and apologetic.

"I guess my body is re-acclimating to freedom." She wiped her palms over her eyes. "They kept waking us up in that jail, it was like—whatever comfort we tried to have, they'd try to steal from us. Sorry if I've interfered with your—our—schedule."

"No problem," I'd said. Which was true. So far.

We'd talked for the rest of the afternoon, and then made dinner. Spaghetti, very chummy. Ashlyn told me (without one hint of irony) about her teenaged aspirations to be a marine biologist, but then how much she "loathed" college. She "could not make it two months in that place" so she dropped out and got a job as a salesperson in a suburban Dayton boutique called Labels. "Totally hip," she said. "And they called me management material." All resume, no smoking gun.

At dinner I managed to ask her, several times, to elaborate about her stepfather and her intimation of abuse. My first couple of tries, she changed the subject. The third time, she surprised me again.

She looked at me across the kitchen table, as if perplexed. "I never said that."

"But—yesterday." Was I wrong? No. I certainly was not. "On the couch. I distinctly remember. You said specifically—" Am I pushing her too hard? "You said your mother hated *you* because of it."

"You must be mistaken." She twirled spaghetti on her fork, watching the spiral of marinara-coated strands. "Did you have a lot of wine?"

It was futile to argue, although she was completely lying. I know what she said. And *she* had the wine. What Ashlyn thinks, and what she decides to reveal, or confirm, is haphazard. Slapdash, offering a tidbit here and a tidbit there, sometimes changing her story altogether. She still hasn't said what really happened to Tasha Nicole, which you'd think would be the first thing she'd want to tell me. If she wasn't guilty.

When Dex had a murder case, he'd never directly ask the defendant whether they committed the crime. "I don't want to know," he'd say. "Because it's unethical for me to lie, or to allow my client to lie to the jury." In this case, there's no jury. Except for me.

Still, even without legal jeopardy, I don't expect Ashlyn to confess quickly. She thinks this is about redemption.

And it is. Just not of her.

Sunday night post-spaghetti, we also covered one more item on my list–the chloroform. *She* thinks we covered it, I mean. It's almost hilarious. Does she think I don't know about Casey Anthony? That case was all about chloroform.

Ashlyn herself brought up the issue. She laughed about it, dismissing Spofford's accusations in the trial. The chloroform "thing," she explained, was her mother's fault. Georgia, she said, was "incredibly gullible" and a health-fad fanatic.

"I came home one day and her teeth were green," Ashlyn said. "She told me she was adding chlorophyll to her bottled water. Can you believe that? Naturally, she had to show me all about it online. When she did a search for chlorophyll, she spelled it with an *f*, and chloroform came up. She can be an idiot."

She'd pointed to my laptop. "Try it," she said.

When I typed in "Chlorof," chloroform popped up as first on the list.

Ashlyn took my plate. "You done?" She'd rinsed the spaghetti dishes herself.

"I see what you mean," I said over the sound of the running water. She wasn't looking at me, but I tried to keep a straight face just in case. "Misspelled" searches by her mother is exactly the excuse Casey Anthony fabricated when confronted with *her* case's chloroform evidence. I can't wait to put Ashlyn's brazenly copycat defense in the book. Murder lessons.

Plus, Ashlyn's mother was a hospital volunteer. Ashlyn could have visited her there. Or pretended to. Done a little chloroform shoplifting. Maybe *with* her mother?

"So there was no computer search for 'chloroform,' you're saying." I pretended to accept that story as original. "It was a spelling mistake. And she did it a few times."

"Right," she said. "And I'm going to bed."

Now we walk a suburban sidewalk on a normal-for-everyone-else sunny Monday. Far from her home, far from her life. I wonder what she's thinking.

"Do you miss Ohio?" I figure that's benign.

"Kidding me?" She turns to me, making a face. "There's nothing for me in Ohio."

"Want to talk about it?"

"Let's just walk, okay?" She gestures at the color-splashed trees, the cloud-dotted sky. A car passes by, windows open, radio blasting, leaving a trail of steel guitar. "Can't believe I was in that cell, for a year, for nothing, you know? So much for justice."

"Yeah," I say.

We stop at a crosswalk, and I watch a line of elementary school students boarding a polished yellow bus. The sun glints off its side mirror, and cars line up behind it waiting for the flashing red stop sign to flap back against the side. Lives unfolding, normal and safe. Sophie will never be one of those kids, and I can barely watch. One by one, each child takes that steep first step up into their future, their shoes huge on spindly legs, leggings and fluttering dresses on the girls. Oversized backpacks. Tasha will never get on a school bus, either.

For a moment, it's overwhelming. The possibilities each of us is born with, and how the doors close, one by one, sometimes— no, *usually*—without our being aware of it. How can it not be overwhelming to *her?* Maybe Ashlyn never knew love. Maybe she's too young.

Maybe she's too guilty.

I'd floated "Ohio" because yesterday in the kitchen, me taking notes on the laptop, we'd also talked about her life there. Ashlyn hated Dayton, "a frickin' map dot" with zero to do. She didn't remember her dead father.

"Sad," she'd said, her voice softening, "how different my life would be . . ." She'd looked away from me, talked to the kitchen wall. "If he'd lived."

Her domineering stepfather, she sneered, spent his early retirement flying his private plane and having affairs. No matter how I tried, I couldn't get her back to the abuse. But I know she said it.

Her mother, doting, traditional, and a fervent housekeeper, spent Ashlyn's high school career grooming her daughter to be prom queen. And, because "Tom" was often out of town, smothering attention on her dogs.

"Dogs don't talk back, she always said." Ashlyn mimicked a derisive falsetto, then took a bite of just-thawed condolence cookie, a few crumbs falling to her lap. She brushed them onto the floor. "Georgia. What a loser."

Now, Monday morning, the rumbling yellow school bus still idles at the corner. A millennial mom in pink kitten heels and a black suit, cell phone to her ear, kisses the top of her son's head before he clambers on board.

Where is Ashlyn's phone? I haven't seen her with one, never thought about it. Has she called her parents? Her pals? How about that boyfriend, or the babysitter?

"Screw that, right?" Ashlyn says.

"What?" I know I didn't ask her anything. And there's nothing unusual here at the crosswalk, unless you count a fluffy-tailed squirrel risking its life to scamper against the traffic. *Road kill,* I think, before I can help it.

Ashlyn turns to me, adjusts her big sunglasses. "Oh my god, sorry, I am such a crazy person," she says. "I was thinking about something else, and must have . . ." She shakes her head, the darkened lenses hiding her expression. "Nothing."

"Do you have a phone?" I ask.

"The damn cops took it." She flips her hand, annoyed. "Quinn's *still* trying to get it back."

A block until Ristretto. It's show-on-the-road time, whether Ashlyn likes it or not. They're paying her to talk to me.

As I predicted, only a few tables are occupied, some with summery umbrellas strategically unfurled, shading the filigreed metal tables and their occupants from the morning sun.

"I'm nervous about our deadline, Ash." I wave her through the wrought-iron entrance gate toward a square metal table in the corner, white tablecloth, a turquoise-striped umbrella in the middle open on a tilty metal pole. A bouquet of orange chrysanthemums teeters in a turquoise ceramic vase, wobbling on the uneven tabletop. "Can we fast-forward?"

"No prob." She pulls out her chair, its metal legs rasping across the concrete patio. She sits, picks up the plastic-covered menu, flips it to the back, then the front again. "That's why we get the big bucks, right?"

I think of my list as I sit across from her, and try to pick a topic. I'll hold off on the big stuff–Tasha's father, whoever that is. Why wasn't *he* a suspect? And the elusive babysitter, Valerie. Why wasn't *she* a suspect? And the strangely absent boyfriend Luke. Why wasn't *he* a suspect? We both fiddle with napkins and silverware.

"Can we talk about Ron Chevalier?" I'll start there. She'd asked for him in that jailhouse call. She'd stayed at his apartment, so said the magazine. "According to *Scoop Magazine,* his nightclub Hot Stuff was–"

"Did you know Hot Stuff was named that because everything in it was stolen? True story. But you're so funny." Ashlyn flaps her napkin onto her lap. "It's been like two days now. Why don't you ask me what really happened to Tasha Nicole?"

CHAPTER THIRTY-EIGHT

Ashlyn's answer puts me as off-kilter as the stripey umbrella, as off-balance as that turquoise vase. I clean my knife, unnecessarily, with the white cotton napkin. "Well, sure," I say, as if it had been my own idea. "I didn't want you to feel as if I'm pushing you."

"Look. People love to hate me." Ashlyn's voice is soft, softer than I've ever heard. Her tone has changed. "I'm really grateful to you, Mercer. I know you're doing this book to help me. And in a way, aren't I just like you? A single mother. Trying to make the best of a bad deal in life. We both lost daughters. We're both devastated. We're both—"

I feel my back stiffen, and my eyes narrow. I will not let her say "we're both" anything on this planet. Her phony sympathy will not distract me. I force my face into a compassionate expression, and hope she can't read how equally counterfeit it is.

A waiter in a black T-shirt arrives. *Ken,* his name tag says. Thank goodness for the interruption. He settles our coffees into place, clattering white china saucers and then white china cups, and then a white china cream pitcher.

Ashlyn has gone silent, and seems to be wiping her eyes under her sunglasses. She's in the lee of the umbrella, half in shadow. After Ken finally leaves, there's only the sound of her spoon as it stirs sugar into her coffee. Then a horn from the street. She looks up again.

"At least *you* have a way out. No one blames you." She points her spoon at me, one coffee drop falling to the white tablecloth.

"At least *you'll* be able to grieve, and get better, and someday, maybe, you'll start over. But me? My daughter's dead. Just like yours. But *my* life is ruined. Yours isn't."

It *isn't?* But I choke back my words, and I'm saved again by Ken's next interruption. Now, "compliments of the kitchen," he's delivering a wicker basket of cinnamon rolls. Their spicy fragrance, usually divine, is sweetly sickening, too strong. I vowed I would not discuss Sophie with this woman. And now she's brought her up. As if we live in the same world.

"But how can I even tell people my name?" Ashlyn selects a cinnamon roll, unfurls the gooey spiral. Looks at it, not at me. "I know what they call me. 'Murder Mom.' And much much worse. No matter what the jury said, no matter what you write, no one will ever believe I didn't kill Tasha. People still think, oh, she must be a *disgusting horrible* person. They *want* me to be guilty. They think 'not guilty' only means I, like, got away with it."

Didn't you? And I want to ask: *If you didn't kill Tasha, who did?* But stop myself. For now.

"But I'm not guilty. I'm not." She drops the doughy cinnamon-coated strip back on her plate, frowning. "I'm like Casey Anthony. She's innocent, the jury said so. But she can't even–I mean, can you imagine her saying her name? *Hi, I'm Casey Anthony.* People would either bolt, or throw up, or try to grab a Facebook selfie. She can never introduce herself with her real name again."

"Did you follow that case?" I ask. *Please admit it.*

A lone tear falls down her cheek, emerging under the rim of her sunglasses. The first tear I've ever seen from Ashlyn. She swipes it away.

"I know I agreed with Katherine," she says. "I agreed to talk to you, and let you write the book. I need the money, just like you, right? I thought I could do it. And you've been so nice to me."

Little do you know, I think. But this is exactly what I wanted her to believe, so I nod, as if modestly agreeing to my own generosity. She ignored my question, but I can push her about Casey Anthony later, if need be.

Ashlyn looks around, furtive, as if someone might overhear, but at this hour, nine-ish, the place is in a lull. Those who have to report to offices have gone; those planning a day in Boston are still herding their kids to daycare. She leans forward, reaching one hand toward mine, not quite touching it.

"I'm so sorry for you," she whispers. "Katherine told me exactly what happened to your family."

And, *thud*. But I guess I'm not surprised. So Katherine used me and my story as currency. Or better, ammunition. I've purposely not opened that personal discussion with Ashlyn, tried to avoid mentioning Dex and Sophie. I suppose it's a line of connection, but I just can't go there. Taking a delaying sip of too-hot coffee, I realize this is how Katherine must have sold the tell-all book deal. Peas in a pod, or some manipulatively odious comparison like that.

"I see." Is all I can manage.

"And thing is, that's the reason I agreed to talk with you. *Only Mercer*, I told her." Ashlyn has both elbows on the table now, her fingers holding her temples as her head barely swivels, eyes searching left, then right, then focusing on me. "You'd *get* it, she promised me. I could trust you, she said. But thing is, now, I'm not sure. About our book."

"Not sure?" I move the cinnamon rolls away from me. Dex craved them. We should never have come here.

"You totally think I'm guilty," she says.

"What? I do not!" I almost choke on my coffee.

"I bet your entire book is about how guilty I am. That's just so . . . difficult for me. I keep wondering if I can trust you. Not to, you know, screw me."

"The book—it's not—it's only in progress." I've got to steer her away from this. She's got to be feeling me out, fishing, so I'll use this time to reassure her. "Of course I don't think you're guilty. The jury said you weren't. I'm just a writer."

"Yeah." She fiddles with her spoon again, turning it over and over. "So can I see the whole thing? What you've written, so far? I'm just saying–everything you ask me sounds like you decided, jury or not, that I *am* guilty. You're being very nice to me, but like you said. You're a reporter."

"But . . ." I lean forward, trying not to make too much of it. Not be too defensive. Since she's right.

"No." She puts up a palm. "I am not guilty. I did not do it. And . . ." She tilts her head, seems to have an epiphany. "It's *my* book, now, too, isn't it? And the whole *point* of it is to–yeah. I'm not sure you're the person to write it."

Okay, Defcon 1. She's serious. And this cannot happen. There's a contract, sure, but it all hinges on her cooperation. If she balks, or tries to pull out–well, it'd be simple enough for Katherine, even with us being pals, to obey the command of the publisher and find another author. An author who won't care about it as much as I do. An author who doesn't need it as much as I do. An author who won't care about justice as much as I do. I muster every scintilla of acting ability in my body.

"Of course you can see it." Old journalism technique, agree with whatever the subject wants, even if you don't intend to do it. And–I just this second realize–I have a big fat ace in the hole.

"And may I tell you something, in confidence, Ashlyn? You cannot ever breathe a word. But it'll prove I don't think you're guilty. It'll prove it beyond a–" I pause. She can fill in the blank.

She looks puzzled. "Prove? Sure, okay. I won't tell."

"Promise."

"I *promise*," she whispers. I take a sip of coffee, getting my story straight. A city bus thunders by, and I hear Ken taking orders from another table. My turn to look around, checking for eavesdroppers, but no one is paying attention to me and the murderer. "There was a juror who . . ."

I pause. Savoring the guarded anticipation on Ashlyn's face. And my own realization.

The universe has provided me a pivotal insight. If I consider it a different way, I can create a new reality from the Juror G debacle. Turn it into a good thing. Use it as ammunition. My voice lowered and leaning toward her, I tell Ashlyn the whole story. About Carmendy, but not using her name. '*So* incredibly guilty,' the juror's quote. Which I may have exaggerated in the retelling. About my recon at the hardware store. And generically, so I'm not ratting out Quinn, I tell what I did as a result.

"The dumpy woman who always gave me the nasty looks?" Ashlyn's eyebrows go up. *"Her?"*

"Well, I don't know." My coffee tastes perfect now. "I've never seen the jurors. They weren't allowed on camera."

"She *hated* me." Ashlyn's poking the remnants of her destroyed cinnamon roll. *"Hated.* I could totally tell. I wondered what happened to her." She sighs, as if playing it all out, envisioning the alternative verdict. "Wow."

"Yeah," I say, agreeing with the movie in her mind. "I knew she thought you were guilty. If I'd been hoping for a conviction, I could easily have kept quiet. If I had, and she'd stayed in that deliberation, you might be sitting in a cell instead of drinking dark roast in a suburban coffee shop."

Take that, Ashlyn.

Ashlyn smiles. Toasts me with her coffee. "Okay. Well, that is—interesting. I must admit. So, okay. Okay. For now. Right? So I'll . . . reserve judgment. So to speak. I'll read the book as we go. And we'll see."

CHAPTER THIRTY-NINE

Crisis averted. After our Ristretto *détente* yesterday, we agreed to start in earnest. No more coffee shop. I'll transcribe what she says each morning, then craft it into the book while she goes off and sunbathes or watches TV or whatever. I'm happy she won't be breathing down my neck as I write. I'm at the desk, laptop open. Somehow we've both decided to wear jeans and T-shirts this morning. Mine is white and hers is black, which is hilarious.

"Ready?" I ask.

"Go for it," she says.

We're talking about a dead child, and she's acting like it's some celebrity interview. But this'll be over soon.

She's appropriated the big wing chair in the study. Where Sophie and I used to read together. I'd put a blanket over it, the ombre pink one Sophie's Grandmother Emily crocheted, to convince myself it's a different chair. Ashlyn's put her second mug of coffee on the mahogany side table. With no coaster. It's that kind of stuff that makes me nuts. She's—careless. But maybe I can use that.

I start with the big one.

"So, Ashlyn? Let me ask you again. And we can figure out how you want it to go in the book," I lie. "What happened to Tasha Nicole?"

She stops, her mug halfway to her lips. Her eyes widen. "Well, that's the whole point, Mercer. Right? I mean, I don't know."

Pants on fire. "Really?" I say. "That's so—I don't know—kind of incredible. Like, you have no idea? At all?"

"No." She shakes her head, and I see tears. She closes her eyes briefly. Opens them. "Can we start with a different question?"

Right. And give you time to come up with a story? Sure, she had plenty of time in that cell to make up something, but maybe now she'll have to work on a new version of reality. Now there's been a trial. There's evidence. And every bit of it has to match.

"Okay, sure, and I hope this gets easier for you as we go," I say, trying to look sympathetic. "I know it must be tough. But it's all for the book, right? A good cause. So . . . when was the last time you saw your daughter? Was it in Logan airport? And why were you there together, by the way?"

"We never were in Boston together," she says, shaking her head.

My turn to close my eyes. I flap down the laptop, trying to hide my annoyance. This is how it's gonna go? Pulling teeth?

"Oh, gosh, really?" I pull open my file drawer, flip through the green hanging folders, pull out the manila file labeled Rogo-wicz.

"You know Detective Rogowicz," I say.

"Asshole," she says.

"Anyway, this police report he filed says he found surveillance tape of you and Tasha in Logan Airport. Just off a plane from Chicago. In some newsstand, playing with a puppy."

"Where'd you get that?" She makes no move to see it.

"Research." I flip through it, seeing Rogowicz's sentences typed on the gridded police form. "So if you say you weren't in Boston together—I mean, I'm so sorry, Ashlyn, but readers will wonder about that video." Old writer trick, deflection, it's not really *me* being pushy, it's the demanding public. "How should we explain it?"

"It wasn't me, maybe? Maybe it wasn't Tasha? Maybe it wasn't either of us? How do I know?" Her voice rises with every question. "I wasn't there. And if it's such a huge deal, why didn't they show it in court? I mean, hey, if they have some tape proving I was in Boston, I gotta think they'd have showed it. Don't you?"

That had crossed my mind, I have to admit. "So you're saying it's not you? Were you ever in Boston during the time Tasha was missing?"

"She was never missing!" Ashlyn stands, throws both hands in the air, paces to the bookshelves, paces to the door, undoing her ponytail and then banding it back in place. "That's the whole point. That's why I have no idea. She was with the babysitter, with—"

She stops mid-sentence. Her chest rises and falls under her black T-shirt. "Valerie. With Valerie. Or, so I thought."

"Right," I say. "And where's Valerie now?"

"I don't know, I don't *know*." Ashlyn's pacing again.

"And how about Luke? Walsh? Was he your boyfriend before or after Ron Chevalier? What does he have to do with anything?"

"How'd you know about Luke?" She stops in front of the book-shelves, faces me, eyes narrowing.

My turn to pause. Luke's been such a part of my consciousness through this whole thing—but how do I know? Oh. I heard about him from Quinn McMorran, which I can never divulge. And from Joe Riss, whose confidence I can't break either.

"So there *is* a Luke?" I go on offense, hoping it works.

"There's a Luke. But he doesn't have anything to do with this."

"Who does, then?" I can't resist asking. But then decide I should pull way back. Being antagonistic won't do any good. I'm trying to tease out a confession. Get something. Anything. One juicy morsel. Before she realizes what she's said.

"You don't understand at all." She stomps to the study door, as if she's about to leave.

"Help me, then," I say to her back. Spider to the fly. "Help me help you."

CHAPTER FORTY

We've switched places. I'm in Sophie's chair now, Ashlyn's behind my desk, reading a section of my—our?—my book. To lure her back to the fold, I'd suggested she read some of it, and then comment. Before she could choose, I'd opened the section about that taped phone call from the Dayton jail, when she'd yelled at her mother. In the long run, it won't matter what she thinks. But this is the short run.

"Oh, see, this part is wrong," she says, scrolling down the page. "I guess it's not your fault, you were only . . ." She shrugs. "I mean, I guess you never thought I'd read this. Or if I did, there'd be nothing I could do about it. Maybe you were trying to be—what you call it—objective. But this isn't right. Not how it was."

She narrows her eyes, still scrolling. I've made separate files, so she can only see one section at a time.

"Did you *hear* the call?" she asks. "How we really sounded?"

I hadn't, of course, I'd just read about it. I pretend to think. "I guess not. There was a transcript in the—"

"Yeah," she interrupts, then, leaning in closer to the screen, reads out loud from the manuscript.

"'You have to get me *out* of here!' Ashlyn insisted. 'It's not up to me,' Georgia replied. Which honestly, was a relief."

She sits up straight, scratches her cheek. She'd high-pitched her voice to recite her mother's side of the dialogue.

"See?" She says in her own voice. "You wrote that Mom *thought* 'which honestly was a relief.' But she didn't *say* that, right? So how do you know she felt that way? You made it sound like she's happy I'm in jail. She's a bitch, but like, not that much of a bitch."

"Well, I . . ."

"Let me go on. Starting with Mom, then me." She clears her throat. "'If you want help, why don't you just tell me? Tell me what–' 'Because I don't know what "happened" to her,' Ashlyn interrupted, her voice rising, taut with scorn. 'Are you kidding me?'"

Ashlyn stops. "You wrote 'her voice rising, taut with scorn'? When you didn't even hear me?"

"Yes, sure, but it's all . . ."

"Wait." She runs a finger down the screen, then picks up the dialogue. "'Ashlyn, don't shriek at me,' Georgia said. 'Are you blaming *me* that you're sitting in jail?' 'Effing right,' Ashlyn retorted. 'Blame yourself,' Georgia snapped. 'For telling lies.'"

Ashlyn stops again. I hear the derision in her voice, so I wait for what she's going to say. Plus, I'd used too many verbs.

"That's so mean, Mercer," Ashlyn says. "I didn't *shriek*. I was terrified. And it *was* Mom's fault that I was in jail. I mean–that horrible cop in the closet thing."

She stares at the page. "All I *actually* say is that I want to get out of jail, and that I don't know what happened. Mercer, how does that make me guilty?" Her eyes well with tears as she turns to me. "You just made me *sound* guilty. *So* guilty."

I try to figure out how to answer that. She's right. If you look at it that way.

"That's why we're going over all this," I explain. "We'll make it be exactly the way you say it was. And I cleaned up the language, right?" I go on, trying to lighten the moment. "If the transcript is correct about what you really said."

"Yeah, well." She rolls her eyes. "Gotta tell you, I remember wishing I knew some uglier words. I was behind bars! For–what? But see? I'm not a reporter like you so I don't know, but seems like you could easily have written something like 'Nothing Ashlyn said sounded like she had any idea of what had happened to her daughter.'" She shrugs. "You could have written it better. And truer."

"Got it," I say, fake-capitulating. "And thank you. But now that you understand we're editing, and that means clarifying, let's go on. Why did you keep asking for your phone?"

She blinks a few times. "How would you feel if *your* phone was gone? And like I said, the stupid cops *still* have mine, can you believe it? Wouldn't you be mad?"

"Yeah, okay. I admit I'm pretty attached to it. But–"

"Exactly," she says. "And I had to explain to Ron where I was. Can you imagine how humiliating it was? I wanted him to hear about this whole mess from *me*."

"People will wonder, though, and forgive me, but why weren't you asking about Tasha? Where she was?"

"Because I knew where she was, of course!"

"Why didn't you say so?"

"Because . . . it was too stupid. I was too angry. I'm sorry for not being perfect, Mercer, but, they'd just *arrested* me for like, telling my mother I'd seen Tasha in person. If they put me in jail for every time I lied to my mother–you ever lie to *yours*, Mercer?"

That made me laugh, which made *her* laugh, and for a minute I had to remember how much I hated her.

CHAPTER FORTY-ONE

had to keep remembering how much I hated her. And why. If she weren't so—I don't know, convincing and resourceful—she'd never have lured so many people into doing what she wanted. When she went to the bathroom, first time I've ever been relieved to see her go there, I reclaimed my desk chair and my position in our relationship. I felt mean-girl about my next move, but I selected the manila envelope from the hanging files anyway. To get myself on track. To *my* justice. My truth.

When she came back into the study, her hair was combed, and the edges around her face wet, as if she'd splashed with cold water.

"So to continue," I say. "It's almost lunchtime, if you're hungry? But first, may I show you something? It's kind of confusing." I half-smile, proving I'm truly nice, and it's all part of the job.

I pull out the photo of her in the wet T-shirt, the Hot Stuff sign behind her.

"Can you tell me about this?" I keep my voice nonjudgmental as I stand, and hand it to her.

"Oh . . ." she says, taking the photo. She sinks, slowly, into Sophie's chair. "Where did you get this?"

"Research," I give the standard answer. I wait.

"This is so. . . ." Her face softens. She swipes a tear from one eye. "Oh, damn."

I feel my frown coming back. She's crying? "Huh?"

"I worked, just part-time, at the community college, you know?

In Dayton. Student union, see S-T-U?" She points to the letters. "And they—they had one of those ice-bucket fundraisers for ALS, and for childhood diseases, cancer and things like that. So it was especially . . ." She grimaces. "Yeah, not a good day to wear a white tee-shirt. I like, ran to the bathroom after that. Put on a sweatshirt. But—all for a good cause, right?" She hands the photo halfway back, then stops. "Unless, you don't need this? I'd love to keep it. This was one of the good memories, you know? There weren't many."

"Sure," I say, perching on the edge of my desk. "Keep it." Katherine will kill me, but how am I going to say no? I can always get it back. We should never have slut-shamed her with that photo. Now I'm feeling sorry for Ashlyn, which is not a good thing. Because it makes me vulnerable. Time to make *her* the vulnerable one. I don't like to be unkind, but she's the one who killed her daughter. Probably her idol Casey Anthony raised money for charity at some point. Doesn't make her innocent.

"Can I check with you about something?" I ignore my conscience. "I wrote a scene which is all from research, and it might be tough, but do you mind reading it?"

"Sure," she says. "Let me put this photo away."

When she comes back, I'm behind the desk again. And I've printed out the scene titled "You Are My Sunshine." That was Tasha Nicole's favorite song, so says *Insider Magazine*. The song the church organist played at Tasha's memorial.

Ashlyn plops into the Sophie chair, tucks her legs underneath her. She looks at me, expectant.

"Why didn't you go to the memorial?" I wince, stopping myself. "I'm sorry, Ashlyn. I should be more gentle. But this is the scene I'm talking about." I hold up the pages. "Tasha's memorial."

She presses her lips together, her face deflating.

I let the ugly words hang between us in the silence. Tasha's memorial.

"Why didn't I go?" She finally says. "Besides being held in jail?"

"The judge said you could go," I remind her. "But you said no. It's a horrible journalist question," I continue, being honest, "but what went through your mind?"

"Oh, Mercer, you're never going to understand this—but, hey. Maybe you will. Did you go to Sophie's funeral?"

I nod. I asked for this. And I can handle it. Briefly.

"And are you—do you—feel closure?"

"Never."

She nods. "Right. But the thing is—and you asked, Mercer, so I'll tell you the truth. I know people might say it's delusional. Thing is, the day of the memorial? I still didn't believe it was Tasha. I still thought she was somewhere else. They showed me that composite drawing, you must have seen it. It didn't look like her. At all. I kept thinking about that, and thinking about that. And what if the DNA test was wrong? It was all I could see in my mind, that there'd be some moment they'd show up with her. I imagined this scene, so clearly, I couldn't get it out of my head, where Quinn would come in, and there'd be Tasha, and they'd say . . ."

"But where did you think she was? With who?"

"I didn't know, I didn't *know,* that's why I needed Ron and I needed my stepfather—did you know they knew each other?"

"What?"

"Right. And did you know why it was really called Hot Stuff?"

"You told me because stuff was stolen."

"I know what I told you. And don't you think it would be . . . convenient?" She cocks her head, untucks her legs. Plants her bare feet on the carpet. "For someone dealing in stolen stuff to have someone with a private pilots' license? Especially someone who'd blown his whole retirement in some stupid investment thing? Sorry to sound like a crime show. But I . . . I somehow got in the middle of it. They knew I'd do anything for Tasha. I wasn't *part* of anything of course, but I knew. . . ."

She leans back in the chair. Talks to the ceiling. "I knew Ron. I knew my stepfather. I knew enough."

"So what happened?" I don't want the desk between us. I wheel my chair out from behind it, and scoot closer to her.

Ashlyn leans forward, our knees almost touching. I smell her baby powder deodorant, and the remnants of coffee and a flowery shampoo.

"Tashie loved her grandfather, and would have gone anywhere with him. Wherever he took her. Wherever Valerie was. *That's* where Tasha was. Tom Bryant knew I'd understand Ron's hold over him, and me, and Tashie, and us, and our lives. If I told what they were doing. If I told what they were having him fly on that plane. And he's her—her *grandfather.* I never thought someone like that, someone who'd loved her since she was one second old, could do anything to harm her. That's why I didn't—couldn't—say anything. All this time, I was hoping, hoping, hoping they'd bring her back, but I couldn't say so. Of course I couldn't say so! And Mercer, why do you think my stepfather refused to testify?"

"But wait, Ashlyn. Ron *testified.* That you were a 'friend' and came to the club." I swivel my chair, once, then again. "Why didn't Quinn ask *him* about this—stolen goods scheme?"

"Mercer, don't you get it? She didn't know! Of course she didn't know. Setting me up for a murder charge back then was a test, of *me,* to see if I would rat them out. See? At that point I wasn't sure it was actually Tasha. I hoped if I kept quiet, they'd bring her back."

I'm silent for a beat, thinking about this.

"So you were willing to roll those dice?" I close my eyes for a fraction of a second, imagining. "You were willing to go prison for life to protect Tasha?"

"Willing?" She stands, so quickly I have to move my chair away.

"I'm not sure 'willing' is the word I would choose. But would I sacrifice my life for my daughter's?"

Her question weighs on my shoulders. I know what her next one will be, and I think, *please don't ask me that.*

But she's going to. I can see it in her eyes.

"Wouldn't *you?*" she asks. "Have sacrificed your life?"

This room is too small, too small to hold me and Ashlyn and two dead little girls. And all those memories. All the choices we make. All the choices I *made.* All the choices I should have made. *Could* have made. This has to stop. This whole undertaking—oh, no, not undertaking, I didn't mean to pick that word . . .

"Mercer? You know what?"

I blink myself back to reality, such as it is.

"I *want* to read about the memorial," she goes on. "I've never talked to anyone about it, never read anything about it. But I think your book—our book—is a way for me to be there for her. Maybe get my closure. Say goodbye. Which I never got to say. You know how that feels, right?"

I don't answer. I can't.

"I've pictured the whole thing, of course," she goes on. "Imagined it. But *you're* better at making stuff up."

"Well, I took it all from research, and—"

"I didn't mean it that way." She holds out a hand. "Let's see."

I give her the pages. Watch her settle back into the pink-covered chair. Reading my words, she'll be going to her daughter's memorial service. She'll envision the garlands of pink roses and baby's breath, hear the piping soprano of the children's choir, a minister in all black, searching for words to comfort the inconsolable attendees and grief-ravaged grandparents. See how on the altar, front and center, sat a glossy life-size photo of her wide-eyed daughter, surrounded by white lilies. That's what I wrote, as gut-wrenchingly poignant and heartbreaking as I could make it.

I'm giving her the feel of real, all right. And it feels—wrong.

I snatch the pages from her hands.

"What are you doing?" she asks. "I wanted to read that!"

"And you can," I tell her. "Whenever you want. But you know what? Let's take a walk. Go to Ristretto. Get lunch. I've got to get outside. I feel like I'm in—"

I almost said jail.

"Yeah," she says. "I hear you."

CHAPTER FORTY-TWO

ladies?" Ken the turquoise-aproned waiter is our old pal now. He pulls a yellow pencil from behind his ear. "The usual?"

Ashlyn and I nod. We have a "usual."

"Two ice coffees, one add hazelnut, two ham and cheese croiss," Ken says. "Coming up."

Ashlyn seems agitated, fussing with her scarf-disguise and fidgeting with her baseball cap. She's chosen a table in the corner of the patio, and sits next to the white brick wall, her profile to the restaurant's gated entrance. The sun is high overhead, but the rickety turquoise umbrella shades both of us. Ashlyn keeps her sunglasses on.

"What?" I ask. "You okay?" Maybe she's upset over the funeral thing. Well, yeah, she should be.

"I'm worried, Mercer." She spins the saltshaker, spilling a few grains. She dabs them up, tosses them over her left shoulder. Moves the saltshaker away. "I shouldn't have told you about the private-pilot thing. Flying the stolen stuff. And Ron. And Tom."

"That's okay, really," I say. "Don't worry. We're like lawyer-client. It's your book. What you tell me is confidential." I am making this up, completely. There's no confidentiality, none at all, in fact exactly the opposite. But she killed her own daughter, somewhere in all this, so all rule-following is off the table. "We'll only use what you want."

"Um, no, I mean . . ." She takes off her sunglasses, and almost looks sheepish. A new face from our Ashlyn. "I mean—because it's not true."

"What?"

She cleans her glasses on a napkin, ever so diligently, then looks at me from under those lashes, as if she's just had an idea. "I mean, that I know of. But it *could* be true. Right? Tom *is* a pilot. And there's definitely something going on at Hot Stuff. Where'd Ron get the money for that whole business? But yeah. I made it up." She puts her shiny sunglasses back on. "It was just a theory."

I'm glad we're in public, because if we were at home, I'd have thrown her out the front door on her too-tight-jeaned rear. Which I cannot afford to do. But I can't help it, I'm pissed. And Dex hated that word, and now I've mentally said it, and now I'm angry about *that,* too.

"Ashlyn? *Seriously?*" I shift in my chair, which knocks a fork off the table, which clatters on the concrete floor, which creates another flare of anger, a jolt of impatience and frustration. I'm annoyed at myself for feeling sorry for her. I totally fell for it.

"How hard is it to be straight with me?" I try to lower my voice to a publicly-acceptable level, but I refuse to diminish the bitter tone. "Listen. Should I call Katherine? Do you want to do this book or not? Why are you screw—messing with me here?"

"Mercer? Merce?" Ashlyn briefly puts both hands over her face, elbows on the table. Some of her hair escapes from under the Sox cap, two softly curled tendrils. "I know you see right through me, you're so good at this. Yes, I'm avoiding the truth. I know I am. But I'm lost. Totally lost. I don't know what to say or do or tell you. My life is ruined, and my family's life is ruined, and I did—nothing, really nothing, but I'm terrified no one will ever understand."

I pick up the fork, point it at her. "Try me."

"Ladies?" Ken puts down our food, seems to sense he's interrupting. As he quickly leaves, we both shift our plates aside. Ashlyn snaps two packets of sugar with a fingernail, rips them open, and dumps them into her hazelnut coffee. Some of the sugar spills onto the tablecloth.

"Okay. Truly. I'll tell you the whole thing. But you have to hear me out."

I gesture with a dubious flip of my hand, *go on.* I don't trust what I'd say out loud. I'll call Kath if need be. We haven't heard from her, but that's typical Katherine. Predictably unpredictable. Ashlyn's worse.

"Tash and I were doing fine." Her voice is soft, as if remembering a favorite story. "It was difficult, but sometimes when you love someone, you can make things seem possible, you know? I loved Tashie so much that no matter how she'd been born–"

"What's 'how'?"

"Let me tell it, okay? I have to get through it."

I gesture again. Intrigued, against my better judgment.

"No matter how she came into this world. I would have done anything for her. Anything. None of it mattered, and frankly, I thought maybe God had given me this gift as a way for me to turn my life around. No more partying, no crappy jobs, but a real reason to live. My *family.* Know what I mean?"

I can't bring myself to answer that, but she doesn't wait for a reply.

"And then Tasha Nicole got sick," Ashlyn says. "Horribly sick. Cancer. And that's why she was suddenly gone. She was in a private medical facility. Tom had connections, because of his Mercy Flight stuff. But there was no hope for her. No hope for my poor baby girl. And that's why I was fundraising at the student union, that's why that photo was so–difficult and wonderful to see."

I need to be open-minded, but this sounds . . . well, improbable, is my increasingly skeptical reaction. At best unlikely. Okay, it *could* be true.

Ashlyn briefly puts her face in her hands again, then pulls her scarf up close around her, shoulders collapsing. "I don't know,

Mercer, sometimes I think God took her, because God knew she was, I don't know, conceived in brutality, and . . ."

Conceived in brutality? She's still talking, and I am utterly fascinated now.

"And she needed blood transfusions, and I was so worried—if they tested my blood, and Tom's, and what if they somehow found he was the father? Tasha? You know? Her name?"

"Huh?"

"Where's Mercer from, why're you named that?"

Where's *this* going? "Well, Mercer's my Mom's maiden name. She wanted us to preserve a thread of history. But what does that have to do with anything?"

"Yeah. Well. Tasha's a family name, too." Ashlyn's tone is sarcastic. "For Tom and Ashlyn. See? He *made* me name her that. Made me promise never to tell. But she died, so they didn't test. And after that, we told the doctors we were taking her to the funeral home, but really Tom and I flew her to Boston, in his plane, we picked it at random, a place with water, where we didn't know anyone. I knew there had been bodies in the harbor before, even a little girl once. Tasha had been so sick, and . . . we just wanted her to rest in peace."

Tom plus Ashlyn equals Tasha? I try to keep the incredulity out of my expression, and probably fail. Besides. There would be some kind of hospital records. So this does not make any sense. I know the world doesn't always make sense. But still.

"Um, Ashlyn? So you and your stepfather put her in a garbage bag and dumped her in the ocean?"

"It was a burial at sea," she says. "It was probably illegal, but no one was ever supposed to know. The duct tape was to . . . keep the fish away."

Is *that* what she wants in the book? Too keep the *fish* away? Is that supposed to be sympathetic? It's only pathetic. I'm not sure I could write it with a straight face. Unless—is it possible that it could be true?

"What hospital? Why didn't you have a doctor testify? Does Quinn McMorran know this? Or your mother?"

"My *mother?* Listen, Mercer. You heard the trial. You heard her admit it. She's the one who sold my photos. Photos of her own daughter and grandchild! For twenty-freaking-thousand dollars."

"You think she's involved? Somehow? Your mother?"

She sits up straight. Takes off her sunglasses. Points them at me. Puts them back on.

"Holy crap, Mercer," she says. "I never thought of it that way. Until you brought it up. You are *so* right. And I am *so* stupid. She *knew.*"

"Knew what?"

"*All* her bogus testimony." Ashlyn opens her arms, encompassing *all.* "All that totally bogus 'oh, Ashlyn was a good mother stuff.' Bull. She wanted to make it look like *she* was the good mother. *Her!* Not *me.* I totally see it now. Thank you, Mercer. She *knew* it wasn't me. She knew what *really* happened. She was lying her ass off. My own mother! To save her precious Tom. Dis*gust*ing. Him. Over me. I cannot believe it. She *knew.*"

"Ashlyn?" Has she gone off the deep end? I wish I had sunglasses to point back at her. "Knew *what?*"

The patio gate squeaks as more people arrive, and they filter toward the empty tables. A shopping-bag-toting mom and two squabbling preteens. A middle-aged man in a barn jacket, focused on his cell phone. Carmendy, I realize, with another young woman in floaty scarf and short skirt, heads together, giggling over a cell phone screen. Ashlyn and I must look like two chatty suburbanites, sharing coffee on an ordinary Monday.

"We have to go." Ashlyn scrapes back her chair, stands up. "Now. Right now."

"What?" Now I'm beyond baffled. I stand, dig out my wallet, stash twenty bucks for Ken under my saucer. The sunlight changes, slashing a band of light across the table, the spill of sugar sparkling like tiny jewels.

Ashlyn yanks down her ball cap, then reaches out to me, touching my arm. "See the guy who came in? Using the cell phone?" she murmurs.

I start to turn.

"Don't *look*," she says. " Never mind. Let's just go."

I have to trot to keep up with her as she winds between tables and out the patio gate. Head down, looking at the sidewalk, Ashlyn is almost running.

I'm almost out of breath as I reach her side. "Ashlyn?" I say. "What was all that about?"

She stops, stock still, on the pavement. The crosswalk light is beeping that it's our turn to leave the curb, but she ignores it. She tucks her arm through mine, pulls herself closer to me. I smell coffee, and, I swear, my grapefruit shower gel.

"Did you believe that story I told you? Buried at sea, I mean?" Her grip gets stronger. "No, right? I know, it sucks. But you're the writer. You can help me make it better. You've got to create a better story, a believable story about what happened. Or else they'll get me, too."

"Create a . . . ?" I extricate myself from her, taking a step back. "Or else—what?"

"Did you see the guy with the cell phone? Emailing or texting or maybe taking a *photo?*" She gestures back in the direction of Ristretto. "I know he saw you. And me. Of course."

"Taking a photo?"

"That was a juror. A *juror!*" She whispers. "I'll never forget their faces, not ever. That guy's another one who I always thought had it in for me—he never liked me. How did he find me? Why is he following me? And following *you?*"

The crosswalk light goes red, the illuminated stick figure now keeping us on the corner. The sun pools shadows at our feet. "And I'm so sorry, Mercer," Ashlyn says, shaking her head. "Since the cops have my phone, I'm completely out of touch. But I'm so sorry. It seems like *you're* involved now."

CHAPTER FORTY-THREE

A blue-and-gray police car—Boston, not Linsdale—careens by us, blowing through the red light, siren wailing and blue lights ablaze. Our heads swivel as we follow the cruiser's progress. It's turned the corner, and is speeding away down Ardella Street. Toward my house? A silly reaction, since it's not like no one else lives around here, and my neighborhood is hardly off the beaten path. I'd be more worried if it were a fire truck.

Cops come when someone is dead. Everyone I care about is already dead.

Ashlyn's gone pale. Guess no matter how innocent she might profess to be, the arrival of a police officer will probably always be post-traumatically disconcerting to her. What's more, I remind myself, no matter what cockamamie story she continues trying to foist on me, she's *not* innocent.

As the siren fades, I can't figure out what question to ask first.

"And you're saying that whole story you told me—about the—" I purse my lips as we walk, mentally playing back her recitation. "The burial at sea thing. Cancer, and the . . . assault by your stepfather. Tasha's name. That's all not true?"

"Whatever," Ashlyn says. "That's not the point. The point is the only way I'll ever be able to participate in this world again, to have a life, is if we can use the book to convince people I'm innocent. That's why I agreed to do it."

"*Are* you innocent?" I can hear the birds again, a tweeting chaos of sparrows and grackles crowded in the spindly branches of the municipal maple that occupies a grassy patch in the sidewalk.

"Are you not hearing me?" She stops, jams her hands into the back pockets of her jeans, and looks to the sapphire of the summer sky, rolling her eyes, as if I'm too dense to comprehend. "We both know 'not guilty' is not good enough. There's nothing worse than killing a child. There are people who think I didn't get what I deserved. Like that juror, maybe. Now they're out to get me. They'll take it upon themselves to punish me. And that is so mercilessly unfair. You have to help me. You *have* to."

My cell phone rings, buzzing in my purse. I ignore it. It's certainly Katherine, wondering how we're doing. And for that, I have no answer.

"The part about Tom is true," she continues. "But I'm putting all that behind me. The question is, will *they?*"

"Ashlyn?" I've stopped now, almost can't walk and digest her ever-changing stories at the same time. She thinks people are out get her? Since she can't be referring to me, even though I am, who's this "they"?

"Who is 'they'?" I ask her. "Who do you think–?"

"Look." She puts up a palm, like a stop sign. "You remember the day I was sick in court? You know how that happened?"

"Food poisoning?" That's what Joe Rissinelli reported.

"Yup." She nods. "And you know from what? From a sandwich they brought me in jail. It was right after Tom tried to come visit. It has to be connected. That was the only time he showed up– my mother never did. Did you know that? *She* turned her back on me. *He* tried to poison me. Or got someone else to. Crap. They're completely cutting themselves off from me."

"What did you start to tell me about your mother, though? In Ristretto?"

"Gimme a break," she says. "Anyway, fine. If that's how they want it."

She whirls, and starts up the sidewalk.

Ashlyn's a complete nutcase. That's all I can think as I catch up and fall in step beside her. If she's trying to get me to believe everything, how can I believe anything? I'll call Katherine back, resign from this whole thing, return the money, count my blessings. Extricate myself from her. Pure crazy.

"Hey." She pokes my arm with one finger as we walk. "Think about the break-in at Quinn McMorran's house. You *know* they were looking for something. *Or* trying to kill me. The graffiti's like, a diversion."

Ashlyn waves a hand across the horizon, as if pointing, past the guy mowing his lawn, past the kid on the trike, past Jenna and Bob Emerson's famous pink hydrangeas and across the Mass Pike to the shattered windows and profane scrawls spray-painted on her defense attorney's home. "I mean, that alone's gotta convince you. But making me sick? Threatening my lawyer because she defended me? Didn't you think it was bizarre she just—left town?"

"They caught those people, right? Kids."

"Come *on,* Mercer. *Exactly.* Kids. *They're* not the big fish."

We'll turn the corner onto Norwalk Street in a minute, and be home, and then I'll sort this out. I'd also been perplexed by Quinn's departure, but thought maybe she was escaping the scrutiny and pestering reporters. Or remorseful she'd let a child killer go free. Or celebrating her victory.

"I *tried* to explain it to Joe Rissinelli, okay?" Ashlyn says. "He wrote about the food, remember? But I don't know, he seemed sort of—out of it. Maybe it's his divorce thing. But he told me about you, that he would contact you, and so when Katherine brought your name up, too, I thought, okay, perfect. We can all work on it together. *That's* why Joe came to see you. Didn't you wonder why he just showed up?"

Wait, wait, wait. Now it's my turn to stop in the middle of the sidewalk. "What does Joe Rissinelli have to do with this?" He's getting a divorce? Obviously that isn't the most important question, but I need a way to keep track of the players in whatever game this is. The sun is blasting full steam. New England can be as brutally hot in early September as it is brutally cold in February. "Does he know you're working with me on the book?"

"Of course he does." Ashlyn takes off her cap, lifts her hair from her neck, puts the cap back on. "But listen, can we talk inside? I don't see anyone, but I'm worried that juror guy is following us. Or he sent someone else to. Or someone sent *him*."

Despite myself I look around. Juror guy? Someone else? Ashlyn is speaking a language I don't understand. But besides the rumble of that lawn mower, nothing and no one disturbs the suburban mid-morning now, not even an idling mail truck or a nanny trundling a stroller.

We round the corner. I see my willow tree. I see my house.

I see that Boston Police cruiser parked across the street. In front of the Rayburns' house? Did something bad happen to Ezra and Liz? Or their son Derek? There's no one inside the cruiser.

"Shit." Ashlyn hisses, then repeats the word under her breath again, and again. "This is about *me*."

"This isn't about *you!*" I whirl, whispering, almost losing it. The woman is a one-person tug-of-war between paranoia and ego. The world is not about Ashlyn Bryant. "That police car is at the *Rayburns*'. Probably Derek got in trouble for speeding again. Or their cockapoo is lost. Or both."

But Ashlyn runs ahead and I have to keep up. She races up my flagstone walk, takes the two porch steps in one, and at the front door turns to me, holding out her hands, imploring.

"Open the damn door," she says. "And do not say one word to the police about me."

My key clicks the door open, and Ashlyn almost pushes me to get inside.

"I'm not going to lie to the police," I say, closing the door behind us. I move the front curtains apart, feeling absurdly cautious, and peer out. "Besides, the police aren't here. There's no one in the car, Ashlyn. The police are somewhere else. You've had too much sugar and caffeine."

She's taken off her sunglasses, and hangs them on the collar of her black T-shirt. Now I can see what looks like fear in her eyes. "I didn't say *lie*. I only said don't mention me. I'm going to my room. Let me know when the cops are gone."

Was it really fear I saw? Hard to tell, and now she's gone. I hear "her" door shut. Setting my canvas totebag on the entryway table, I scan the living room, ridiculously looking to see if anything is out of place. But of course it isn't.

And then the doorbell rings.

The last time I heard the doorbell it was Katherine, with Ashlyn in tow. This time, when I check the peephole, it's not Katherine.

It's—and I only know this because I saw him on the witness stand—Boston Detective Bryce Overbey. I remember that face. "Dissolute," I'd written in my manuscript. But up close, he's more attractive, almost gentle. He's wearing maybe the same brown tweed jacket he wore to court. My mind is racing to figure out why he's here. Her paranoia aside, it's got to be about Ashlyn. Have they come up with new evidence? What if they're here to arrest her? For what, though?

Or wow, what if they found the real killer? Except—that's Ashlyn. Funny how I have to keep reminding myself of that. And if they'd arrested someone, no reason for them to come tell me. *Oh.* Is it about the accident? It can't be about the accident. That was an accident.

The doorbell rings again. He's got to have seen me checking. I can't stall any longer.

"Detective?" I say as I open the door.

"Detective Bryce Overbey," he says at the same time. "Boston Police." He flips me a gold badge in a black-flapped wallet. "Mercer Hennessey, correct? May I come in?"

There had been two people in the car. Where's the other cop?

I open the door wider, but not quite letting him in. Trying to catalog my rights and his legal responsibilities, but I haven't done anything wrong so there's nothing to fear.

"How can I help you?" I ask. I look over his shoulder, but he's alone. His partner, at one point, was Koletta Hilliard, the detective who tracked down Baby Boston's identity. And the origin of the duct tape. Not that it mattered.

Overbey somehow walks by me, into the entryway. I watch him scan the front closet, the hallway, then the living room, almost faster than I can follow. Has Ashlyn left any of her possessions around? But I suppose they'd look just like mine. Be ironic if Ashlyn were hiding in the closet so she could listen. But I know she isn't.

"We're checking on the whereabouts of Joe Rissinelli." Overbey takes a spiral notebook from an inside pocket. "No one has seen him in the past few days. His wife's upset. More than upset. Any idea where he might be?"

CHAPTER FORTY-FOUR

s he okay?" Not a brilliant question. If the police don't know where Joe is, they certainly don't know if he's okay. "I mean," I say, gesturing Overbey to the couch, "I mean–I guess I don't know what I mean. Why would you think I had any idea?"

"Yours was the last number he called. On his cell phone. But that phone's at his house. So's his car. *He*"–Overbey sits on the couch, without invitation, crosses one leg over the other. Jeans, black leather shoes–"isn't."

Two things I'm juggling now. One, of course, concern for Joe. He's not old, maybe late forty-something? And certainly world-savvy. Is he dead in a culvert somewhere? Or mugged? Couldn't be a car accident, they'd already know about that. But he's a reporter. He'd never leave his phone. Especially if he's on assignment. Unless he has another phone.

The other thing is not exactly fear, but apprehension and confusion. My number is the last he called? I never got a call from him. That I know of.

"Hey!" I say. I wasn't sure whether to sit, so I'd stood by the wing chair, but now I take a few quick steps to the entryway table. Grab my purse, paw through it. "I did get a call, Detective, a little while ago? But I was in the middle of something, and ignored it, so could be that was–"

"That was me." Overbey cocks his head in the direction of the Rayburn house. "Your very helpful neighbors across the street told me you and your girlfriend had gone for a walk. 'As usual,' they said. Does your girlfriend know Joe?"

"*You* called my cell?" I'll avoid his girlfriend reference. "Where'd you get my number?"

"From Mr. Rissinelli's phone, ma'am," Overbey says. "Your name showed up in the contacts. And your address is listed. Just like *Law & Order*."

"Sorry. Of course." I'm an idiot. And somehow nervous. But that means this visit has nothing to do with developments or new evidence in the Tasha case. Not directly. "This is so disturbing. What do you think happened?"

"So." Overbey smiles, so very pleasant, so very patient. "He's a what? Friend? Colleague? Something else? I didn't tell his wife we were coming to see you. Or that her husband did. Yet."

He pauses, as if to let that semi-threat sink in. What does he think I've done?

"He's nothing," I say, "I mean, he's a colleague." I almost say 'was,' which proves how disquieting police questioning can be. "And I heard . . ." Oops. Dumb, Mercer.

"Yeah?"

"I heard he's getting a divorce." Of course I can't say who told me that, so I backfill, hoping he already knows this. "Just through the grapevine."

"Yeah. So any idea where he might be? His wife says he took both their passports. And some of her jewelry. That jog your memory? Why he hasn't been home for three days?"

"No." I widen my eyes, wondering why telling the truth is coming out like it's not the truth. "He's a freelance reporter, so he gets assignments, all over the world I guess, maybe he's on one of those? Did he post on Twitter? He uses that a lot. But there's no reason for him to tell me anything. We only worked together, sort of, informally, covering the Ashlyn Bryant trial," I explain.

If he asks me how that started, or why, I'll have to say I called him. But it was for the book, so there's nothing sinister about that. After this morning, though, seems like Ashlyn knew about it. *She destroys everyone's life she touches.* How many times have I thought that?

"I see," Overbey says. He still has his notebook out, purses his lips at the still-blank pages. "Did you attend the trial?"

"Ah, no. I watched on TV. That's how I knew who you were," I explain. "I was—am—writing a book about it."

Overbey nods. "And Mr. Rissinelli was 'helping' you? What was your relationship with him?"

I can't gauge whether his questions are straightforward, or if he's laying some kind of trap that I don't recognize. This may be a cop trick, to ask a sincere-sounding question, then lower the boom after the answer. Whatever he thinks the boom is in this case.

"Nothing," I say. "We talked about the trial. We had pizza. I haven't seen him, or heard from him, since"—I calculate—"since the jury went out."

"I see." Overbey stands, takes a business card from a flap in his notebook. Hands it to me. "All right, then. Call me if you hear anything. I mean—anything. I'm scheduled dayside, Wednesday through Sunday, eight to four. In the Schroeder building. Show this card if you want to talk in person. But call me anytime. I mean—*any* time."

He eyes the front door, and I feel a ridiculous sense of relief as he heads toward it. I try to remember what I've written about him. I know he's a veteran cop with an impressive conviction rate. Ashlyn Bryant's case did not help his numbers. I bet he's not Ashlyn's biggest fan.

"Detective?" I am pushing my luck here, following him to the door, but I can't help it. He's a major player in a murder trial. I'm the jury now. "For the book I'm writing? I saw your testimony. That must have been so disturbing, seeing Tasha Nicole at Castle Island."

He turns to me. Looks me up and down. Puts his hand on the doorknob. Doesn't answer.

"Detective?" I'm going for it. And crossing fingers Ashlyn isn't eavesdropping. "Even given the not-guilty verdict. Is there a possibility someone *other* than Ashlyn Bryant killed Tasha?"

Silence. But he takes his hand off the doorknob.

"I can't talk about that. Ma'am."

He doesn't move. Okay, I'll try another tack. "Do you know who Tasha's father is? Where he is? Was?"

He doesn't say a word. But doesn't leave. I take this as the go-ahead to keep pushing. Maybe he's waiting until I come up with the question he wants to answer.

"Did you ever see the surveillance video? The video of Ashlyn and her daughter arriving in Boston? Why wasn't that used at trial?" I take the tiniest step closer to him, don't want to crowd him, but I need to keep my voice low. No way to tell if Ashlyn is listening. The guest room is not that far away. She'd have to be right up against the wall to hear—but I still turn my back to the hallway. "Wouldn't it have proved they were both in Boston? Together?"

Silence again. I open my mouth to try another question. But he speaks first.

"Off the record?" he says.

I probably look as surprised as I feel. It's truly unlikely that he would talk to me. Maybe he has an agenda of his own.

"Sure," I agree.

"It got lost. The thumb drive with the video. By a Dayton cop. Just a screwup, he didn't download it, shit happens—sorry, things happen. He seems to be an okay guy."

I rewind my brain. "Rogowicz? Wadleigh Rogowicz."

"Yup. Maybe you should ask him about that," Overbey says. "The newsstand didn't keep a copy, they tape over every month or whatever. Huge snafu. So"—he shrugs—"the judge decided to keep out testimony about it. Rogowicz said you couldn't be certain who it was, anyway. Still. So the cookie crumbles."

"Are you looking for some other killer, though?" I regret the words the moment they come out. It's a cliché, after the O. J. trial. I try to undo. "I mean–are you investigating now? The case would still be open, right, if you think she didn't do it? Or not?"

At this, Overbey's hand goes back onto the doorknob. "Ma'am? You know anything about what defense attorneys do?"

I do, in fact. They marry you and be wonderful and then get killed in car accidents.

"A little," I say out loud.

"Then you'll have noted, as any good defense attorney would, how often Royal Spofford said 'only Ashlyn.' Remember that?" He scratches his head, fingernails at one temple of his graying hair. "If they charge someone else, it'll be damn tough for a different DA to say to a new jury–'well, on the other hand, ladies and gents, maybe it wasn't Only Ashlyn.' Spofford created instant reasonable doubt, Miz Hennessey. This sucker is closed, no matter what the verdict."

I nod, seeing his point. Ashlyn's only a few yards away. Is she hearing this?

"Do *I* think she's guilty?" Overbey takes one step out the door. Turns back to me. Over his shoulder, I can see his cruiser now has someone in the front seat. "Guilty as hell. From day one. Not that it matters."

He adjusts the collar of his jacket, rolls a shoulder. "She's bad news," he says. "That woman wrecks everything she touches. And now I've gotta go find Mr. Rissinelli."

CHAPTER FORTY-FIVE

et's get out of the house," Ashlyn insists. "Go into the back-yard."

I'd told her what Overbey said, not the part about her being guilty, but about Joe being missing. The wife, the passport, the phone call. Now she's tense, frowning, fussing with the couch.

"And turn on some music," she says, over her shoulder. After lifting each white cushion, patting and examining, she's stacked them on the living room floor. She runs her hand along the back edge of the couch frame, as if she's looking for lost change. "I don't like that the cop was in here. Did he go into any other rooms? And where was his partner? She's the bitch who my mother let hide in her kitchen, you know. He could have left a bug. And now they're listening to everything we say."

While I try to decide how to deal with that—in a way that doesn't include laughter or the suggestion of Prozac—she shoves the cushions back into place, then yanks open the sliding glass door to the backyard. I follow her, baffled.

The picnic table is still there. The grass is still green, and smells just-cut, thanks to the monthly yard guy, but seeing the deserted white-fenced enclosure, you might think no one lives here. Dex was the gardener. He said deadheading the daisies and killing weeds made him feel as if he had some control over the universe. Wrong. Now the daisies are dead, too. Sophie used to play out here while her father battled Mother Nature, but when spring arrived this year, I had her redwood swing set carted away. That left a rectangle of holes in the ground, signifying where something used to be. Right.

"What are the holes?" Ashlyn asks. "Sophie's play house?"

"Swing set," I say. End of topic. I slide the door closed behind me, step into the glare of sunshine and soft heat and almost-autumn swish of leaves. "Why would that detective plant a bug in my house?"

"Well, got to think he suspects you're connected with Joe being gone. In some way." Ashlyn peers over the fence, the end facing the sidewalk and street. She turns back to me, hands on hips. "Did he ask about me?"

Because the world is about *you,* even when a person is missing?

"He didn't," I say, not really lying. *I* asked *him* about her. But come to think of it, he never followed up on my "girlfriend" that the Rayburns reported. He's not a dumb cop, that's for sure.

What if he knew Ashlyn was here? And his partner Koletta was watching the house, maybe from the Rayburns' living room. Maybe they've been watching ever since Ashlyn arrived. But why?

This is the problem with being a writer. It's natural to make up the scariest possible scenario, with the most sinister plot, because that's the best possible story. Real life is seldom as dramatic.

But Joe Rissinelli is missing. In real life. That's why Overbey was here, not because of Ashlyn. I shade my eyes from the afternoon sun with one hand and watch her.

She seems to be walking the perimeter of the yard now, lifting her chin and standing on tiptoe to see over the top of the fence every few steps.

"So, Ashlyn? What are you looking for? Joe?" I'm kidding, hope she knows that, as I drag out one of the picnic table benches, making a semicircle gouge in the grass. The redwood is warm as I sit. "Seriously. What's going on? Do you know anything about where Joe is?"

She gives up her reconnaissance and perches against the table, facing me, legs outstretched. Whatever Ashlyn was doing, she still hasn't explained.

"Why would I know where he is?"

The answering a question with a question thing is annoying— an interviewer technique, in fact, but she's not the interviewer.

"Why does Overbey's visit upset you so much?" I ask.

"Kidding me?" She loops her hair out of its ponytail and adjusts it into a new one, her nervous tell. "There were times, sitting in that cell for a *year,* you know? I worried I'd never feel the sun again. And then, just as I begin to believe in the possibility of closure, just as I start hoping the book will save my life and reputation, and I'll maybe have some sort of income, that cop rings your doorbell. That *specific* cop. And you know who his partner is. They're out to get me, I can tell you that. I don't see them out there any more, though. Jerks."

She stands and turns away from me, hands on hips, a petulant child.

"It's not connected to you, Ashlyn," I say to her back. And no matter if that's true or not, I've got to steer her to Tasha. I'm seriously concerned about Joe, but there's nothing I can do. The book is due in ten days, Joe or not. As for "saving her life," as she says, that's hardly gonna be the result. "They're *local* detectives. Joe's a *local* case. They're done with you."

When Ashlyn turns back to me, tears are streaming down her face.

"They'll never let me go." She holds out her palms, entreating. "This is exactly what I was trying to explain. Why the book is so important. Why you have to make the book convincing. You have to create a story that's true enough for people to believe."

"Why do I 'have to' make something up? That's what I don't understand. What's wrong with telling me what really happened?"

"I can't let you write what really happened!" She runs her hands down her face, looks at the sky, then at me. "Because that's the only thing worse than me being guilty. Which I am not."

Before I can come up with a question, she points a forefinger at me.

"You have to figure something out. A story that's like, an *accident,* an unavoidable accident. One that was no one's fault. Like what happened to your daughter. Everyone believes that, right?"

"Because it's true."

"Because everyone *believes* it's true."

"But it *is*–" This is going nowhere. And it's not about me. It's about her.

"But *I* couldn't come up with something true enough. When *I*"–she points to her own chest, then to me–"tried out my story on you, you almost bought it. Almost. But then you didn't."

Part of me wants to stand up and yell: *You are a batshit lunatic.* But yelling is never a good tactic. Especially with someone this volatile. And paranoid.

"Listen. The cops coming to your house?" She points one forefinger at me again, then taps it to her other one as she ticks off her examples. "Joe missing? That juror following me? Or maybe following *you?* I'm so sorry, but I'm starting to believe, I *have* to believe, that it all adds up to–listen. It means I'm in trouble. And I need you to write a story for me."

"But I am. I'm writing the truth."

"No! Don't you see? The real truth will kill me. But listen. If you don't make this book sound true enough, if you can't make me sound innocent enough–I don't know, Mercer. I think you're in trouble, too."

CHAPTER FORTY-SIX

What?" I stiffen my back, which hits against the redwood table as I sit up straight. Earlier today she'd said I was *involved*. "Ow. But—me? I'm in trouble? How the hell am *I* in trouble?"

"Who knows what they think *you* know? Right?" Ashlyn paces to the left, then back toward me, talking as she goes. Gesturing with each point she makes. "You're the big reporter, always getting the story. I agreed to do this for—like Katherine said. To clear my name. But maybe that's impossible. Maybe they're just too powerful. Maybe they think I told you too much. Or I'm about to. I don't know." She throws her hands in the air as she whirls, lets them flop to her sides. "Maybe they don't trust me. Maybe it doesn't matter. Maybe they don't care. Or maybe it's already too late. Maybe I should have run when I had the chance."

How do crazy people talk? I'm trying to remember my abnormal psych classes, oh so many years ago. Some people truly believe their personal universes. "They"? Are "too powerful"? This is all good for the book, I reassure myself. Loonier the better. Except that the loony is living in my house. Do I tell her to leave? Reprise the meet-you-at-the-Holiday Inn idea? But talking can't hurt. Talking is what I want her to do.

"Still. It's odd. Don't you think it's odd? I do." She keeps talking, jittery. Hyper-excited. Like she's having a conversation in shorthand, mostly with herself. "This whole thing? I mean—what could it mean?"

She straddles the bench, one blue-jeaned leg stretched on the grass, the other under the table. Leans toward me. "Let me ask you. When was the time closest to before your husband died that you talked to Katherine Crafts?"

A motorcycle roars down the street, which sets some dog barking, which sets off another dog. "Rocco, hush!" someone yells. A door slams. Normal life continues, but only outside my backyard fence.

I stare past her, through the still-green leaves of the maple across the street and on past the wisps of nimbus marking the turquoise sky. I know when it was. Exactly.

"Why?" I ask.

"Humor me," she says. "When?"

"The day he and our daughter were killed," I say, still looking off in space. "Katherine and I went for brunch, at Ristretto, in fact, to celebrate the new job she was getting at the publishing company. I did errands on Saturday mornings, and always took Sophie, but she'd tipped over her Cheerios, and she was supposed to go to a birthday party, it was a mess, and I was frazzled, and running late, so Dex said he'd stay with her at the party. Then Kath called and said *she* was running late, so we had to push it back an hour, so I wasn't late after all."

I stop, wondering if I can find the voice to go on. Or if I need to. I'd have to say the next thing I knew, they were dead. But I'm not sure I can form those words out loud.

Ashlyn reaches out, touches my arm, so I have to look at her. "It's not your fault," she says. "Though of course, I understand you must feel like it is. Could I ask—did Katherine come to the funeral?"

No. No, it wasn't my fault. I'd imagined more than my share of murky what-if scenarios, but it was an accident. Of course, I had replayed it, over and over, if I hadn't made that brunch date, if Sophie hadn't spilled her cereal, if I'd been more flexible, if we'd all just stayed home. I'd give anything if only.

"The funeral? No," I say. "Katherine was . . ." I shake my head. What's the difference. She was out of town. *Could* it have been my fault?

"And then the next time you heard from her, right?–after I'm sure she said she was sorry a few times and sent flowers or whatever– was when I went on trial for murder. Suddenly she's back at your door. Or did she call you? Pushing you, I bet. Convincing you. She made a big deal of how guilty I was. Right? She was trying to sway your opinion. Mold it from moment one."

"I never thought of it that way," I say. This is absurdly unsettling. Meaningless. Besides, Kath *did* call. For a while. "No. That's not true." I amend my answer. "She called me a bunch of times."

I just stopped calling her back. This is reminding me of guilt I've tried to bury–*bury!* My fault? My tightrope jiggles. Bounces.

"Oh, right," she says. "Trying to be your friend. Smart. I bet she also knew your husband. Before, I mean."

"Well, of course." I search for steady footing. "Sure. We'd hung out. They'd planned my surprise birthday party together. She'd sent his law firm business. So what?"

She narrows her eyes. "And then Joe Rissinelli shows up at your door. Did he tell you Katherine sent him? Or did she?"

Sent? I remember the day they arrived, the day of closing arguments, one soon after the other. I remember I'd noticed they knew each other. But they'd both worked at *City,* so it seemed logical.

"No. Neither of them said that." I'm trying to untangle what Ashlyn is getting at. See if she has a reasonable point. She's nuts, I need to keep remembering that. I'm simply playing along with her non sequiturs.

"Exactly. So now your husband is gone. And Joe Rissinelli is gone." She holds out a finger as she says each name. Nods, as if she's reached some conclusion. Then adds another finger. "Katherine knows me, too. She brought me to you, remember? Did you know she's from Ohio? She never told you that, I bet."

"Ohio? Yeah, she did. I knew that." My brain used to work, I know that. I also know that for the past month I have pushed my limits, sleep deprived and emotionally frazzled, working to untangle the murder of a child whose face insists on morphing into my own daughter's. I've struggled, every day, to keep these things separate, though it's impossible, but the world goes on and I'm doing my best, I tell myself, sitting here in the sun with a crazy person. Doing my best to save my own life. Sometimes it feels like I'm succeeding, sometimes it doesn't.

I stare at the rectangular holes in the ground where the swing set used to be. It's really hot out here. I need water. I need to go inside.

"Exactly." Ashlyn nods, as if she's now discovered the solution to a difficult problem. "Dayton. Ever wonder how she and I got together? Why I'd agree to see her? A reporter, or—whatever she calls herself, editor?"

"She *is* an editor." I frown. I can feel my forehead furrowing. A drip of sweat trickles down the middle of my back. My T-shirt is sticky, and my feet are hot. It had crossed my mind to ask how Kath got access to Ashlyn, but she's spent her life as a journalist. She has connections. That's why she's successful.

"Of course she is," Ashlyn says. "But ever wonder what she does in the other part of her life? How often she might go back home to Ohio? Where she might hang out? Like a certain night club?"

Katherine? At a night club? I wonder if we're talking about the same person. Or in the same language.

Ashlyn stands, looking down at me, shading her eyes with one hand.

"Hey. Did she know Ron Chevalier?" She persists, not waiting for my response. "You know that's not his real name."

"Yeah, I wrote that," I say. "You think she knew Ron? Wait. You knew her in Ohio? She never mentioned that."

"I'm not surprised." Ashlyn shrugs, sits back down on the

bench, flaps one leg over the other. "She probably only told you what she needed to tell you. Next time you talk–hmm, I bet she hasn't called recently, has she?" She's nodding, like she's reading the expression on my face. I'm glad I can't see it because *bafflement* is surely an understatement. "Next time she does? Ask if she knows my stepfather. Well, if you do, she'll lie, so whatever," she says. "She's not going to admit it. It's probably part of the plan."

"What plan?" I stand, stretch my shoulders. I am stiff from sitting too long. My brain is frying. I am about to faint from the heat. I have no idea what Ashlyn is talking about.

"But you're all about the research, right?" She's smiling as she points at me, again, with one forefinger. "Check it out."

CHAPTER FORTY-SEVEN

The smoke detector is shrieking. In the middle of the night. I hit the ceiling, it feels like, then peel myself off as I leap out of bed, heart in my throat. I know the stupid alarm sometimes does that–when the humidity gets too high, or there's dust in the "sensor lens," the instructions had explained. Still, it's terrifying. My first thought is never "it's a false alarm." It's always "I'm going to burn to death."

Ashlyn almost crashes into me in the hallway. I'm in one of Dex's law school basketball shirts. She's in a black camisole and underpants.

"Is something on fire?" Her hair is crazy askew, her eyes wide.

"Do you smell anything?" The shriek of the alarm forces us both to yell, and we clamp hands over our ears. "The alarm sometimes does this, but–"

"The fireplace!" She points down the hall to the living room. "You think they set a *fire?* I'll check there! Or the kitchen!"

"I've gotta turn it off in the basement," I yell over the unrelenting noise as I head to the door in the dining room. Ashlyn dashes down the hall.

Do I smell something? Maybe. Kind of. I try to clear my brain and cover my ears as I rush down the gloomy back stairs. Stupid smoke detector. Dex always promised to get it fixed, but it refused to malfunction when the electrician was here. It never woke Sophie up, the good news and the bad news. That always worried us.

"Dammit!" The pile of video-equipment boxes I'd dumped at the bottom of the stairway almost splats me on the concrete floor. I grab the wooden banister for balance and kick the packing boxes out of the way with one bare foot, my continued swearing obliterated by the intensifying noise.

I find the breaker box. I pull open the dented aluminum door. Dex always handled this. It hasn't happened since he was gone. I find the label—in Dex's blocky printing. I flip the black plastic switch.

Silence.

"It's the kitchen!" Ashlyn calls out.

"What?" I race back up the steps two at a time. Now the alarms go off in my head instead. "What?"

She's holding the toaster cord in her hand, and a wisp of dark smoke rises from a piece of charred bread still in the slot.

"It wasn't a false alarm," she says.

The kitchen reeks of burned toast. "Did you make toast?" I say. Ridiculously. My feet are gritty from the basement floor.

"Huh? Did I—?" she says. "It was turned up all the way. You trying to burn down the house or something? Hey. Kidding. But maybe the thing shorted out, or whatever? Did *you* maybe . . . leave a piece of bread in here? And it stuck? I don't know how these things work."

"Me either. Maybe. Thanks." *Did I?* I'm grateful for a solution, anyway. And the silence. And the lack of a spreading fire. Stupid toaster. "Good thing the alarm woke us up."

"I'm used to alarms. Better this than some guard calling a bed check." Holding its black plastic handles, she dumps the dead toaster into the stainless steel sink, then jams the blackened bread down the disposal. "So this is only a coincidence, right? Crossing fingers. Let's go back to sleep."

"Coincidence with *what?* Why crossing fingers?" The kitchen clock reads 4:31, but these comments of hers—*you think they set a fire?*—aren't throwaway lines.

She shakes her head. Shrugs. "I'm overthinking. I guess. You know? Quinn's house?"

"Ashlyn? There's no connection to—they *caught* those people. Right? But you think someone would set a *fire?* Who?"

"Really. Forget it. Your toaster sucks. So there's nothing."

"But today, in the backyard, you were talking about—" After her ravings about Katherine and Ohio, she'd gone inside to watch TV, then went to her room with a bag of barbeque potato chips and a glass of white wine. I'd tapped on her door for dinner, but she said she just wanted to sleep. So much for working. "You were talking as if you were afraid of someone."

"Yeah, I know." She yawns, fingers her hair away from her face. "I probably panicked, you know? Seeing the police? It brings back so much—so many terrifying memories. And like you said, Quinn's house. I knew I should have disappeared somewhere, right after the verdict. I never should have agreed to this book thing. But honestly, Mercer, I don't think they'd set a fire. Really. No. Like you said, this is not about me, right? Like you said, they caught the guys." She smiles, as if she's admitting her own personality flaw. "Go back to bed."

No way I'm going without answers. And *she's* the one who brought up Quinn's house.

"Ashlyn? They *who?* They—the people who I think you're saying took your daughter? Or killed her? Those they?"

She adjusts the strap of her camisole, then seems to realize she's wearing basically underwear. I see a pink star tattoo on the swell of her breast, just like Quinn described.

"I've got to figure it out," she says. "How much I should really tell you. How much is safe for you to know. It's probably fine." She purses her lips, begins a frown. "I sure hope Joe Rissinelli's okay. You hear from anyone?"

I'm exhausted, and frazzled, and feel like I've had a narrow escape, which I might have, I guess, if the smoke alarm hadn't worked. I understand that she's trying to change the subject, and I'm concerned about Joe, too, but I'm not going to let her distract me with her on-again off-again stories.

"No," I say. "Nothing about Joe. But about tonight, Ashlyn. It's hard for me to decipher what things you tell me are real. Is there someone who even *might* have set a fire? The stuff you told me about Katherine? Quinn's house aside, okay? It makes writing a true-crime book kinda difficult. Since I don't know what's true. You're the only person who does."

"Trust me," she says. "We'll figure it out."

"But you don't have to 'figure out' the truth."

"Yeah," she says. "You do." She touches the toaster in the sink with one finger, then flattens her palm on it. Then turns the faucet on it, dousing it with water. "Let's get some sleep. We have work tomorrow." And she's gone.

It's impossible to sleep and think about a fire at the same time. It's too hot in my bedroom now. And in my imagination. *Quinn's house.* I stick my bare feet out from under the blanket. Stare through the predawn gloom at the swirls on the white ceiling. Could someone set a fire in my house? How? Who? Who's *in* this house anyway, the pizza delivery guy? Ashlyn? But she put it out. And it was only my unreliable toaster. I'm ridiculous. I'm making up stuff again. And embarrassed to be considering a pizza delivery arsonist. I turn on my side, struggling to get comfortable. Did I forget I was making toast? I could have. I guess.

But something else haunts me. I was the one who'd contemplated burning the house down myself, maybe a month ago. And when I heard that alarm, I wanted to live. What does that mean?

I punch the pillow into a different shape. Ashlyn. I don't understand her at all. She's not behaving like—well, yeah. How do I know how someone who'd murdered her own child would behave? She wouldn't go around crying all the time. Unless she thought that was the way someone who *didn't* kill her own child behaved. So a murderer would pretend to be sad. Ashlyn's not sad, real or pretend. Except about herself.

I close my eyes, not only in exhaustion, but in confusion and emotional defeat. How would I appear to someone who'd just met me?

Finally I get up, shower, and write on the mirror, 480, trying to regain my bearings and share the story, but somehow Dex and Sophie don't help. "Please don't leave me," I whisper, touching the edge of the four. "Please."

Ashlyn's up too, and in the kitchen. She presents me with coffee. Skim milk. "You look tired, Mercer," she says. "And listen, I trashed the toaster. So you don't have to think about it."

CHAPTER FORTY-EIGHT

We bring our coffees to the study. Ashlyn's more talkative this morning than she's ever been. She's right, I'm tired, but I'm awake enough to know she's still giving me nothing. She's prattled–that's the only word–about Tasha's birth (horrible until they finally gave her drugs) and seeing her daughter for the first time (tears) and how unhappy she was to be living at "Tom and Georgia's."

"I needed to find a real job," she says. She's standing, her back to me and facing the bookshelves, as if she's fascinated by my collection of journalism memoirs and true-crime books. "And I was hoping it'd be out of town. Dayton was–well, not good. For so many reasons."

She steadfastly dodges questions about the identity of Tasha's father.

"Was it *your* father?" It makes me cringe to do it, but I have to ask. She'd denied it a couple of days ago, insisting I'd "remembered it wrong" because of the wine. But that's ridiculous. Typical Ashlyn. I know she said it. And it seems so repugnantly possible to me. Plus, *she's* the one who had the wine.

"Stepfather," she says, turning to face me.

"Stepfather." Only marginally less hideous. "Was it?"

"Here's the deal." She pulls a book from the shelves. I can't see what it is, but being Ashlyn, she won't put it back, so I'll look later. "I'll tell you about that as soon as I decide how to do it."

It's like talking to quicksand.

But we're almost to the place in the Ashlyn-and-Tasha time-line where, according to all my research, Ashlyn connects with Ron Chevalier and Hot Stuff. If we continue at this pace, the facts (if such a word means something to her) about Tasha's disappearance and death should be coming soon.

Day 5 goes by. Day 6. Day 7.

She's driving me crazy. I'm taking her step-by-step through the trial, transcribing what she says, and then trying to craft that into an outline. She has an explanation, sometimes several of them, for everything. Someone's out to get her, and they took Tasha. Her stepfather is involved. He's bad, he's good, he's rich, he's cash-strapped. He's a child molester, look what he did to me, who knows what he did to Tasha. Her mother knew. Her mother didn't know. Tasha was dying. Valerie is still out there, she must be part of it. Ron is involved. There were drugs at Hot Stuff. There might be drugs. Everything was stolen. Ashlyn knew too much. Ashlyn didn't know anything.

How am I supposed to write anything from this? I've asked her a million times. *Tell me the truth. Tell me what happened.* And she does. Then does it again. Differently. How much of it is fantasy? Or, and I can't stop myself from considering it no matter how I try to avoid it, is it reasonable doubt? I know what I *believe* to be true. But if I don't know for certain, might another story be true?

Anyway, she's constantly underfoot. We'll reach for a paper towel at exactly the same time. Or the TV remote. She drinks the last Diet Pepsi. Doesn't change the toilet paper roll. Leaves towels on the shower rod so I can't close the curtain. Puts dishes in the sink instead of the dishwasher–apparently she thinks I'll clean up after her. The book she'd been examining was the Marcia Clark memoir about prosecuting O. J. Simpson, which would be interesting if it weren't so obvious. I can't even use that detail; people would think I made it up.

It's probably half the pressure and half the impossible assignment–I recognize that–but I'm feeling caged. Imprisoned by a deadline. Trapped in a jail of my own journalistic making. Sharing a cell with a murderer. Trying to search for the answers that'll set me free. Or something. I'm running out of clichés.

Funny that Ashlyn seems to feel just the opposite. She's luxuriating in it all, the couch (where she's claimed the right corner, with the end table and clicker), the fridge, the TV. Her using the bathroom still creeps me out, but Dex and Sophie, back again, thank heaven, have agreed they understand.

We talk in the mornings, and then I work in the study while she sits in the backyard. She's out there now, with an *InStyle* magazine and the sunscreen she took from my linen closet. At least she asked first. I have not said so out loud, but the study, my domain, is still off limits for her, unless I'm there, too.

I'm struggling to hide my annoyance and disdain. And my goals. It's important that she believes I believe her. How many times did I hear Spofford remind the jury that Ashlyn gets rid of whoever is inconvenient? In her way? I don't want that to be me.

We've only been out once, the day after the fire, to get a new toaster. At Home Depot, which was weird. The duct tape displays were still up. And I kept looking for Kelsie. We're getting food delivered from the grocery service now (I save the receipts for Katherine) and Ashlyn flirts with that delivery guy, too. Once I think she let him in as she put the food away—I heard voices from the kitchen. But when I came in from the study to check, she was alone.

I stare at my computer screen. It's already Saturday now, a week since she arrived. Truth is, I'm stalling about the actual writing, and mostly watch trial videos. She thinks I'm working like mad, but I don't want to get invested in her make-believe. If I write it all and she finally tells what really happened, I'll just have to unwrite it. I'm running out of time, though. I know that. Rolling the deadline dice.

She still hasn't confessed, not even close, or given me a pathway to nail her.

It should have been easy to prove whether Ashlyn fabricated the tale about Katherine, but Kath's still not answering her cell or office phone. Predictably unpredictable. I left messages, another one just a minute ago, so she'll certainly call back. She'd told me she lived in Dayton, so that's either something or nothing.

Talk about something or nothing—I haven't heard from Joe Riss either. Or anything about him, and that's bothering me, too. We're not really friends, and never hung out together until the trial, so it's not as if he's suddenly missing from my life, but he's a good guy. I mean, I guess, except for that passport and jewelry thing Overbey made sure I knew. Maybe it's a messy divorce, and the wife is difficult. There's been nothing in the paper or on TV about a missing person, so that's reassuring. Joe's probably on some hush-hush assignment. I would have heard if something had happened.

I hope he's okay. *I'm* sure not. I wish I had someone else to talk to, bounce ideas off, or provide a second opinion on Ashlyn's mental state. But I have to rely on myself.

"Good morning," she says, as she comes into the study, cutoffs and flip-flops, coffee mug in hand. She sits, as usual, in the Sophie chair, which I struggle not to refer to as the Ashlyn chair. "You hear from Katherine?"

Katherine again. "Nope. But she knows we're writing. She'll call, when it gets closer to the deadline."

"Pretty close now, though, right? It's like, Saturday. A week to go. Seems odd." She sips her coffee. "Was she acting weird, or anything? Last time you saw her? I mean, before I came? Like worried? Or upset?"

I save the manuscript page I was sort of working on, and think about that. In fact, yes. Kath *was* upset. There was the bomb scare at Arbor Books. And she thought she was being followed by someone in a silver car. But I don't need to tell that to Ashlyn.

"No more than usual," I lie. I add a smile. "She's an editor, she always worries."

"Really? No?" Ashlyn seems to consider that. "She told *me* she was freaking out over being followed by somebody in a silver car. And there was a bomb scare at her office. And she told me she'd told you that stuff."

"Oh, right." So begins the cover-up. "Guess I forgot."

"You forgot. Yeah, okay. You *forgot.*"

I open the manuscript to a different section, preparing to change the subject. Wondering why Kath mentioned that to Ashlyn.

"Why does that matter?" I can't believe I'm taking the bait. And now trying to make my lie make sense. "It could have been anyone. There's a bomb-scare *thing,* schools and stuff. Your trial. It's a constant problem in Boston. And people drive like maniacs in Massachusetts."

"Sure," Ashlyn says. "Or else . . ."

Silence.

"Or else—someone was trying to warn her to stay away from this story."

Silence. I cross my arms on the desk, lean forward. "Listen. Ashlyn? If you know something, why don't you just tell me? Is Katherine involved in—" Oh, *stop.* I am not getting sucked in to this. I try to keep the impatience out of my voice. "Is there something I need to know?"

"You already know it. I did not kill my daughter." Ashlyn extends her arms above her head, fingers stretching to the ceiling, her black T-shirt lifting to expose a pinkly tanned abdomen. Then she points to me with two forefingers. "But you won't let yourself believe it. If that guy Royal Spofford and a slew of cops and detectives couldn't convince a jury I did it, why do you think *you* can? But you're so full of your writer self—you think I'm guilty, and you're creating a whole reality to prove I am."

"That's just not true." Where's this coming from? "We've had this discussion, Ashlyn."

"I know, right? With you trying to persuade me you're like,

'open to the real story.' But I can totally tell you're not. I've told you some perfectly logical ways Tasha could have–" She stops. Screeches to a halt, midsentence.

"I'm looking for the truth, Ashlyn," I say in the silence. "That's all. I want to write the truth. Wouldn't it be . . . easier? To simply tell me that?"

She covers her face with both palms, and her thin shoulders quiver, her hair tumbling over her hands.

"My daughter is dead," she wails through her fingers, and when she takes her hands away, her face is splotched with red and her wet lashes glisten. "You never ask me about *that*. Never ask me if I miss her, or how I can live without her, or anything, *anything* like that. Every night I cry and cry and cry into my pillow, terrified you'll hear me." She wipes the tears from her flushed cheeks, one side, then the other.

"I'm her mother," she whispers. "Her *mother*."

CHAPTER FORTY-NINE

She ran out of the room after that, and I heard her flop onto her bed. I mean, the guest bed. I thought about going in to comfort her, but is that my role? My list asks *Why A not sad abt Tasha?* Maybe she is. Maybe I subconsciously didn't want to go there, so I never brought it up. But she didn't either. But then again, I didn't either.

I stare at the open manuscript now, the words swimming in front of me and the task looming impossibly, like I'm trying to write in a foreign language.

Is she trying to convince me she's innocent? Or is she trying to get me to see there are other ways Tasha would have been killed? And as a result, make me understand there's reasonable doubt? And if there is . . . who am I to raise the bar on justice?

Leaning back in my chair, I feel the beginnings of a deadline headache. No matter what I ask, Ashlyn won't give me more details about Katherine. My theory is that she concocts the beginning of a story, then can't come up with a believable way to finish it. She'd bragged to Sandie DiOrio that she was good at making stuff up. But maybe not as good as she thinks. This is me she's talking to. I already know the real story. Or, most of it. I think.

I look at my trusty list of questions, only some of which are getting answered. I hear her open, then close, the slider to the backyard. Good. Let her calm down out there. And in here, I'll cure my deadline headache by planning my next move.

She emerges for dinner—pizza again. *I missed it so much,* she'd said. *Thanks for letting me binge.* She seems to be over her sorrow, and her suspicions of me, so I pretend her tears and accusations never happened. We avoid reality, whatever that is, and a few tentative hours go by.

I'm back on my tightrope. Waiting for the right moment to tackle another item on the list. The duct tape.

There's no way she can explain away the duct tape. It clearly came from Ohio, so said the witness. And that's about the only thing in this whole saga that's unwaveringly true.

"Can you believe we've been together a whole week?" I pour her another glass of white. We're into our late-night sitting-on-the-couch ritual, which I think encourages the increasingly sun-baked and possibly wine-vulnerable Ashlyn to talk.

"I know you're sad, and I'm so sorry." I go on, lying, but refuse to go as far as "I know how you feel." "You better now?"

She says nothing, takes a sip. I wait.

She clicks on Lifetime, some show about tumble-haired teen-age girls and a cute-but-sinister science teacher. I wait.

"The duct tape on the fridge at your house." I finally broach it over our third glass, after she's clicked through a few shows on Hallmark and SyFy, and finally left the TV on, but muted, showing *Law and Order.* The woman has no sense of irony. "I'm thinking, how do you explain that? I mean, how do *we* explain that?"

"Explain? Duct tape on the fridge?" Ashlyn smiles. We're two chums chatting on a Saturday night in front of an empty fireplace and a humming TV. "Well, the thing on the bottom kept coming off, so Mom fixed it with duct tape."

"Yeah, that's what she and Detective Hilliard testified. But you know what I mean, Ashlyn. How do you explain that the same duct tape was on–in–" I don't want her to start crying again. "Involved."

Ashlyn swirls her chilled sauvignon blanc, watching it spin in the stemmed glass. "Remind me. Did anyone ever testify the duct tape on the fridge was the same *roll* as the tape used in the—" She looks at me. "Involved?"

I scratch my head, pretending I had to think about that. "No."

"So what's the big deal?"

"Well, the tape on Tasha, forgive me, was Ohio tape. And there was tape like that in your home."

"And millions of other homes in Ohio, certainly, or that company would be out of business." Ashlyn drains her glass. "And it wasn't *on* Tasha. If you remember. So your question is?"

"How do we explain that connection, though?" I persist. "Of all the duct tape in all Ohio, how did it get used in a crime that took place in Massachusetts?"

"Explain." Ashlyn tilts her head. "Explain? You know what? I gotta say I still kind of don't get this. You're going through the whole trial with me. Like I have to *prove* I'm not guilty. But—" She runs a finger around the rim of her wineglass. "But the jury already *decided* I'm not guilty."

I begin to apologize, then switch gears. I'll go with the old "best defense is a good offense."

"You want to stop? That's okay, seriously." I keep my voice polite, even sympathetic. To prove I'm not threatening her. You don't want to threaten Ashlyn. "I'm only the hired hand. Katherine and Arbor Books are paying me to write your redemption. Correct?" I don't pause to let her respond. "That's what I agreed to do, Ashlyn. But, and I don't mean to sound harsh, really I don't, but if you can't handle the hard questions, then how am I supposed to provide the answers? Questions aren't criticism. They don't mean I'm against you, or trying to hurt you. They're just questions that need to be answered. I'm only doing my job. *My* part of *our* job."

She takes a tube of lip gloss from a side pocket of her thin gray jersey hoodie. Slides out the sticky applicator, smooths a glow of transparent raspberry over her lips, back, and forth. Pauses, holding the still-glistening wand.

"Ever hear anyone say I didn't love Tasha?" she asks.

"Ah, nope."

She jabs the lip gloss at me. "Did you ever, ever hear anyone say the slightest thing, not counting Spofford trying to make me sound like a monster, but some real person, witness, or friend, or cop, even my parents, say anything that ever sounded like Tashie and I were anything but happy?"

"No, but–"

"And don't you think, *Mercer,* don't you think that if there was anyone, *anyone,* who would have been able to say anything specific at all about my horrible motherhood, *anything,* that Spofford would have put that person on the stand and dragged every disgusting part of my life into the spotlight? On international television? But there was nothing, right? And no one."

"Ah, sure, I completely understand." I'll let her think she's making a point. This 'good mother' stuff is meaningless. As if you would hit your kid in front of someone.

"All the so-called evidence is circumstantial." She tucks the tube away. "And the jury, thank God, understood that. So why do I have to explain anything?"

"Because for the book–" I begin.

"Remember when McMorran brought on the crime scene tech person to testify?" She cuts me off. "Let's watch that part. It was pretty short, if I remember right." She tilts her wineglass at me. "And I do."

"Sure," I say. "But it's so late. Maybe let's wait until tomorr–"

"No," she cuts me off. "I'll run to the bathroom. You go get your tablet. Now or never."

When I get back, she's back, too, and has poured more wine in both of our glasses. I find the clip, and hold the screen so both of us can see, and push Play.

We watch Quinn McMorran as if in another life, because we don't know where she is now, march across the brown courtroom carpeting to a glowing projector. The screen is still white, and blank.

"That's where Spofford just took down the crime scene photos," Ashlyn says.

"Did you look? When he showed them?" I've already asked her that, but I want to see if she's keeping track of what she's told me.

"Kidding me?" she says. "I have enough nightmares without seeing what happened—somehow—to Tasha. And like I said, I was still half-believing it wasn't her."

In the video, McMorran snaps off the projector switch. As the courtroom lights come back up, she returns to the defense table, walking deliberately.

"What were you thinking right then?" I ask.

"I was in another world, kind of," she says, her voice soft. "I think she touches me and, yeah. See?"

Video Quinn stands behind video Ashlyn, and puts a hand on her client's shoulder.

"Then I did look," Ashlyn says. "At that cop on the stand. See how she hasn't budged? Here comes the part I want you to remember. Listen."

"Officer Ruocco," McMorran is saying. "Is there any evidence in those photos, tragic as they are, that links whatever caused whatever happened to the little girl—is there any evidence that links that death to my client? Anything at all?"

The entire courtroom stayed still, I remember that. Not a breath, not a motion, not a sound.

The woman on the stand—blinking in restored light—touches one of her gold earrings. She shakes her head.

"No."

"And that's all." Ashlyn pushes the stop button on the video. "That was the end of her testimony, right? There was nothing, nothing, nothing. And they don't even know how Tasha died."

"Do *you?*" I can't resist asking.

Now the living room is more silent than silent. The air thick with emotion and history, and the fate—not fate!—of a little girl. And the future of her mother.

"Let me ask you this, Mercer. Like the lawyers do. Just yes or no. Do you think I did it?" She points at herself, poking one finger into her chest. "Killed my own daughter? After the jury decided I didn't?"

"Of course not." What else am I gonna say. She left out the proved beyond a reasonable doubt part. And I'm the jury now.

"Because if you're trying to . . . I don't know. I'm so scared," she says. She's full-out crying again, and looks at me, lashes wet, snuffling. "No one believes me. No one. I bet the jury still thinks I did it. That's why we *have* to—do you *promise*—"

I pick up my wine.

"Wait. That's mine," she says. "Not yours."

"No, it isn't," I say. "I don't think." I remember my glass was more full, but she'd topped them off while I was gone.

"Drink this one." She hands me the other glass. "Don't want you to get my cold. I guess I moved them while you were getting the tablet."

"Fine," I say. And take a sip.

"Do you promise you're writing to save me?" She wipes her eyes. "You and I, Mercer, we're still alive! I know you're sad, I know you miss your daughter. Don't you think I know exactly how you feel? But it's unfair if you take everything out on *me.* You promise, sacred word of honor, on the souls of your daughter and your husband, that you're writing the redemption book?"

Promise on Sophie and Dex?

She keeps talking, doesn't acknowledge that I haven't answered her repulsive *sacred word of honor* demand.

"Because, Mercer? I need to show the verdict is true. But the parts of our book I've seen—*your* book really—sound like I'm the most horrible person on the planet. That the jury was wrong. And I'm a . . . a murderer."

"Ashlyn. Listen. It was a draft. And even you have to admit, the book would've been written that way if you were found guilty. Right?"

"But now—"

"Exactly." I raise my glass to her, then take another drink of the now-tepid sauvignon blanc. "Now we're writing it that you're *not* guilty."

Not guilty in the jury's opinion. But exactly the opposite in mine. It's like Schrödinger's cat, dead and alive at the same time. That's Ashlyn and the book. Guilty and not guilty at the same time.

CHAPTER FIFTY

How are you feeling?" Ashlyn's already in the kitchen, up before I am this morning. It's just after ten. She's washing the wineglasses.

"Huh?" I say, guessing she's being polite. Maybe she can tell I have a headache. Another headache. "Fine, how about you?"

So thirsty. I get a bottle of water from the fridge. Maybe this will erase the bad taste of Ashlyn's cross-examination of my motives last night. I'm struggling to wake up, too. I'd slept like "long," as Sophie used to say. But we've got to get this show on the road. I'll say whatever it takes to get her to talk. Keep her happy.

"I'm sorry about last night," she says. "Being kind of a bitch. Too much wine, maybe. But . . ."

"You're still up for this, aren't you?" I take a big slug of water. "Should I call Katherine and say we can't do it? I hope not."

"What's the diff? Katherine told us, like sitting right in this kitchen, you guys would write the book with or without me, remember?" Ashlyn drapes the string of a mesh bag over the back of her chair—my chair—and pulls the sugar bowl across the kitchen table toward her. "I don't have much choice."

"So, truce, then?" I put in a coffee pod, get out the milk. Last Sunday morning at this time Ashlyn and I had spent one night under the same roof. Now a week later, it seems like a lifetime. "Let's start with the premise you didn't have anything to do with it."

"Okay, yeah . . ." She spins the sugar bowl, once, twice. "Isn't that what we were *always* doing?"

"Exactly." Oops. I have such a headache. But I press on, all congenial as I join her at the table. In Sophie's chair. "So since that means the story Royal Spofford told *didn't* happen, we can't avoid talking about what *did* happen. I mean, at some point, we've got to face it. State it. Clarify it. That's the whole point of the book, Ash. We need to give the public some answers."

Ashlyn stirs her coffee. "I told you I don't know—"

"Yeah," I say. "But like—where you were. What you were doing. We could do a timeline. Hang on." I reach back and open my junk drawer, repository of a tiny screwdriver, a few old matchbooks, random wine corks, and a million rubber bands. I rummage through and find the cheap little calendar, the one I remembered the life-insurance guy left. It's been there since—well, as the bathroom mirror knows, I don't need a calendar to count exactly how many days it's been since I saw *my* daughter alive. "Here. Show me. When was the last time you saw Tasha?"

"Okay." She points to a week the year before last. "Somewhere in here."

"When, though?"

She points again, touching the flimsy page. "That Tuesday. I dropped her at Laughtry Drive. As usual."

"And did you pick her up?" I circle the day on the calendar.

"I . . ." She takes a breath. "I called my parents to say I'd get her the next day, and if that was okay, I was going to Ron's."

"And then?" I take the calendar back, rip off the page, tuck it in my pocket. Shove the rest back into the drawer. Wonder if there's Advil in there.

"The next day I went to pick her up. And she wasn't there. My mother wasn't there, either. My father told me—I wasn't to say a word."

"Your father."

"Stepfather."

"What did he tell you? Not say a word about what?"

"Is this what we're supposed to be doing?" She gets up, puts two English muffins in the new toaster. Her cutoffs are very short, but she's twenty-something, and I suppose that's what they wear. "Aren't we supposed to be going over the trial, like we were before?"

"Sure, we'll do that. But Ashlyn, why didn't you tell anyone you'd dropped her at your parents and she wasn't there the next day? I mean, isn't that an instant 'not guilty'? Wait—are you saying now your *parents* killed Tasha? And tried to frame you for it? Your stepfather? Your mother? Your stepfather didn't testify. Is that why? If Quinn *knew* all that—"

Ashlyn nods.

"—why didn't she call him?" I finish my sentence. "Or why didn't *you* testify to that?"

"I wanted to! I truly wanted to." She leans toward me, pushes her coffee away. "I wanted to get up there and rip that jerk Spofford's face off. But Quinn wouldn't let me. She said she was pretty sure I'd be found not guilty—there were no forensics, remember? They couldn't prove when and where and how Tasha died. I remember her exact words about me testifying. I'll tell you if you don't use them."

I hold out both palms, agreeing. She makes such a big deal out of everything.

She opens her mesh bag and takes out a tube—my tube—of citrusy-sweet sunscreen, and squeezes a melon-colored strip onto her bare leg.

"She told me, 'you'd better keep quiet.'" Ashlyn smooths on the orange goo, wipes her hand on her—my—cloth napkin. "She said, 'The only thing you could do is screw it up.' Exact words."

The coffeemaker beeps that it's out of water just as the muffins pop from the toaster.

Ashlyn coats her other leg. Then stands. "I'll go get the newspaper," she says.

Screw it up. I mull that over. Quinn was only invested in a not guilty. It's the verdict that matters to her, not the reality. But if

Ashlyn knew what happened, or offered some remotely plausible explanation, wouldn't Quinn have followed that reasonable doubt to the ends of the earth? Why not show who the real killer is? Why not set up a sensational Perry Mason moment and hit the verdict out of the ballpark?

I smell the sweetness of mango sunscreen before I see Ashlyn in the kitchen door. Does it take this long to get the paper?

She puts the thick Sunday *Globe,* encased in its yellow plastic wrapper, on the kitchen table.

"Is there a cat in the neighborhood?" she asks.

"I don't know," I say. Cat? "Why? Did you see a cat?"

She shrugs. "Nope. But there was a dead chipmunk on your front steps. A baby."

"What?" I stand, thinking of my bare feet and wondering where I put the dustpan. The English muffins lose their appeal. "Poor little thing," I say.

"Yeah," she says. "I got rid of it."

CHAPTER FIFTY-ONE

I peel off my T-shirt, push back the shower curtain, turn on the faucet. We're meeting in the study in fifteen. Wonder what Ashlyn's story of the day will be.

It's naive of me to expect her to make sense. She's a liar. *That's* why she didn't testify. Of course I haven't forgotten her "they're out to get me" and "you're involved, too" pronouncements, but she dodges every time I ask her to clarify. Changes the subject, or says she was kidding, or says it doesn't matter. Truth is, she was lying.

She admitted lying to Joe Riss, too. Wonder if Katherine knows he's missing? If he's missing. I haven't heard from her. Or him. So I have no one to ask. Should I call Overbey? Or does that make me look suspicious? That's ridiculous, but who knows what he thinks. Besides, I could never let Ashlyn know I called him.

Quicksand.

I reach a hand into the shower, testing. I have to admit, though, with a whole week gone by, I'm losing hope I can trick Ashlyn into confessing. In truth, I'm flat-out failing. Like Wadleigh Rogowicz. And like Royal Spofford, who—as Ashlyn herself reminded me—wielded the power of law enforcement and the entire judicial system. *I'm only a writer,* I reassure myself as the shower water finally heats up enough. There is a truth, there is a justice, but maybe I'm not the one who can find it. I have *such* a headache.

Immersed in soapsuds, I feel like I'm washing more than a dead creature off me, even though I wasn't the one who disposed of it. Maybe I should decide that whatever her story is, fine. I'm paid to write it. Besides, the only thing worse than letting a crazy murderer go free is a crusading reporter getting it wrong.

When I write our numbers on the mirror, 484, I try hard to connect. "Is it possible she's innocent?" I whisper. But Dex and Sophie don't answer. "Would it be okay if I let go? If I gave up on this?" No answer to that either. I have *such* a headache. Might as well face reality. I have a hangover.

I open the medicine cabinet for ibuprofen, and as I take out the white plastic bottle, I see my labeled prescription container of Ambien. Which is not where it usually is. Or is it?

Advil, hand lotion, aspirin. All where I left them. Tiny faceted perfume samples. Three lipsticks. All in place. And the Ambien. Which is not.

The sleeping pills are mostly there for backup. I haven't taken one in months, but it's reassuring to know they're available. I put down the Advil and secure the towel I've wrapped around me, cinching it tighter. I twist open the Ambien bottle, rattle the pills. What I'm looking for, I don't know. I have no idea how many orange ovals were left.

I twist the bottle closed. This headache is a hangover. Too much wine.

Wine. I think of the wine. And then Ashlyn's insistence that I had the wrong glass. If someone—Ashlyn—put pills in my wine, she certainly wouldn't be so stupid as to essentially point it out. If you're gonna drug someone, you've got to be more subtle than that. If she'd blown it, she simply wouldn't drink hers. And try her ploy again later.

Plus, wouldn't I have tasted it? You can't just put medicine in wine and expect someone not to notice. Unless it's the third glass, maybe.

But what would be her goal?

I turn on the water in the sink to splash my face. When I bend over, my towel falls to the floor. The chill I feel may not be only because I'm naked. The running water reminds me of this morning. When I came into the kitchen, Ashlyn was washing the wineglasses. I thought she'd decided to be helpful.

I wrap the towel again, and slug down four ibuprofen. When I put back the pills and close the mirrored cabinet, my numbers are gone.

What are Dex and Sophie trying to tell me? I open the cabinet again, take out the pills. Clutching my towel and pill bottle in hand, I take the two steps into the hall, then one step into my bedroom. Close the door. Think.

Am I the crazy one?

If Ashlyn gets rid of whatever gets in her way, and she's decided I'm in her way, and she tries to kill me, that'd be completely stupid. She'd be the first suspect. But wait. My shoulders sag, and I lean against the closed bedroom door. If she runs? They wouldn't even look for her. No one knows she's here. Except for Quinn. Who's gone. And Kath. Who's been out of touch. And Joe. Who's strangely unavailable.

And yeah, I'm the one who hid her from the cops.

Am I the crazy one?

I open the top drawer of my dresser, scoot aside the folded underwear and my passport and my envelope of secret money—secret from who?—and stash the pill bottle way in the back. Like that's not the first place someone would look. But no one is going to look. I take the pill bottle out, and push it between and mattress and the box spring. Like that's not the second place someone would look. Maybe I should just dump the pills down the toilet, flush, and then they'll be gone. And with that flush, I'd punish only myself, since I've made up this entire drama about a pill bottle that may or may not have moved.

I *am* the crazy one.

But I'll leave them under the mattress for now.

Ashlyn's in the study. Standing in front of my desk. Almost blocking it from me. Shadows from the shutter slats behind the open curtains make prison bars on her face.

"Hi, Merce," she says. As if we hadn't just been talking. "Can I confess something to you?"

My face must have some kind of surprised look, I can feel it, but this is the last thing I'd expected. Confess? Hey. Maybe to get what you want, you have to give up the quest and let go. Maybe I'm wrong about the pills. I'm dry and dressed. The ibuprofen seems to be working. If Ashlyn the Drama Queen wants to confess, I don't care if she was in the study alone. I'm ready.

"Confess?"

"Yeah. I took one of your Ambiens," she says. "I've been feeling guilty about it all morning. You probably wouldn't miss it, but I couldn't sleep, not after last night, and I was so upset. And then I–like this morning, I couldn't remember if I'd put the bottle back in the right place, so, I don't know, I didn't want you to worry. Or like, think I was a sneak or something."

"I didn't notice," I lie. Now I'll have to put them back. Because she'll certainly look the next time she's in there. Checking to see if I'm telling the truth.

But wait. Does she mean she "took" it? Like swallowed it? Or took it? As in–took it from the bottle and put it in my wine? I certainly can't ask. And whatever the answer, it might not be true. But I still have to put the rest of the pills back. It's a signal, almost, that I trust her. Which I don't.

"So I owe you, now," she's saying, smiling as she perches on the edge of the big chair. "And really, thanks for your patience. I tend to be kinda mood-swingy, you know? I can't get past that I'm always waiting for the bad thing to happen, like it always does, and I can't do anything to stop it. But fire up that laptop, okay? And I'll tell you an important part of the story."

"Okay," I say. Ambien episode over, apparently. As I open a new file, I think–will the truth be true this time?

Ashlyn's scooted back into the big study chair, the soles of her bare feet on one upholstered arm. Sophie used to sit that way, but I'm not thinking about that. Sophie's legs were much shorter, and

I loved how her bright-blue stripey dress matched the narrow stripes in the chair.

"Let me ask you something, Mercer," Ashlyn is saying. "Who do you think Tasha's father is?" She gives a tiny smile. "I know you talked to Joe Rissinelli about it."

She knows? How? I had my uncertainties about Joe, but it's odd that he told her that he told me. Although, since I know that part is true, it's possible Ashlyn's finally about to spill something else that's true. I need to encourage her to keep talking.

"Joe's a colleague, sure. But he's never told me he met with you, or interviewed you. Let alone revealed whatever you might have said." I'm twisting the truth a bit here, trying to protect a fellow reporter. Wherever he is. I've continued leaving messages on his phone, but he doesn't have it. Or didn't. And the police still haven't called. "Did you tell him who Tasha's father is?"

"Was." Ashlyn corrects me, pointing a finger. "I told Joe, like, off the record? That Tasha's father was dead. Killed in a car accident before Tasha was born. But to prove I trust you, I'll confess about that, too. I made that up. I had to protect myself, didn't I? From having people know the real truth?"

My brain shuffles possibilities, then reshuffles them. I can almost hear the sound of it. Protect? Real truth? Joe had told me Tasha's father was killed in a car accident. No way could I forget that. And his name was . . . ah. Unusual, like–Marker. Darker. Barker. Barker . . . Holt.

"But Mercer," Ashlyn goes on. "Who do you think would be the one person, the *one,* that would not only ruin my life, but Tasha's and my so-called family's?"

"Ashlyn? The one person?" I flap down the laptop so I can see her. "I–I don't want to guess."

"Tom. Tom. Tom." Her voice darkens each time she repeats her stepfather's name. She draws her knees close to her chest. "Mercer? My stepfather raped me, more than once, and threatened he'd kill me if I told. He said no one would ever believe me, that no one—"

I shouldn't interrupt, but this is exactly what I'd been getting at for the past however many days. She claimed she hadn't told me anything like that. I remember her denials perfectly. Because I didn't believe them. That "Tom plus Ashlyn" thing had been pretty darn convincing.

"But Ashlyn, when I tried to bring that up the morning after you first mentioned it, you insisted—"

She puffs out a breath. Her arms tighten around her legs. "It's not that fun to talk about. I've never discussed it with anyone. Not *any*one. But that's why I've been so—I don't know. Difficult about this."

I let that hang for a moment, wondering if the truth has a different sound.

"I'm so sorry," I feel I need to say. "But Ashlyn, if you knew . . ." Thin ice here. "If you knew your stepfather was the father of your child—why did you—I mean, why didn't you . . ."

"It was a *life*, Mercer. How could I take a life? What mother could do that?"

And with that she bursts into tears, and I can't help it, I do, too. I go to the chair, crowding next to her, and put one arm around her shoulders. We're both crying, and I'm thinking of Sophie, and how often I comforted her in this very chair, for her earache, or a stubbed toe, or something she wasn't even old enough to articulate. My poor tiny little Sophie, and I can't help it, I'm crying too hard, and Ashlyn is, too. I can feel her body trembling, and she's so thin I can feel her bones and the sharp jab of her shoulder blade, and I think about Dex, and how much Sophie loved him. And me. And us. And here's Ashlyn, twenty-something and single, and her baby daughter relying on her for the entire world, not knowing, consciously, that she was missing a father.

It's almost awkward, the muffled sounds of our tears, and being so close to her, and now the silence. The ghosts of our loss. I'm not her friend. But I cannot ignore her. No matter what, I know how she must feel. She must.

I have to get up, somehow get us back to an equilibrium, balancing not only our shared, or not-shared, grief, but our roles in this project.

"Want some water?" I say, edging toward the door. My nose is probably red, and my eyes, too. Hers are, as she looks up at me.

"It was probably selfish, to keep her, I mean," she whispers. She wipes her eyes with a corner of her pink T-shirt. "I couldn't promise a wonderful future for that sweet baby inside me."

She adjusts herself in the chair, straightens her back. Shakes her head as she continues. "But when I finally faced the fact that I was pregnant, it was probably too late anyway."

"I'm so sorry, Ashlyn." Being genuine now. I mean, who wouldn't be sorry.

She slaps her palms on the arms of the chair, one on each. As if closing a chapter, and opening another. "But. Tom." Her voice goes harsher, and she tosses her hair. "Tom insisted he'd make my life miserable if I said a word. He told me to 'make up' a father. A one-night stand, or something. He even said, 'You're such a party girl, no one will be surprised.'"

"Really?" I perch against the edge of the desk. Talk about harsh.

"Yeah. He said my baby would be taken away. I couldn't decide how I felt about that, a creature who'd been given life by mistake, what would be the best? I was so confused. And then, so, I had to get out of the house and I had to get away, and I wouldn't, couldn't, could *never* tell my mother or anyone, not anyone . . ."

I try to picture all this as Ashlyn's words spill out faster and faster. Try to compare what I know with this new reality. But what do I know is true? I'd read about the Bryants in newspapers and magazines, that's how I "know" what they did and said and thought. But all that's only what some writer like me decided to *make* true.

Ashlyn's still talking but my brain is spiraling into meltdown. Maybe I've spent the last week trying to ruin someone's life, ruin it more than it was already ruined. Maybe I should be using the power of the written word–*my* words–for good. Instead of . . . whatever I thought I was doing.

If I decided in advance not to believe a word she says, how can I be a fair jury? I'm exactly like Juror G, making up my mind without the facts. But unlike Juror G, I'm still in a position to make a horrendous decision. And make it public. And accept a lot of money for my lies. My heart begins to race, I can hear it, I swear, the rush and pounding in my ears.

I'd kept asking Ashlyn to explain. She came up with answers, but then, every time, she confessed they weren't true. But if she truly doesn't know, as she keeps saying she doesn't, she wouldn't be *able* to tell me. No matter how many times or how cleverly I ask.

Will it help Sophie and Dex if I write a book saying she's guilty if she's not? What if–I feel my brain take a tentative step–what if she's innocent?

Maybe this is what Dex and Sophie have been trying to tell me. That I'm wrong. *I'm wrong?* Someone else killed Tasha Nicole? But who?

I begin to rearrange the puzzle as Ashlyn talks. Undo my own Rubik's Cube. See if the pieces might fit together in a different way. A predatory stepfather. A hateful jealous mother. Stolen goods. Ron? Drugs. Valerie? Luke? Ashlyn's chloroform explanation, what if that's true? No chloroform was found, not anywhere.

So how could she have killed Tasha with chloroform? No one ever explained that. The jury certainly didn't believe she did.

Even the wet T-shirt. She had a perfectly innocent explanation for that, too.

She has an explanation for everything. But what if it's not "explanation"? What if it's truth?

Ashlyn as victim. As *terrified* victim. Ensnared in the lies of others. I test the possibly reality of this new vision, the colors clicking into a new pattern.

A pattern that means I've misjudged, assumed, let my own depression poison another human being's life.

Maybe Katherine's right. Maybe this *is* a redemption book.

Redemption of *me*.

"Ashlyn?"

She stops, mid-sentence. Looks up at me.

"I'll make everything okay, Ash," I whisper. "Trust me."

CHAPTER FIFTY-TWO

Ash?" I call out. She's not in the kitchen this morning. She's not in the bathroom, since I was just there writing my numbers, 485. The study door is closed. The guest room door is open. Her bed is unmade, a dresser drawer open but not empty. She's not there. "Ashlyn?" She's not in the living room.

Holding my coffee, I look out the sliding doors into the backyard. "Ashlyn's" green-webbed lounge chair is there on the grass, the white plastic cube table next to it. A magazine she left out overnight is dimpled with dew. But she's not there.

"Ash?" I call for her again.

We'd talked the rest of yesterday, sharing stories, both of us, and although I told her more about my life, and Dex, and Sophie, than maybe was necessary or prudent, I think we made some book progress. I made emotional progress, too. I'm open to the truth. I can handle it, now, whatever it is. Even if she's innocent. Which—she might be. Maybe I can actually do good. Help her. And seemed like she's decided to trust me. I'm invested. We'll do this together.

I can't "explain" to her that I'm more open-minded about her innocence now, since she didn't know I wasn't before. Still, it's fine. All I have to do is continue to pretend I was always telling the truth.

"Ashlyn?" I come back inside. Did she go out? Maybe to get reconciliation croissants or something? But why didn't she leave a note?

"In here, Mercer."

I turn, and now the study door is open. Ashlyn stands in the doorway with one hand high on the doorjamb. One tanned leg extended, like a fashion model. She holds out a little packet, looks like a facial tissue folded up.

"What're you . . . what's up?" I say. Détente or not, I don't like that she's apparently been in the study again. She invaded my territory yesterday, and now again today.

"First," she says, offering me the packet, "here's your sleeping pill back. I know you said 'no problem,' but yeah. You were probably lying about that, too."

I take the tissue, confused. Stash it in my jeans without looking at it.

She doesn't budge from the doorway, her chest rising and falling under a black T-shirt, tight cutoffs, flats. I get the impression she's keeping me out of the study. *My* study.

"No, it's really—" I begin as I take a step forward.

She doesn't move. Narrows her eyes.

"Please tell me it's true that your daughter died, Mercer. Or were you making that up, too? So you could be all what do you call—empathetic?" She sighs, puffing out a breath. Her lips are glossed and raspberry. "I don't know why I believe *anyone* about anything. Do I look like a stupid person? Or some kind of—"

"Hey, no, I understand, I'm so sorry, keep it." I take out the pill and hand it back to her. Maybe she's acting nuts because she's tired. I certainly know how that feels. But I'm trying to untangle this. "But Sophie? Not sure why you're asking me that, Ashlyn. I'm sorry, and I know you're worried and unhappy. But that's over the line."

"Oh." Her eyebrows go up. "*I'm* over the line. Okay, sure, definitely. I'm *over* the *line*. So sorry."

She waves the pill away, keeps talking. "But can I just ask you? Over the line about what? Do I lie or manipulate or make up stuff to get you to tell me things? Is that what you're implying?

Because, yeah, if you are, I guess you would recognize the technique, right?"

She backs away from me, putting one foot onto the study rug, and then another. And another. Her eyes stay on me.

Then she whirls, goes behind the desk, pulls a piece of paper from under the laptop computer. "Recognize this?" She holds it between two fingers, fluttering it. "Do you?"

I squint toward it. Hold out my hand. "Can I see?"

"Oh, you've seen it, I'm pretty sure," she says. "And I have, too." She holds it out, keeps fluttering it, facing it forward.

It's my list.

"Yeah." She shakes her head in dramatic contemplation. "*Inter-esting.*"

"Well, sure." Damn. This is such an invasion of privacy. I can't believe she was snooping. Or maybe I can. And I do understand why she might be upset, but I need to nip this paranoia in the bud. "Every writer needs notes, Ash. Otherwise we'd never remember anything. A book's a big project, you know?"

"Yeah," she says again, making it into three syllables. She presses her lips together as she looks at the paper. "Great list, Merce. Of all your brilliant questions about the trial. Or should I say, of all the 'holes' in my story."

"No, I, well, there's nothing sinister about it, Ashlyn. It's just notes. Gee." I push a step further, reassure her. "Go ahead, read it."

She sits down. In my desk chair. "Oh, trust me. I have."

She makes a *tsk* sound, disapproving, then slides the list back where I'd hidden it under the keyboard. Pats it into place.

"But Ashlyn," I say. "Those *would* be the most important topics. The things I'd want to know. Anyone would." I'm not pretending anymore. I do see her side. But now whatever I say will ring false. She thinks she's found my smoking gun. Maybe she has.

"'The most important topics'? Yeah, in one way of thinking. The *guilty* way." She's leaning back in my chair. "The chloroform. The 'issues' with my mother. And Tom. Sure. But you know what's not here? Anything like—who'd want to hurt Tasha? Who'd want to hurt Ashlyn? Other people's motives. Anything like—who's the real killer?"

She covers her face with her hands, just briefly. "And to think, yesterday I decided to buy it. Truly believe you, that you were on my side. I am such an *idiot*."

"No, Ashlyn, really," I try again. "Believe me, I—"

"Believe you? Give me a freaking break. Do I need to make it clearer, Mercer? Forget about it. Forget about everything. There's *nothing* on your little agenda about how innocent you think I am. It's all about how guilty. It's your—road map to convicting me."

"Come on, that's not fair." I come closer to the desk. "I wrote those before I knew you, right? Plus, it asks who killed Tasha Nicole, and that's the whole ball game."

"It also asks 'who is Tasha's father.' Bet you were psyched when I spilled *that* whole thing yesterday. But, hmm. Did you buy that story?"

"So it *wasn't* your stepfather?" I take another step closer. Maybe I can turn the tide here. "Who was it, then?"

"Was?" Her face darkens. "Why would you say *was?*"

Damn. That was from Joe. And I've already said he hadn't told me anything.

"Was. Is. *You* said was. I didn't mean anything specific by it." I'll keep trying to pivot. "So he's alive?"

"Don't try to change the subject, Mercer. I'm not stupid. Or . . ." she lifts her chin, eyes narrowing. "Or *insane.* Yeah. I was especially fascinated, I must say, to see your list says 'Ashlyn *insane?'* In all big letters. *INSANE?"*

She smiles, fake-prettily, batting her eyelashes. "You think I'm insane?"

Oh. Shit. I back up two steps, almost lose my balance and fall into the seat of the Sophie chair. "Oh, no, Ashlyn, that's only—I was simply—the list was only my partial notes from the—you know there was a possibility of the insanity defense."

"You are such a *liar*," she says, almost a hiss. "Instead of understanding my grief, supporting me, showing the world I'm truly innocent, like you *agreed* to do, like you're being *paid* to do, you decided to trick me. Make me look guilty. *'Insane'* for crap sake. You told me, your very words, 'It's just another job for me.' Liar."

She stops. Almost smiles. Cocks her head. Stands, and picks up Dex's Aegean rock. "What if Joe Rissinelli was found, just for example, killed by chloroform? If the police checked the search history on your computer right now, what would they find?"

"That's ridiculous," I say. "You were just showing me about your mother."

"Was I? *You* typed it."

She hefts Dex's rock from one hand to the other, back and forth. It's the same size as her fist, and I gauge its weight as she shuttles it. Should I try to grab it?

She shifts the rock again. "I suppose it all depends on what *your* prosecuting attorney would say. And what *your* jury would decide. Guess you better hope Joe's okay."

"Do you have a point, Ashlyn?" Is she threatening me? I stay near the door. Just in case. It dawns on me, with a goosebump chill, that no one I can contact knows she's here. If she bashes me in the head with Dex's rock, there's no one who would notice. Not soon.

She sets the stone down, placing it with a solid thunk. Puts both palms flat on the desk. Leans toward me. "Reporters," she says, as if the word tastes bad. "Did you think you'd lured me to 'confess'? I saw your face when I said that word. You were totally salivating."

"I never—"

"Mercer?" She puts up a palm. "It's too late now to screw around. You're trying to con me. I get it. But remember that dead chipmunk? On the porch?"

Okay, she's lost it. "Yeah."

"And the texting guy in Ristretto?"

"Yeah."

"Did you recognize him?"

"No. You said he was a juror, but I never saw the jurors."

"Exactly. And the kitten heel woman on the cell phone at the school bus stop? The toaster fire?"

"Ashlyn?" This makes zero sense. I'm embarrassed she found the list, and embarrassed she's accusing me of something that's true, and relieved she's put the rock down, but I'm also confused. And more than a bit uneasy. What if I'm wrong again? What if she's a nonsense-babbling murderer? Who might now have decided I'm in her way. "Why does any of that matter? What are you talking about?"

"Let me ask you. Ever see any other dead animals?"

Dead *animals?* I pat my back pocket for my cell. This is way disturbing. Should I call . . . someone? The police? Does Katherine understand how scary-weird Ashlyn is? Where the hell is Kath, anyway? I'm calling her. Like, now. Emergency level. And tell her to haul this woman away. I gambled, I lost. I have no idea if she's guilty or innocent. But I'm not going to risk any more.

"Ashlyn, listen. We're done here. I'm—"

She pushes the chair away behind her. Comes around the desk. "Seriously, listen. Stop. Put away the phone. Don't call anyone." She stands across from me, palms together, touching her fingertips to her mouth, as if in prayer.

She takes in a deep breath. I see her chest rise and fall.

"I'm taking a huge risk telling you this," she says. "The texting guy? He's not really a juror. But the chipmunk? The kitten heel woman on the phone? The fire? All of it? All that kind of stuff happened to me, too. Before Tasha Nicole disappeared. They're *warnings.* I learned that too late. I know it's hard for you to trust me, but even though you're a liar, you're another human being. And I have to tell you."

Part of me wants to run. Part of me wants to laugh. Part of me wants to hear the rest. Is she testing me? Seeing how I'll respond?

"Warnings?" I say. "What are you talking about?"

"Fine. You don't believe me. As always. Don't, then." She dismisses me with a wave of her hand. "I've done all I can. It's your funeral."

CHAPTER FIFTY-THREE

With that, she brushes by me, runs down the hall, and opens the door to the guest room. Slams it closed behind her.

"Ashlyn?" I follow her, stashing my phone in my back pocket.

"Don't come in here," she calls out. "I'm packing. I'm leaving. Never mind. You can tell Katherine I bolted. Whatever. Make something up. You're great at that."

"What?" The door doesn't lock, so I start to turn the knob. She's invaded my privacy, so I can—but wait. I can still respect hers. I take my hand down. "Ashlyn, let's talk."

"Leave me a*lone.*" She's raised her voice, not yelling, but I can hear her perfectly. "I read every word of your 'book,' Mercer. Every word. Of your so-called truth."

Read my book? My so-called truth? I tap on the door, trying to make my knock somehow sound supportive. "We're so cooped up in here, Ashlyn. And you've had such a frightening time. Maybe it's too much pressure, too soon? Reliving the whole thing? Maybe we can call Katherine and get an extension on the deadline."

"No!" She yells. "Get away. Nobody can ever understand!"

I hear noises, the closet opens, and slams, and drawers, maybe?

"I've had it, totally had it!" She's almost screaming now. "Your stupid list. Your twisted book. Your *constant* lies. No one will believe me! My whole family is gone . . ." Her voice trails off, and it sounds muffled. Maybe she's not near the door anymore. "There's no reason, Mercer, no reason at all for me to—oh, Mercer, please, please, please, just this once do the right thing. Tell them I'm innocent, I'm innocent, and I'm so sorry it had to end this way. . . ."

Silence.

"Ashlyn?" Nothing. End this way? I press my ear to the white-painted door. Silence. She's such a drama queen, but what if she's–oh, I don't know. This is completely absurd. But she's so volatile. And completely off the deep end, threatening me, if she was, with Dex's rock and chloroform. And then saying "end this way."

I open the door.

She's at the window. Not dead. Or almost dead. A gauzy curtain flutters back into place. Her suitcase is nowhere to be seen.

"Are you okay?"

"Of course I'm not 'okay.'" Her face is blotchy red. From crying? Or anger? "*You* are a stone liar. And out to ruin my life. Even more than it was."

On the floor, under the window, is box four of Dex's boxes. Not on top of the pile any more, but canted to one side. Open. I know the boxes were stacked, my tower of memories, when I brought Ashlyn into this room nine days ago. Was she pawing through Dex's boxes? Snooping, or stealing? Did she touch his posessions? That's disgusting. Only I have the right to do that. But first I better see if she's still driving the crazy train.

I shake my head, trying to look conciliatory. "I'm so sorry you feel that way, Ashlyn. And we should talk about it. But, um." Damn. I can't help it. I gesture to the box. "What were you doing with that?"

"Doing? Me? Nothing. I was trying to listen to you and that cop, and needed to get closer to the wall. So I had to move the boxes to do it." She shrugs. "Didn't you hear this one hit the floor when I dropped it?"

"No," I say.

"Well, I was gonna put it back before I left. So you wouldn't notice. But then the top opened—it was only flapped shut, that one strip of tape, and it came apart."

I draw in a calming breath, try to hide my annoyance. Was the box like that when I checked the room a while ago? I hadn't come all the way in. She's invaded my study, my desk, my computer, my refrigerator, my linen closet, my bathroom, looked in my *mirror*— why is this any different? But it is. *She wrecks everything she touches,* Overbey said. She was trying to eavesdrop. Did she succeed?

"I'll get out of your life, Mercer." She's apologetic. Sounds like it, anyway. "You think I'm guilty, and I understand, but I can't deal with that. And I don't need to live with your lies. As for your box, whatever, I'm sorry. It didn't sound like anything broke. Want me to tape it back up?"

"That's okay." I'm sick of this. I'm tired. And I'm not sure what to think or how to think it. It's just a book. But it's *the* book! If she's leaving, that means no more book. I need that book. That's why Dex and Sophie wouldn't let me off the hook this morning. They *want* me to write it. And Ashlyn needs it, too—she's always talking about the money. I can make the deadline, it'll be over, she'll be gone. I don't have to *like* her to write about her.

But right now it kills me that she's messing with Dex's possessions. They're—sacred. They're all I have.

"I'll tape it myself," I say.

Ashlyn steps aside, back to the wall, as I shift the box flat, then open the flaps so I can tuck them closed again. On the top there's a photograph, in one of those molded clear plastic frames. The rest of Dex's frames are black wood, so this one is different. It's of Dex and Sophie. In Pallisey Park where we always played, and where they had their private Sophie-and-Daddy days. "Just the two of us," Dex would insist. "*I'm* two!" Sophie once crowed. Her first sentence.

In the photo, Sophie, beaming, is holding Bunno and a white balloon. They always got balloons, brought them home. Tears brim as I remember, and I turn the clear plastic over, just a reflex.

Someone has drawn a big heart on the back of the photo, in thick black Sharpie. A heart? There's an inscription, too. *Remember the happy days. Katherine.*

"What?" It doesn't sound like my own voice. Not sure I've seen this photo before, come to think of it. Who took it? A heart?

"What is it?" Ashlyn doesn't move, but I can feel her looking over my shoulder.

I step back, holding it out. That lets her read the inscription, too.

"Oh, Mercer." Ashlyn's voice is soft. I can barely hear it through the roar of the tidal wave in my head. "That's what I was trying to—she poisons everything she touches. I'm so sorry."

"Did you write that?" I whisper. Is that Kath's writing? Could be. Or not. "*You* wrote that. That is *so* nasty."

"You're a good person, Mercer," she says. "I know you're hurt. You don't mean to accuse me of something horrible. Like you do in your book."

I'm still staring at the photo. A heart? Katherine?

"I know, you thought she was your friend. That's awful." Ashlyn touches my shoulder, just one fleeting moment. "Listen, I understand what grief can do. Maybe you were mixing up my daughter and yours. Mixing up my life and yours. So I–I kinda forgive you. You were doing your job, trying to get the biggest story you could, even if you had to be sneaky about it. But see? I'm the innocent one. I'm as much a victim as Tasha Nicole. Except *I* have to live with it."

"Huh?" I say. *Dex and Katherine?* I calculate, looking at Sophie. Bunno is smudgy-white and flop-eared. Not new. He was our gift for her eighteen-month birthday. So Sophie's maybe just turned three in this? So—not long before. The accident.

A heart? I let the photo fall back onto the still-open box. It lands face up. Dex, Sophie, Bunno, white balloon. The ugly secret on the back is hidden again.

"Let me ask you, and just a thought," Ashlyn goes on. "Maybe

Katherine hired Dex to represent her? For something? She met him while he was with your daughter? And he never told you?"

I can only shake my head. It's just a photograph. It's nothing more. Maybe. "Just the two of us," Dex would insist when they went off together. I thought it was fatherly and adorable. Was he actually keeping me away? So he could meet Katherine?

Ashlyn takes my arm, leads me away from the photo, away from the box, out of the room. "Well. Now maybe you'll believe me. Seems like *you* might be her victim, too. Let's get you some water," she says. "Or wine."

We get to the kitchen, my nerve endings fried. I'm trying to calculate what I missed and when I missed it. Or if. I'm sure it's nothing. It's just a photograph.

With a heart.

CHAPTER FIFTY-FOUR

Wine," Ashlyn says, handing me a stemmed glass. It's one in the afternoon. I down the entire thing, and sit at the kitchen table. In my chair. Dex's chair, and even Sophie's, look different, somehow. Dex's for sure. Did he have another life? And I didn't know? I mean, we had . . . I guess they were fights, sure, especially after Sophie. Little stuff. Disagreements. Like everyone does. The white kitchen. Vacations. And of course he stayed late at work, he's a lawyer. Was that truly why he stayed? When I put my head in my hands, I hear the trickle of more wine being poured.

"I know you must be trying to figure this all out," Ashlyn is saying.

I look up long enough to take a sip. And another. I wondered, too, about Dex's cell phone. At some point after the accident I'd found it on the desk, and tried to use our password to open it. *I need to save his photos,* I'd actually thought that. But seemed like he'd changed the password. Which I hadn't cared about. Then. But why would he do that? We'd always had the same password. He'd changed it, hadn't told me. Another sip. Were there other things I missed? Smart, happy, married, clueless me?

"You know, Mercer," Ashlyn says, pulling her chair, Dex's chair, closer to me. "I thought I recognized the warning signs. But when you showed me that photo, that proved it. Katherine did not tell you the truth. Or me, either."

"About what?" I manage to say.

"But *you* haven't told me the truth either, Mercer." Ashlyn doesn't answer me. "And that's why you still can't accept what was going on between your husband and your friend Katherine."

"Truth about—what? About the book, you mean?" I rally, struggling to keep a clear head. "We talk about this every day, Ashlyn. I thought you trusted me."

"I do," Ashlyn's face has a look. "But you haven't told me the real story, have you? All this time, you're trying to get *me* to confess. So funny."

"I–"

"Don't even go there." She puts up a palm. "When it's really you who needs to confess, isn't it?"

"About?"

"'About?'" She repeats, almost mocking me. "I know it's difficult, but I'm doing this for you, Mercer. For your emotional well-being. Don't you want to stop pretending? Be free? Don't you want to face it?"

"Face—Dex and Katherine?"

"That too, if it's easier."

"Easier than what?"

"Why do you think your husband and daughter were killed? And not you?"

I look up, and she's laser-focused on me. Hard. Taut. Intent.

"I–"

"I won't try to trick you into confessing, Mercer," she says. "I'm not cruel. And I know the cops ruled it an accident. Before Katherine told me, I'd assumed Dex was driving, and you were home or someplace. But you weren't. *You* were driving."

Outside it's pouring rain, one of those relentless downpours that rivers down the windows and extinguishes the sun. The kitchen's overhead light hits Ashlyn's face, making dark circles, and lines, and mottling her skin, as if she's aged twenty years in the last half hour. I might have, too.

"It was raining that day, too," I whisper. "And they say I must have–"

Ashlyn nods. "I know. I know all of it. Like I said before, Katherine told me the whole thing. Joe told me, too. Everyone knows. People are pretty careful with you. They watch what they say. Joe told me I should be careful, too. Everyone's worried you'll go under again. Like you did for all those months."

The darkness, I call it. But I don't tell her that.

"But Mercer? Think about it. I'm sorry, but here's the only reason I'm bringing it up. Don't you see? I'm trying to prove you're innocent."

Innocent. The word hangs in the air.

Innocent? Of what? It was an accident.

An accident means it's no one's fault. An accident means there's nothing anyone could have done. Nothing I could have done.

Ashlyn drapes one arm over my shoulder, the weight of it, a human touch, so unfamiliar.

"I can't imagine how you feel," she says. "Crashing your car into a tree. And only you survived. I am so, so sorry. How can you live with yourself? It must be horrible."

I close my eyes. See the darkness. *No.* I open them again.

"You *still* must be thinking," she goes on, "like every minute, why didn't I pay attention? Why didn't I keep my eyes on the road?"

I don't know which is worse. When she talks, or when it's silent.

"And if Dex had been driving, *you* would be dead, you know?" she whispers. "I just thought of that."

If Dex had been driving, like he always did, I'd be dead. And he'd be the one with three cracked ribs, two black eyes, and a fractured conscience. Would his life be as miserable as mine? Would he have moved on? What a stupid, *stupid,* selfish thing to think.

"So which would be better? To have you dead? Or your husband dead? You must think about that all the time. Seeing that tree."

Maybe I'll just take another drive. Go visit that tree. I can almost picture it, the rain . . .

"Mercer? You know what? Maybe you didn't really cause it," Ashlyn continues after a beat. "Or even the rain. I don't want to be—well. Could it be that maybe someone didn't realize you were picking up Dex and Sophie after you left the restaurant?"

"Someone?" I'm at the kitchen table. The shiny white kitchen table. The rain is only outside.

"I mean, you've driven in the rain millions of times, right? That very same way? Nothing ever happened before, right?"

"No," I say. "I mean—I mean, right. No."

She stands, begins to pace. I feel the warmth on my shoulder where her arm had been.

"I'm so sorry, and stop me if you don't want to think about this, I totally understand. But did you feel okay after that brunch?"

"Did I . . . yeah, I guess so."

"You told me you and Katherine were celebrating her job. What did you have to drink?"

"We had . . ." I know this, perfectly, I've thought about it ten million times. "Prosecco."

I look up at her.

She raises both eyebrows.

"One glass," I whisper. "Or two. With food. But they did a blood test, in the hospital. It was zero percent."

"Oh, no, no, of *course,* I knew you wouldn't drive like that, Mercer. But I just mean—did your drink taste funny?"

What did a glass of wine taste like a lifetime ago?

"Wait." Ashlyn holds up a forefinger. "Did you get to the restaurant first? Or did Katherine? Had she already ordered the drinks?"

"She had, but—"

"Never mind." Ashlyn shakes her head. "I'm being stupid. But I just can't believe it's your fault, you know? You'd never kill your whole family. I'm just trying to figure out the truth of what really happened."

The truth? *It was an accident,* my brain screams. I might have said it out loud, I'm not sure.

Ashlyn sighs. Leans against the kitchen counter by the sink. "I know, honey," she says. "Listen. Was your car driving okay? Did the police check your brakes, and all that? Can I just say— and just an idea, a little idea—maybe she thought you'd be in that car alone. And crash—alone. And *she* would have Dex and Sophie."

"She—Katherine?" My brain struggles to focus. The police said they'd checked the brakes. Must have. "But she couldn't have been certain there'd be a crash."

"True. Of *course*. But she could have simply tried again. But she didn't need to, did she? If that's what happened. I'm just putting it out there."

"But why would she send *you* to me, then? Why wouldn't she just stay out of my life?"

Ashlyn gives a big shrug. "Money, for one," she says. "For two, she gets you on her side, makes you a bestseller, keeps you from being suspicious. I'm just a convenient pawn. She convinces you to focus on me—so you won't focus on your own loss. And what really happened"

Does that make any sense? How can I remember what happened when my brain sees only darkness?

"Oh, you're the only one who can do it," she says in a sing-song voice. "That's what Katherine told you, right? To get you to do the book? Did you think that was a compliment?"

"Well, I—" I had, in fact. Stupid gullible me.

"Sometimes the tiniest thing reveals the truth, you know?" Ashlyn's gentle smile is full of sympathy. "After we search and search, the truth simply—appears. A scrap of paper, or an opened door. A photograph of a little girl with a stuffed rabbit and a white balloon. Inscribed with a heart."

I take a gulp of wine.

Ashlyn's certainly seen Katherine's handwriting. She stayed at Katherine's house.

"You really didn't write that?" I have to make sure. "On that picture?"

"I almost wish I had," she says. "Seeing how unhappy it's making you."

I drain my entire glass.

Ashlyn refills it.

"This is *me*, Merce. I *know* what it's like to have been set up. Don't you think it's weird? Like, 'suddenly' you can't drive? That doesn't seem wrong? Listen. Katherine is not a good person. I know her. Way better than you do. She takes what she wants, and she wanted your husband. You were a good mother, honey."

"I was," I whisper. I wipe the tear, quickly, so she won't see. "I was."

"I can tell." Ashlyn sits next to me again. Clamps one hand on each of my arms. "You would never drive your daughter into a tree. Someone did this to you."

"Truly?" The rain has stopped. I think.

"Mercer?" She squeezes my arms. Hard. Looks me in the eye. "Trust me. What you need to investigate is not *my* daughter's death. It's *your* daughter's death. And your husband's, too."

PART 3

THIS MORNING, as I wrote 486 on the bathroom mirror, I thought again about Sophie.

I remembered how I used to read out loud to her from T. S. Eliot. She was too young, but it was just as much for me as for her. And I wanted her to love the sound of words, and their power, as much as I do. In *Old Possum's Practical Cats,* Eliot tells how all cats have three names: the one we give them, the one that's a special name, and the one that only the cat itself knows, "the deep and inscrutable singular name."

Is that how the truth is, too? With three possibilities. What we think it is. How someone presents it to us. And what it really is. The deep and inscrutable singular truth.

Maybe we can never know that truth, since it's so inescapably transformed by our own point of view. As a magazine writer and a reporter, my task is to uncover whatever I can, convince whoever I can, to get me closest to the real truth. But that can't be what a trial is about, since in a courtroom, two sides are offering different versions of the same story.

Same as in a marriage. Two sides, two different versions of the same life.

One of them has to be wrong.

Or maybe they both are wrong.

CHAPTER FIFTY-FIVE

The door to Sophie's room hadn't made a sound as I opened it this afternoon, the first time in . . . months, I guess. I heard the still-familiar quiet tap of its edge against the shelves of stuffed animals and books we'd installed too close to the door. I'd kept the lights off, on purpose. Strange enough to be in here at all, much less illuminate everything that used to be. I risked a sniff to see if any Sophie-fragrance is left, baby lotion, or cleaning wipes, but there's nothing. Not a trace. The shutter-rattling rain won't stop, and the rumble of thunder underscores my growing unease. The gloom makes Tuesday afternoon feel like Tuesday night.

I'm sitting in the white wicker rocking chair where I'd fed her and cradled her and rocked my baby girl to sleep, the chair where I'd read to her, and heard her say "good night moon" for the first time. The unblinking eyes of her stuffed animals—snuggled bears and a silvery unicorn and a comical plush hedgehog—stare at me in plastic surprise. Bunno is with Sophie. Now I rock alone, and in my lap, instead of my daughter, a flickering iPad shows me videos of a murder trial.

I swish through the files of the witnesses—Overbey, Hilliard, Al Cook. The medical examiner, the crime scene tech. Duct tape guy. Georgia Bryant. The trial plays back, the story resetting and reorganizing and retelling itself, scene after scene presented by Royal Spofford as true, then the second storyteller, Quinn McMorran, offering her own interpretation. For the past week,

Ashlyn's given me *her* version. Several of them. The same events, each time making a different pattern.

Do the stories of our lives spin out the same way? We think we know the script, and the role we play, and have some inkling of how we hope the story will evolve. But everyone else sees our lives from a different point of view. Like Dex. Like Katherine. Like Ashlyn. The big unknown is the ending, and it's our human nature that we don't dwell on that.

Sophie, happily, had no concept of death. Tasha either.

Katherine.

She's the actor who's missing in all these scenes. But was she missing? Maybe she lurked behind the scenes, directing or producing. Writing the script. Maybe that's what she thinks I'm doing now, following her script. But why hasn't she called? Predictably unpredictable.

I rock silently, the trial flickering forward, playing out again on my lap. I see my own reflection in the screen, overlaying a close-up of Ashlyn.

Katherine. *And Dex?*

I push that thought away, but its replacement is also disturbing. Have I been so focused on Ashlyn's guilt that I didn't see another side of her story? That maybe the jury was right? Every time my brain went there, I'd dismissed it. But if she's truly innocent, and someone else killed Tasha, it means that person is still alive. Out there.

My mind is going too fast to reconcile this. But—Katherine. The woman from Dayton. The woman who killed my family.

The woman who made *me* kill my family.

If that's what happened.

"Mercer?" Ashlyn's voice. She's a shadowy silhouette in the doorway. Even Ashlyn, murderer or maybe-not, would not step uninvited across the threshold into Sophie's room.

"Yeah." I click off the tablet. Stand up. We'll go into another room. Whatever she did or didn't do, I still don't want her in this one. "I need some water."

I close the door.

"Did you decide?" she asks, as we walk side by side down the hall. "What I asked you this morning? We only have a few more days."

I laugh, the harsh sound mixing with a clap of thunder outside. As if I didn't know the deadline.

"Do you want to know the truth?" She persists. "Or not?"

That's the impossible question that possessed me for the last three hours, rocking, watching trial videos, lost in some alternate world. Truth? Or not?

The photo. Dex. Katherine. Dex and Katherine. All the white spaces in our lives that I ignored, or accepted or dismissed. Last minute trips. Sudden errands. Late-night client calls. I'm consumed by a world that contains a new truth. Not only that Dex might be a different Dex. What makes me yearn for the darkness is one soul-crushing irony.

I killed my own daughter—but Ashlyn didn't kill hers? She's innocent—and *I'm* the murderer?

CHAPTER FIFTY-SIX

We're back in the kitchen now. We don't have much choice. Our tiny constricted world is living room, study, backyard. Bedroom, bedroom. Bathroom. Deliveries come, sometimes the mail. Today I got a glossy palm-treed postcard from Patrick and Lita in Aruba, all solicitous. The phone is silent. My emails are mostly ads for investment planners and meal deliveries and the occasional—and instantly deleted—announcement of a "back-to-school bargain."

Ashlyn and I, we're trapped here, like a prison. A prison Katherine sentenced us to. She knew she was doing it. But I don't know why.

"Look," Ashlyn says, pouring herself wine. And me. "I'll tell you exactly what happened. Hand to God, I will. Tell you the truth. On Tasha's soul."

I blink, incredulous. Stare at her across the kitchen table. She's swearing on her dead child? Could any mother lie after saying that?

"But it all adds up to one dead certainty, Mercer," Ashlyn says. "Katherine. Joe. Maybe even Quinn. They're targeting *us* now. They're watching *us* now. The only way for us to be safe is to let them know we understand. That we'll never say a word. Or else we're both next."

"They?" I manage to say.

"But if you *write* the true truth, Mercer, here's the thing. No one but Katherine will ever read it. If you hand in that book? That book will vanish. Because Katherine will know I told you.

And boom. Gone." She picks up her empty wineglass, puts it down again. Shakes her head, once, twice, dismissing. "Who knows. It may already be too late."

I watch the downpour muddle the window, my front yard change into an impressionist painting of unrecognizable green and brown and gray. Or maybe that's my brain. Maybe it's the four-in-the-afternoon wine. Maybe it's impossible for me to see anything in the world as it really is any more. "Too late for what?"

"Or maybe not." She puts up two palms, as if stopping her own thought. "Listen. Katherine's got to contact you soon. She'll act like it's to see if we're making the deadline, but it'll really be to find out whether you've gotten me to 'confess.' If you say yes, then she'll know she's got a problem. That I talked. She and her pals will also realize that you know too much."

"I? 'Know too much?'" My wineglass is empty, too. We're going through a lot of wine. And we keep using the same words. "I don't know *anything.*"

"That's what you think. But maybe you do. You don't really know, right? And that's my problem. Our problem. It only matters what they *think* is true."

"But there *is* a truth, Ashlyn. There *is* what happened to Tasha." I'm clearheaded enough to remember that, at least.

"So what? All that matters is what they decide to believe. Just like a jury." She stands and paces, like she always does, this time from kitchen window to the back wall. I turn my head like a tennis game to follow her.

"Look. Katherine set *both* of us up. Not just me. From you, she wanted Dex, obviously. And now she can't have him. Obviously. Right?"

She stops, her expression sympathetic, head tilted. "And you're the one who caused his death, you know? I'm sorry, it sounds awful, but in *her* mind, you did. In her mind, it's all *your* fault. You ruined her life. And she sees you as the reminder of that. Plus, she's relying on your self-guilt. That you're thinking–*if only I had been a better driver. A better wife. A better mother.*"

"Ashlyn!" I stand, almost crashing my chair over. "Come on. That's cruel. Completely cruel. Responsibility? *Me?* I spent my whole life–"

She backs off. "Well, okay, but you might have died, too, you can't deny that. And if you had died, she'd be totally off the hook. But you didn't die. You just killed the rest of your family. Sorry to say so, but you did. If you're facing reality."

She's right, of course. I've beaten myself up with that every day for the past 486 days. Every single day. But I never connected Katherine with the accident. And I still can't.

"Look, I've thought about this," I say. "Katherine *meant* to kill me? She cut my brakes? Drugged me? Or something? So she could be with Dex and Sophie?"

"Oh, now you *remember?* Your brakes didn't work? That's pretty interesting, right?"

I sit down again. Cross my arms over my chest. The brakes were fine. I'm pretty sure. "No. That's totally insane."

I'm so enraged that I say insane on purpose.

But she just keeps talking. And pacing again.

"But what if." She holds up one finger as she heads back toward the sink. "They sent me to you–to test me. To see if I'll keep my promise not to talk. Katherine herself set you up for it." She mimes air quotes, makes her tone cloying and obsequious. "'Oh, Mercer, you can get her to tell you *every*thing.' Am I right?"

She is, but it would've been easy for Ashlyn to guess that.

"Katherine gave you that wet T-shirt photo of me, didn't she?" Ashlyn persists. "To make me look bad. But she completely misrepresented that, didn't she? Ever wonder who gave it to her?"

I try to answer, but she keeps talking.

"So. If *I* fail the 'test,' and tell you what really happened–I'm dead. And you are, too. But Katherine would win anyway, because she has control. If you write something they don't want made public–she can easily make sure that book never sees the light of day."

I don't believe any of it. But what worries me is that in some twisted world, I can semi-envision it. I'm relieved the thunder did not clap at that point. It would've been too ridiculous. Instead, it keeps raining.

"On the other hand." Ashlyn pulls up a chair next to me, scoots it closer, out of its normal place. "If *you* fail, and I *don't* tell you the truth–that's our only chance. Katherine still wins, because her secret is safe. But she'll think I kept my promise and duped you. She doesn't care if you don't get me to confess. She wants us to *lie*. That's what she *wants*."

What's the word–stupefied? I'm sure that's how I look.

CHAPTER FIFTY-SEVEN

Y ou look like you've seen a ghost, Mercer. But I'm telling you. That's the only answer." Ashlyn nods, agreeing with herself. She stands, and opens one of the kitchen cabinets, then another. Yanks out a bag of pretzels, and opens it with her teeth. Salt spills onto the kitchen floor.

"Listen." She sets the bag on the table, open end facing her. "It doesn't matter what you think or believe. About me, or about anything. We've—you've—got to write a story that proves to them you don't know. You've got to make something up. In the end, Katherine gets a book, and you get a book, and I get to be truly free."

"Make something up?"

"That a new concept to you?" She whaps my arm with the back of her hand, as if she's told a good joke. "Making up a story?"

I move my arm away from her. She pulls out a pretzel, stabs a finger through a loop. Takes a bite. Then another.

"Who is *they*, though?" My turn to talk. She's never gotten close to telling me that. Or maybe she has.

"Mercer, for crap sake, do you not understand what I'm telling you? You don't want to know that!" She swallows, then puts her hands together in front of her mouth, breaths into her prayer-like palms. Then points them at me. "Listen. If you get too close to the truth in what you write, I'll stop you. But it's better for you—trust me—if you don't exactly know."

Still no thunderclap, thank goodness. "Make something up?" I repeat.

"It's only a book, for god sakes." She rolls her eyes. "Right? If it's true *enough,* there's no law that says it has to be the whole real story."

Feel of real is how Katherine herself had put it. But screw her, right? Although I'm still not entirely convinced about her and Dex. I wish I had analyzed what was in his dresser drawers before I trashed everything. Wish I had researched our credit card bills, even looked at them, but I never had. I never questioned his dinners out "with clients."

"You're a reporter," Ashlyn waves a pretzel at me. "They always make stuff up."

My turn to roll my eyes. No, we don't. I suppose.

"But if we do that, Ashlyn, make something up, the public will never know who killed Tasha Nicole. Don't you care?" If she loved her daughter, wouldn't that be an unthinkable outcome? "That person will never be brought to justice."

"I understand that, right?" She drags her hands down her face, as if wiping her expression away. "But listen. Which is more important? Meaningless 'justice' for my poor dead Tashie—or saving your own life? And frankly, mine?"

"You honestly think . . ." Crazy? Or not? Did I want to find out? And I realize I said "the public will never know who killed Tasha Nicole." As if I'm accepting Ashlyn didn't. "You honestly think, and I cannot believe I'm saying this, you honestly think we're in danger?"

"Oh, yeah. Definitely. But we don't have to be. If you want the truth, fine. I'll tell you. But then we—you—have to come up with a *different* story. A plausible, believable story. It'll be a big bestseller for you, like, you'll be the *only one* who could convince the truly innocent Ashlyn Bryant to *tell the real story.*" She makes air quotes again. "If they go for it, we'll both be safe. Otherwise—"

"Otherwise what?"

"Otherwise I don't know. Or maybe I do. Another accident."

Truth? Or not?

Maybe I'm beyond comprehending what's true. Maybe it's unknowable. What does it matter what's in some book? I'm only a writer. No matter what anyone writes, people believe what they believe.

Have I been living a lie? That's all that matters to me now. Easier to create someone else's reality than to face my own.

"Okay," I say, toasting Ashlyn with my empty glass. "Let's find you a new truth."

But how will I find a new one for me?

CHAPTER FIFTY-EIGHT

don't see anyone watching us," Ashlyn says. First thing she did after coming into the living room this morning was go to the front window, pull the edge of the linen curtain liner in front of her face, and try to look outside without being seen. Her second Wednesday morning—and last, thank goodness—in my house. "But I guess we wouldn't be able to tell. How're you doing on the book?"

I drink the last of my coffee, place the mug on a *People* magazine Ashlyn left on the coffee table. I'm in jeans and a T-shirt, frazzled and exhausted. I'd stayed up late last night working on the book—honestly trying to write. But it's more difficult to originate fiction than to embellish reality, and everything I wrote was terrible. Phony, coincidental, ludicrous. I deleted it all. When I put 487 on the mirror this morning, I saw dark circles under my dark circles. I'm working in the living room today, instead of the study. Computer on my lap and not the desk. Maybe a change of scene will give me inspiration.

"No one's watching us," I say, not answering her question. "What's there to see?"

She sprawls onto the striped wingchair, cutoffs and bare feet, and I'm hoping she hasn't slathered on that orange sunscreen. The chair survived Sophie, but it couldn't survive that. Yesterday's rain has stopped, but Wednesday can't decide whether to go gray or golden.

"I have an idea," she says.

"Terrific," I say. Which is a good thing, since *I* certainly don't. I'm trying, and failing, to write a true-crime book that's not true. Because all I want is Ashlyn out of my life. And Katherine out of my life. I can't think about her and Dex. When this book is done, Ashlyn and Katherine will disappear. The rest of it never will.

"What if . . ." She crosses her legs on the chair, yoga style. Her cheeks are still pink from the sun, her lips glossed, her hair in a soft ponytail. No dark circles. "I'm not saying this is true, obviously, just what if. What if my stepfather was like, running drugs. When he did the Mercy Flights. I know he flew to Boston, all the time. That's real. He knew about the Boston airport. And, you know, the harbor. But what if he was a drug mule for maybe Ron Chevalier? And at some point, they got caught. And Katherine, who like I said before, knew Tom from Ohio but is now in Boston and has connections, suggested Dex be their lawyer."

My terrible ideas were more plausible than this one, but as long as she's talking, I'll listen.

"I mean," she goes on, "there'd be no reason for Dex to tell you about some piddly drug case from Ohio. But if *Katherine* sent it to him—Oh! like *she* sent *me* to *you,* remember? Wow. Two birds with one stone? Right? Anyway, possibly Dex didn't want to mention it to you, because of, you know. Or didn't want to say anything about her connection?"

"What connection?"

"Whatever we decide it was." Ashlyn rolls her eyes. "I mean, we haven't come up with that yet. Did Dex tell you about every case he got? Like, before he knew you?"

"I guess not." My bare feet are propped on the coffee table, and I can feel my knees getting stiff. I tuck a throw pillow behind the small of my back, and pop the laptop screen to black. *Before he knew you.* "He told me about some of them, sure, but not all, I suppose."

It's true, I didn't know everything about his entire life. Clearly not. I'd met Dex on an interview for a story about a financial blackmailer I was writing for *City*. He and I we pretended the only reason we had drinks afterward was to continue talking business. That charade lasted about an hour. We were married within a year. But I am no longer thinking about that. I'm not. Or anything that happened afterward.

"So how about that for a beginning?" Ashlyn says. "Say the drug people used Tasha as a hostage, told me they'd kill her if I ratted them out. People would believe that, right? You can take it from there."

"Not really, Ash." I shake my head. "You can't simply make up actions and motivations out of thin air. The book's got to include what was presented in court, and use that to explain your side of the story. There's no evidence about drugs, or Mercy Flights, or your stepfather. Nothing at all. Your story has to feel *realer* than that."

"Oh right. Good point." She shifts position in the wing chair, dangles her bare legs over one side and rests her head on the opposite armrest. "Hmm. Let me think."

I stare at the keyboard in my lap, reconsidering. Yesterday I was scared, then sad, and hurt, and—okay, drunk, and basically completely out of it. But "making something up" is a terrible idea. Ridiculous. Bizarre. When the time comes, I'll tell Katherine I can't make the deadline. Or something. Not sure how I'll deal with her, though. That's what kept me up last night.

"So. About Katherine." As if Ashlyn's reading my mind. She sits up, plants her feet on the carpet. Leans forward, earnest. "She's got to be involved with this, because, and this part is true: *Tom* sent Katherine to me. Suggested I tell my story to her. My mother wanted Tom and her—Mom I mean—to stay totally out of my life, but now I'm thinking. What if Tom worried about keeping me quiet? And wasn't sure he could do it alone? I mean, they're like, on a cruise in the Caribbean now. Can you believe it? How'd they pay for *that?* And what if she never comes back? Like, drowns or something?"

316 Hank Phillippi Ryan

"What?" I say. Now Ashlyn's cribbing from another tabloid story.

"Just *saying*, Mercer. A cruise! Anyway, Tom was probably counting on me being convicted, then it wouldn't matter what I said, it'd just be the ravings of a whacked-out murderer. But once I got that not guilty—*wait*. Maybe that's where Dex came in. They needed legal advice about whether they could get me convicted of something else."

That, I know is wrong. Do I have to say it? "Dex was dead then."

"Okay, okay, right." She grimaces briefly. "That's why I need you, to keep this all straight. Okay, so he and Katherine must have been involved before. During the drug case."

"What 'drug case'? You just made up the drug case." I put the laptop on the coffee table. Check for coffee, but my mug is still empty. A tiny ray of sun attempts its way through the front window. "'He and Katherine?' Meaning Tom and Katherine? Or Dex?"

"We'll figure that out. Maybe *Dex* was why the cops were hanging around here last week. Because maybe Joe Riss was involved, too?"

Ashlyn stands, then paces again, front window to the sliding back doors, then back to the living room, back and forth. She sits on the couch, facing me. "Seriously." She tucks one leg under her. "Not for the book, but for real. Joe Riss and Katherine—did they know each other?"

I remember closing arguments day, and peanut-butter sandwiches on this very couch, and Dex's boxes arriving, and Joe's tattersall shirt. When everything seemed semi-normal. "Of course they did. You know that. You told *me* that."

"Oh, right. And *Dex* and Katherine knew each other."

"Thanks for reminding me. So what?"

"So now you need to find out how the *three* of them are connected. Joe. Dex. And Katherine. Not for the book. Not for me.

For real life. For *you*." She nods, pressing her lips together. "You're doing this for *you*. Listen, do you think you could get into your husband's law office? Look at his files? I'll go with you, if doing it by yourself would be too difficult. Because of what you know about Katherine."

"It's only a photograph." I hear the edge in my words. "It doesn't mean anything." It's so unnerving that I introduced Katherine and Dex. But wait, that's wrong. She knew I interviewed him for that blackmailer story—but I thought it was my idea. Did she send me to him? Set us up? "So what if they knew each other? Nothing sinister about that."

I make it true by saying it.

"And I just cannot believe, not for a moment," I go on, persuading myself, "that Dex would do that. To me. And Sophie. And us. No."

"Okay, fine. End of discussion." Ashlyn stands, brushes off her palms. "Forget the heart. We'll just agree there's no connection between them. Or between them and what happened to Sophie. Not to mention Tasha. Write the book any way you want."

She takes a few steps toward the hallway, then turns back to me. "And Mercer, listen. I'll shut up about it. I promise. If you don't want to know the truth about your own life, like, if it's easier not to know it, or makes you happier not to know it, great."

"I care about the truth," I say. "But it's only a photo."

"Right. Listen, I'm only trying to help here. Say . . . if you went to his office. You could get like, schedules. Diaries. Letters. Maybe there's something. And if there's nothing, all good, right? Because then you would know for sure."

"I *do* know for sure, Ashlyn. Dex loved me. Beyond question."

"Good then," she says. "More power to you."

"Great." So that's over.

"I'm just saying, you know," she points at her own chest, "if I thought *my* husband was having a big affair with a good friend, or like, my boss, it'd kill me. But you're okay with it. The possibility I mean."

"The poss—"

"Because it's not like you're going to stop thinking about it, right? Even if you pretend you are."

I hate this. The suspicion of Katherine is a glowing ember in my chest. Every time I try to extinguish it, it burns brighter. Every word Ashlyn says stokes it. It's like one of those awful birthday candles. When you try to blow it out, the flame shoots back, and higher.

"Can you live out the rest of your days, never ever knowing?" She takes a step into the room. "Never being sure? I know what happened to Tasha, even though it's hideous. But you—still wear your wedding ring. How do you feel, now, when you see that? You have no idea about the truth of your very own life."

I look at the platinum band, and envision what's engraved inside. *Until the end of time.* I couldn't decide whether to bury Dex wearing his matching one. Some of me wanted to wear it myself. But if we were married until the end of time, I finally decided, he'd need his ring.

"Did you write that on the photo?" I ask. "Swear on Tasha."

"No," she says. "I swear. On Tasha."

"There's nothing in Dex's office anymore," I say, "It's all . . . in the boxes."

CHAPTER FIFTY-NINE

Forget the book. Forget everything else. I need to catalog every-thing in Dex's boxes. I need to know. Ashlyn's helping. So what if she touches his stuff. It's already tainted. The guest room is now getting wallpapered in yellow stickies, all marked in my blocky printing. The flurry of Post-its shows years and months, and then categories: Schedules. Clients. Decisions. Clippings. Cases. The only clear space on the carpet is where we're sitting, cross-legged, encircled by piles of paper and legal pads and manila fold-ers. I'm a researcher. This is what I do. Now I'm not researching Ashlyn's life. I'm researching my own.

We arrange each item underneath its designated yellow square, organizing it to see if we can make it mean something. Reveal something. Where Dex went. What he did. Dex and So-phie were always having "adventures." Now I realize Sophie couldn't have told me about them. *Pop-si-cle,* she would say. *Ba-lloon.* If she'd said *Kath-rine,* I wouldn't have blinked. And Dex, as always, would have explained it beautifully.

Sophie was shy. Hesitant to talk. But soon, she'd have been say-ing full sentences. Like: *Daddy and Katherine went to a hotel.*

Dex. I print a yellow stickie with his name. Slap it onto the wall. Dex. Had insisted he didn't want to be with Sophie at the birth-day party that morning. The more I think about it, the more I realize I'd nagged him into doing it. But Dex involved with trying to *kill* me? Impossible. Unless, once in motion, there was no way for him to stop it. No. I won't believe that. Katherine was probably—I close my eyes for a second. Does *everyone* lie about *everything?* I push away the darkness. Truth is the light.

"Was there anything of Sophie's missing? Before the crash?" Ashlyn asks. I'd loaned her a pair of my gray sweatpants and a utilitarian T-shirt. It's disconcerting to see her in my clothes. "I kept noticing Tasha Nicole's toys were not where they should be. Before she—disappeared."

"Things were always getting misplaced," I say. "Mail, stuff like that. Dex's passport once."

"Hmm," she said. "Interesting. Joe Riss's wife said his was missing, too."

Ignoring the time, we scrutinize each document. There's so much paper. Seems like Will Pritchett, or maybe Theo, had simply swept everything in, jumbled and unorganized. Every time I see Dex's handwriting, my stomach clenches. My suspicions fester, fueled by the possibly of what might explode in the next document, or the next.

"Look for billing information," I instruct her. "Client names."

"And timesheets, maybe?"

"Exactly."

We finished box four first, since that was already open. But the only photo is the heart balloon. I know Dex *had* others, so where are they? We rip open the box numbered one.

Ashlyn and I slug down coffee, needing the caffeine. Ashlyn has a PB and J for dinner but I'll never be hungry again. Around two in the morning she brings cheese cubes and crackers and water from the kitchen. She fell asleep on the floor around 4 A.M., and I guess I did, too, but we woke up at dawn's light and kept working. By breakfast time Thursday, coffee and Pop-Tarts, the corners of the untouched cheddar cubes are softened and sweating. For lunch we have more coffee, and the stale cheese and crackers. Box two. I roll the sticky packing tape into a ball, toss it into the wastebasket. The box is crammed with paper.

"Look for anything about Katherine," I say, handing her a stack of files. I stifle a yawn.

"You're so tired." She offers a sympathetic smile. "Shouldn't you–"

"I'll sleep when I'm dead," I say. "Or maybe never again. And look for Ohio."

"Like what in Ohio?"

"I'll know when I see it," I tell her. "If you think it's questionable, tell me. Names. Places. We'll sort first, then see what's there."

When the sun starts down on Thursday, the guest room looks like it's festooned with the scribbles of some wacky–or determined–mad scientist. A formula in progress. An emerging theory. We're scraggly and need showers. But I'm on a mission, and I've conscripted Ashlyn.

She sorts manila folders, like playing cards, into three piles. "Did your husband ever act worried about anything?"

"Give me a break," I say. "Worried? Dex was a lawyer. And a father. Of course he worried."

"What did he say about Katherine?" She puts a folder under the stickie marked timesheets.

"Unless you find something, don't talk about her," I say. I'm done with Katherine. Did she worry that I'd find that photograph? She was here when the boxes arrived. I'm pretty sure I told her I'd never open them. She thinks I'm focused on writing a book. For her. And I am. But now I'm thinking it'll not only be Ashlyn's "redemption," but also a bigger story. For me, anyway.

If Katherine denies it, that'll only prove it's true.

All this time she's been lying. Now she's taking advantage of me, again, to write this manipulative book. "Feel of real," she had the nerve to say. Because of Katherine, I pledged my soul to Sophie's memory. Nothing will ever be pure or right again. Katherine can take her book and shove it.

I'd sneaked in my numbers when I made a bathroom trip, no time for condensation, just on the bare glass. I'd stopped, my finger paused mid-four. What if I've spent the last 488 days mourning a complete fantasy life?

Still. I head back to the guest room. There must be clues. Dex didn't think that Saturday morning would be his last on this earth. He would not have left incriminating evidence at home. It must be here. Somewhere.

"You know," Ashlyn says as she pages through a file. "If Katherine caused the 'accident,' it definitely makes you not guilty. But Mercer? It also means she's not the only one who *is* guilty. Right? It takes two to—whatever that saying is."

Tango, I almost say. And then it hits me. Solid in the gut. Ashlyn's right.

Dex killed Sophie.

His duplicity and his betrayal and his selfishness killed her. And now it's destroying me. I'm sitting in my own house, on the carpeted floor, feet bare and in my own sweatpants instead of Dex's, by the window that faces the street. And I'm dying.

"Here's something. Newspaper clippings." Ashlyn's head is in box two, her voice muffled. "Some stories are by Joe Rissinelli. Did your husband know him?"

"I have no idea," I say. Joe, though, is haunting me. I haven't heard from the police. There's nothing in the paper—that's either the good news or the bad news. I left him yet another voice mail, despite Overbey saying Joe didn't have his phone. I emailed, too. Maybe he's working undercover. Maybe he didn't tell his editor. Maybe he emailed his wife and she didn't get his message. Maybe he doesn't care if I know where he is. Maybe he doesn't want me to. Maybe he's dead. There's barely enough room in my brain to speculate.

"Car-accident stories." Ashlyn holds them up.

"Well, Dex did handle personal-injury cases." I hold out my hand for the clippings. "Drunk driving. Drugs. Things like that."

"Told you." Ashlyn meshes her fingers together. "My stepfather. Ron. Drugs. Katherine. Dex."

For a moment, the only sound is paper, pages turning, files shuffling, and our soft breathing.

"Oh," Ashlyn says.

"What?"

She hands me a little white card. A business card.

Katherine's.

"Where did you find that?" I hear the flat tone of my own voice. Suspicious. Bitter.

"In the clippings," she says.

"With what article?" It's a business card. Everyone has them. Everyone loses them, or they get swept up in some pile of papers and misfiled. "Can you tell?"

"I'm not sure. I'm so sorry, I mean, it kind of fell out. There's this one about a drug bust in a night club." She hands it to me. "But not in Ohio. Oh. Or it might be this one. About a car accident where a little girl was killed."

"Set them aside," I say. "Keep looking."

We keep looking. In four boxes of Dex's files, except for that damn business card, we'd found no further evidence, that we recognized at least, of a Dex-Katherine connection. The car accident clipping led nowhere.

"Time out," I say, making the sign. "I know we've got one more box. But I'm brain-dead. I'm bleary. And we're gonna miss something. Let's finish tomorrow."

"Sold," Ashlyn says. "With ya. Pinot or Chardonnay?"

We both stare at the seven o'clock news on TV, our feet propped on the coffee table. Ashlyn's drinking more than usual. We'd nuked popcorn for dinner, so buttery we brought in a stash of paper towels with the big red bowl. When it got dark outside, we didn't even bother to turn on the living room lights.

During a commercial about Halloween costumes, out of nowhere or maybe out of the pinot, she puts the TV on mute.

"Mercer?" she says. "Listen. One day Tasha Nicole disappeared. I knew why. I absolutely did."

"Why?" I say. "Did you tell the police?"

"No way," she says. "I had to keep pretending. That Tasha was okay. Or else, um. Or else they'd kill her. They told me that."

"Who?" This feels like the real story, not the made-up story.

"I didn't say a word. But they did it anyway," she whispers. "*They* killed her." The front of her T-shirt was soggy with tears when she managed to stop crying. "Not me."

"But who's they? Why?"

She shakes her head. "I can't, I can't. I need to protect you," she says. "And me. I don't want to die."

I click the TV off. The room is dark. Darker. Darkest.

She's crying again. Her head in her lap, her shoulders shaking. She looks up, and I can almost see her face.

"At least they didn't make it look like *you* did it," she whispers. "At least your mother didn't turn on you. At least they let you *believe* it was an accident."

CHAPTER SIXTY

wake up this morning still on the couch. I'd dreamed about Katherine, and white balloons on curly ribbon strings. She kept giving them to Sophie, so many that they floated Sophie away. Katherine, while I watched, took a photograph of her in the air, and gave it to Dex with a big heart. I almost couldn't breathe as I finally opened my eyes, wondering how the real-life balloon picture happened and what it might mean. I hardly knew what to believe. If anything.

Friday, I tell myself, struggling to put my brain straight. Book deadline—moment of truth, ha ha—is Tuesday. I write my numbers on the mirror as usual, 489, and even with everything, I try to communicate with Dex and Sophie, but somehow the connection feels fragile. Am I losing that, too?

The police investigated, four hundred eighty-nine days ago. The rain, the slick street, the tree. An accident. They *decided* that. And I've consoled myself, a hundred times a day, with my belief that Dex and Sophie never felt a thing. That they were here, and loved me, and then were gone. And they never knew it.

I was left to bear it, comforted only by the knowledge that it was an accident. That there was no "why," only a random tragic universe.

Was it not random after all?

Just because Dex had a mushy picture from Katherine doesn't mean they were having some affair. Necessarily. And certainly doesn't mean Katherine is a killer. Necessarily.

"You ready?" Ashlyn's voice from down the hall.

I throw on a T-shirt and jeans, the first ones I see. As I get to the guest room, I hear tape ripping.

Ashlyn's holding a wide translucent strip in her hand, shards of cardboard still attached. "Here we go," she says, crumpling the tape and dropping it on the floor. "The last box. Maybe what's in here will give you answers. But let's start on the law books. Maybe there's like, a note hidden in one of them."

I stare at that brown cardboard cube full of terrifying possibilities, and my brain, confused and fraught and destabilized, cannot take it another moment. I am so hungover, so sleep deprived, so everything-deprived, I probably wouldn't recognize my own name.

"You look awful, Mercer," Ashlyn says. "No offense. Are you okay?"

"Okay" is a concept I may never experience again.

"I'm fine." Hearing the old me, saying what I used to say, I know it's even more of a lie. How will I ever face Katherine again? But I signed a contract. If I don't write the book, write *something,* my career is over. Not that I feel like that matters much now, nothing does. But ridiculously, I promised Ashlyn and Katherine the redemption book. Three days to deadline. "Sorry you had to sleep in this mess, Ash."

"You poor thing." Ashlyn closes the box, folding down the bottom flap, then the side, then tucking in the top. "Get some sleep. In your own bed. We'll start again later this afternoon. Even tomorrow. It's okay. Whatever's here will still be here."

I hoist myself to my feet, knees creaking, hold on to the sill for support.

I'm surprised when the blind clatters down, hitting my knuckles, shutting out the day. Ashlyn has pulled the white cord, and the room goes darker.

"Hey," I say, stepping back. I rub my hand. "Ow."

"Tuesday is the deadline." Ashlyn's voice is soft. Not accusatory. Even sad. "And you still think I killed Tashie."

I blink in the altered light, and step back, trying to read her expression.

"No matter how you try to convince me, no matter what story you've promised me you'll make up for this damn book, you've spent every day trying to prove I'm guilty." Ashlyn twists the blind cord, twisting until the white ball on the end pops up at the tip of her finger. She points down, and the cord twirls away, swinging back into place.

"But you're such a good person. I can't bear that you think I did it. That's why, risky as it was, I told you as much as I did last night. About them taking Tash. But, Mercer? Please. Let the police do their jobs. Let *them* find who killed Tashie," she says. "After all, they accused *me,* right? That horrible detective in Dayton, Rogowicz. And Overbey. And his sidekick. *So* unfair. They *owe* me. Right?"

I can't tell her that Overbey still thinks she's guilty. I wish I could collapse in Sophie's armchair, but I'm afraid I'd pull the crocheted Afghan over my head and sleep forever, so I stand by the door.

"Thing is." Ashlyn goes on, taking one step closer. "In your case, they stopped investigating. But that's what *you* need to do now. Investigate. I'll even help you." She shrugs. "*No one* can help *me* at this point, except for you. But you don't want to."

Even more tired than I've ever been, even with that photo of Dex and Sophie stained with Katherine's name, even unsure about Ashlyn, even then, I need to keep a grasp on reality. I plop onto the chair and sort of toss my hair, to prove I'm still in charge of my life.

"Okay, Ashlyn. Tell me. If you didn't kill Tasha Nicole, who did? I don't care about any consequences—what could be worse than what's already happened to me? Tell me the truth. That's the only thing that will let me believe you."

"I know it sounds . . ." Ashlyn half smiles, shakes her head. "See, thing is, you can decide for *you*. But you can't decide for *me.*

Listen. I did not kill my daughter. But I might be taking my own life in my hands if I tell you who did. Do you want to take responsibility for that? Take responsibility for another death?"

I blink at her through the gloom. I never thought about it that way.

"Or," she says, "do you want to take responsibility for *yourself?*"

CHAPTER SIXTY-ONE

Taking responsibility for myself. That means finding the truth about Katherine. And Dex. Yes. I want to know. I need to know.

Yesterday's scour of Dex's law books found nothing. We'd eventually opened wine and ordered yet another pepperoni pizza for Friday dinner and watched *You've Got Mail,* which she called "an old movie." Both of us actively avoided reality. But after I dragged myself to bed, reality wouldn't let me go. Sleepless, thrashing and hearing noises, I'd conjured images of Dex and Katherine, skin and sweat and whispers and secrets. Hell with sleep, I thought, pounding the pillow into another shape. Hell with the deadline. Ashlyn's right. This is about me now. *Me.* I need answers. I need my truth.

Only Ashlyn can help me find it.

And I thought of a great idea where we can start. The balloon guy at Pallisey Park. It's Saturday morning now, he'll be there. Maybe he remembers seeing Katherine with Dex and Sophie. Maybe more than once.

"We have to go find him," I tell her. We're in the kitchen, stoking up on coffee.

"Why 'we'?" She stirs in sugar.

"Because *you* have to talk to the balloon guy. He might recognize me."

"Huh." She adds more sugar. "Well, what if–okay. You should leave by yourself, with, like, an armload of dry cleaning."

"Dry cleaning?"

"Yeah. Because if Katherine, or whoever, is watching, it's better if I'm still inside, and you're on some errand. We're supposed to be working on the book. How about you drive to the cleaners, in case they follow you, but they won't because you know, dry cleaning. Then I'll sneak out the back so they don't see me, and meet you at Pallisey Park. It's not that far. I've seen signs for it on the way to town."

Even if it's silly, it's not worth it to argue.

We go get the photo, which I've put in the study. "Bring this to show him," I say. "But be careful." I may need to confront Katherine with it. Maybe.

"Okay." Her eyes dart to each corner of the room. "We shouldn't talk in here, though."

"Why?"

"It just crossed my mind—what if there's a bug in all this electronic video equipment they brought? Katherine arranged for it, right? Maybe it wasn't just for the trial." She flips some switches on the monitor and a power strip, then pries open the back of the silver mouse. Two black double-A batteries clatter onto my desk. "You let that cop inside. Like I said before, who knows what he planted. Joe's been here, too, right? Was he ever in this room alone? How about Katherine? Why haven't they come to pick this stuff up? Haven't you wondered about that?"

It almost makes enough crazy sense to be possible. Closing the front door behind me, I welcome the late morning sun. I love our—my—house, but I feel held hostage by the place. By tragedy, and then grief, and then the book and the trial, and then Ashlyn, and now by raging uncertainty.

I drop off the cleaning, two sweaters from last winter and some jeans I don't even wear. Forty minutes later, as planned, I meet Ashlyn at the Pallisey Park bandstand, a whimsical pale-green octagon of elaborate columns entwined with lushly blooming sweet autumn clematis. The now-landmark bandstand on the park's greensward was a gift in memory of village patriarch Pallisey Linsdale. His family is long gone, but his descendants bequeathed this pavilion for those remaining in their namesake town.

"I found balloon guy." Ashlyn pats the white-slatted bench beside her, signaling me to sit. "He's not the one who's usually here, so I gave him the photo to show to the one who is. He says come back tomorrow."

I hate that photo, but I sure wouldn't have given it away. I sit arm's length from her, and open my mouth to challenge her decision.

"Come on, Merce," Ashlyn says. "I used your copier. The original is safe. Trust me, okay?"

I stretch my legs onto the pavilion's wooden floor, wide panels scuffed and mottled by years of folding chairs and music stands and musicians' feet. The clematis fragrance is intoxicating. I can almost see, like a movie of another lifetime, Dex and Sophie and me on the grass, splayed on our green plaid blanket, with contraband white wine and a tippy tray of cheese and crackers, Sophie and her Bunno waddling toward any congenial-looking newcomer, especially if they had a fluffy puppy or a toddler of their own. The music of a Fourth of July concert, Sousa and the Beatles, lilting determinedly from the makeshift local band. I'm sure it was the same this year. Just not for me. Or them.

When I hear music, I'm almost confused. But it's my phone. I pull it from my jeans pocket. Unknown number.

"Where are you, kiddo?" Katherine's voice. The sun darkens, but only in my world.

"Hi, Katherine." I use her name so Ashlyn knows who it is. "Where am I? Why?"

Ashlyn widens her eyes. Mouths, "Don't tell her."

It's not strange that she's calling right now. It's not surprising. It's not. The Ashlyn book is due in three days, and part of Kath's job is making sure I write it. But what if she *was* watching us?

"Checking up on me, huh?" I fake-laugh as I continue, like this is amusing and normal and I don't hate her. "Where are *you?* Where have you been?"

Oh. Maybe she's calling about Joe. I try to swallow back my laugh. "Listen, Katherine? Have you heard about Joe Rissinelli?"

"Why would I hear about Joe?" she asks.

"Why would you hear about Joe?" Again I repeat, for Ashlyn's sake.

Ashlyn purses her lips, nodding. As if to telegraph, *told you so.*

"The police came to my house, almost a week ago, and told me he's missing," I say. "Didn't you know that?"

"Missing?"

"Yes, missing. Didn't they contact you?" I shrug at Ashlyn, making a *who knows* face. I shift on the bench to keep the sun out of my eyes.

"No," she says. "But why would they? I'm sure he's okay. That's strange, though. The police. But listen, quickly, yes, I'm just checking up on you. I'd stop by your house but—"

"You want to come over?"

Ashlyn is shaking her head now, full out frowning.

"No, no, thanks for the invitation, but not necessary," Katherine goes on. "So you making progress, you two? You connecting? Has Ashlyn told you what really happened?"

These are all perfectly logical predictable questions. But somehow, even in the sweet suburban sunshine, with clematis shadows on my arms and the last of the summer's bees nudging the white lavender-edged blossoms, the words Katherine uses take on a hint of menace. *What really happened.*

"I just went to the dry cleaners," I say. "We're doing fine."

"Has she told you the whole story?" Katherine persists. "That's going to make or break the book, Merce. You're the perfect person for this. You can get her to talk, if anyone can. Right?"

She's using the exact words Ashlyn said in the study. How does Katherine know that?

"Um, has Ashlyn told me the whole story?" I hope Katherine doesn't think I've lost it, repeating everything.

Ashlyn draws a finger across her throat.

"Not yet," I chirp, trying to communicate writerly optimism. Holy crap, I am so good at making stuff up. "But you are so right, if anyone can get her to talk, I can. And I know we're hitting deadline. I'll keep you posted, okay?"

Ashlyn looks pleased, gives me two thumbs up as I click off the call.

"That confirms it." Ashlyn stands, drags her fingers through her hair, then looks out over the park. "Katherine's totally in on it."

A few moms and their kids arrive, fringe-visored strollers and a Dalmatian puppy, rambling toward the playground. Where Dex and Sophie used to hang out. With, apparently, Katherine. I try not to picture that. Stare at the floor instead. Then decide.

"Ashlyn?" I say. "This is it. Make or break. In on *what?*"

Ashlyn clears her throat, thinking. She nods. "Okay. First. What're the odds Katherine doesn't know about Joe?" She rounds her thumb and forefinger into a circle. "Zero. Right?"

I have to agree. I stand, brushing down my jeans. "Well—"

"And *Katherine* made me stay with you. Remember how she manipulated that? Like I keep saying, that was to set up the test. To see if you could get me to tell."

She puts her hand on the wrought-iron stair rail. Then stops. *"Oh!"*

"What?" I shade my eyes with one hand. "Are you okay?"

She takes the pavilion's three steps down to the grass. Turns to me, looks up at me, her face bathed in a shimmer of sunshine. A puff of breeze ruffles her hair.

"Mercer? I don't want to mention this. But I'm sorry. I have to. What if Katherine sent those people to Quinn's? To scare me out of there, and scare Quinn away, and make it *logical* that I stay with you? She completely knows where Quinn lives, right?"

"Yeah, sure but—"

"And she knew I was there."

I try to think. "Did she?"

"See? She's amazing." She shakes her head. "People are never what they seem, are they?"

Katherine sent whatever bad guys to Quinn's house? And then used that disturbing episode to make it seem compelling for Ashlyn to stay with me? *Only with you, Mercer,* she'd said. "You mean—to get rid of Quinn? Because she was too close to revealing the truth?"

"Oh my god, Mercer. Yes. You're brilliant. Come on. Now *we* have to take charge." Ashlyn starts to walk away. Then turns, beckoning me. "Come *on.* I'll tell you everything. But not here. And you have to promise, word of total sacred honor, never to tell. Ever."

CHAPTER SIXTY-TWO

Our shoes tramp in unison across the grass, and then crunch onto the gravel of the parking lot. "We can't talk at your house, either," Ashlyn says.

She looks around, scouting, eyes shaded with one hand. "No one could have tampered with your car, I guess. We'll talk there. But this will be the only time we'll discuss it. Okay?"

I'm not sure about any of this. "Okay."

"If they followed you here, or me, we're screwed." She shakes her head as we walk, then waves her arms, gesturing at the lush maples, and the rows of coppery mums, and the parallel lines of fresh-mowed lawn around us. "But, hey. We're not in *prison*. We're allowed to go to the park, that's reasonable, right? Let's drive. Like yes, nice time at the park, now we're going to, I don't know, the mall. There must be a mall. I'll watch and see if anyone follows us."

"Okay." I say again. I think about "reasonable doubt." My whole life is doubt. Question is, what's *reasonable?*

I click the gadget to unlock the Subaru. Not many other cars in the lot, and they all appear to be empty. I can't believe I'm looking. Driving is not my favorite anyway, though usually I'm fine. "They don't know what you've told me, Ashlyn," I say, half pretending and half serious. And I'm somehow saying "they" as if it's an actual entity.

"They wouldn't hurt us at this point," I go on, opening the door, "because they don't know what I know." There's nothing to gain by arguing, or dismissing her. I push the ignition. Feel ridiculously relieved the engine rumbles instead of exploding. "Right? They don't know if you've passed or failed."

"Unless they're listening." Ashlyn jabs on the radio, some Top 40 station. "All I can say is Mercer, you have to help me. You *have* to. The people who killed Tasha Nicole were out to punish me. Listen. I'd told them they shouldn't use Hot Stuff to sell drugs. I told them, someone's gonna find out. That's why I was always at Ron's—trying to convince him. That's why I kept asking for my phone. To call him. To warn him."

"Warn him of what?" I pull onto Witherby Street and wind up behind a chugging truck, keeping to the speed limit as we head to the highway. The car works normally. It's not raining. Fine. The mall.

Ashlyn flops her head against the back of her seat. "I'd . . . told someone else about it. The drugs. Then he died. In a car accident." She fusses with her seat belt, and at the stoplight I glance at her. She's staring out the windshield. "Was it them? I don't know. Maybe it *was* an accident. I don't know. But I was terrified. And they said they didn't like *rats*. That's what they thought I was, a rat."

The light turns green. The music thumps, a bone-jarring bass. We're in four-lane traffic now. I navigate to the middle. Ashlyn is still talking.

"And one day when I thought she was at a play date, they stole Tasha. And threatened to murder her. To pay me back for telling. I honestly didn't think they would—how could you kill a poor defenseless child? But it's—you know. Drugs. Money. Power. They're . . . I can tell you who they are, sure, but it wouldn't mean anything to you. Anyway, I guess they decided it would be worse for me, worse than killing me, if they could frame me for my own daughter's murder. At least Quinn convinced the jury I didn't do it. But if we reveal the truth about them . . ."

She rubs her hand over her face. "Then we're both in danger. That's why I keep telling you—we need a story that's true enough to convince everyone it was an *accident*. Like what happened to you. That'll stop the police from looking for the real murderers. When that happens, I'm safe. You're safe. Because 'people' will think you believed me."

We're at the exit for the mall, air conditioner full blast, my left turn signal blinking, its mechanical click an underscore to the progression of my thoughts.

"So you didn't tell the police about it," I say.

"Please," she says. "Don't be stupid."

"Did you explain this to Joe Rissinelli?" We have the green arrow to go onto Route 1, but I wait, wanting to see her reaction.

"Oh my god." Her face has gone white, a ghost against a black leather seatback. "I kind of did."

The possibilities shift and shuffle. Say for a moment her story is true. If Joe's a good guy, and Ashlyn revealed more than she should, he may be in danger, too. If he's a bad guy, he knows Ashlyn has a big mouth. Either way, it could explain why he's gone.

"Either he's in trouble, or he's involved." Ashlyn sums up my own conclusions. "And it's all my fault. You have to help me. You have to get me—*us*—out of this."

There's something in her voice. True fear? Or, I must also consider, she's a nut job. How risky are the consequences if I make the wrong choice? Someone pulls up behind us. They honk. I flinch, and accelerate onto the highway.

"Silver car," she says.

"Millions of cars are silver," I say, but I'm looking in the rearview. It's not there anymore.

"You know what?" Ashlyn says. "Let's get back to your house. They think we're working on the book. We should do that. We don't want them to wonder where we are."

CHAPTER SIXTY-THREE

Now, just after midnight, the fifth box remains untouched. I'm aching to get in there and rip it open, but Katherine's call was a reminder that she's monitoring me, and she's expecting this book.

In two days.

I sit, elbows on my desk, propping my chin on my fists. There's no question I have to give up what I want to do–find the truth about Dex–and fulfill that obligation. Even if Katherine was sleeping with my husband. My first goal has to be to protect myself. And, I suppose, Ashlyn. We have to do exactly what we promised.

Here in the gloom of my study, I yearn to ask *someone* for advice: What should I do? What do I believe? What's right? The cursor on my computer screen blinks at me, awaiting my decision. Until 491 (it's after midnight) days ago, I'd consult Dex. Or talk to an editor. In college, my best friend, Kristin, always knew what to do. In the very old days, I'd go to my mom.

But now I have no one. No touchstone for reality. Dex is gone. My friends and colleagues are gone. Katherine is definitely gone.

As for the missing Joe Riss, Ashlyn's now convinced her bad guys are responsible. "Holy crap, they got him, too," she said as we drove home. She was crying, dabbing her eyes with a napkin from the glove box. "And it's all my fault."

You have to help me! I can almost hear her voice. What if the jury got it right? That would mean I'm putting Ashlyn in danger because of my own—I don't want to say obsession. But maybe my own one-woman conspiracy? I wanted to be the jury. But if I'm the executioner instead, that makes *me* the guilty person, not Ashlyn.

Ashlyn is long asleep. She became so agitated after her realization about Joe that she made me take her to Walgreen's for pills, and closed the door to her room at 8:30. We both knew I had Ambien of my own, but offering her one was a touchy subject. We'd ordered Pad Thai, neither of us ate much, and silently watched the news on TV. Almost silently.

"I'm not going to say another word," she told me. "It's all on you."

Since then I've been sitting at my desk, procrastinating. Deciding. The manuscript draft is due in forty-eight hours. What am I supposed to write? Did Ashlyn kill her daughter? How can I untangle all the stories?

The computer screen goes to black again, tired of waiting for me. Truth is, I'll never know the truth.

Covering a trial seems so simple now. You listen to testimony, you choose the best parts of what witnesses said, you add thoughtful analysis and reaction. It's up to the jury to make sense of it and agree on a decision. The jurors in Suffolk Superior Courtroom 306 had to decide whether, beyond a reasonable doubt, Ashlyn Bryant murdered her daughter. They said no. The jury set her free.

Who am I to argue? Whatever happens now, that verdict cannot be undone.

I can hear her voice, now, pleading with me.

You have to help me!

Ashlyn insists I need to save her life by giving her a new truth. I suppose it'd be easy enough—I'm a storyteller—to concoct a believable story.

I have an idea.

YOUR CHILD, TOO

"Please, please, please," Ashlyn begged Luke and Valerie. The three crowded together against the drink-laden bar at Hot Stuff; Valerie a tousle-haired millennial and newcomer to Dayton, whose permissive parents allowed her free rein and unlimited credit card access, and Luke, a big-shot money manager of some kind out of Chicago, Ashlyn wasn't sure. First time he came to town on business, he'd hit on her. Each time he came to Dayton after that, he called her. Now it was her turn to get a favor.

"Please say Tasha and I are coming to Chicago to visit you, okay?" Ashlyn smiled as she asked, knowing just the angle to tilt her head to make her eyes luminous. "Just if anyone asks. They won't, no one will. But just in case? Cover for me?"

She was so thankful they both agreed. And without asking any questions. Later, she'd thank Luke in the only way men really understand. As for Valerie, (*fill in here—ask Ashlyn*)

The whole mess had started a month ago. And maybe just maybe, it would all go away. Maybe no one would ever find that little body. So far, everyone—except her stepfather Tom, of course—actually believed the story that Tasha was simply somewhere else. But her mother, increasingly insistent, was beginning to ask questions. And that was a problem. Ashlyn had to protect her. Even if it meant alienating her.

All of Tasha's possessions, though. They tormented her. Tashie's pink bedroom, as if it were waiting for her to return. Her four Tiggers, all lined up. Her Donald Duck inner tube. If Ashlyn was keeping up the charade that Tasha was alive, she couldn't dispose of them. *Dispose,* she thought. And, hiding in a solitary metal bathroom stall, she burst into tears again before she regrouped, reset, and hit the bar again. She had to keep up appearances.

She'd barely managed those first two miserable days, hiding in Ron Chevalier's cramped apartment, unable to eat anything, lying to everyone, pretending to enjoy the *Joy Ride* movie, with her poor dead daughter in the trunk of her—she couldn't bear to think of it. But Tom insisted it was the only way.

"We have to make sure no one knows," he'd told her as they stood over the lifeless child in their backyard that day. The front of his maroon country club golf shirt was soaked with sweat, and both knees of his khaki pants grass stained. Minka and Millie, inside, scrabbled their claws on the sliding glass doors, frantic to get out.

Ashlyn, shaking in horror and overcome with sorrow, pulled out her phone to call 911.

"Put that phone away." Tom grabbed her arm, hurting her. "No way they'll believe it's an accident. We'll be—dammit, it'll be all over the newspapers. The club. The golf course. We'll be accused of, I don't know, neglect. Child abuse. Murder. Why in hell did you let her go on the swing standing up?"

"I didn't! She—I turned my back for *one* second, and . . ." Ashlyn had to admit she saw a glimmering of her stepfather's point. Poor thing was already dead. They'd covered Tashie's motionless face with her beloved white blanket. There was no way to bring her back to life. "I don't know. It was an accident. It *was* an accident. People will believe it was an accident."

"With *your* night life? Your reputation?" Her stepfather's words had stung, stung with the harshness of truth. "And now you let your own child get killed?"

"She's yours, too." In grief, the truth came out. She couldn't bear to look at Tasha; the child's hair, like tawny seaweed, matting across her face. She couldn't bear to look at Tom. Disgusting, pushy, manipulative Tom. His face was all red, veins in his hideous neck bulging. Maybe Tasha Nicole was never supposed to live. Maybe this was meant to be. "*Your* child, too."

"Get a trash bag. Get two," Tom ordered. "And the big cooler. The plastic one."

Within minutes, the tiny body—so light, Ashlyn realized as she lifted her, perhaps for the final time—was encased in heavy green plastic. Tom used three short strips of duct tape to make the blanket-covered shape less recognizably human. Ashlyn, in a rush of remorse, had snatched up Rabbie just in time, and tucked the beloved stuffed animal into the bag to comfort Tasha in heaven.

"I'll tell your mother I have a Mercy Flight to Boston, where that big cancer-kid doctor is," Tom said, pulling out his cell phone. "In two days. Meantime, you put the cooler in the trunk of your car. Add ice or something. Park somewhere else. Figure it out. And then we'll take the cooler to Boston. Act normal, for chrissake. Tell your mother you and Tasha are visiting a friend. Or shopping. Everyone will believe *that*."

Using both palms, Ashlyn wiped the tears from her cheeks, tears of sorrow and fear and guilt. Come to think of it, this disaster wasn't completely Ashlyn's fault. Tasha was not supposed to stand on the swings at all, much less alone. It was the girl's own fault for disobeying.

"And what will they believe when they never see Tasha again?" she asked.

Tom narrowed his eyes at her. "We'll think of something."

Which obviously was not successful. For Ashlyn, anyway. She was eventually arrested for murder.

That version of the story raises a lot of questions, most immediately why anyone would do such a gruesome thing, but I'll face that when I get to it in the narrative. If Ashlyn agrees this could be what happened, her stepfather is not gonna be happy, but he's not happy anyway. As long as he doesn't sue me for libel. Or her. Ashlyn told me neither parent is speaking to her. She says they never want to see her again.

Lovely people.

It's tempting to go back and read my old "Ashlyn is a murderer" story, like poking the place where a tooth was pulled to see if it still hurts. Instead I'll need to revise it, fast, and make sure there are no howling loose ends.

Because truth has no loose ends. Before the verdict, I thought I knew the truth. Can I prove myself wrong?

One-thirty in the morning now. I read over my new scene, trying to envision it through the mind of an objective person.

My reimagining of the story needs more tension, maybe, between Ashlyn and her handsome but aging money-craving stepfather. And where was Georgia during all this, do I need to include that? It also needs more setting in the first paragraph about Hot Stuff, maybe some disco-lighted, bass-thumping, alcohol-fueled, body-scented description. Maybe I should include what Ashlyn was wearing. I'll ask her about that.

Then I remember.

I'm making it up. If this scene never happened, how could Ashlyn tell me what she was wearing? I'm confusing myself. It's late, and silent, and all my realities are tangling into each other.

But my new truth, same story and evidence but crafting the reportage differently, doesn't have to be entirely true. It only has to be true enough.

Chin propped in both my hands, I stare at the screen until my words blur. I feel my eyes close, and I let them.

CHAPTER SIXTY-FOUR

Morning sun slants through my kitchen window. And on the table, a printed-out copy of last night's scene, pages numbered one through five. Sometimes it's easier to revise if the words are printed on paper—makes them seem more real.

Fifteen minutes ago, as I wrote 491 on the bathroom mirror, I tried talking to Dex, and then Sophie. Our connections seemed different, maybe because I'd been given a possible subplot to their deaths. Katherine.

True? Or not. One simple choice changed everything.

"What happened?" I whispered to them through my reflection. I could not bear to "ask" Dex about Katherine's signature, those blocky words in smeary Sharpie, that scrawled heart. Could not, yet, allow my soul to believe it. I still half-believe Ashlyn wrote it, imitating Katherine's all-too-available handwriting. But why would she do that? To mess with my mind? To shift the focus from *her?*

I wait for the numbers to vanish with the condensation. Ashlyn will be awake soon, and I need to keep my numbers to myself. I pause, the world stopping, as I realize those numbers are supposed to represent my only reliable truth. What have I actually been counting?

The thunk of the Sunday paper on the front porch jolts me back.

I open the *Globe* as I bring it to the kitchen, and page through, scanning, waiting for my coffee. Nothing about Joe Rissinelli. I add milk, then stir. I've gotten no calls from the cops. No response to my emails or texts.

"Hey Merce." Ashlyn is at the archway to the kitchen, hair in a topknot ponytail, wearing my sweatpants but a T-shirt of her own.

I watch her get out a coffee pod and a mug, familiar with my kitchen. It creeps me out how it seems so natural to her. As she putters, I half-expect a call from Katherine, since I woke up this morning after yet another dream about her. She was behind a glass wall of some kind, and talking to me, but I couldn't hear. Then a phone rang in the dream, and I opened my eyes.

Ashlyn's coffee water burbles as the machine heats up.

"So I did some work on the book last night." I've decided to think of my role as "messenger." Katherine wants a book about the so-called redemption of Ashlyn Bryant, phony as it is, and that's what she'll get. Ashlyn wants a book to create a cover story that's believable and yet doesn't pin the blame on some mysterious and possibly fictional "bad guys" she's terrified of, and that's what she'll get. I don't care. The book is supposed to be a compelling true-crime story. If they pay me, that's the crime story I'll write. Minus the true. I'm only the messenger.

"Here." I hold up the printed pages. "Could you read it? See if it makes any sense?"

I can't believe I'm asking Ashlyn if something makes sense.

"You're amazing," she says. "Let's see." She yanks out her chair—the one that used to be mine, the only one I'm comfortable with her using—and takes the manuscript. I hear her coffee hissing from the machine, splashing into her mug. The kitchen smells like dark roast.

"I'll get your coffee while you read." I remember how she brought *me* coffee, that first day she came to stay. I remember how certain I was that she was a murderer. Now I'm helping her. To everything there is a season. The metal spoon scrapes the bottom of the ceramic mug as I stir in her sugar, two lumps. I watch Ashlyn, reading the life I made up for her. She turns over page

one. I try to read the draft through her eyes. Try to gauge her expression as she starts page two.

"Just so you understand," I begin, "I had to make you somewhat–
well, I couldn't make you perfect. It's not believable, you know? If
you were perfect, you would have called 911. Or watched Tasha
more carefully in the first place. I have to balance and juggle to
make your motivation's convincing."

"Let me read it." She doesn't look up from the page.

I'm annoyed with myself for feeling anxious. For hoping she
likes it. Writers are nuts. The clock on the coffeemaker shows
8:14, then 8:15, then 8:16. I actually begin to pace. Ridiculous.

Ashlyn puts down the manuscript. Props her elbows on the
table. I see her eyes close. Then open.

She's smiling.

"I love that you used Valerie and Luke," Ashlyn says.

So silly. Praise, even from her, makes me happy. Writers really
are nuts.

I pull out my chair–Sophie's–and point to the manuscript.
"Yeah, but what will they think when they see this?"

"Who?" She takes a sip of coffee.

"Valerie and Luke. I mean, it makes them either dupes or liars.
Or both."

Ashlyn throws her head back and laughs. The sound hits the
ceiling and falls to Earth again.

"Oh, holy crap," she says. "I made them up. I had to make it
seem like Tasha was somewhere. So she wasn't *missing*. I created
'Valerie' and 'Luke,' because if they didn't exist, no one would be
able to find them to prove she *wasn't* with them."

"Valerie and Luke are made-*up?*" I struggle to grasp this. "You
can't just make people up."

"Guess you can," she says. "Everyone thought they were real.
Everyone was looking for them, and wondering why they didn't
testify. I know *you* wondered, Merce. I read your list. Remember?"

Ashlyn smiles, triumphant, like she's proved a point. "Waffle?"

She gets up, pulls the plastic bag from the freezer. "No?" Pops one into the slot.

So Valerie and Luke are fiction. Real-life fiction. I take back my pages, tamping them straight on the tabletop. The toaster ticks as Ashlyn opens the fridge for butter.

Katherine had told me they'd thought Valerie was dead–but then, she wasn't. Then there was nothing more about that. No wonder Katherine had the "wrong" Valerie. There is no "right" Valerie. I'd asked Kath who "they" were, I remember that. But she'd never answered. Katherine again.

Valerie and Luke. What else might not be real? I think of my list again.

"Let me ask you something." I shift the handle of my coffee mug back and forth. "About the Skype. With Tasha in Chicago? With Valerie?"

"Oh, please," she says. "There's no Valerie. There's no 'Chicago.' And that Skype was taped."

"What?"

"My mother is beyond lame with computers. And so predictable. Tasha could barely talk, anyway. I'd recorded a Skype with her, like, from the living room to the bedroom at a friend's house one day. You know, Sandie? DiOrio? Just for fun. Tasha loved it. I'd put it on a thumb drive, on my keychain. And then, when my mother got all pissy and demanding, it was easy to set it up before anyone else came into the room. Tom thought it was genius."

"But how did . . ." I'm trying to remember the dialogue. "I mean, Tasha had a conversation with your mother."

"Did she?" Ashlyn's slathering her waffle with butter. Her knife crunches through as she cuts it in half. "I read your manuscript, remember. There's nothing in it that Tasha says directly to my mother. Look again."

It had crossed my mind at the time, briefly, whether that Skype was somehow faked. But it was never used in the trial, so its veracity was never questioned. And I can't look at it "again" because I've never seen it. I only heard Georgia Bryant's recitation on TV. She believed it was real. I simply believed *her.*

"Why would you save a Skype video?"

"I'm surprised you'd ask that, Mercer," Ashlyn says. "Didn't you save videos of *your* daughter?"

I had, of course. But I hadn't tried to use them to trick anyone.

"Wasn't that risky, though? Weren't you worried she'd figure it out?"

"You're kidding, right? *Her?*"

The machine is gooshing out my second coffee. Right. So either Ashlyn's mother is super-savvy enough to protect her husband by covering up his crime, or she's so super-dumb she can't understand how a computer works. There's not gonna be enough coffee in the world to understand this.

"How about that surveillance video of you at Logan Airport? With Tasha? That implicates your stepfather."

"You ever see that?" Ashlyn asks, gesturing with the waffle-square stabbed onto her fork. Almost flutters her eyelashes. "I never did."

Detective Overbey had admitted to me that the tape wasn't clear. What's more, it was lost. So now, like Luke and Valerie, it doesn't exist. And can't undermine Ashlyn's story.

"I better keep writing," I say. I don't even know who *I* am anymore.

"Good," Ashlyn says. She's picked up the *Globe.* "Let me know what you come up with."

CHAPTER SIXTY-FIVE

Litigation hypnosis.

That's what Dex called it. It's when lawyers have a blazingly guilty client, who, at first, they despair of getting acquitted. Then, as their trial prep proceeds, the lawyer devises an alternate theory of what happened—a reimagined narrative of the facts designed to persuade the jury their client is innocent—and eventually begins to believe that story. Buy into it. Completely. They've hypnotized themselves.

Dex once lost a drug-conspiracy case and came home devastated; tie askew and with the slack-shouldered demeanor of Eeyore.

"Guilty," he intoned, shaking his head, as if saying apocalypse or doomsday.

"But you told me the guy was guilty as all get-out," I reminded him. "That there was no way he'd be acquitted."

"Yeah," he said. "But then I convinced myself he wasn't. And now I'm totally bummed out."

Do I have litigation hypnosis? I tap my fingers one at a time, pattering a random rhythm on my desk. I have not typed one word since breakfast. Two hours ago.

I keep thinking about Ashlyn's story. Now that I've created the swing-set scenario, it's difficult for me to *un*create it. What if it's true, and Ashlyn didn't want to admit it? If Tom confessed to what happened to help clear Ashlyn, he'd be culpable, *too*.

My fingers continue to tap the desk. Another possibility. What if Ashlyn fabricated the drug deal/bad guys/rat story? It's damning, but maybe she thought the reality it creates put her in a better light than the one about conspiring with her stepfather to cover up the negligent death of her own daughter. *Their* own daughter?

But gee, when she was charged with murder—I have this conversation with myself since there's no one else to have it with—wouldn't she have owned up to the real reality then?

I wish Dex were here. I wish someone were here, at least, some lawyer, to tell me what crime it would be. Unlawfully disposing of a body? Maybe child neglect, too. But anything is better than facing life in prison for chloroforming your own daughter, and then shoving her into a plastic bag and dumping her.

Still. The jury decided that's not what happened.

But why would Ashlyn risk a jury trial?

So maybe the stolen-Tasha threat-to-Ashlyn story *is* true?

How can I write a true-crime book—if what's true is unknowable?

"Ahhhhh!" I stretch both hands above my head, hoping my brain does not explode all over the carpet and wallpaper. "You just have to write a story," I instruct myself out loud. "Not the *true* story. A *plausible* story."

When the jury acquitted, my story changed, too. Now the duplicitous Katherine and her exploitive publisher are paying us to write an "as told to" book. Ashlyn's redemption. Her explanation of what happened. As told to *me*. Okay, fine. I can decide what she'll tell.

Whatever way the story unfolds, at some point, Ashlyn was in Boston. She told it one way—that Tasha was not there. The DA told it another—that Tasha was. But what if they'd found that missing airport video? Then whose story would be true?

Mine would.

WHAT'S DONE IS DONE

Two hours from Dayton to Boston. In a single-engine Cessna with no bathroom. Ashlyn raced into Terminal B, hit the Ladies, and then joined the confident hustle of the big-city airport. She must look like shit. Her eyes puffy, no makeup. Her damn Cubs hat screaming *outsider.*

On the trip over, looking down at the cottony clouds, the sun baked the Cessna so hot she worried Tom would fall asleep. It was another world. Like, heaven. Which reminded her of their gruesome cargo. *If I jumped out of the plane, would I just float into the clouds? And be gone, like my Tasha?*

She tried not to picture it, any of it. What's done was done. She had to move on. She could not bring back Tasha, who was so young she'd almost not had a life. But Ashlyn—well, she had a future. And she refused to give it up. Life goes on.

First thing, she decided as she joined the crowd in the bustling concourse, get a new cap. A Boston cap, so she'd blend in. She saw a Hudson News place, where they'd have souvenirs, and candy, too. Ten minutes until she was supposed to meet Tom at the taxi stand. He'd carry the cooler. "No one notices a cooler," he'd assured her.

This would work. It would be sad. And then it would be over.

She'd almost reached the metal display rack—pink Red Sox caps seemed cute—when a little girl toddled by wearing a lavender pinafore and a floppy hat over her sandy curls. So like Tasha that Ashlyn had to push her own heart back into place. She could be brave, if that was the word, and pretend reality away. Until reality stared her in the face.

The girl ignored her. Ashlyn watched the harried young woman who must be her mother trying to keep one hand on her roller bag, one eye on her daughter, and battle an annoying credit card machine.

"Puppy!" The girl held out one chubby arm, pointing to a Chihuahua writhing in a traveler's arms. The dog's owner put the tiny speckled pup on the terrazzo floor for the child to see.

"Hannah!" the mom called out, glanced over her shoulder as she signed a receipt. "Stay with me, honey."

Ashlyn couldn't stand it. She stooped down next to Hannah. They both reached out to pet the dog at the same time, and when their fingers touched, Ashlyn almost fainted.

I blink at the computer screen, trying to envision this. So far, it certainly matches how I remember Rogowicz's description of the airport video. In that, I think the toddler–Tasha? but not in this version–runs off, and Ashlyn goes with her. In my version, they also leave. But not together.

My writer brain outlines what happens next. Ashlyn meets her stepfather at the taxi stand. They put the cooler in the trunk of a cab, they maybe tell the cabbie to go somewhere benign, then change to another cab just in case. No one would notice anything unusual. Then maybe a third cab to Castle Island. They're picnicking on the beach, just like everyone does. They have trash, just like everyone does. They wade into the water, just like everyone does.

Well, no. They have to get the body–yeesh–farther out into the harbor.

I imagine it another way. They take some sort of harbor cruise, with the cooler, just like everyone does. Well, wait. Would someone check what was in the cooler?

Okay, another way. They rent a little J-boat from Boston Sail, and load up the cooler, just like everyone does, a father and daughter taking an afternoon picnic out into the harbor. Peaceful. And private enough.

Could that have been the way it happened?

I feel my foot jiggling. I save my draft of the airport scene.

But I have questions.

My cursor blinks. Demanding: what next, sister? I realize

there's no need for me to research my files about this. The primary source is in my living room.

"Ashlyn?" When I get there, she's sprawled on the couch, watching a movie. *Sixteen Candles,* if I'm right. She clicks the TV to black.

"You have more?" she asks. "Can't wait."

Piece of work, I remember Joe Riss saying. He was right. Where the hell is he?

"I have a question," I say. "Or two."

"Sure." Ashlyn looks expectant. I wonder if she takes my questions as challenges, seeing if she can come up with a plausible answer. Or maybe she's telling the truth.

"The Dayton police found evidence from TSA," I begin. "Your plane ticket, showing that you and a lap child had flown to Boston. Before Tasha's body was found in the harbor." It's still odd that I can say those words to her—in another life, it would be unacceptably impolite to be so crass. I get queasy when someone mentions a car accident, and people are always sheepishly apologetic when they forget.

Ashlyn doesn't seem distressed by my words. "So?"

"So, you told me you and your father flew in his private plane to Logan Airport. And okay, fine. But you didn't use a ticket for that, so you clearly were also in Boston, at Logan Airport, another time."

"That was before we went with–I mean, before the cooler."

"So you were in Boston before? And then came home? But there was no return ticket. We need to deal with that in the book. It's a provable thing."

Ashlyn looks at the ceiling. I look up, too, then realize she's thinking. She sighs. I wait.

"Okay," she says. "It was after we put it there, but before they found it. Her. It was part of Tom's idea to prove Tasha was still alive. Like you said in the book, he told me he'd think of something. We were going to say Luke lived in Boston, and we were going to visit him. See? It would prove Tasha was alive. So we got a kid to come with me, and we dressed her like Tasha. On some airlines, you don't need ID for a lap child. And anyway, all girls that age look the same."

Ouch. No. They don't. "But that's dumb, Ashlyn. It proved you were in Boston. And when you came back—how'd you do that, anyway?—Tasha wasn't with you anymore."

"Well . . ." she says. Shrugs. "What can I tell you. Tom is an idiot. I guess he never figured it would matter. Lucky for me, that janky cop lost the thumb drive. Yeah. Quinn told me. Because that video would have—well, whatever. I know you'll figure out a way to write it. Cannot wait to see what comes next."

CHAPTER SIXTY-SIX

She's taking a nap. A *nap!*

I'm at the living room entryway again, after spending the last three hours trying to come up with a believable story about how a terrified daughter and her overbearing stepfather dump their sickening cargo in Boston Harbor, then fly back to Dayton, all distraught and second-guessing each other (to make them more sympathetic to readers), and then debate how to convince a meddling Georgia Bryant to stop asking after her darling granddaughter's whereabouts. My fists plant themselves on my waist. Ashlyn's *asleep?* On the *couch?*

It's past one in the afternoon. I needed Ashlyn to help fill in the considerable holes to the "feel of real" in her story. I mean, my story. Our story. The story. Whatever story means Tasha's death was not her fault. And not some fictional sinister kidnapping. I was going to suggest we talk over lunch.

But looking at her, stretched out and face down on my white couch, her feet bare and one arm dangling to the floor, it appears she's already had lunch. That's based on the two curved pizza crusts, leftovers from the other night and nibbled up to the edges, discarded on a paper towel. And the tipped-over empty beer can. That beer's been in the fridge for—a long time. Dex's. I couldn't bear to throw it away. Guess it's still good.

I stare at her, lying there oblivious. Do I think she's guilty? I hardly think of that when I'm writing. Now I'm just telling a story. Ashlyn's redemption, as promised. If I let my mind wander from

356   H a n k   P h i l l i p p i   R y a n

book-path, it goes to Katherine. It wonders if every time Dex was on a business trip, or late coming home, or distracted, there was actually something else causing it. Some*one* else. And right now, that's feeling pretty damn real.

I'll focus on the questions I *can*–fictionally at least–resolve. Like, how could Ashlyn exist without leaving a trace while that Dayton cop Rogowicz looked for her? And if she and her stepfather flew a Cessna to Boston, what was she doing in Terminal B? That's only for commercial flights.

She'll have some answers when she wakes up, no doubt. I could probably concoct some on my own, but it's supposed to be *as told to*. And that's my journalistic cover.

I also need to ask sleeping beauty about Barker Holt. If Tom Bryant wasn't Tasha's father–just saying–and it was actually Barker Holt, that might make Ashlyn a more sympathetic character. A young woman who thought she was in love, and found herself– I'll think of a better way of putting that–pregnant. Maybe the guy wouldn't marry her? And left her? Or maybe, and this would be better, he *wanted* to marry her, and all the plans were underway, and then he got killed, and she was never the same. That's plausible. And it's essentially what she told Joe Riss.

At least, he said she did.

That means I need the details on Barker Holt's accident. If there was an accident. I know there was a Barker Holt. Though, again, only according to Joe.

Where *is* Joe?

There are two people who may have answers. Maybe it's time to pay them a visit.

And since Ashlyn wants to sleep? Perfect timing. Before I can second-guess myself, I write a note to Ashlyn, saying: *Cemetery. Back soon.* I half-cringe, hoping that's not blasphemous. I tuck the note under her pizza plate, grab my car keys and a plastic bottle of water, and go.

As I push the ignition, I get a twinge of unease about leaving Ashlyn alone in my house. But, hey. What harm can she do? Swipe a few more Ambien?

I back out of the driveway. Accelerate on autopilot, lost in thought. I check the rearview as I reverse into the empty street, and–*what?* A silver car speeds toward me. *At* me?

He's going too fast. Too fast. *Too fast!* I slam on the brakes. The wheels lock. My car jolts to a stop. My seat belt straps me in place. The silver car zooms by. I bang the car into park, half into the street, put my hand to my chest and close my eyes, struggling to reset, feeling my heart hammering off the charts. If I hadn't looked out the rearview at just that moment, if I'd accelerated out the driveway a fraction of a second earlier–I *felt* that car go by. Its velocity. Its intent. It happened so fast, it stopped time. There's somehow a void, a silent space where the nothing happened. A silver car.

I twist in my seat, heart still in flames, but my brain demanding *get a license number!* But it was going too fast, it'll be long gone.

I'm wrong. Instead the silver convertible slows, and top down, veers into the Rayburns' driveway, still idling while their automatic garage door opens. In the front seat is Liz and Ezra's nutcase drag-racing son, what's his name. Derek. Stupid guy almost killed me.

The car disappears into the white garage, a segmented door rolls into place. I almost laugh, but it's not quite funny yet. A silver car. Like the one that "followed" Katherine. "All the way," she'd told me. Well, yeah. The guy lives across the street. Another mystery successfully solved. Stupid Derek. Katherine will be relieved. Like I care about how she feels.

But I–some kind of shrill noise begins, echoing and reverberating and taking up all the space in my head. I feel the blood drain from my face. Every bit of heat in my body is replaced with cold. The trees outside blur into a mass of green, and all I hear is the noise, the *noise,* louder and louder and louder. I clench the steering wheel, smash my foot on the brake. Hold it down, force it down, hard as I can, hard as I can. I hear sirens and more sirens, see swirling red lights and flashing blue lights and shattering glass and people yelling and screams and screams and screams.

CHAPTER SIXTY-SEVEN

When I open my eyes, the dashboard clock shows me less than a minute has passed. No sirens, ambulances, no screams. No exploded airbags. The windshield is clear and pristine. No stabbing shards of glass cover my hair and clothing and my bleeding arms and face. Dex is not moaning. Sophie is not motionless. The sun highlights my willow tree. A blazing scarlet cardinal lands in the nearest branch, followed by his wrenny mate. They trill to each other, *pretty pretty pretty.*

I lift my foot from the brake. Unwrap my fingers from the steering wheel. The buzz in my head softens, subsides, vanishes. I'm behind the wheel. Motionless, but moving through time. And safe. I'm safe. Nothing happened. *Nothing happened.*

A flash of something outside my window. A knock on the–unbroken–glass. *What the–?* I recoil, spooked. Heart in my throat.

Ashlyn.

"You okay?" She's holding a beer in her hand, a can. Bare feet. "Why're you just sitting here half in the street? Want me to come with you to the cemetery?"

"Cemetery" was an awkward lie, especially now, but I have to stick with it.

"Oh, no thanks. And I'm fine," I say. That might even be true. I gather my strength, what there is, and try for a brave smile. "Just thinking. Guess I spaced." I take a swig from my water bottle, then flutter my fingers. "I've got errands to run, too. See you soon."

I ease onto the now-deserted street, shaky but determined. I have to do this. I will not let the past ruin my life. In the rearview I see Ashlyn saunter back into the house, close the door behind her.

Looking out the windshield now, road clear and neighborhood quiet, I rebalance on my tightrope. Nothing happened. I'm fine, it's all fine, it's over.

Still. That was *so* damn close. The doomed Hennessey family, the newspaper stories would report, all tragically destined to die in car crashes. Two separate ones. Not today, though. *Not today.*

I accelerate, gently, then make myself more confident. Reclaiming normal.

I did it. I made it through that moment. And came out the other end. Plus, I know it was only the Rayburn kid. I'm safe. He's an idiot. And my life goes on.

I brake, gradually, as I approach a STOP sign. My brain is working again. And it reminds me, gently, that what just happened doesn't mean the Rayburn kid's silver car was the one "following" Katherine.

Katherine again. The book was her idea. Ashlyn staying with me was her idea. Maybe Katherine even confessed her "relationship" with Dex–*ah*–to Ashlyn that night at her house. Maybe she sent Ashlyn to find out if I know about her and Dex. On the other hand, if *Ashlyn* wrote those words on the photo and Katherine is innocent, that ruse makes Katherine a victim, too.

Or. Maybe Ashlyn was as surprised as I was. Maybe the signature is real. It's impossibly confusing.

There's no other traffic, so I stay at the STOP sign, thinking this through. Talk about confusing. I'm increasingly aware that even writing this book as fiction, I can't come up with a way to manipulate the actual evidence enough to plausibly explain that Tasha's killer was not Ashlyn.

Because who else could it be? I can't use the "bad guys" Ashlyn says she's afraid of, presuming they're even real. She insists that story—her truth—would put her in danger. And me in danger, too.

My main suspects were Valerie and Luke. But they don't exist. I've tried storylines blaming Ron Chevalier. Tom Bryant, of course. I'd even considered a jealous or abused or betrayed or deranged Georgia. But nothing makes "Ashlyn didn't do it" have the feel of real.

Who can I finger as the bad guy? I look both ways, take my foot off the brake. Then put it back. Stop.

Wait. Okay. I know who else might have killed Tasha. My brain revs through the entire plot. Yes. It could work. And it's so obvious, it's right out of a Lifetime movie.

Barker Holt. Right? He kills Tasha, because of . . . something. And then gets killed. By—I have no idea. Or! He kills himself. Yes. Out of remorse? That could be.

I keep my foot on the brake, thinking. Fingers tapping on the steering wheel. It's all about the timing.

Joe Riss told me that Ashlyn told him that Barker Holt died before Tasha was born. But when I talked to Ashlyn about it, she admitted she'd made part of the story up. I assumed that was because—disgustingly—stepfather Tom was actually Tasha's father. But maybe that's the lie she told *me*.

It makes more sense that Barker Holt really *was* Tasha's father, and she lied to Joe about the "before Tasha was born" part. What if Barker Holt is still alive? Could it be that Ashlyn doesn't know that?

A car pulls up behind me—not silver—and beep-beeps to get me to move along. I wave, all good. I don't even flinch. I truly am fine. But I'm so hot on this Barker Holt solution that I almost make a U-turn to go home and run it by Ashlyn.

If it's true that Barker Holt killed Tasha, I can't use that in the book.

Talk about confusing. The truth is the only thing I'm *not* allowed to write.

At the entrance to the Mass Pike, I slow for the yield sign. Do I change plans? No. I have a mission.

I accelerate onto the eight-lane highway, soon hitting seventy, though other cars are passing me. It feels so different to be out of the house. Free. Even with wacky Boston drivers, even seeing the scruffy billboards and the bleak graffitied backs of cinder block buildings. The real world. I've been out of it for so long. Fearful for so long. I roll down all the windows, letting in the day. No darkness. The Rayburn kid is a moron. I'm fine.

My plan is to go to the cop shop, see Detectives Overbey and Hilliard, crossing fingers they're there, and ask for Ashlyn's phone. It's all a ploy, and I could have called and made an appointment, but that'd give them time to cook up some story about where the phone is and why Ashlyn can't have it. Obviously they won't release it to me, but now I want to talk to the cops all the more, and I figure that could be a good way to start.

Bryce Overbey told me he still thinks Ashlyn is guilty. So he and Koletta Hilliard must know something I don't. Maybe, in the privacy of their office, they'll tell me.

CHAPTER SIXTY-EIGHT

In the lofty-ceilinged lobby of the police headquarters, I show the uniformed receptionist the business card Overbey gave me. It seems the equivalent of saying the secret word. It's almost unsettling how quickly the cadet ushers me into the chaotically file-stacked detectives' office on the third floor, an open-plan room with desks regimentally spaced behind a double-wide glass door. The door pings as it opens, pings as it closes behind me. There's only one person in the room. Place smells like coffee, which almost makes me laugh.

Then I actually do laugh, although I think I hid it. It was like seeing a movie star in real life. Koletta Hilliard, all business in a navy twill blazer, black jeans, and a tight bun, gets up from her desk, second from the front, smiling. Holds out her hand.

"Detective Hilliard," she says. "So you're Mercer Hennessey. Bryce said if you ever called or showed up, you were top priority. He's out. I'm his partner. What can I do for you? Coffee? Have a seat." She gestures at the glass pot on a warming stand, then at a padded swivel chair.

"Sure, just milk," I say. "Thanks. And you know, I watched you at the trial. On TV."

Offering coffee means she wants to talk. Accepting it means I get to stay longer. As she putters with the coffee stuff, I watch her, fascinated. I envision her hiding in the Bryant's kitchen, waiting to pounce on Ashlyn. She's the one who took the refrigerator duct tape to be analyzed. Sent the clothing to the pollen analyst. She's the one who vowed to call every police department in Ohio until she found the place with a missing little girl.

I begin to feel–embarrassed. Kind of humble. Dilettante-writer me convinced myself I could crack this tragic case. Hilliard tried it in real life. She's the one who took the stand in Courtroom 306 and said "only Ashlyn." She must still believe it.

That's why I'm here.

"We know she's at your house, by the way," Hilliard says, handing me a navy ceramic mug. "Ashlyn Bryant. If you're planning on lying about that, or being cute about it, let's not go there, okay?"

Whoa. She's tough. "Great," I say. I shift in the swivel chair, its wheels squeaking on the dingy gray carpet. "Which brings me to why I'm here."

"You heard from Joe Rissinelli?" she asks.

"Well, no." Interesting that's the subject she brings up. It's been more than a week. Are they still looking for him? Do they still suspect I know something? "Have you?"

Hilliard scratches her cheek, once, with an unpolished forefinger, as she leans against the edge of her desk. It's uncluttered, no photos or mementos or painted pots of curling ivy. A stack of manila file folders, edges aligned, crowds one corner.

"We're no longer concerned," she says.

"But–is he–" I wonder, with a pang of conscience, if I should tell her Ashlyn's theory that Katherine's connected with his disappearance. I don't get through the whole thought before I decide against it. "Is he okay?"

"When there's something we can share, we will," Hilliard says. "You understand. So. What brings you here?"

"Ashlyn told me you were holding her cell phone," I begin my rickety cover story. "With the other evidence. And she really wants it. She's–" I search for a word as I take a sip of coffee. "She's reluctant to ask you for it, and her lawyer is out of town."

"Her phone?" The detective purses her lips, crosses her arms in front of her chest. Shakes her head, *no.* "We don't have her phone. Or any of her possessions. We gave all that back to her, right after the trial. In fact, her father called, too, wanting it all returned to him."

"Her stepfather, you mean."

Hilliard shakes her head. "No. Her biological father. You're referring to Tom Bryant, correct?"

"Yeah, he's actually–"

"No. He's not." Hilliard's gesture, a STOP-sign palm, rejects this entirely. "He's not her stepfather. No way. Trust me, I know everything about that girl, Ms. Hennessey. Where'd you even hear that?"

I know she must read the surprise on my face. I regroup, first looking away, then staring into my coffee cup, as if the future is contained in that dark liquid. Ashlyn made a huge deal of her dead father. Then, after crying and withholding and changing her story, she'd finally "confessed" the bitter truth about her stepfather's actions. She'd corrected me, over and over, when I called Tom Bryant her father. If none of that is true, what else isn't true?

"Ms. Hennessey?" The detective's voice is soft, encouraging. "If Ashlyn Bryant has told you something, anything, that might lead to finding out what happened to Tasha Nicole, we need to know. She's been with you for almost two weeks now. We understand you're writing a book about–"

I look up, questioning.

"Yeah," she says. "Why do you think my partner gave you that business card?"

"Because of Joe Riss," I say. "Inelli."

She nods. "That, too. But Ms. Hennessey? Be straight with me. You're not here to retrieve Ashlyn Bryant's phone."

The coffeemaker hisses. A fluorescent light buzzes above. Detective Hilliard buttons her jacket, then unbuttons it.

"She *has* her phone," the detective says. "The day she was acquitted, we gave it back. Let's see now. Why do you think she told you she doesn't have it? Ashlyn concocts her own realities, Mercer. As you certainly observed from the trial outcome, she's very good at it. But a courtroom is not the only place to find justice."

The detective lets her thought hang in the coffee-scented air, in a room filled with stacks of files, and flashing silent phones, and the occasional ping of an elevator in the hall. Justice. I used to think I could fashion it on the printed page. Choosing exactly the right words, telling a story, illustrating how people think and why they do what they do. But four hundred and ninety-one days after my own reality exploded against that oak tree, I'm still searching for justice, justice for my child who wasn't even old enough to understand the word. Truth is, justice for Sophie cannot exist. But for Tasha? The story of Tasha Nicole isn't about *my* life. It's only about hers.

If Ashlyn is innocent, that's fine. But I need to know the whole story. The real one. The police do, too.

I hear Detective Hilliard spool out a breath. "Listen. You can help us." She pauses. "Because, Mercer? This is not about you writing some *book*. This is about you helping a murderer get away with a horrible crime."

CHAPTER SIXTY-NINE

After half an hour and two cups of coffee each, I've told the detective everything. That Ashlyn says Valerie and Luke are fictional. That she says the Skype was taped. That Ashlyn as much as told me that Tom, who she said was her stepfather, was Tasha's father. Hot Stuff. The detective, sitting at her desk, takes notes with a blue plastic ballpoint into a Boston PD spiral notebook. Even at top speed, her precise handwriting stays between the lines. When I mention Hot Stuff, she lifts her pen.

"Did you see that photo? The wet T-shirt contest at Hot Stuff?" Koletta almost sneers. "She probably didn't show you that."

I blink, thinking about this. "She didn't, but I mean yeah. I've seen it. But she said it was a charity event at the student union."

Koletta's laughter fills the squad room. One peal of short, pure disbelief. She swallows, regaining her composure. "No," she says. "It wasn't."

She closes her eyes, shakes her head. Then looks up at me. "So, go on, Mercer. What else did she say?"

I tell her about the cancer. Mercy Flights. The Cessna. I almost describe the Chihuahua in the airport, but just in time remember I made that up.

"But it's suspicious," I go on. "How do you think her stepfather— I mean, father—and Georgia are paying for that cruise they're on now?"

Koletta narrows her eyes. "Mercer? The Bryants are home. In Dayton. You think we're not keeping track of them?"

Come to think of it, it's my in-laws who are on a cruise. Did Ashlyn appropriate that palm-tree postcard?

"You think they were involved?" I ask. "Tom and Georgia Bryant?"

"No. They're cleared. Those two are simply baffled—and unlucky—middle-aged suburbanites with a psychopath daughter. Every unhappy family is unhappy in its own way."

That stops me, briefly, unhappy families. But this is not about *my* story.

"Detective? You know that break-in at Quinn McMorran's house?

"Intimately," she says.

"Was Ashlyn almost killed?"

Koletta waits a beat, as if evaluating my sanity. "The taggers were punks. We've got them, slam dunk. They didn't come close to really getting inside. Didn't even want to. No one was in danger. What'd *she* tell you?"

"Never mind." Okay, Ashlyn exaggerates. We know that. Being self-aggrandizing doesn't mean she's a murderer. It means she's scared. Maybe. But Koletta—we're on first-name basis now—is my lifeline. Someone with the same agenda. Someone objective, and knowledgeable. I can tell her anything, and she won't judge. She knows a verdict doesn't necessarily represent the truth. But it might.

"So I was thinking," I go on. "If I'm going write a true-crime story, I need to know the truth. What if Ashlyn is innocent? What if she's making up stories—because she doesn't really *know* the truth?"

"I see." Koletta leans toward me, elbows on her desk. She seems authentically interested. "Do *you* have a theory?"

"Barker Holt," I say. What's the harm? I know a lot about this case, but I'm not Nancy Drew, and I don't have the law enforcement power to investigate, so I might as well tell the police. If my solution is true, and Ashlyn is innocent, that's gonna be—well, it would be a big freaking deal. And a big freaking story. "You know of him?"

Koletta nods. "Yup."

"Well. Ashlyn told Joe Rissinelli that Barker Holt was Tasha's father. And that Holt died before Tasha was born. So I never thought of him as a suspect."

"Obviously," Koletta says.

"But then Ashlyn told me she'd made up part of that story," I go on. "What if *that* was the part she made up? The timing of his death. What if he didn't die until after Tasha was killed? No one knew who he was, or that they had a connection."

"Except Ashlyn," Koletta says.

"Right." I'm so into this. "So no one was looking for him. In reality, well, he might have asked for visitation, something like that, and she felt obligated, or something, to allow it. And then he killed Tasha . . ."

"Somehow," Koletta says.

"Right. It could be a million ways. And let me ask you—do you think it's possible that someone's *blackmailing* Ashlyn? Maybe framed her for Tasha's death? Maybe Barker Holt himself? Maybe he's alive?" I know I'm talking too fast. "Do you think Ashlyn *was* maybe involved? Or that she didn't know? Or *still* doesn't know? Or she's still covering it up?"

"We'll wait to get the evidence, okay?" The phone rings on an unoccupied desk. Koletta ignores it.

I'm right. I knew it. This book is going to be—as we used to say in college—kickass. I'm getting that feeling, hard to describe, that comes at the end of the final draft of an important story. It almost brings tears to your eyes. Because it seemed impossible at the outset, but then it all *worked*. Plus, talk about justice.

"And Koletta?" Pushing it now, but I can tell she respects me. "Joe Rissinelli was in close contact with Ashlyn. She told him things. Do you think Joe's disappearance connects with what happened to Tasha?"

Koletta nods, listening. She takes a sip of coffee, and I can almost see the wheels turning in her brain. Clichéd, but in this case precise.

"Why don't you call him and ask?" she says.

CHAPTER SEVENTY

"Call? Joe? Rissinelli?" I say. Is this a trick? "He doesn't have his phone. Right?"

Koletta stands, flaps her spiral notebook closed, tucks it into an inside pocket of her blazer. "He does now."

She doesn't look sly or conniving, or like she's trying to trap me, but what do I know about police deceptions?

"I emailed him right after Detective Overbey came to my house," I say, standing. "And texted, and he didn't answer. Again and again. He hasn't tweeted. For days. Like, a week."

"That was then," Koletta says.

Now it's the wheels in my own brain that are turning. After all, these are the cops who were trying to identify a five-year-old Hispanic girl. The ones who charged the possibly-innocent Ashlyn Bryant with murder. What might they do to *me?* What might they have misinterpreted or gotten wrong? Is this exactly what happened to Ashlyn? The police are now mistakenly blaming *me* for—something?

But at this point I can hardly refuse to call Joe. Can I?

I pull out my cell. Koletta's gone back to the coffee pot, and I see her selecting a fluted filter paper and opening a plastic-topped canister of Dunkin's coffee. Her back is to me. I click my phone contacts, take a deep breath, and call.

One ring. Two.

"Rissinelli."

"Joe?" I say. Koletta doesn't turn around.

"Mercer? Hey, how are you? Long time no talk."

My brain sputters and goes out. "Where have you *been?*"

"Uh, nowhere, really," he says.

I think his voice sounds funny, but I don't trust my powers of observation much right now.

"What d'you mean by 'been'?" he goes on.

Koletta raises my empty mug, inquiring. I shake my head. Wine maybe. But that doesn't seem to be in the offing.

"I mean—where were you? I mean . . ." I close my eyes for a second, try to collect my thoughts. Truth is good. Especially with the police in earshot. "The police came to my house. They were looking for you, said your wife was worried, said I was the last person you called, said you didn't have your cell. Said no one knew where you were."

Silence on the other end. "I *did* call you," he finally says. "On closings day, remember? But anyway, I've 'been' out of town since then. With my other phone. It was kind of a misunderstanding."

What the hell kind of misunderstanding? I want to yell at him. But maybe that's not appropriate. I turn away from Koletta and face a bulletin board, its cork crumbling under thumbtacked layers of union notices and wanted posters. And a DO YOU KNOW ME poster of Baby Boston. "What happened? Are you *okay?*"

"Yeah, sure," he says. "I'm fine. It was—personal. My wife is sort of . . . well, it's all fine now. What's new with you?"

What's new? What's *new?* I don't know what to say first. And I don't want to have a whole conversation in the detective's office, especially asking how much Joe knows about Ashlyn. About what really happened. Or what she told him. Joe doesn't know she's at my house. Does he? I'm still not sure he's a good guy. Although the cops—*is* this a trap?

"Have you seen Katherine?" Is the first thing that comes out.

"Katherine?" A pause. "Listen, Mercer? Maybe it's better to talk in person. Want me to come over?"

Just like la-dee-dah normal? Like you haven't worried the hell out of me for a week? I don't know whether to laugh or cry or scream or kill someone. Do I trust him?

"I'll call you back," I say.

I jab off the phone, confused or angry, I can't decide. Why didn't he call me? But then, why should he? If he were simply "out of town" for "personal" reasons, there'd be no reason for him to check in. I emailed him, but we're only colleagues. He wasn't missing or bleeding in a damn alley somewhere or, as I secretly feared, dead. Those disasters were all in my imagination. Doesn't mean I can't be annoyed by it.

The double door pings as it opens, then pings as it closes behind Detective Bryce Overbey. He stops at the office entrance, looks at me, then Koletta. Scratches his neck, as if surveying a crime scene. He mirrors his partner, navy blazer and black jeans. Plainclothes, supposedly, but as much a uniform as any regulation blue outfit.

"What's new?" he asks. "Is there coffee?"

"Hey. Detective. Remember me? Joe Riss was just out of *town*?" I'm kind of mad about this, take a step toward him. It wasn't only Ashlyn who planted the "bad Joe Riss" seeds. The cops, Overbey in particular, made me worry about him, too. "And you never bothered to inform me of that?"

"Hi, Bryce." Koletta's leaning back in her desk chair, legs crossed, paper cup of coffee in hand.

"Yeah, sorry about that." Overbey half-shrugs at me. "Between us? It was personal. Turns out. Nothing to worry about. He's a fine upstanding citizen. If you can call a reporter that. But ah, we gotta let *him* tell you about it."

I stare daggers at him, but he doesn't seem to care. In the silence of the squad room there's only the slosh of the coffee into his paper cup, and then a plunk as he adds a mini-container of half and half. So. Apparently Joe wasn't embroiled in some drugs and murder plot with Katherine. As Ashlyn encouraged me to believe. My imagination will be the death of me.

"Listen, Bryce," Koletta finally says. "Mercer here has a theory. Or two."

"Ashlyn has an evil twin? Tasha is still alive?" Overbey says. At Koletta's glare, he retreats. "Fine. Do tell. We're all ears."

I'll ignore his sarcasm. Rise above it. After they hear my theory, they'll be sorry they scoffed. I can find out about Joe later.

It takes me less time to tell Overbey my Barker Holt idea than it took to explain it to Koletta. Overbey nods, the whole way through, and makes his way to the desk at the back of the room, me following him, still talking, and Koletta following me, pulling a wheeled swivel chair behind her.

He gestures me to keep going as he boots up his computer, and waves me to the chair. Koletta perches on a neighboring desk. Overbey's typing now, and I figure he's taking notes.

"Hey, Bryce," I hear another voice. Coming from—the computer?

"Hey, Wadleigh," Bryce says. "I'm here with a . . ." He looks at me.

"Writer," I fill in his blank. Wheeling my chair closer, I get a glimpse of his computer screen. It's Skype. And on the other end is, unmistakably, Dayton Detective Wadleigh Rogowicz. He's distorted, with the jaundiced light and peculiar camera angles Skype displays, but I've seen his image on so many TV stories and once, I think, in *People*. Funny, how much I've written about him, his thought processes, his determination, his pursuit of the Tasha case even under pressure to drop it. Wonder how much of that is accurate. I do know he hid in the Bryant's front hall closet, though. How incensed must he be that Ashlyn was acquitted?

"Reporter," Overbey says instead. "And she has a theory we want her to run by you. Mercer Hennessey, meet Detective Rogowicz. From Dayton. Go for it, Ms. Hennessey. Gotta love Skype, right?"

CHAPTER SEVENTY-ONE

Detective? Do you know Barker Holt?" I blurt it out, not phrased very professionally, but I'm fueled by how psyched this Dayton cop might be to find Tasha Nicole's real killer. "Could *he* have murdered Tasha Nicole?"

"Yup. Nope." Detective Rogowicz looks like the cowardly lion with a crew cut, round-faced and world-weary.

I pause, seeing my own face boxed in the upper right of the Skype scene. It's tiny, but large enough that I can read my own look of surprise. Why is he so sure? I should have laid the groundwork better, pitched him a more complete idea.

"Tell her why," Overbey says. He's tilted back in his chair, the front wheels off the battered carpet.

"Died before Tasha was born," Rogowicz says. "Month or so." I see his dour face attempt a smile. "Too bad for our Ashlyn— Holt mighta been a good alternative. But hey, just because a jury says she's not guilty doesn't mean she didn't do it."

"Got that right," Overbey says. "Anything else, Ms. Hennessey?"

I don't see why they couldn't have simply told me this, and it's clear they're making fun of me. But whatever. I can take it. I get to see Rogowicz in real life, and hey, I'm still supposed to be writing a book so I might as well take the opportunity to ask him some questions.

"Yes, in fact, there is," I say. "How did Holt die?"

"Car accident." Rogowicz says.

"You have the police file?"

"Yup."

Pulling teeth. "Could you–"

"Hang on," he says. And disappears from the screen.

"Any other theories?" Overbey is flat-out mocking me now. I know people hate reporters. This guy's probably been burned by a few. Probably only putting up with me because Ashlyn's at my house.

"It was a good idea, Mercer." Koletta flashes him another *lay off* look. "I think my partner was assuming you wouldn't have believed us if we'd told you we'd look into it. Reporters never believe the police."

"Thanks," I say. Koletta's conciliatory, and I'll pretend to be unaware of Overbey's attitude. Plus, he owes me for Joe Rissinelli. "Could I ask you, Detective–Koletta says you gave Ashlyn back her phone? After the verdict?"

He nods.

"Do you know the number?"

"I'm back," Rogowicz's voice comes from the computer screen. "Here's the file," he says, holding up a thick manila folder. He pulls out a black-and-white form. I can't read it as he holds it up to the camera, but I see there are boxes checked and the space where the responding officer fills in the details is crowded with handwritten notes. "It's on paper, we only went totally computer two years ago. I can scan and send," he says.

"Great," I say. "But can you just tell me what happened?"

"Rainy night, car crashed into a tree."

It takes a fraction of a second for me to recover and reset, but I do. This is not connected. Not about me. "Why?" I ask.

"Yeah well, some cokehead ran Holt off the road. Stole a car from a parking lot, went nuts. There was a witness, some driver going the other way called it in. We found the car later, license was off of it, but the VIN, you know, we traced it. Car's owner had a solid alibi. We caught the cokehead. Wasn't his first rodeo.

Plead to everything, drug dealing, drug use, possession with intent, reckless driving resulting in death, buncha other car thefts."

My big idea hits a dead end. But at least they'd checked out the—wait, though. "How did you know who Barker Holt was? That he was connected to Ashlyn? And when did you make that connection?"

"Can't reveal sources, ma'am," Rogowicz says.

"I'm sure you're familiar with *that,*" Overbey adds.

"Might want to ask Joe." Koletta winks at me.

Joe told the cops what Ashlyn told him? That's interesting. That means they didn't check Holt out until *after* Ashlyn's arrest. During the trial.

"Before you go, Detective," I say to the Skype screen. "Just a detail for my story. What was the car owner's name? The owner of the car that got stolen, I mean."

"Ahhh." Rogowicz runs his finger down the page. "He's a Denholm L. Shaw, from Dayton."

"Where's he now?" I ask.

"Do you have a point with this?" Overbey says. "Or are you just playing cop?"

"I didn't hear all that," Rogowicz says. "Are you talking to me?"

Of course. They looked at Barker Holt's death *after* Joe told them that name. Of course they would. That was the first time Barker Holt's name had been mentioned in connection with Ashlyn. Being dead, and his death adjudicated, they crossed him off their suspect list—I imagine with some relief, since that reinforced their certainty that Ashlyn alone was guilty.

But I'm a writer, and I understand how we never quite know where a story begins. And in a book like mine, I have to follow the threads of Tasha's murder both ways—forward through the cover-up, but also backward all the way to the beginning.

Now, sitting here staring at a cop seven hundred miles away in

Dayton and feeling the derision from two cops in Boston, I imagine what might have happened, and why, and what happens when a person is so single-mindedly determined to answer one question that they ignore another. The police were focused on investigating Tasha's death. When they also should have been—maybe—investigating Barker Holt's death.

And of course, they thought they had the Barker Holt death solved.

"Sorry to keep you, detectives,"-I say.

· "Nothing but time." Overbey looks at his watch to let me know he's being sarcastic.

"Huh?" Rogowicz says.

"Don't mind them," Koletta says.

"Were there fingerprints in the Shaw car? I mean, other than Denholm Shaw's." Whoever that is. I can find out if need be.

"We knew from other thefts this genius always wore gloves," Rogowicz is saying. "So not sure they ever—hang on." Over the Skype I hear the sound of pages turning. Rogowicz, head down and wire-rimmed glasses perched on his nose, must be leafing through the file. I see the top edges of each page flip by.

"Yeah," he says, without looking up. "They printed the car. Nothing from the perp—but again, gloves." I see the file close. He looks into the camera again. "But yeah, fingerprints. Shaw's. And a few others. But no matches."

Koletta has crushed her paper coffee cup, and tosses it past Overbey and into a wastebasket. I remember what I wrote about the reporters in the press room, waiting for the Ashlyn verdict, one of them—was it Joe Riss?—doing exactly the same thing with a cup. I wonder if Ashlyn is asleep on my living room couch again. Ashlyn, who always gets rid of whatever's in her way. Ashlyn, who makes her own reality.

"Here's what I'm thinking," I say.

CHAPTER SEVENTY-TWO

There's nothing more timelessly serene than a New England September twilight. The Linsdale streetlights glimmer, almost unnecessarily, and a pin spot highlights the stark carillon tower of the white-shingled Congregational Church. The bronze Minuteman statue stationed on the town green grasps his musket, forever at the ready. A sliver of moon glows in the steely pale sky. Not quite day, and not quite night. Or some of each.

It's a balance, seeing the world two ways at once.

Ristretto has put stubby votive candles on the outside tables and it's cozily crowded. Parents sharing chicken fingers with fidgeting kids, a white-haired couple deep in conversation, and a twosome that I peg from their starts and stops of conversation as on a first date. Or maybe the final one.

Ashlyn and I are well into wine and apps. She was back on the couch when I got home, but who knows what she was doing while I was with the cops. Probably chatting on her supposedly nonexistent phone with—who knows. I'd told her I was famished, and needed to unwind after my cemetery visit. She seemed to buy it.

The candlelight reflects in her sunglasses, which she refuses to take off. Otherwise we almost match, like Detectives Hilliard and Overbey. We're in T-shirts and jeans, both with little crossbody purses. I wonder if hers contains that phone.

"Did you see your neighbors moved away?" she asks, examining the bruschetta. "Those people across the street? Where the cops were parked that day. The moving van woke me up, like at about two. They had tons of stuff. Took, like, hours."

So she was either sleeping or watching out the window all that time. Good. Whatever occupies her. At least she wasn't going through my drawers.

"Yeah, you know their son is a nut," I say. I take a sip of water, ignoring my wine. I'm tired of wine. "He almost gave me a heart attack when I pulled out of the driveway. Just before you came out, actually. He's a maniac."

Ashlyn drinks her pinot as I describe what happened. Takes a bite of bruschetta. A chunk of tomato falls to her plate. "Yow. Nine lives, Merce. You could have been killed. Again."

Again. The sounds of the restaurant fade, and in one chilling out-of-body moment I picture what she means by "again," my vision of it as dazzling and realistic as a big-screen movie. I'm driving the car, almost like this morning, turning the corner toward the oak tree. Rain pelts the windshield. Wipers slash. Dex is buckled in beside me. Sophie, blue-striped dress smeared with birthday cake frosting, is car-seated in the back, pretending to sing along with the radio like she always did. In the rearview I glimpse Sophie flapping her arms, pointing through the sunroof window at the storm. Sophie, fearless, loved storms, loved thunder and what she called "light-ting." Hurrying to get home, I accelerate around the corner and into that turn. The thunder crashes. "Look!" Sophie calls out. "Light-ting! Mama, look!" We always looked.

Maybe I looked.

Maybe I swerved. Maybe hit a puddle, then, or a gully, or some random wrong in the pavement. Maybe I was trying to avoid the stupid Rayburn kid. I've emotionally censored what happened, made that into the darkness, I know that. But maybe the kid sped on, without a scratch or a backward glance. No one would ever know.

And we were left—I was, at least—to pick up the pieces.

An accident.

"You okay?" Ashlyn says. "I ate the last bruschetta thing."

"We should go." I close the door on my vision. Wipe under one eye with a forefinger. Wipe the picture from my mind. I do not want to discuss death, anyone's but Tasha's, with this woman. "Let's bang out another chapter or two. I'd hate to miss our deadlines."

"Oh, you heard from Katherine again?" She drains her wine.

"Nope." Such a mean girl. As if I needed reminding about Katherine. "Or Joe either." I'm so pleased with my lie.

"I checked my Twitter," she says, forehead furrowing, "and Joe hasn't posted for a while. That's so scary. So sad. I really fear for his–" She stops. "I mean . . ."

I say nothing, waiting to see how she'll weasel out of this. She's specifically told me she has no phone. I know she does. I have my laptop with me, as always, so she couldn't have used that. She's careless. And now she's blown it.

"I *did* have my phone, how dumb am I?" She pulls down her sunglasses so I can see her face, all wide-eyed, *such a silly girl.* "It was in the pocket of my roller bag. I guess Quinn must have stashed it there, when she packed my stuff. I never knew, can you believe it?"

No, I think. Not a word of it. "That's great," I say. Like no big deal.

"Anyway, it scares me that he hasn't posted." She glosses over her lie, as if it never happened. "Clearly he's in big trouble. I wish . . . we could help him somehow."

"I'm sure he's fine."

"You are? I'm not."

"The police are on it, Ash." I'm playing along now, playing with her like she did me. In the end, I'd told the police about Ashlyn's "bad guys out to get me" story, about drug dealers kidnapping Tasha and killing her and threatening Ashlyn to keep quiet. The cops couldn't stop laughing. I had to agree. And I'm

sheepish for more-than-half-believing it. Now it's almost enter-
taining, since she persists in floating ominous stories about Joe.
Stories I know are not true. I check my watch.

"Let's go," I say, standing.

"But I *told* him, you know? About everything? And now Joe's . . .
whatever." She looks out over the town center, as if she might see
him there. "I'm sure they got him, Mercer. It's horrible. And it's
all my fault."

"It's very worrisome." I make it sound dramatic, just to enter-
tain myself.

As we walk, it gets darker by the second, as early autumn nights
do. The edges of the buildings soften in the dusk, the glow of the
streetlights take over. Ashlyn takes off her sunglasses.

"Heard from your parents?" I ask as we cross Lincoln Street.
"How're they doing on that cruise?"

"I told you, they're out of my life. And I'm never going back to
Ohio," she says. "Dayton is like, a zero. I'm thinking–California.
Someplace they don't know me. I'll start over, be someone new."

"But maybe the book will make you famous," I say. "Good-
famous. Maybe you'll be on all the talk shows, the poor victim
of the misguided justice system. The grieving young mother who
was almost unfairly sent away for life. They could make a TV
movie, you know? A big star might play you."

She looks at me, intent, the most interested she's ever been. We
arrive at my front walk. She pauses at the first flagstone. Adjusts
the strap of her shoulder bag.

"Can you write it that way?" she asks.

"Let's give it a try." I walk past her, unlock and open the
door. "Kitchen or study?"

"Study."

"Good call," I say.

CHAPTER SEVENTY-THREE

slide behind the desk, click on my computer. Make a few adjustments, open my manuscript. It's exactly where I left it. I click a few more keys, make a few more adjustments. Type a few words.

Ashlyn's on the wing chair, one leg slung over the upholstered arm, shoulder bag on the floor. She's leafing through a magazine. Appropriately enough, it's the new *Insider* with her on the cover. Ashlyn Free says the headline. She's ignoring me. Perfect.

"So I have a couple of quick questions," I say, still typing. I pause, waiting, and then it's time. "Ah, okay. How well do you know Denholm Shaw?"

"Who?" She narrows her eyes at me, with an expression of hate that goes by so quickly I might have missed it if I hadn't spent the last sixteen days with her. She throws the magazine onto the rug.

"Freaking *Luke*," she says. "How did he find you?"

Luke? She'd said there was no Luke.

"He didn't find me," I say to cover my astonishment. "How'd you get Luke from that?" *Luke?*

"No one wants to be called *Denholm*." She grimaces. "Ugh. Luke's his middle name, so I call him that. But why would you ask about him? Did you hear me talking to him? When he called the other night? Damn. I thought you were dead asleep."

She stands up, steps closer to the desk.

The other night? Maybe that's the phone ringing that I thought was in my dream? Or when I thought she was talking to the delivery guy in the kitchen. She was on the phone. I'm glad to have two feet of solid wood desk between us now.

"So there *is* a Luke." I say. "You said he was made up. You said his last name was Walsh."

She's picked up Dex's rock again, shifts it from palm to palm. I remember the first time she did that, when she semi-threatened me with the chloroform search. I was suspicious then. Now I'm certain.

"Of course there's a Luke," she says. "I only made up the last name. I had to keep him out of it all, right? Easier if he doesn't exist. When my book is done, we can be together again."

"Because he didn't kill Tasha," I say.

"Oh, I'm sure not," she says. "We all flew to Boston, one happy family, and, you know." She pauses. "Oh, it was so very, very, deeply sad. I never saw her again. I have *no* idea what happened."

The rock thunks into her other hand. "I'm com*ple*tely innocent. The jury said so, right? And no one can change that."

"Yeah." I don't like her with that rock. "Is Valerie real?"

"Geez Lou*ise*," she says. "No, okay?"

Her face changes, like something has surprised her. She looks down at her shoulder bag. Which is vibrating.

"Your phone." I say. "Better answer." I come around from behind the desk, put out my hand. "I'll take that rock."

As soon as I grab it, I go back behind the desk. Stash the rock in the drawer. Cross my fingers.

"Luke?" She's pulled out her phone, says the name out loud. "Why are you calling me? You were only supposed to call me if it's an emergency. What's the fricking emergency?"

She glances up to see if I'm paying attention. I pretend to be fascinated by my computer. Which I actually am. She turns her back on me, hunching over her cell phone.

"The cops told you—what? Shit. You've got to leave town," she says. "*Now.* Just let me know where you are."

At that the closet door opens.

"Fool ya once," Overbey says as he emerges. "Shame on you."

"Fool ya twice?" Rogowicz's voice comes from the Skype I'd set up on my computer. I swivel the screen so he can see her—and she him. "Still shame on you."

CHAPTER SEVENTY-FOUR

There's no way they'll let me write the inside story of Ashlyn Bryant's arrest for the murder of Barker Holt. I know that. It's doubly annoying Joe Riss gets to write it for the *Globe*. And triply annoying that in this continually role-reversing world, he's going to be interviewing me for it later this morning. Everyone covered her arrest, of course. But "details" as they say, are "sketchy."

That's because I'm the only one who has them. *Only Mercer.* Ha ha.

Katherine's put my book on hold "until we see what happens." "You are *awesome*," she'd said on the phone. Like there was nothing else between us but the book. I'll finish with this interview, then get on with my own truth. Who knows if that'll include the book. Or Katherine.

I'd watched the blue-and-gray police cruiser, with Ashlyn hand-cuffed and sulking in the back seat, speed away. Then I ripped the sheets and the comforters from the guest room bed, grabbed up all the towels she used, and my grapefruit body wash, and my sunscreen, and threw it all in the trash. The new toaster, too. With Ashlyn gone, the whole house changed.

Then, in what felt like an exorcism, ten at night, I pulled down all the multicolored stickies from the guest room walls, taking solace from hearing the repetition as each one peeled away from the pale yellow paint, like removing a layer of doubt. I crumpled the little squares and destroyed them, including all the unhappiness and suspicion they stood for. I stacked the books and stomped on the boxes and crammed everything, including the unopened box five, into green trash bags—horrible but the only color I have—and threw that all away too. All of it.

Okay. I kept the heart photo. For now. But whatever happened with Dex, he—and Katherine?—had nothing to do with Ohio, or drugs, or Ashlyn or Tasha. That was all Ashlyn's re-created reality. But in some ironic consequence, Ashlyn's contagious manipulation had stampeded me to open boxes of the past I'd vowed not to. And allowed me to find—nothing else. Nothing I needed, or ever would need. When I finished erasing the past and trashing the baggage of unnecessary memories, all of Dex's boxes were gone. As my life continued to unfold, whatever Dex would mean to me was not contained in those boxes.

I was almost out of breath with the tension of it, or the relief, as I finally stared at the only alien things remaining in the guest room. Ashlyn's empty suitcase, and her few clothes in the closet. What was I supposed to do with that? Finally, I yanked everything off the jangling hangers and scooped her possessions from the dresser drawers. The whole mess teetering in my arms, I tried to unzip her roller bag to shove everything inside. That gray hoodie, the one she wore so often, slid onto the carpet. It sounded different than I expected. I dumped the jumble of what I was still carrying into the suitcase, then picked up the hoodie. Something in a pocket had made the noise. I dumped it out.

An amber plastic pill container rolled onto my palm, rattling a few pills inside. It had the logo of a local drugstore, the medicine prescribed to Katherine Crafts. I squinted at the tiny print. Ambien. Ten milligrams. I stared at the bottle, the story shifting again. Ashlyn had sleeping pills. Exactly like mine. From Katherine? Did she steal them from her? Or did Katherine give them to her? Why?

I put my hands over my eyes, trying to squeeze out the truth from my brain.

Had she taken one of mine at all? Had she given me back one

of these? Had she put one in my wine, then pretended she didn't? I'll never know. But if she'd done it to make me feel unfairly suspicious of her, it worked.

She makes her own reality, I'd thought of that that so many times. And, like Koletta said, she was good at it.

I thought over the past two weeks. Tried writing it into a different story.

That fire in my kitchen. What if Ashlyn simply parlayed my unreliable toaster into an arson conspiracy? The bomb threats. The food poisoning. The graffiti and break-in at Quinn's. Katherine's silver-car mystery. Seeing the "juror" and the woman in pink kitten heels on the cell phone. She *used* all of those, twisted them, to fabricate her own reality. To make a new story. To scare me. To convince me those random events—some real, and some maybe not, was there really a dead baby chipmunk?—were connected to *her.* She *used* me. And my grief. To make her own reality.

The depth of her deception was astonishing. Almost brilliant, now that I understand what happened. She'd even appropriated Joe, turning his absence into a tragedy. Again, all about her. I knew, I always *knew,* she wrote the heart on that balloon photo. I guess.

Maybe.

But there are two stories that need a truth. Tasha's death, of course. She'll never be punished for it, but I'm confident of that one: Ashlyn is guilty. But what about the deaths of Dex and Sophie? Is someone—besides me—guilty of that?

I trust my husband.

I trust my friend.

Maybe.

CHAPTER SEVENTY-FIVE

et's do the interview first," Joe says. "How'd Rogowicz find Luke? I mean, Denholm Shaw?"

Joe and I are in my living room, Monday morning at ten-fifteen, talking about Ashlyn. At opposite ends of the couch, morning light filtering through the front windows. Some of the leaves on my willow changed to yellow overnight. But not all of them.

Joe's still being cagey about where he was for the past week. But clearly it had nothing to do with Ashlyn's imaginary bad guys. I'm embarrassed for having suspected him. But he'll never know.

We're up to the part about the double-city sting that resulted in Ashlyn Bryant being charged with murder.

"Easy," I say. "Shaw wasn't hiding, you know? No one ever connected him with Ashlyn. He answered the door when Rogowicz went to his house. Boom. Off to the Dayton cop shop."

I pause, remembering. It was pretty funny when I showed Ashlyn my Skype screen. And got to see her reaction when her boyfriend Denholm "Luke" Shaw was right there with Rogowicz. Shaw had called Ashlyn from the Dayton PD, Rogowicz by his side.

Hard to come up with a lie when the other half of the conspiracy has thrown you under the bus. Shaw had an alibi for the night of Holt's "accident." Now Ashlyn will have to prove she had one too. Cops are betting she doesn't.

"Why'd Ashlyn kill him? She was pregnant with his child,

right?" Joe's writing in a reporters' notebook, old school. "Did Holt not want to marry her or something?"

"The opposite," I tell him. "Apparently he *insisted* on it. Wouldn't let go. According to Shaw, Ashlyn told him Holt was about to make a big public stink over her pregnancy. Problem was, she'd set her sights on bigger things. Shaw was a better catch. Richer, to be specific. Holt was in Ashlyn's way.

"So yesterday, when the cops showed Shaw the fingerprints, he ratted her out. Boom. His only choice. He told them she'd borrowed his car that night, and insisted he knew nothing about why. When Holt was found dead, she admitted she'd run him off the road, but said it was to scare him, not kill him. She only wanted to get him out of her life. So she said."

"Don't want to get in Ashlyn's way," Joe says.

"Tell me about it," I say, thinking of Dex's rock. "Anyway, as a cover story, Ashlyn convinced Shaw to ditch the car and pretend it'd been stolen. Lucky for them—I guess lucky is the word—the cops arrested the wrong bad guy. For that incident, anyway."

"Why didn't they check the fingerprints bef—oh, I get it," Joe says. "Even if they did, Ashlyn's weren't on file at that time. So they wouldn't have a match."

"Yeah," I say. "So dumb. She could have said she and Shaw were an item, and 'of course she was in the car' at some point. But she got careless. Like she does. Too late now for that lie."

"She lies to everyone." Joe clicks his ballpoint pen. "Half the time, I think she believes it. A complete sociopath. You knew this when you brought Ashlyn back to your house yesterday?"

"Yeah, it crossed my mind, I gotta tell you," I say. "But I also knew Overbey would use the key I'd told him I always have under a rock by the front porch and be there, already hidden, when we arrived. So hey. It wasn't that risky."

I roll my eyes, replaying it. "On the other hand, yeah, I guess it would have been risky if Ashlyn *hadn't* fallen for it. How would I have gotten Overbey out of that closet?"

Joe stops writing. Looks at me, smiling. "You've been so great through all this, Merce."

"Thanks," I say. "Big story."

"Can I ask you something?" he says.

Isn't that what you do in an interview? But his eyes have softened, and—what if he's *not* going to ask about the Barker Holt murder? How will I answer?

"Mercer?" he asks again. He looks at his watch.

"Yeah?"

Joe shifts position, turns his whole body toward me. Looks at his watch again. "Who do you think really killed Tasha Nicole?"

"What?"

"Yeah, I mean—there's still no answer to that."

I take a deep breath. Not exactly what I thought he was about to ask. But, okay. Who killed Tasha Nicole? How many times have I wondered about that? Ashlyn would deny it, but what she'd told me yesterday sounded like a confession. For sure. But was it *"Only Ashlyn"?*

"Maybe it happened exactly the way Royal Spofford described," I say. "Maybe the Skype was real. Maybe the chloroform was real. We might never be sure. And maybe not 'only' Ashlyn. Wadleigh Rogowicz says the name Denholm Shaw *is* on the passenger manifest of the plane Ashlyn took to Boston—so that puts them both in Boston, and *with* Tasha, like she told me. But doesn't matter, because they can't charge her again for Tasha's murder. And if they charged Shaw, well, he'd be acquitted, too. Talk about reasonable doubt."

"True," Joe says.

"And it's a tightrope," I tell him the clincher. "He could make a deal that he won't testify against Ashlyn for the Barker Holt murder unless they give him immunity for everything else."

"People can get away with murder," Joe says.

"Yeah," I say. How well I know. But they can never get away *from* it.

392   H a n k   P h i l l i p p i   R y a n

Joe is quiet for a moment, and I am, too.

"It haunts me, you know?" I finally say. "If that black Lab had found the body sooner. If the composite drawing had been more recognizable. If Wadleigh Rogowicz hadn't lost that video. If there'd been *one* fingerprint of Ashlyn's on that duct tape. And maybe it's—in a way, my fault. That one juror, Juror G, who talked to her daughter and got dismissed. Might it have made a difference if she'd stayed on the jury? I can't stop thinking about that. And now, it feels like Tasha's death is not . . . like there's no justice for Tasha."

"Ashlyn's in custody," Joe says. "Maybe that's enough?"

I think of that face, and those pink leggings, and the purple butterfly barrettes. "Guess it has to be. Justice is not an exact science."

When the doorbell rings, Joe gets up, faster than I do. Follows me to the front door. I look through the peephole.

Katherine.

CHAPTER SEVENTY-SIX

Mercer?" Joe says again as I go to the door. "I need to—"

"Hang on." Now I have to face it. *Katherine. Dex and Katherine.* How will I deal with her? I try to assemble my facts, and Ashlyn's lies, if they were lies, and my quandary about that photo. What still haunts me, relentlessly, is that not *everything* Ashlyn said was untrue.

Which is this?

I haven't seen Katherine, or heard from her, for two days. Mainly because I'm avoiding her calls. Now that there's no way to send her to voice mail, I'll play it by ear. See where she takes it. And if I decide to confront her over the photo, I certainly won't do it while Joe is here.

"Hi, sweetheart," Katherine says as I open the door. "And hi, Mercer."

Before I can unscramble her greetings or read her expression, she's inside, the fingers of one hand intertwining with Joe's.

I close the door. Every time Katherine arrives, it's *The Twilight Zone.*

"Yeah," she says, before I can remember how to talk. "We wanted to tell you first. We're—Joe's wife is—they're—ah."

"That's what I was going to tell you," Joe takes over. "Kath and I are, um, together. And last week we—took off. Of course we didn't want anyone to know. It would have been fine, except my wife—who I'd told I was out of town on business—went nuts. Called the police. We'd been having trouble for a while." He shrugs.

"And she was getting back at me. She's incredibly suspicious, and I'm not a very good liar. The cops tracked me—us—down pretty quick. Exactly what my wife wanted to happen, complete with the embarrassment."

"Is it too early for wine?" I ask. Kath and Joe? So that means the whole Dex and Kath thing is—well, no, not necessarily. Joe's wife is a married woman, too.

"I'm so sorry," Katherine says. "That's why we both showed up at your house on closings day, remember? Joe had three coffees? We just wanted to be together, somewhere we could really *be*."

Does every story have another explanation?

"You crazy kids," I say, trying to keep my balance. I still don't know what's true. "Listen, Joe, can you give us a sec? I want to show Katherine something in the study."

It takes one minute for me to take the photo from my desk. Fifteen seconds for her to look at it. Ashlyn hadn't been lying about making a copy. She'd left the original. To torment me, I'd decided. We'd never gone back to check with balloon guy, of course. Her arrest got in the way.

"Aw," Katherine says. "Yeah, that's so sweet. Balloon day. What about it?"

"Did you sign that?"

"Sure," she says, flipping it over, and back again. "Balloon day. I took this, Merce. Then Dex took one of you and Sophie, then some kid took one of all three of you, and all four of us. Last time I was in Dex's office—planning your surprise birthday party, I think—he had them all on his desk. I signed on a whim. Put hearts on the others, too."

I blink, looking at the picture. Where are those others? Ah. We never opened the last box. And now it's gone.

"Balloon day? I was there?" I squinch my face, trying to retrieve any fragment of that day. I look at Sophie's funny little mouth. *Pop-si-cle.* "Wait—blue popsicles. Right?"

"Right. You were still pretty sleep deprived, sister. Good thing

Dex loved you so much." She hands me back the photo. "Sophie's terrible twos were brutal, remember?"

"Yeah. They were." I open my desk drawer. Take out an amber plastic pill container. "Katherine? Ashlyn had these."

"That bitch." Katherine takes the bottle, examines it, shaking her head. "Piece of work, huh? I wondered where those were. I only had five, and I was hoarding them." She twists open the top. Shakes the orange pills onto her hand. "Four," she says.

"One more thing." I pull a bit of paper from my jeans pocket. "Did you give this business card to Dex? It was in his files. With your cell number on the back."

She takes it. Shakes her head. "Nope," she says. "Couldn't have, honey. See? It's an Arbor Books card. I didn't have those until—you know. After."

"An Arbor Books . . ." I totally spaced on why it was impossible for Dex to have that card. So why . . . *Oh.* "Wait. Did you give one to *Ashlyn?*" She might have planted it in the files. Ashlyn obviously hadn't checked. Careless.

"Yup. Definitely gave her one." She hands me the card. "Anyway, what's up with this?"

"Nothing," I say, taking it back. And, at that moment, I'm also taking back my truth. All the familiar puzzle pieces of my life resettle into place, right where they were before Ashlyn took all my truths and scrambled them. I'll never be how I was back then. Never be that happy again. But I was, once. I *was. We* were. And that is as true as anything can be. "I just couldn't remember where it came from."

Lame, but Kath's floating in her own romance-novel world.

"Great. So what do you think about Joe and me?" She tucks her arm through mine, pulling me close, and leads me back into the living room. Her perfume is lemony-sweet, and her hair has the scent of flowers.

Seeing her like this, I cannot believe I doubted her. Well, I guess I can, Ashlyn's a pro. But I'm relieved Kath will never

know the truth. Our friendship was almost another of Ashlyn's
victims. *She ruins everything she touches.* But not this.

"Isn't he terrific?" she asks. "We really *get* each other, you
know? Just like you and Dex."

She stops. Frowns. "Oh, I'm sorry. I didn't mean to–"

We're mid-hallway, right beside my gallery of family photos.
Dex and Sophie are watching me. Smiling and happy. Like they
always were. Like they always will be.

I reach out, stopping her mid-sentence, and throw both my
arms around my one true friend. A quick hug, but full of the
future.

"I'm happy for you, honey," I tell her. "I am. You're fabulous.
He's wonderful. You deserve every bit of joy. Savor it, you know?
Both of you. Should I shop for a bridesmaid's dress?"

Kath's laughter encircles me. "I promise you'll be the first to
know," she says. "We're under the radar, though, being careful,
until the divorce. But I really do think. . . ."

Katherine keeps talking, and I tune out her bliss. Some people
meet new loves, some people go to prison. I only write about it
all, write about what I believe is true. But the truth is not what I
choose to believe. It's what's true.

"Okay?" Katherine is asking. "He should be here any second."

"Who?" I ask. Joe's writing in his notebook, feet propped on
the coffee table. He's talking on his cell phone, holding it between his ear and his shoulder.

"The *guy*. Weren't you listening to me? To get your courtroom-
feed equipment. They'll try Ashlyn for the Barker Holt murder in
Ohio, so you won't be needing it."

"Listen to this," Joe taps off his phone as he stands, holds it up
as if to show us who he'd been talking to. "Quinn McMorran
confirms the cops have now found all the guys who tried to
break into her house. Local yokels, she told me, coked up, they
hate all defense attorneys, everybody's guilty, whatever. But it

made Quinn so mad, she's gonna get a special dispensation from Ohio to go there and defend Ashlyn again."

"Gang's all here," I say. "Hey. Maybe I'll go to Dayton, too? Cover it myself? And add it to the book?"

Katherine tilts her head, raises one eyebrow. I know that look.

"Brilliant!" she says. "But she might get off, you know. *Again.*"

"She might," I say. "It's a good story, either way."

The book on Ashlyn Bryant's life is not closed, and I hope I'm there to write the next chapter, too, the final version of *Little Girl Lost.* The true version. Ashlyn was lost, too, after all.

The doorbell rings. Again. Maybe this morning is not so much *Twilight Zone* as madcap sitcom.

"I'll get it," Katherine says, talking as she heads to the door. "That's gotta be the guy for the video gear. It's his last day at the production company. He's got some great new job in New York, doing . . . Hey, Max."

"Hey, Katherine. Hey, Joe. And you must be Mercer," he says, coming into to the living room. Plaid shirt, Levis. Tortoiseshell glasses. Unruly hair. Wide smile. Nice eyes. "We've got to stop meeting like this."

Oh. I recognize that voice. I mean—that Voice.

I burst out laughing. Purely, openly, laughing. At least I got Voice right. And as tears stream down my face, tears of surprise, and relief, and reality, I wonder—how many days has it been since that happened?

EPILOGUE

The next morning, I still write on the mirror. Of course I do. We need rituals, we need remembrances, we need the private connections that make each of us unique. The web of our individual lives, the combination of love and fate and luck and timing and coincidence that creates the tiny space in the universe that only we inhabit.

Did the Rayburns' reckless son spook me and Dex and Sophie to crash into that innocent tree? Or was it Sophie's *light-ting?* I'll never know, just like I'll never know what Sophie might have been, whether Dex and I would have been happy forever, or how long the sun will shine.

What is the deep and inscrutable singular truth? There are things we can't know. And that we certainly can't understand.

There are truths, though. We have one life, we do the best we can. We love, we laugh, we grieve, we breathe. Some doors close. Some doors open. We find forgotten rooms.

This morning, I use one finger to write on the steamy mirror. First, I draw a line down the middle. A line of demarcation. On the left, before. On the right, after.

On the left, as I have for so many months, I write the number of days away from my old life. Four hundred ninety-three days. 493. The ghost of every number will always be there.

On the right side of the line is my future.

With a single motion, and sending a tender message to the stars, I write: 1.

ACKNOWLEDGMENTS

Unending gratitude to

Kristin Sevick, my brilliant, hilarious, and gracious editor. You are endlessly wise and patient, and you made all the difference. The remarkable team at Forge Books: the incomparable Linda Quinton, the indefatigable Alexis Saarela, and copy editor Nancy Reinhardt, who noticed everything, even kept a list of the numbers. Thank you. And thank you, Faceout Studio, what a cover! It is astonishing to see this story come to life. Bess Cozby, I am so grateful. Brian Heller, my champion. The inspirational Tom Doherty. What a terrifically smart and unfailingly supportive team. I am so thrilled to be part of it. Thank you.

Lisa Gallagher, my stellar and incredible agent. You changed my life and continue to do so every day. I am so honored to work with you.

Francesca Coltrera, the astonishingly skilled independent editor, who lets me believe all the good ideas are mine. Editor Chris Roerden, whose care and skill and commitment shines on every page.

The artistry and savvy of Madeira James, Mary-Liz Murray, Nina Zagorscak, Charlie Anctil, Mary Zanor, and Jen Forbus.

Sue Grafton. Mary Higgins Clark. And Lisa Scottoline. And Lee Child. Words fail me. (I know, a first.) Erin Mitchell. Barbara Peters, Joanne Sinchuk, and Robin Agnew.

My amazing blog sisters at Jungle Red Writers: Julia Spencer-Fleming, Hallie Ephron, Roberta Isleib/Lucy Burdette,

Jenn McKinlay, Ingrid Thoft, Deborah Crombie, and Rhys Bowen.

My dear friends Mary Schwager, Laura DiSilverio, Elisabeth Elo, and Paula Munier. And my treasured sister, Nancy Landman.

And my darling husband, Jonathan Shapiro, of course, who made this possible.

Do you see your name in this book? Some very generous souls allowed their names to be used in return for an auction donation to charity. To retain the magic, I will let you find yourselves.

Sharp-eyed readers might notice I have tweaked Massachusetts geography a bit. It is only to protect the innocent. And I adore it when people read the acknowledgments.

Keep in touch, okay?

http://www.hankphillippiryan.com
http://www.jungleredwriters.com
http://www.careerauthors.com

CPSIA information can be obtained
at www.ICGtesting.com
Printed in the USA
BVHW020723190323
660733BV00025B/593